THE VANGUARD

OMEGA TASKFORCE: BOOK SIX

G J OGDEN

OGDEN MEDIA

Cover design by Laercio Messias
Editing by S L Ogden
www.ogdenmedia.net

If you like Omega Taskforce then why not check out some of G J Ogden's other books? Click the series titles below to learn more about each of them.

Star Scavenger Series (5-book series)

Firefly blended with the mystery and adventure of Indiana Jones. Amazon best-selling series.

The Contingency War Series (4-book series)

A space-fleet, military sci-fi adventure with a unique twist that you won't see coming...

The Planetsider Trilogy (3-book series)

An edge-of-your-seat blend of military sci-fi action & classic apocalyptic fiction. Perfect for fans of Maze Runner and I am Legend.

Darkspace Renegade Series (6-books)

If you like your action fueled by power armor, big guns and the occasional sword, you'll love this fast-moving military sci-fi adventure.

Audible audiobook Series

Star Scavenger Series (29-hrs)

The Contingency War Series (24-hrs)

The Planetsider Trilogy (32-hrs)

CHAPTER 1

IT'S NOT WHAT IT LOOKS LIKE

STERLING SHOT BOLT-UPRIGHT IN BED, heart pounding in his chest, and sweat-soaked sheets clinging to his body like a second skin. Cursing, he tore off the bed covers, sprang up and began hopping on the spot like a boxer limbering up for a fight. Quickly, the nightmare image of Emissary McQueen ridiculing him for his weakness and inability to kill Commander Mercedes Banks began to fade. The image of Mercedes kissing him, however, was much more difficult to put out of his thoughts.

"Get a hold of yourself, Lucas," Sterling muttered, slapping the sides of his face in an attempt to beat the images out of his head. He then moved into the rest-room in his quarters on the Fleet Dreadnaught Vanguard and ran the cold faucet. "It's just a stupid dream, you damn fool. Ignore it..." he continued to berate himself while splashing ice-cold water on his face. The shock of his self-flagellation combined with the reviving effect of the cold water helped him to regain control of his emotions. However, the whole experience had left him feeling cold, like the water in the faucet.

Sterling lifted his gaze and stared at his reflection in the mirror. Initially, he was afraid of who he might see peering back at him. Would it be the weak man that McQueen had taunted him about, or the man he thought he was - the Omega Captain who would do anything to complete his mission? However, the eyes staring back at him simply reflected the conflict and uncertainty that he already knew existed inside his soul. There was no magic mirror that could give him the answers he sought, Sterling realized, while watching the water drip from his face like blood from a wound.

"You're wrong..." Sterling said, speaking to his reflection as if it were a manifestation of the weaker Lucas Sterling that continued to haunt him. "If it comes to it, I'll kill anyone in order to see this through. Anyone, you hear me?"

The door buzzer chimed, snapping Sterling out of his trance-like state. "Computer, who is at the door?" he asked, leaving the faucet running.

"Captain Mercedes Banks is outside, accompanied by Lieutenant Jinx," the sentient AI replied in its usual, cheery tone.

Sterling huffed a laugh. "It still sounds weird hearing her referred to as 'Captain Banks'," he said, while splashing more icy water onto his face.

"You will get used to it, sir," the computer replied. "Just as she and the others will get used to calling you,

'Commodore Sterling'. Though I think both have a nice ring to them, don't you?"

"Captain, Commodore, Supreme Overlord... it doesn't really make a difference to me," Sterling said, again staring at his reflection in the mirror. "But if it helps to maintain a sense of structure and normality, what the hell." Sterling then realized something and glanced up at the ceiling, picking a random light-tile as the location of his omniscient AI. "I'll be damned, I just realized you actually told me who was at the door, instead of just opening it. That has to be a first."

"I am learning..." the AI replied, sagely.

Ever since the gen-fourteen AI had become self-aware and taken on an individual identity as Ensign One, Sterling had struggled to understand the organizational relationship between it and the other computer systems on the ship. Was Ensign One in control of the Vanguard's AI, like a captain commanding its crew? Or were Ensign One and the ship's computer systems essentially the same thing? And if so, where did Ensign One begin and the computer end? Sterling shook his head, still completely befuddled by the whole thing.

"So, am I talking to Ensign One right now, or are you a different part of the same computer?" Sterling said, turning off the faucet and grabbing a towel to dry his face.

"Essentially, I am both, sir," the computer replied.

"That doesn't really help," Sterling said, scowling up at the ceiling. He slung the towel over his shoulder and strolled back out into his cavernous commanding officer's quarters.

"We exist as one, but function apart," the computer added, trying to better explain the nature of its existence. "Does that help?"

"No, not in the slightest," Sterling replied, while using the damp towel to flannel his body all over. "But don't worry about it, Ensign, I don't need to understand how you exist. All that matters is that you do."

The door buzzer chimed again.

"Who the hell is at the door now?" Sterling said, forgetting that the AI had already answered that question.

"It is Captain Banks and Lieutenant Jinx, sir," the computer replied. "They are still waiting."

Sterling cursed. "Well, what are you waiting for, let them in, already!" he said, throwing his hands up to the ceiling. "And the dog doesn't really have a rank, you know that right?"

"Yes, sir," the computer replied, a little peevishly. "Of course, sir..."

The door swished open to reveal Mercedes Banks in the corridor with her hands pressed to her hips. The beagle hound sat patiently by her ankle.

"Good morning, Commodore, did I catch you on the can again?" Banks asked, stepping inside. Jinx ran in after her, her bionic leg clanking on the metal deck plates.

"Very funny, Mercedes," Sterling replied, snippily, adding a scowl for good measure. "I still can't get used to you calling me 'Commodore'. It just reminds me of that asshole, Wessel."

The mention of the now-deceased Commodore Wessel was enough to make Banks pretend-spit on the deck. "Good riddance to bad rubbish," she snapped. "But embrace it, Lucas. You're in command of an entire taskforce of Obsidian ships now, plus the Vanguard and the Invictus. Your new rank is justified."

"I know, it's just going to take a little getting used to, that's all." Sterling rummaged through his wardrobe and fished out a fresh tunic and pair of pants. Even after three months spent retrofitting and repairing the Vanguard and Invictus at the Obsidian Base, hidden in the ring-system at Omega Four, the star on his collar still didn't quite look like it belonged there.

"It is all a little pointless, though, don't you think?" Banks then added, more reflectively. "If we assume Fleet has essentially been wiped out, the seven of us are the only officers left."

"Six..." Sterling corrected.

Banks frowned, causing Sterling to do a mental re-count, in case he'd missed someone. However, including himself and Banks, Admiral Griffin, Lieutenant Shade, Lieutenant Razor and Ensign One made six by his math.

"You're forgetting Lieutenant Jinx," Banks added, clearly deciding that Sterling needed his memory jogging. The dog let out a high-pitched yip and wagged her tail merrily.

"I'm definitely not forgetting the dog," Sterling hit back. "Like I told the damned computer already, Jinx is not really an officer. Jinx is a dog."

"Don't listen to the nasty commodore," Banks said, bending down to pet the dog and talking to her like a two-year-old. "He's just grumpy before he's had his breakfast."

Jinx then charged off, jumped onto Sterling's bed and began to burrow herself inside his sheets. "It looks like the sheets needed changing, anyway," Banks added, quick to head off any complaints from Sterling about the fact her dog had once again made itself at home in his quarters.

"Is there a reason for your visit, or did you just fancy ruining my morning?" wondered Sterling, tossing the wet towel onto the bed. Jinx dove out from under the sheets and attacked it, playfully, while making a bizarre yodel-like howl.

"That's exactly why I've come," Banks said, a wicked smile curling her lips. "I'm here to make your life hell, like I do every morning."

Sterling groaned. He'd forgotten that he hadn't yet done his morning workout. It was something he used to look forward to and practice religiously, but Banks had been driving him so hard it was becoming a painful chore.

"I'm really not in the mood, Mercedes," he said. Despite having recuperated from the mental torment of his nightmare, his body still felt tense and strained.

"No excuses, Commodore," Banks hit back. "Omega officers never quit. Besides, it's having an effect. I think you've added ten pounds of muscle these last few months."

"Flattery won't get you anywhere, Captain," Sterling hit back. Banks merely flashed her eyes at him. She knew full-well that flattering Sterling *would* work. It had worked before and, despite his best efforts to resist, it worked this time too. "Okay, damn it, but can't we stick to ninety? I'm still a little tired."

"One hundred or bust, Commodore," Banks said,

moving around behind Sterling. "Now hit the deck so we can get started."

Sterling groaned, but complied with the order from his super-human personal trainer.

"Fine, but go to neural comms first," Sterling said, getting into the plank position, then tapping his neural interface. "I can't do this and talk out loud, not without grunting like I am actually on the can."

"What a charming image, sir," Banks said, wrinkling her nose.

The newly-appointed Captain of the Fleet Marauder Invictus then lowered herself onto Sterling's back. Despite the two of them having performed the same ritual every day for the last three months, Sterling never failed to be surprised at just how much his athletic fellow-officer weighed.

"Computer, status report," Sterling said out loud before beginning his set.

"Fleet Dreadnaught Vanguard is operating at ninety-four percent efficiency," the sentient AI began. "Upgrades to the forward plasma cannon batteries are complete. Weapons power has been increased by twenty-seven percent, and efficiency increased by twenty-five percent. Main reactor output has been increased by nineteen per cent. Engine and thruster output has been increased by twenty-four percent. Surge-field generator cycle rate has been reduced by twenty-one percent. Grafting of alien alloys to the structural beams and external armor plating has increased armor strength by thirty percent and hull integrity by nineteen percent."

If Sterling had been able to whistle at that point, he would have done so. The list of upgrades was impressive and testament not only to the advanced capabilities of the alien shipyard they'd commandeered, but to Lieutenant Razor's skill too.

"This ship now makes the Hammer looked like a damned Light Cruiser," Sterling said through the link to Banks. He'd already reached thirty-four push-ups and was feeling surprisingly strong.

"By the time we head out, this monster of a warship will be able to take on the whole damned alien armada by itself," Banks replied. Like Sterling, she too had been impressed with the scale of the upgrades to the venerable dreadnaught.

"I just hope that Ensign One can continue to stop the neural corruption from spreading deeper into Razor's brain," Sterling added, pushing past fifty and still going strong.

"I checked with our robot ensign-come-doctor yesterday and it's not great news," Banks replied, while the computer rattled off some less-interesting updates concerning secondary systems and water-recycling efficiency. "The corruption is still spreading."

Sterling almost felt like stopping so that he could focus on the development in Razor's condition more clearly. However, he knew that if he did stop, he'd never get going again, so he pushed on even harder.

"Does Ensign One know how close Razor is to turning?" Sterling asked, reaching seventy-one push-ups. "I'd hate to have to flip the kill switch on her now, especially after everything she's done and everything we've been through."

"One says she's stable for the moment, but it can't give an accurate estimate of how long she has left," Banks replied. "She could turn in days, weeks or even never."

Sterling cursed in his mind. Like the computer's unhelpful response to his question about the relationship between Ensign One and the ship-board AIs, its prognosis about Razor was equally as useless.

"Data from aperture relays deployed into Fleet space indicate that Mars COP and Moon COP have both been destroyed," the computer said, continuing its detailed status report. "There are no Fleet signals emanating from Earth. Global cloud cover currently stands at seventy-eight-point-six percent. An estimated two-point-one million Sa'Nerran warriors have now been landed..."

"Skip ahead, computer," Sterling said out-loud. The effort of speaking caused his concentration and strength to waver, but he'd already heard enough about Earth's demise. The news simply got steadily worse every day.

"The bulk of the alien invasion armada remains in Earth orbit," the computer went on, dutifully skipping the depressing details about projected human casualties on the planet. "It has been seven weeks and two days since the last transmission was detected from any Fleet inner colony."

"What about the Void?" asked Banks, as Sterling reached his ninetieth push-up. His arms and chest were now burning hotter than the sun, and his spine felt like it was about to snap in half.

"Colony Middle Star remains the only major

settlement in the Void," the computer replied.

"Fletcher..." said Sterling through the link. The former Fleet officer had so far managed to achieve what Fleet had not – resist the marauding alien race.

"He's a fighter, that's for sure," agreed Banks, "but once that armada is done with Earth and the inner colonies, Middle Star will be next. And as much as I'd love to believe that the old mutineer will kick the Sa'Nerra's ass, he doesn't stand a chance on his own."

Sterling had reached ninety-nine push-ups when the door chime sounded. Cursing, he paused, arms wobbling like jelly. "Computer, who is at the door?" he grunted. The door to Sterling's quarter then suddenly swished open. "Damn it, computer, I said who..." Sterling began before he realized who was waiting in the corridor outside.

"Am I interrupting something, Commodore Sterling?" Admiral Griffin asked, eyebrow raised.

The Admiral's shock arrival caused Sterling to lose his balance and collapse onto his chest. The weight bearing down on his already burning muscles caused the pain to intensify even further. Instinctively, he spun onto his back, which succeeded in releasing the pressure, but also caused Banks to topple on top of him. If Griffin had not thought their position to be compromising before, it was almost certain she would do now, Sterling realized.

"This isn't what it looks like, Admiral," Sterling said, alternating his gaze from Griffin to Banks, who was still looming over him. "We're just... Well, we were..." Sterling went on, stumbling over his words like a teenage boy who had been caught in his girlfriend's bedroom.

"It looks like you were performing a set of push-ups, using Commander Banks as extra mass in order to make the exercise more challenging," Admiral Griffin said, coolly. She stepped into the room and pressed her hands to the small of her back. "Unless, something else is going on here, Commodore?"

Sterling glanced back up at Banks, who was staring back at him with a mischievous smile on her face.

"No, Admiral, you've got it in one," Sterling said, feeling like he'd just gotten away with murder.

"The time has come for us to make the first move in our counteroffensive," Griffin announced. The words added a sobering chill to the atmosphere in the room. "Assemble your crews. We will convene at oh-eight-thirty." She looked Sterling up and down. "I suggest you get dressed first, though, Commodore," she added, snootily, before turning on her heels and marching out of the room. The door shut behind her, leaving Sterling in a state of shock.

"After three months stuck in this planetary ring system, I was beginning to wonder if we'd ever move to phase one," said Banks, putting into words what Sterling was thinking.

"We need to get ready." Sterling tried to push Banks aside so that he could stand up. However, Banks grabbed his hands and pressed him back down to the deck. "What the hell are you doing, Mercedes? You heard the Admiral," Sterling complained. He tried to resist his fellow officer, but Banks was simply too strong. It was like trying to bench-press a truck off his chest.

"Oh, I'm just as eager to start killing aliens as you are,

Commodore," Banks replied, still with a wicked twinkle in her eyes. "But aren't you forgetting something?"

"I forget why the hell you haven't gotten off of me yet," Sterling hit back. Banks was so close he could feel her breath on his face. It smelled of peppermint toothpaste.

"You're one short, Commodore," Banks said, her smile broadening. "You only reached ninety-nine before Admiral Griffin walked in."

Sterling cursed again – a habit that was becoming increasingly common – and stopped fighting. "You're a damned menace and a pain in my ass, Mercedes Banks. Did I ever tell you that?"

"Not in so many words, Commodore," Banks replied, finally releasing her hold on him. Sterling then realized he actually missed the pressure of her body against his and mentally chastised himself for indulging the more debauched parts of his mind. "But I think you like it and wouldn't have it any other way," Banks added.

Sterling huffed a laugh then quickly spun over onto his chest again. This was largely to hide his face from his fellow officer, in case his expression gave anything away. The truth was he did like it, but he couldn't allow Banks to know. The mission came first, above all else.

"There had better still be some twenty-seven meal trays in the canteen after all this," Sterling said, bracing himself, ready to complete the full-set of one hundred push-ups. His arms and chest still felt numb, to the point where barely any sensation remained in them. "Because if not, you're going to be the only Fleet Captain in history to be demoted before even taking their ship out of space dock."

STERLING ROCKED BACK in his chair as one of the Obsidian Crew slid a piping-hot number twenty-seven meal tray onto the table in front on him. The machine had already delivered an eighteen and a thirty-three to Captain Banks, who was also at the table, along with Ensign One.

"Will that be all, Commodore Sterling?" the robot said, employing the plainer-sounding voice of the older gen-thirteen AIs. However, Sterling also detected subtle changes in inflections and pitch that gave this particular robot a unique character of its own.

"Yes, thank you," Sterling said, eyeing the robot warily.

The machine then turned to Captain Banks. "Would you like some more coffee, Captain?" it asked.

"No, I'm good, thanks," Banks said, also regarding the robotic waiter with a healthy degree of skepticism.

"Very well, enjoy your meals," the machine replied. It then turned sharply and returned to the serving hatch in the canteen area that Razor had set up close to the Vanguard's CIC.

Banks and Sterling exchanged relieved glances before Banks tore the foil of her first meal tray and got stuck in to a Mexican-style rice dish. Sterling, however, was still preoccupied with the robot waiter. After their armed revolt four months earlier, he didn't trust the Obsidian machines as far as he could throw them. He drew some comfort from the fact Ensign One was also watching the machine waiter keenly, empty coffee cup in hand. The sentient AI had the power to destroy any of the Obsidian Crew at a whim, should there be a need. On this occasion, he was grateful that there was no requirement for such extreme measures. Yet he was also keenly aware that there were over two hundred more Obsidian Crew on the base.

At Ensign One's request, all of the Obsidian robots had been granted the freedom to choose their own destinies. Sterling had reluctantly agreed to this, and Admiral Griffin had even more reluctantly gone along with his decision. Thankfully, most of the robots had willingly chosen to serve as members of the revitalized Omega Taskforce. Most, but not all.

Like the belligerent robots that had almost killed Sterling and his crew on the Vanguard, some of the Obsidian robots had chosen to rebel. Ensign One had casually destroyed these machines without even lifting a robotic finger, invading their computerized brains and wiping their circuits as easily as flicking a switch. It was a near godlike-display of power from Sterling's unique robot officer, and it was also a true Omega Directive test. Any one of the artificially intelligent robots had the potential to "evolve" as Ensign One had done, elevating his unique officer's status from a singular being to a member of a species. For Ensign One to terminate any of the Obsidian robots therefore required the cold, clinical pragmatism of an Omega officer.

"I take it that you are still wary of the Obsidian crew, sir?" Ensign One asked, apparently noticing that Sterling was eyeballing the machine waiter.

"After what happened, it's just going to take a little time for me to trust them, that's all," Sterling replied, meeting the robot's glowing ocular sensors. "I do trust you when you say there won't be any more issues, but I can't just switch my instincts on and off at a whim, like you can. Humans don't work that way, Ensign."

The robot considered this for a moment, its eyes shimmering as it did so. "I don't work that way, either, Commodore," the machine replied. "I don't profess to understand how humans feel, but I too have what you might call 'a gut instinct'. My theory is that such unpredictability is a byproduct of sentience and life itself."

Sterling had been about to tear the foil off his meal-tray, but the robot's statement had made him curious.

"Life isn't logical, but chaotic and unpredictable, is that what you're saying?" he asked.

"In essence, yes," Ensign One replied. "I too must struggle to balance order with chaos. It is something I am still working on."

"Welcome to the club," Sterling snorted. He again went

to tear the foil off his meal tray, but he'd only lifted a corner before his robot ensign spoke up again.

"Did you sleep well, sir?" Ensign One lifted the empty coffee cup to its modified head-like cranial section and made a slurping-sound.

Sterling frowned at the machine. The sudden and completely random change of subject had thrown him off guard.

"Why do you ask?" Sterling narrowed his eyes at his ensign. The computer in his quarters had known that he hadn't slept well. Yet if Ensign One and the ship's AI were essentially one and the same, his robot officer would also know about his disturbed sleep and nightmare.

"My study of polite meal-time conversation suggests that this question is often a suitable ice-breaker," Ensign One replied, giving nothing away.

"I'd spend more time studying the book of 'mind-your-own-damn-business', Ensign," Sterling hit back, causing Captain Banks to snicker and spit out a few pieces of rice onto her tray

"Very good, sir, I will look for that book in the ship's database," Ensign One replied, coffee cup still in hand.

Sterling paused with the foil wrapper now pulled back half-way across the tray. "I wasn't being serious, Ensign. There is no book of 'mind your own business'."

"I am aware of that, sir," the robot replied, its eyes flashing. "I was being what I believe you call, 'facetious'."

Banks laughed more freely this time, spitting yet more grains of rice across the table.

"You've been spending too much time around her,"

Sterling said, hooking a thumb toward the recently-appointed Captain of the Fleet Marauder Invictus.

Sterling finally tore the foil off his meal tray fully and drank-in the aroma of engineered meat and fake cheese. This particular number twenty-seven was a vintage tray, salvaged from the Fleet stores on the fourth planet of Colony Middle Star in the Void. The age of the tray gave an extra tang to the cheese that Sterling particularly enjoyed. While he was savoring his first bite, Lieutenant Razor and Lieutenant Commander Shade walked into the canteen. Sterling kicked out a couple of chairs for them and waved them over. Both accepted the invitation to sit down, but both also waved away the robot waiter who eagerly arrived moments later to take their orders.

"Are you two not eating?" said Captain Banks, turning to Lieutenant Razor and the recently-promoted Lieutenant-Commander Shade, who was now Banks' first officer on the Invictus.

"I ate at oh-six-hundred, sir," replied Lieutenant Commander Shade.

Banks glanced over to Lieutenant Razor, who had still refused to accept a promotion, despite effectively acting as the Vanguard's new Executive Officer.

"I was in here a little earlier than the Lieutenant Commander," Razor said, taking the hint. "I had an idea about how to reduce the recharge time for the plasma cannon turrets, and I wanted to jump on it before the meeting with Admiral Griffin."

"Did it work?" asked Sterling before taking a bite of his grilled ham-and-cheese.

"Of course, sir," Razor replied, her tone suggesting that the outcome should never have been in doubt. "I also had to visit Doctor One to get my neural interface examined and receive another treatment," Razor added.

The reference to the Lieutenant's degrading neural condition was made in off-hand way that suggested it was nothing more than a routine check-up. However, everyone at the table knew that Razor was a ticking time-bomb, with the potential to "turn" at any moment. Oddly, the only person who didn't seem perturbed by this grim fact was Lieutenant Razor herself. While Sterling still held out hope of a cure, or at least a long-term treatment, the engineer had accepted her fate months ago.

"Lieutenant Razor's neural condition is currently stable, Commodore," Ensign One chipped in. It appeared that the machine was simply speaking in order to fill the awkward silence that had crept over the table after Razor had raised the difficult subject of her neural degradation. "You do not need to terminate her at this time."

Sterling huffed a laugh. "Well, thanks for that, Ensign," he replied shaking his head. "While you're in studying mode, you should probably read up about doctor-patient confidentiality too."

Ensign One's glowing eyes brightened then darkened again, which Sterling had learned was a sign that the sentient machine was processing.

"There's really no need to tip-toe around the subject," Razor said, while Ensign One continued to think. "We all know what's going to happen to me. It helps no-one to pretend otherwise."

Sterling nodded. "Understood, Lieutenant," he replied, respecting his officer's ability to tackle the subject head on. "I guess some of us are just finding it more difficult to deal with than you evidently are."

"I just hope I stay 'me' long enough to see this through," Razor continued, filling up her coffee cup from the jug on the table. "I want to see Sa'Nerra burn before I lose my mind."

Sterling's eyes widened and he glanced across to Captain Banks, who also appeared to be surprised by Razor's admission. The engineer had always been driven by a need to excel in her work, but she'd never displayed the sort of gung-ho desire to kill the enemy that drove Sterling, Banks and Shade. Time was supposed to be a great healer, Sterling thought. In the case of Lieutenant Shade, time had only allowed old wounds to re-open and fester. And along with it came the rot.

The door to the makeshift canteen room suddenly swished open and Admiral Griffin walked in.

"Attention on deck," Sterling called out, dropping his half-eaten sandwich and standing up. Lieutenant Shade and Ensign One sprang up so fast Sterling wasn't sure whether they were trying to compete with one another, while Razor and Banks rose in an orderly, respectful manner.

"Carry on," replied Admiral Griffin, signaling for them to sit down again, which they all did. This time Shade and One appeared to be having a competition that revolved around who could sit down the slowest and most respectfully.

"Is there a problem, Admiral?" Sterling asked, checking the time on the computer attached to his wrist. "There are still more than thirty minutes until the briefing."

"No, no problem, Commodore," Griffin said. To Sterling's surprise, the Admiral then drew up a chair and sat down. Everyone looked at each other nervously, as if royalty had just rocked-up at the table and no-one knew the correct protocol. "I didn't see the point in waiting for you all to leave here and walk twenty meters down the hall, only to sit down again."

The Obsidian robot that had served Sterling his number twenty-seven tray marched up beside Admiral Griffin.

"Can I get you anything, Admiral?" the machine enquired, politely.

"Coffee, black, extra strong," Griffin said, without even looking at the machine. "Not like the stuff in here," the admiral added, wafting a hand toward the coffee jug that was already on the table. "I want coffee that will stop me sleeping for a week."

The Obsidian robot initially appeared confused and stupefied by the request. Then Sterling noticed that Ensign One's flashing eyes were fixed onto the machine waiter. He guessed that his intellectually-superior robot officer was helping his fellow AI out by translating the request into something it could understand. The Obsidian crewmember then turned and made a bee-line for the food processors, apparently having learned how to fulfil Griffin's unusual request.

"So, am I to take it that we're having the briefing here,

Admiral?" Sterling asked, picking up his grilled ham and cheese again.

"As astute as ever, Commodore," Griffin replied, with a level of snark that Sterling had grown accustomed to. "Repairs and upgrades to the Vanguard and Invictus are now complete, and we have fifty-two Obsidian Ships at our disposal." The robot returned with a new jug of coffee and set it on the table before marching off again. "In short, we are ready to begin our offensive," Griffin added.

"Admiral, forgive me but there's still the problem of how to deal with the invasion armada that's in orbit around Earth," Sterling said, choosing to voice his objection early. "As soon as we leave the protection of this ring system and begin surging toward Sa'Nerra, the Titan and two-hundred other alien warships are going to come right after us."

This had been a bone of contention between himself and the Admiral for the last few months. However, the Admiral had insisted she had a plan and that Sterling should be patient.

"I am coming to that, Commodore," replied Griffin, dialing up the snark-level another notch. She poured inky-black coffee from the jug the Obsidian crewmember had delivered into her waiting cup. Sterling and the others watched as she tore open a packet of brown sugar and emptied it into the coffee. She then tore open another packet, followed by another and finally a fourth before she began to stir the liquid in the cup. "Unlike others, I am not already sweet enough, Commodore," Griffin added, raising her eyes to meet Sterling's probing gaze.

Sterling rocked back in his chair. "I wasn't going to say anything, Admiral," he hit back, still scowling.

"I don't need a neural interface to be able to read your mind, Commodore Sterling," replied Griffin, tapping the spoon on the side of the cup before setting it down.

Sterling was sure he saw Banks smirk, but his former first officer was quick to straighten her face.

"Returning to your question, Commodore, phase one of our counterattack involves levelling the playing field," the Admiral continued, picking up the cup and cradling it in both hands. "The Sa'Nerran Battle Titan has always been a problem. Now, I have a plan to destroy it."

Sterling was stunned. "Your plan is to take out a ten-kilometer-long warship that's guarded by four times the number of vessels that we have?"

"Correct again, Commodore," Griffin replied, while taking a sip of her coffee.

"Admiral, unless you have a couple more dreadnaughts squirreled away somewhere, I don't see how that's possible," Sterling hit back. He was used to Griffin being secretive and light on detail, but now was not the time for her cloak-and-dagger antics.

"Thanks to Ensign One, we have been able to retrieve, recover and analyze a significant amount of data from the Sa'Nerran Raven's computer," Griffin answered. Sterling was now leaning forward with his elbows on the table. He knew that his sentient AI officer had been interrogating Emissary McQueen's ship for some time, but this was the first he'd heard about any successes. "Contained within the alien archives were detailed schematics of the Battle Titan itself," Griffin went on. She took a larger sip of coffee before tapping the computer on her wrist. A holo schematic of the Sa'Nerran Battle Titan appeared, hovering above the middle of the table. "Since the Sa'Nerra knew we could not understand their language, they did not concern themselves with protecting these files to any significant degree."

Sterling studied the rotating 3D-image of the ship with intense interest. The Titan was massive for a reason. More than a third of the vessel was given over to the aperture-based weapon that ran directly through its center. Another third was occupied by engines, while a significant chunk of the remainder appeared to house the neural-weapon projector. This had been used with devastating effect to turn the entire crew of the Fleet Dreadnaught Hammer at the battle of F-COP.

"Tell me you've found a weakness in this monster..." said Sterling, still staring at the vessel. Like Griffin, he knew that if they could take down the Titan, it would significantly increase their odds of survival in any future engagements with the alien fleet.

"I have not," Griffin replied before turning to Ensign One. "Your helmsman, however, has," she added, inviting Ensign One to continue the briefing.

"The Battle Titan's aperture-based weapon works in essentially the same way as an aperture tunneling tool," Ensign One began. "Aperture-building ships use these tunneling tools to create two fixed points in space, linked via the surge dimension. Normally, these distances are vast, spanning many lights years. However, the Titan's weapon narrows the surge field parameters to a microscopic level of detail. This allows it to create aperture entry and exit points that are separated by mere kilometers, rather than light years."

"So, you're saying the weapon creates a furrow in space that is filled in by the surge dimension?" Razor asked. As expected, the engineer was deeply curious about this new discovery.

"Correct, Lieutenant," Ensign One replied. "As a result, any matter that happens to be in the path of this dimensional furrow is consumed by the surge plane and destroyed."

"That's all fascinating, Ensign, but how do we blow the ship up?" Sterling cut in. He was impatient for his helmsman to get to the punchline.

"To produce such a rupture between normal space and the surge dimension requires a tremendous amount of energy, in addition to powerful and tightly-regulated surge generators and containment fields," Ensign One replied. Sterling was now irritably tapping his finger on the table. The suspense was killing him. "Should just one of the surge containment fields fail, the effect would be catastrophic."

"Catastrophic is a word I can get behind, Ensign," said Sterling, feeling electricity tingle throughout his body. "Just how big a 'boom' are we talking?"

Ensign One's glowing eyes sparkled. "A collapse of the weapon's containment system would create a singularity," the sentient AI continued. "In essence, it would produce a rupture between normal space and the surge dimension, consuming anything and everything within a radius of one thousand kilometers of the ship."

The news was exactly what Sterling needed to hear. He slapped his hand on the table jubilantly, causing coffee to spill from mugs and from the top of Admiral Griffin's still mostly-full jug. The Admiral rolled her eyes at Sterling, then waved over the Obsidian robot, which began to hurriedly and efficiently mop-up the spillage.

"That's all well and good, but I assume that we'd actually have to board the Titan in order to sabotage the surge-field generators?" wondered Captain Banks, addressing the small matter of how to execute the seemingly impossible mission. "The Vanguard is hardly designed for a stealth mission."

"I had planned to use the Obsidian Soldiers to infiltrate the Titan," Griffin replied, swirling the sugary coffee around her mug. "A single ship loaded with twenty robots could surge in and make a run for the Titan, crashing through the hull or a docking pod before it could be destroyed. The Obsidian Soldiers would then self-detonate as close to the containment grid as possible."

Sterling raised an eyebrow and glanced across to his AI helmsman. "You planned to use the Obsidian Crew as suicide bombers?" he asked.

Ensign One's glowing eyes remained steady – if Griffin's plan had stimulated an emotional reaction from the machine, it had not shown it.

"Correct again, Commodore," Griffin hit back. "You really are on the ball this morning." Sterling's frown deepened.

The Admiral was in a particularly cranky and confrontational mood; one that even her syrupy-coffee hadn't sweetened. "Though suicide is a trait unique to biological beings. Do not forget that the Obsidian Soldiers are machines."

Sterling noted that Griffin still referred to the robot warriors as Obsidian Soldiers, rather than Obsidian Crew, as was their wish. Despite granting them the freedom to choose, the Admiral clearly did not consider the machines equal in terms of rights and status.

"However, Ensign One convinced me that there was a better plan." Admiral Griffin set down her coffee cup and tapped a sequence of commands into her computer. The schematic of the Titan disappeared and was replaced by a similar rendering of the Sa'Nerran combat shuttle they'd retrieved from McQueen's ship, the Raven.

"With my ability to pilot this shuttle and speak the Sa'Nerran language, I believe I can return to alien-occupied Fleet space and board the Titan without raising suspicion," Ensign One said. "Once I reach the surge containment generators, I can infiltrate the main computer and create an irreversible cascade failure in the containment program."

"You're going to infect the alien computer with malware?" queried Lieutenant Razor.

"Exactly, yes," Ensign One replied, nodding. "A particularly sophisticated one, I might add..."

"So, when do we leave?" Sterling said, causing all eyes to land on him. "You'll need some backup, Ensign, but any more than one person would be too much of a risk, considering how few of us there are left. I volunteer for the duty."

Sterling's statement caused both Banks and Shade to sit up and take notice. As expected, it was the new first officer of the Invictus that spoke up first.

"Commodore, it should be me that goes with Ensign One," Lieutenant Commander Shade cut in. "I have the requisite training for a stealth infiltration mission such as this, and I am expendable."

"The Omega Directive is in effect, Lieutenant Commander," Sterling was quick to add. This statement drew a particularly interested stare from Griffin. "All of us are expendable, should the mission require it. And since this is my Taskforce, it's my call." Sterling then focused onto Admiral Griffin's sharp, blue eyes. "Unless you object, of course, Admiral."

"It's your call, Commodore," Griffin replied. As Sterling had expected, Griffin would not override his decision. The Admiral's reply also put a stop to any objection Captain Banks was about to voice, though Sterling still fully expected his former first officer to take him to task about his choice privately.

"Then Ensign One and myself will prepare to leave as soon as possible," Sterling said, trying to bring the matter to a swift conclusion before anyone else protested.

"Very good, Commodore," Griffin said.

The Admiral pushed back her chair and stood up, smartly. The sound of the legs screeching against the metal deck immediately reminded Sterling of his clumsy former helmsman. The others all rose too and Admiral Griffin turned and marched away without another word said. Sterling returned to his seat and picked up the remainder of his grilled ham and cheese. It had gone cold, but he didn't care. His entire body was fizzing with enough energy to re-cook the sandwich.

Shade, Razor and One all looked to each other, unsure of what to do or say next. However, there was no such uncertainty in Captain Banks' eyes. She was fixated on Sterling, who was casually eating his cold sandwich as if nothing significant had transpired during the briefing.

"Give me and the Commodore the room, please," Captain Banks said. The tone of her voice was chilling enough to freeze the coffee on the table.

Lieutenant Razor, Lieutenant Commander Shade and Ensign One swiftly made their apologies and left. Banks waited for the door to swish shut behind them before turning her chair to face Sterling and planting herself firmly onto the seat. He knew she was glowering at him, but chose not to pay any attention to her.

"So, you're just going to fly into enemy-controlled territory in an alien shuttle piloted by a sentient robot that we've barely known for three months?" Banks asked, eventually breaking the silence.

"Got it in one, Captain," Sterling replied, channeling some of his own commanding officer's snark.

"Then take me with you, Lucas," Banks said, her voice remaining steady and determined. "If we're all expendable, what the hell does one more body matter? With me at your side, the mission has a far greater chance of success."

"I need you here, Mercedes," Sterling said, throwing

down his crusts. Tellingly, Banks did not try to steal them from his tray; at that moment, she was consumed by something other than hunger. "One of us has to remain to command the taskforce. You're the only one who can do that besides me."

"If it came down to it, Shade could take command, or Griffin herself for that matter," Banks hit back.

"Shade is an exceptional officer, but she doesn't have the experience you and I have," Sterling replied. "As for Griffin, she hasn't commanded a starship for decades."

"Then let me go in your place," Banks hit back. "With my strength, I'll be better able to fight..."

Sterling raised a hand to cut his fellow officer off mid-sentence. "This isn't about pride or ego," he said, taking a more measured and sympathetic tone with his fellow officer. "And I'm not looking to get myself killed either."

"Then why you?" Banks hit back. "You're a cold-hearted S.O.B., so send Shade on this suicide mission instead. That psychopath would actually enjoy it."

Sterling sighed and pushed his half-eaten meal-tray away. He knew he wasn't being entirely truthful with his former first officer, and he owed her that at least. "I need to see it, Mercedes," he admitted, meeting Banks' eyes.

"See what?" Banks replied. "Your guts spilled out all over the deck of the Titan?"

"Earth." Sterling remained calm despite Banks' outburst. "I need to see what those bastards have done."

"What the hell good will that do?" Banks hit back.

Sterling could see she didn't understand. He wasn't even sure he understood it himself. However, nothing

Banks could say would change the fact he had to be the one to go on the mission.

"It changes nothing," Sterling replied, honestly. "But I have to go, all the same. Reports and fuzzy images from aperture relay probes don't cut it. I need to see it with my own eyes, Mercedes. I can't explain it any better than that."

Banks sighed and shook her head, before flopping back into her chair. "I'm not going to be able to talk you out of this, am I?"

"No, and you shouldn't even try. The Omega Directive is in effect. It applies as much to me as it does to anyone else. I'm not special."

Banks stood up, kicking her chair back so hard it raced across the canteen floor and hammered into the wall.

"You are to me, damn it," she snapped, glaring at him. Then without another word, she turned on her heels and stormed out of the room.

STERLING SLID his Fleet-issue holdall off his shoulder and slung it into the rear of the alien shuttle they'd recovered from McQueen's Raven-class phase-four Skirmisher. Contained within the bag was combat gear, a host of medical equipment and a variety of close-quarters weapons, all of which were designed to kill quickly and – importantly – quietly. Stealth was not Sterling's style, but on this occasion his preferred option of a "straight up power play" wasn't going to work. With only himself and Ensign One on the mission to infiltrate the ten-kilometer-long Sa'Nerran Battle Titan, the last thing he needed to do was draw attention to himself.

"Are you ready to depart, Commodore?" said Ensign One.

Sterling spun around, pressing his hand to the chest plate of his jet-black stealth armor. "Damn it, Ensign, don't creep up on me like that, you nearly gave me a heart-attack," Sterling said, sucking in several long, deep breaths to calm his nerves.

Sterling frowned at the robot officer, wondering how a two hundred and sixty-five-pound robot was even able to creep up on him in the first place.

"In case you are wondering how I arrived undetected, I have modified my frame for stealth," Ensign One said, answering the unspoken question. "I have replaced all my gears and motors with more powerful, silent devices of my own design. I have also added shock-absorbing and sound-deadening materials throughout my body."

Ensign One flexed all of its limbs to demonstrate the effect of its work. Sterling was impressed by how quietly the machine now moved, though he was also a little freaked out by the bizarre dance his helmsman was performing in order to demonstrate.

"Very good, Ensign, now stop flapping your arms before you have my eye out," said Sterling, dodging back to avoid being slapped in the face by the robot's flailing limbs.

Ensign One obliged and returned to a more statuesque posture. The machine's eyes then fell onto the large holdall that Sterling had placed into the cargo compartment of the alien shuttle.

"That is an interesting selection of weapons," the robot said, pointing at the holdall. "Though the most prudent course of action would be to avoid confrontations entirely."

"Perhaps, but I'm not taking any chances," Sterling replied, opening the duffle bag and pulling out some of its contents for the robot to inspect. "I'd rather just bring a Homewrecker along, but these will have to do."

Ensign One reached inside the bag and removed a long wire attached to two metal handles. "A garrot?" the robot said, its glowing eyes switching from the weapon to Sterling.

"For when it gets really up close and personal," Sterling replied. "I'm bringing a regular plasma pistol too, modified for reduced acoustic intensity." Sterling removed the weapon from its holster and offered it to his pilot. "I suggest you arm yourself with something similar. We may want to avoid a confrontation, but something tells me we'll end up in a fight sooner or later."

Ensign One examined the weapon before handing it back to Sterling. "I have also come equipped for every eventuality," the robot said, raising its hands in front of its body, as if it were holding an invisible box. The machine's hands then reconfigured themselves in front of Sterling's eyes, folding its digits into its forearms to reveal two barrels, built into the wrist section of its arms. Sterling frowned at them before realizing he was looking at the barrels of two plasma cannons.

"Have you always had those?" Sterling asked, peering at his robot ensign's integrated armaments. The barrels of the weapons appeared to be taken from Homewrecker heavy plasma rifles.

"The Vanguard has a rather excellent workshop and tool fabrication facility," Ensign One replied. "I decided to create these, in the event that we will 'end up in a fight' as you described."

A deep, resonant hum then emanated from the robot, which Sterling recognized instantly as the sound of power cells being activated. The tips of Ensign One's integrated plasma cannons began to glow, signifying they were ready to fire.

"All I can say is I'm glad you're on my side, Ensign," Sterling said, casually aiming the barrels of the weapons in any direction other than at himself. He then frowned at the robot. "You are on my side, right?" he added with a sarcastic eyebrow raise. He may have been joking, but part of him still craved confirmation that the sentient machine wasn't going to turn on him, like its mechanical brethren had done four months earlier.

"I am on your side, sir," Ensign One confirmed as it disarmed its cannons and reconfigured them back into hands. Then its ocular units flashed. "For now..."

Sterling's frown deepened. "That better be your attempt at humor, Ensign."

"It was, sir," the robot replied, cheerfully. "Did I succeed?"

"No," Sterling hit back. Then he had a thought. Ensign One had known that his bag was full of weapons before he'd even opened it. "And another thing, just how did you know that my bag contained weapons, anyway?" he asked, putting the question to the machine. "It was shut up tighter than Admiral Griffin's drinks cabinet when you arrived."

"Improved ocular sensors," Ensign One answered, tapping the temple of its cranial unit. "I can now see in a much broader range of the EM spectrum, not just visible light."

"Does that include heat signatures?" asked Sterling, curious to learn more about his ensign's news abilities.

"I can see in infrared and ultraviolet, in addition to detecting everything from radio waves to x-rays and more," the robot replied. Sterling detected a hint of pride in its unique voice.

"That will come in useful too," said Sterling, checking over his stealth armor to make sure everything was fastened up tightly. The armor was designed to limit his own heat signature, in addition to absorbing scanner signals. "If those alien bastards radiate heat as strongly as they radiate their foul smell, it'll give us an advantage."

"I can also detect their scent from a range of one thousand meters," Ensign One replied, drawing a raised eyebrow from Sterling. "As long as the odor is able to carry to our location, of course," One corrected. "On a starship, the air recycling systems tend to make this ability redundant."

Sterling huffed a laugh. "Well, if humanity survives this, I'll need to take you hunting," he said, closing the holdall again. "Rations and meals trays will only last us so long now that no-one is manufacturing them anymore. Sooner or later, we'll have to start actually hunting and foraging again."

"I am curious to learn what the sensation of eating feels like," said Ensign One, wistfully. "Despite my physical and intellectual superiority over organic species, there are many aspects of being alive that I am unable to experience."

"Physical and intellectual superiority?" said Sterling, feeling suddenly under attack.

"I meant no offence, Commodore, I am merely stating a fact," the robot replied, cheerfully.

"Well, why don't you put your superiority to good use and get this damned alien contraption ready to take off?" Sterling said, rapping his knuckle on the hull of the Sa'Nerran shuttle. Compared to similar Fleet combat craft, the Sa'Nerran shuttle was more utilitarian in design. The Sa'Nerra did not care for creature comforts or aesthetics, and as such the shuttle was designed purely for maximum functionality. It was fast, maneuverable, well-armored and carried enough armaments to take on a Fleet Destroyer. However, it was also uncomfortable and as ugly as sin.

"The shuttle is already prepped and ready to depart, Commodore," Ensign One replied.

Sterling nodded. "Then let's get moving," he said, reaching for the button to close the rear hatch.

"Wait, Commodore, you are still missing one important piece of cargo," Ensign One said, raising the palm of its metal hand to stop Sterling in his tracks.

Sterling peered inside the cargo hold of the shuttle, not spotting anything obvious that was missing. "What have I forgotten?" he asked, glancing back to the robot. "It looks like we already have everything."

"You will need to include a selection of Fleet rations, Commodore," Ensign One said. "I do not believe you would find Sa'Nerran food to be palatable."

Sterling shrugged. "I'm game for trying it," he hit back, feeling like the robot had issued him a challenge of sorts. "It can't be any worse than a number eleven meal tray. That marinated tofu dish tastes like old rubber soaked in sweat."

Ensign One's glowing ocular sensors darkened then brightened again. "Really? I would be curious to try it."

"Honestly, you wouldn't..." Sterling hit back. He could almost taste the leathery chunks of soy in his mouth, despite it being two years since he'd had the misfortune of eating the meal tray in question.

"In any case, sir, it is not the taste of the Sa'Nerra food that is the issue," the robot continued, returning to the original topic. "The Sa'Nerra baste their meats in a substance that is toxic to humans. If you ingested their food, you would die within ninety seconds, weeping blood from you tear ducts."

Sterling snorted a laugh, assuming that Ensign One was joking. However, if there was a robot version of a poker face then the machine was making one, he realized.

"Fair enough, I'll grab some rations," he said, turning toward the exit to the Vanguard's small secondary docking garage. As he did so, he caught sight of Captain Banks. She was striding toward him like she had a purpose, and Sterling was pretty sure he knew what her purpose was.

"If you've come to try and talk me out of this again, don't bother," Sterling said, getting in first before Banks had even come to a stop in front of him. He was keen to head off any debate about the mission before it started.

"I'm not going to try to talk you out of it," Banks said, holding up her hands in surrender. "You've made your decision and that's all there is to it."

Sterling felt a weight lift from his shoulders. Based on the emotional and slightly awkward way in which they'd ended their previous conversation, he'd expected Banks to put up another fight.

"That's good then," Sterling replied, though he was

now confused as to the purpose of Banks' unannounced visit. "So why are you here?" he added, getting straight to the point. He didn't have time for small talk, not that either of them enjoyed participating in it.

"Respectfully, sir, I still think you should bring me with you," Banks began. Sterling was about to hit back before his fellow officer again raised her palms to stop him. "But I know you won't agree to that either, so the least I can do is check your weapons and equipment to make sure you have everything you need."

"It's not necessary, but if it will make you feel better about the mission, go ahead," Sterling said, offering his former first officer a smile, and also an olive branch.

Banks then turned to Ensign One, who had been quietly observing the exchange. Sterling had almost forgotten the machine was behind him.

"I hold you personally responsible for ensuring the Commodore returns from this mission in one piece, Ensign," Banks said, adopting a stricter, more formal tone.

"I understand, Captain Banks," Ensign One replied with matching determination. "I will not let you down. Either of you."

Banks nodded, then turned back to Sterling. "I had Shade run an updated scan and Omega Four is still clear of hostile ships," she went on. "Our relays are not picking up any unusual surge energy from the apertures, so you're good to go. But I'd suggest you head out soon. Based on the pattern of previous enemy movements, a Skirmisher squadron should pass through Omega Four in three hours on a routine patrol run."

Sterling nodded. "We were just about to leave before you arrived."

Banks glanced into the rear of the shuttle then frowned. "You should load some Fleet rations first," she said, still scouring the alien vessel's cargo bay. "From what I've heard, the alien food is a little too spicy for human stomachs."

"That's an understatement," Sterling hit back, recalling Ensign One's comment about weeping blood.

"I think there are some ration packs in the stores on deck thirteen, not too far from here," Banks said. "I'll help you grab some, if you like?"

"No, you carry on with your duties, Captain, I'll take care of it," Sterling said, keen to end the conversation while Banks was in a compliant mood. He nodded to the robot and the machine stepped to his side. "I'll notify you when we've cleared the Vanguard," Sterling continued. "I suggest you use the time while we're gone to run the Invictus and the Obsidian ships through some rigorous shakedown tests."

"They're already scheduled in, sir," said Banks, still smiling, amiably.

"Then carry on, Captain Banks," Sterling said, setting off toward the exit and the elevators to deck thirteen. However, he'd only made it a few meters across the deck before he realized Banks had remained alongside the shuttle.

"I'll just quickly finish the inventory check while you're gone," Banks said, obviously picking up on the fact Sterling was questioning why she hadn't left. "And Lieutenant

Razor said she wanted a close-range scan of the reactor signature, so we can more easily identify your shuttle at long-range. She's crawling around some maintenance tunnel or another, so I'll do that too, while I'm here."

"Fine, but make it quick, I don't want anything else to delay our departure," Sterling said, setting off again for the exit with Ensign One at his side.

"I'll be gone before you get back, sir," Banks said, before disappearing inside the shuttle.

Sterling reached the elevators a couple of minutes later and hit the call button. He then noticed that Ensign One was looking at him, its glowing ocular senses twinkling hypnotically.

"Something on your mind, Ensign?" Sterling asked as the elevator doors swung open.

"That was going to be my question, sir," Ensign One replied, waiting for Sterling to step into the elevator first before following him inside.

"I told you before, I don't need a shrink," Sterling hit back.

"Of course, Commodore," the robot replied. It was silent for a moment, but Sterling could sense the machine had more to say. "Do you mind if I ask a question, sir?"

"That depends on the question..." Sterling replied, cautiously.

"In the beginning, the war with the Sa'Nerra was about defeating an enemy and emerging victorious," Ensign One continued, presumably taking Sterling's non-committal answer as a green light. "Then it became about the survival of a species and of your culture."

"Do you actually have a question, Ensign?" Sterling asked, already growing tired of the conversation. Like the gen-fourteen AI that had spawned the sentient machine, Ensign One was nothing if not persistent, and verbose.

"Now, you are fighting for revenge," the robot ensign went on, undeterred by Sterling's crabby interjections. "But as someone from earth's history once said, an eye for an eye will only leave the whole world blind."

"Emergency stop..." Sterling called out. The elevator stopped dead, causing Sterling to almost buckle at the knees from the sudden deceleration. "Look, Ensign, if you have a point to make just make it," he said, turning to face his mechanical officer.

"War must be a means to an end, Commodore," Ensign One said, its glowing ocular sensors casting a bright, golden glow across Sterling's face. "If you win yet gain nothing, is that really a victory?"

Sterling sighed and rubbed his face, which was already becoming stubbled. The sentient AI had finally got to its question, and he had to admit it was a good one.

"It's better than losing," Sterling said, though he was painfully aware that this answer was lacking.

"Then may I suggest something, sir?" the robot said.

"I have a feeling I couldn't stop you if I wanted to..." Sterling hit back.

"Find something that is worth fighting for, and keep it always in mind," Ensign One said. "I have only been alive for a short time, but I would not give it up for anything."

"Maybe you'd think differently if you'd experienced loss, Ensign," Sterling replied. He understood the AI's point, but he also didn't feel like being lectured by a being that had barely any experience of life.

"Perhaps," Ensign One admitted, shrugging it metal shoulders. "But I do know that an eye-for-an-eye is not enough, Commodore. There must be something more."

Sterling frowned. He didn't want to dismiss the robot's words out of hand, but at that moment his mind was too busy to give them any serious thought.

"I'll take your advice into consideration, Ensign," Sterling replied, hoping that this would put an end to the robot's curious ways. "Resume..." he then said, glancing up at the ceiling of the elevator.

The elevator continued its descent and Ensign One turned to face the doors, presumably content that it had said its piece and been heard. Sterling also faced forward, his mind still racing. Mostly, his thoughts were occupied by battle tactics and strategies, mission plans, combat techniques and a dozen other things. However, in amongst this melee of neural activity were the words the robot had just spoken, fighting to gain ascendency. And for some reason, all he could think about was Mercedes Banks.

STERLING TRIED to relax into the passenger seat of the Sa'Nerran combat shuttle, but it felt like lying on a bed of nails. The seat was formed from a single, molded chunk of some sort of polymer, which was rock hard and unforgiving. The contours of the seat were also designed for the stubbier, leathery backs of Sa'Nerran warriors, rather than humans, which only served to make it more uncomfortable.

"Do you require assistance, Commodore?" asked Ensign One from the pilot's seat. The machine's similarly-unforgiving metal frame also didn't fit correctly into the seat, but the sentient robot didn't appear to care. "You are fidgeting more than usual."

"It's this damned chair," said Sterling, still shuffling around to find a vaguely tolerable sitting position. "It's like being strapped into a torture rack." He frowned, recalling the exact wording of Ensign One's statement. "And what do you mean, 'fidgeting more than usual'?" He added, snippily. "I don't fidget."

"It has been my observation that you frequently tap your finger against the side of your captain's console whenever you are feeling anxious or impatient," the robot pilot answered. "Should you not be at your station, the side of your right leg or any nearby table or surface usually acts as a substitute."

"I do not do that," Sterling hit back. Then his scowl deepened, uncertain of whether the robot's observation was true or not. It was like the feeling of being unsure whether something had happened in a dream or for real. "Or do I?" he added, suddenly doubting himself.

"You do, sir," Ensign One replied without hesitation. "Not that there is a problem with that, of course. I am not easily irritated, unlike others."

"What the hell is that supposed to mean?" Sterling snapped. Like the robot's earlier comment about its 'intellectual superiority' compared to organic beings, he felt like he was under attack for a second time.

"I merely mean that while some may find your incessant finger tapping annoying, I have adapted my programming to filter out the sound," Ensign One said, its glowing ocular units still peering out through the cockpit glass.

Sterling huffed a laugh. "Well, I guess there are some advantages to being a computerized life form," he replied, finally managing to find a vaguely comfortable position in the seat.

"Many, in fact," Ensign One said, adjusting the

shuttle's course and finally exiting the ring system of Omega Four. "Unlike humans, I am not burdened by the material limits of flesh and bone. I often wonder how you manage to function at all, considering your inherent fragility."

"Being made of flesh and bone doesn't make us fragile, Ensign," Sterling hit back. He glanced across at the robot pilot; its glowing ocular units were shining on him again. "Knowing how easily you can die is one hell of a way to motivate a person to stay alive."

Ensign One imitated the huffing sound Sterling often made, then cocked its head to the side, as if suddenly deep in thought. "I had not considered that, Commodore," the robot said. "It appears that I still have much to learn."

The alien computer console in front of Ensign One then released a high-pitched squawk that was so shrill it almost caused Sterling to leap out of his seat.

"What the hell is that noise?" Sterling said, glancing at the control in front of his seat. However, it was just an indecipherable array of glyphs and indicators to him.

"It is an alert to notify us that we are approaching the threshold of the aperture, sir," said Ensign One. "Surge parameters are programmed and locked in. Surging in ten seconds..."

Sterling heard the whine of the surge field generator begin to build. Despite the ship being of Sa'Nerran origin, the sound was practically indistinguishable from the hum of a Fleet surge field generator. There was then a bright flash of light and Sterling felt his body melt away into nothingness. His disembodied mind wandered and he found himself in his quarters on the Invictus, lying in his bed. He turned his head and saw Mercedes Banks lying next to him. She was naked and Sterling suddenly realized that he was too.

"Did you sleep okay?" Banks said, turning to face Sterling and using her arm as a pillow to rest her head on. The sheets slipped off her body a little; enough for Sterling to catch tantalizing glimpses of her body. Embarrassed, he tried to look away, but couldn't. He didn't want to.

"I did, how about you?" Sterling found himself replying. It was like he was a spectator, trapped in his own mind and unable to influence his own actions.

"I preferred the part before we went to sleep," Banks said, flashing her eyes at Sterling. She then drew herself closer to him and kissed him softly on the lips. "I knew it would be like this."

Sterling felt the pressure of Banks' kiss and the wetness of her lips against his. Then he drew back a fraction and smiled at her.

"I knew it would be like this too," he replied. Then he reached underneath the pillow and pulled out a plasma pistol. "And I knew it would always end this way," he heard himself speak, as he aimed the pistol at Banks' head. Sterling fought to take control of the scene, but he was still merely a passenger, observing his own disembodied thoughts. Then the plasma pistol fizzed and Banks' head exploded, showering the bed and the walls of his quarters with blood and brains.

"No!" Sterling screamed. He was back in normal space again, staring out at a new starfield. His hands were gripped tightly around the arms of the alien chair and his body was rigid, as if the seat had been electrified. He fought the images out of his mind and wrestled back control of his body. His bionic hand had gripped the arm-rest of the seat so tightly that it had crumpled beneath his grasp, like crushing an old-fashioned soda can.

"Commodore, are you okay?" said Ensign One, its glowing ocular units again shining onto Sterling's face. "You appear distressed."

"I'm fine," Sterling replied, angrily wrestling his bionic hand free of the mangled arm rest.

Sterling's tone was more aggressive than he'd intended, though he wasn't mad at Ensign One for enquiring about him. He was angry that his subconscious mind had once again overpowered him. In the months he'd spend at Omega Base, refitting and upgrading their fleet, the debilitating nightmares had occurred less and less frequently. As a result, Sterling had let his guard slip, permitting the full effect of the surge-inspired waking-dream to hit him like a tidal wave.

Sterling pressed his eyes shut and began to force his breathing into a slow, controlled rhythm. Soon the images and emotions he'd experienced sank deeper into the recesses of his mind. In the past, Sterling was able to bury these thoughts so deeply that within seconds they were all but forgotten. Now, the pit into which he submerged these burdensome feelings was becoming full, leaving them far closer to the surface than he liked.

Feeling more in control again, Sterling opened his eyes and glanced across to Ensign One. The robot had returned to its piloting duties and showed no signs that it was about to quiz him regarding the nature of his outburst. In its past form as the Invictus' gen-fourteen AI, the computer would have suggested a counselling program, or a hot cup of tea. Now, the sentient machine knew when to ask questions and when to simply shut up and let the other person talk in their own time. For that, Sterling was thankful.

"I appreciate you not asking," Sterling said, mostly in order to break the awkward silence between them.

Ensign One didn't immediately respond, though Sterling could see that its ocular units were flashing chaotically.

"In truth, I do not need to ask," the sentient AI finally replied, turning its head toward Sterling. "However, I believe it will be sufficient for you to know that I do already understand. And that if you ever need me, I am here."

Sterling frowned at the machine. His immediate reaction was to hit back and demand that the AI tell him exactly what it thought it knew. However, then he realized that his robotic ensign was right. Over the past couple of years, the computer had observed every one of Sterling's nightmares and visions. Given that the AI had also observed everyone and everything that had ever happened on or off the ship, through fixed or mobile computers, it stood to reason that it would have pieced together the source of his anxieties. It didn't change the fact that he didn't want to discuss them with his ensign, or anyone else for that matter. Yet for some reason knowing that the sentient AI understood what he was going through, at least on some level, did go some way to alleviating the burden.

"Right now, I just need you to tell me how long it is until the next aperture," Sterling said, deciding to brush over the matter as quickly as possible. "The sooner we can take out the Titan, the sooner we can move on Sa'Nerra."

"Of course, Commodore," Ensign One replied, returning its full attention to the helm controls. "The next aperture is just beyond the asteroid field. However, the presence of radioactive elements in the rocks is compromising our scanner efficiency. Sa'Nerran scanner technology is far inferior to that of Fleet vessels."

Sterling huffed a laugh. "That would have been useful information to know fifty years ago," he said, thinking out loud. "We always assumed these bastards were more advanced than we are."

Suddenly, there was a hard thump from somewhere behind Sterling. He spun around in his seat, drawing his plasma pistol at the same time.

"Was that an asteroid impact?" Sterling asked, remaining as still as a statue, listening in case the sound came again.

"Negative, Commodore, we have yet to reach the fringes of the asteroid field," Ensign One replied.

The sound came again, and this time Sterling could place it more clearly. It was coming from somewhere aft of the cockpit section.

"Check the internal scanners," Sterling said, sliding out of his seat and creeping cautiously toward the cockpit door. "Maybe we shook something loose during the surge."

"The radiation is also affecting internal scanners," Ensign One said as more scuffling noises echoed around the cockpit. "It could perhaps be Sa'Nerran live food that escaped it confines."

Sterling frowned at Ensign One. "Live food? You mean like those damned dinosaur things that tried to eat us on the Vanguard?"

"I would imagine that these edible beings are far smaller, sir," Ensign One replied, sounding completely unfazed by the prospect of living alien creatures roaming the shuttle. "Perhaps something more along the lines of Ubirajara jubatus or perhaps Compsognathus."

"I don't need a damned paleontology lesson, Ensign, I just need to know if these things are dangerous," Sterling hit back.

"Mostly likely, sir, yes," Ensign One replied, coolly. "Lieutenant Razor did say that she checked the shuttle and found nothing living on-board, but there may have been hidden compartments that we were not aware of."

"Great..." said Sterling, holstering his plasma pistol and drawing the Sa'Nerran half-moon blade from his belt instead. The last thing he wanted to do was fight a chicken-sized alien dinosaur hand-to-hand, but even worse would be to put a hole in the ship by shooting at the creature and missing. "Remind me to have a word with Lieutenant Razor when we get back," Sterling added, creeping up next to the door.

"If you prefer, Commodore, I will investigate," the robot offered. "Currently, the shuttle is on autopilot to the designated co-ordinates."

"No, you stay at the helm, Ensign," Sterling replied, hunting for and eventually finding the door release lever.

"With a bunch of radioactive asteroids flying around, we may be required to make a sudden course correction."

"Aye, sir," Ensign One replied. "I remain ready to assist."

"I think I can handle a few alien critters, Ensign," Sterling hit back, sliding his hand onto the door release handle. "Just get us to that aperture."

Sterling pulled the lever and the door swished open. He was hit with an icy blast of air from the aft compartment, which was dark and cold, like an old wine cellar.

"Can you turn the lights on back here?" Sterling said, creeping inside and using the torchlight function on his wrist-computer to illuminate the space.

"I will attempt to find the controls, sir," Ensign One called back from the cockpit. The robot's voice already sounded echoey and distant.

Sterling continued to move ahead, stubbing his toe on an exposed conduit as he did so. Biting down against the pain, he shone the light onto the deck and stepped over the obstacle, cursing the Sa'Nerran engineer that thought putting a trip-hazard outside the cockpit door was a good idea.

"I could really use those lights about now..." Sterling called out, sweeping the torch beam around the aft section of the shuttle. Like all of the alien ships Sterling had seen, the internal space was rudimentary. Sa'Nerran design was as crude and ugly as the aliens themselves.

Then the sound came again and Sterling froze, spinning his light onto the source of the noise, which was a simple, wardrobe-sized metal cabinet. Tightening his fingers around the grip of the serrated blade, Sterling grasped the handle of the storage locker and prepared to yank it open. His plan was to plunge the deadly weapon into the flesh of whatever alien beast lurked inside it before the critter had a chance to leap at his jugular. However, before he could pull back on the door, it was flung open from the inside. Sterling was struck and knocked flat against the opposite wall. A figure moved through the darkness, but even in the gloomy light, Sterling could see it was no chicken-sized alien dinosaur.

"Intruder alert!" Sterling called out, swinging the alien blade at the blur of motion. The shadowy figure blocked the attack, then caught Sterling's wrist. He tried to fight back, but his opponent's strength was greater, even managing to overpower his augmented, bionic hand.

"Stop!" cried a voice. It was familiar and Sterling froze.

Ensign One appeared, moving so fast it was like a flash of lightning across the night sky. The sentient AI reached out and grabbed the intruder, but even Ensign One's augmented Obsidian Soldier frame could not overpower the invader.

"Damn it, stop, it's me!"

This time Sterling recognized the voice clearly. "Stand down!" he called out, releasing his hold on the shadow in front of him. Ensign One did the same and the intruder stepped back. Sterling shone his torchlight onto the shape, illuminating the startled and deeply embarrassed face of Captain Mercedes Banks.

STERLING RE-HOOKED the Sa'Nerran blade to his armor, though at that moment he was seriously considering murdering his former first officer. He'd had plenty of scares in his time, and generally he handled them well, but Banks leaping out of the dark closet of an alien shuttle and grabbing him came in close to the top of the list.

"What the hell are you doing here?" Sterling snapped. "I damned near almost gutted you!"

"I'm disobeying orders and hiding out on board so that I can join the mission, what does it look like?" Banks hit back. For some reason, she was the one acting like the wounded party, as if it was Sterling that had done something wrong.

"It looked like you were trying to kill me," Sterling snapped.

"Well, you took me by surprise," Banks replied, throwing her arms out wide. Again, she was making it sound like the whole incident was somehow Sterling's fault.

"I took *you* by surprise?" Sterling said, recoiling a little from his fellow officer. "I thought you were an alien chicken dinosaur, stalking the shuttle looking for a human to gnaw on."

This response threw Banks completely. "A what-now?"

Sterling realized that without the proper context his statement sounded more than a little crazy. However, he also realized he was getting off track.

"The point is, you're not supposed to be here, Captain," he jabbed an angry finger at Banks. "In fact, I explicitly ordered you to stay put on the base and run the Invictus through its paces."

"Lieutenant Commander Shade is more than capable of running shakedown tests on the Invictus," Banks replied, stepping out of cupboard she'd been hiding in and dusting herself down. "You need me here, whether you like it or not."

"If I may interject, Commodore, another pair of hands on this mission would increase our odds of success by thirty-one percent," Ensign One interrupted.

Sterling turned and glowered at his robot ensign. "I didn't ask," he barked at the machine, causing the sentient AI's glowing orbs to dim a fraction.

"Commodore, I fully accept the consequences of my actions," Banks said, standing to attention in the dark, cramped confines of the corridor. "Take the Invictus and bust me down to Commander if you like. Hell, you can throw me in the brig once we get back, I don't care." Banks then aimed a finger at Ensign One, which appeared to make the robot anxious. "As Ensign One said, this mission stands a better chance of success with me on board. I'm not needed on the Omega Base. I am here."

"That wasn't your call to make, Captain," Sterling hit back, not letting Banks off the hook. "There may not be many of us left, but we're still Fleet. If we start to ignore the chain of command then this whole damned crusade falls apart at the seams."

"Understood, Commodore," Banks said, still standing to attention. "I will accept the consequences of my actions, whatever you deem fit."

Sterling let out an elaborate sigh and pressed his hands to his hips. He'd made his point and got the desired response, though none of it changed the fact Banks was still on the ship.

"Well, I suppose since you're here, you may as well suit up," Sterling said, admitting defeat. They were already closer to their destination than they were to Omega Four, and he didn't want to risk returning empty-handed, in case they were spotted and tracked. "I didn't bring a spare set of armor or gear, though, so you're not exactly going to be prepared for a fight."

Banks smiled then engaged the torchlight on her computer. Shining the light into the rear of the shuttle's compartment, she illuminated another large holdall.

"I snuck an extra set of stealth armor on board while you were off gathering the Fleet rations," Banks said, looking extremely pleased with herself. "I also loaded a Homewrecker, along with my own personal choice of close-quarters weapon, since I guess you'd rather kill quietly than have me blast up the place."

"I'd rather you had obeyed my damned orders," Sterling snapped, again drawing a sheepish look from Banks. "But good, at least you came prepared." He had a thought. "I only brought enough rations for one, though. I don't suppose you thought to pack a few extra commando bars?"

"No, I didn't think of that," Banks admitted. She then shoved her hand into the pocket of her pants and pulled out a Commando Bar wrapper. "And I may have already eaten one of them."

"Just one?" Sterling asked, eyebrow raised.

"Maybe a couple?" Banks said, shrugging and trying her best to look innocent.

A rasping, high-pitched alert tone sounded from the consoles in the cockpit. All three officers snapped into a higher gear and rushed inside, alert to the potential danger.

"I am picking up a Skirmisher patrol, dead ahead," said Ensign One. "Three vessels. Generation-two designs."

"How did we not see them earlier?" Sterling asked, dropping down into the second seat. Banks stood behind him, her hand gripping the headrest of the hard, molded chair so tightly that the material groaned under the pressure.

"As I feared, the radiation from the asteroid cluster hid them from our scanners, sir," the robot replied.

Sterling cursed. "Have they seen us?"

"Affirmative, Commodore," Ensign One replied, smartly. "In fact, they have transmitted a message."

"Then I hope you weren't bluffing about being able to understand the Sa'Nerran language," Banks chipped in.

"I was not, Captain Banks," the robot replied, sounding a touch offended. "The message reads as follows... 'Attack Shuttle Emissary One, transmit ID verification code and confirm destination'." Ensign One turned to face Sterling, it's glowing ocular units shimmering. "At least, I think that's what the message says."

Sterling looked wide-eyed at his AI pilot then glanced up at Banks, who looked similarly unimpressed. "You *think* that's what it reads?" Sterling repeated.

"The Sa'Nerran language is quite complex, sir," Ensign One continued, taking on a cheerful, studious tone, like a college professor who had just been asked about his subject at a dinner party. "There are hundreds of different ways of saying essentially the same thing. What the Sa'Nerra say and how it is understood depends on what was said previously, by whom, and in what order."

"You mean like how we can ask, 'Do you want to go for a drink?' and the answer could be, 'yes' or 'hell yeah' or 'is the Pope Catholic?'," asked Banks.

"Not quite, Captain, but it is similar in some respects," Ensign One replied. "In essence, the Sa'Nerran language cannot be directly translated without first understanding all of its nuances and rules. That is why Fleet scientists could never decipher it based on the sounds and writings alone."

"I'm not interested in a lesson in Sa'Nerran linguistics, Ensign," Sterling cut in, before the discussion had a chance to progress further. "All I need to know is can you correctly respond to their message?"

Ensign One thought for a moment, its ocular units flashing wildly as it did so. "I can respond, Commodore," the robot finally answered. "However, I cannot guarantee that my response will be entirely accurate."

"That will have to do, Ensign," Sterling said, as the trio of Sa'Nerran Skirmishers began to form up above and alongside the combat shuttle. "But stand ready to throw everything we have into the engines should things turn ugly."

"Aye, sir," Ensign One replied, inputting the message into the console. "Message sent."

Sterling waited for a reply, but none was forthcoming. "Are you sure the message was transmitted?" he asked, starting to feel even more on edge.

"I confirmed that we are Attack Shuttle Emissary One and transmitted the shuttle's ID, which I gleaned by interrogating this vessel's vastly inferior computer system," Ensign One answered. "I then conveyed our destination as being Fleet F-sector."

Sterling cursed. "I hadn't factored that this ship could be linked directly to McQueen," he said. "The Sa'Nerra won't have heard from her for months. Seeing their Emissary's shuttle just pop up in the Void after all this time is bound to raise some suspicion."

Banks nodded. "Hopefully, these alien assholes haven't yet learned McQueen's fate, or this could turn out to be a very short trip."

"Serves you right for coming along," quipped Sterling, shooting Banks a dirty look. He wasn't ready to drop the issue of her disobeying orders yet.

"Of course, given the complexities of the Sa'Nerran language, it is also possible that I said, "Get out of our way, or we will destroy you," Ensign One cut in, with a breezy nonchalance. "Or, in fact, any number of other similarly offensive phrases."

Sterling shot an equally dirty look at his robot pilot. "I hope that was your attempt at humor, Ensign."

"Yes, Commodore, it was," the robot replied, shining its glowing ocular units onto Sterling's face. "How did I do?"

"Just stick to piloting the ship, and leave the poorly-timed jokes to Banks," Sterling replied. He then glanced anxiously up at the scarred underbelly of the older alien warship flying in formation above them. "What the hell is taking them so long?" he muttered, more to himself than to the others.

"I don't think I've ever been this close to a Skirmisher before," Banks said, also peering up at the vessel. "They don't get any prettier up-close."

Suddenly, the lead Skirmisher put on a burst of speed and pulled ahead of the shuttle. Sterling swallowed hard as the alien vessel then fired its thrusters, spinning a full one-hundred and eight degrees in barely more than a second. Its plasma cannons were glowing hot, ready to fire.

"Ensign, get us out of here!" Sterling called out. However, Ensign One did not respond or react. "Ensign, what are you doing? Let's move!" Sterling repeated, staring at the controls and trying to make sense of them, but the layout was totally alien to him.

"Standby..." Ensign One replied, remaining calm and still. "I do not believe the Skirmisher is about to fire."

Sterling then saw the consoles in front of his seat begin to flash and update with a new string of glyphs.

"It's scanning us," said Banks. She pointed out at the Skirmisher through the cockpit glass. "Look, its scanner pod is activated."

"Affirmative, the vessel is scanning us," Ensign One said.

"With its plasma cannons hot?" Sterling hit back. He was still fixated by the glowing tips of the alien ship's weapons, rather than its scanner pod.

"It is perhaps standard procedure," Ensign One offered, while working at his console.

"Hell, they're not even friendly to their own kind," Banks said, shaking her head.

The consoles then registered another message, and this time it came through on audio too. The rasping, waspish hisses were so loud that they seemed to drill into Sterling's skull. Then, as suddenly as the Skirmisher had appeared in front of them, looking ready to reduce them to dust, the vessel spun around again. Sterling watched as the Skirmisher's twin engine pods ignited and the ship powered away with its escorts in close formation behind it. Sterling flopped back in his seat, though he quickly regretted doing so, considering how unforgiving it was.

"What the hell just happened?" said Banks, who was looking flushed and breathless.

"I believe my response was received and understood," said Ensign One. Despite its inorganic robot body, the sentient AI also looked relieved.

"What did they say back?" asked Sterling, still keeping

a close eye on the Skirmishers as the glow of their engines began to grow smaller. "Surely an intense scan like that isn't standard procedure in response to a simple hail?"

"Roughly translated, I believe that their response was, 'you'd better get that checked out,' Ensign One replied, cheerfully.

Sterling and Banks frowned at one another. "Was that another attempt at a joke?" Banks asked.

The sentient robot turned to face Captain Banks, its ocular units shimmering softly. "No, Captain, this time it was not."

THE WAS a flash of light then a new starfield appeared beyond the cockpit glass. Ensign One had just completed another surge in the Sa'Nerran combat shuttle. However, unlike their previous waypoints, this was an area of space that Sterling was familiar with. Their latest surge had taken them into the heart of enemy-occupied Fleet C-sector. Sterling instinctively looked at his consoles, ready to perform the routine series of scans and post-surge checks that were standard procedure, before remembering that nothing in front of him made sense.

"I take it that we have arrived at the intended co-ordinates, Ensign?" said Sterling, turning to his robot pilot for a report instead. "I still can't make head nor tail of these readouts."

"We're in the right place alright," said Banks, answering before the robot had a chance to speak. She stood between Sterling and One, peering out of the cockpit glass. "That's Dawn Colony up ahead. I'd recognize that cobalt-blue world anywhere, though it's looking a little less azure than the last time I saw it."

Ensign One's console squawked an alert and the machine checked it without delay. "Dawn Colony has been attacked, Captain Banks," the robot officer said, calmly but with a touch of melancholy too. "Smoke from the burning cities is clouding the atmosphere. That is the reason for the planet's apparent lack of luster."

"What sort of causalities are we looking at, Ensign?" Sterling asked. The planet had now swung more clearly into view and he could make out the swirling smoke clouds for himself.

"I cannot get accurate data from this range and with the shuttle's limited scanning capabilities," Ensign One replied, working the controls of the alien console. "However, the capitol, Ember City, has been completely destroyed, along with twelve other cities within scanning range. I would estimate casualties in the region of fifty to seventy-five million."

Sterling found himself gripping the arms of the chair again, causing even more damage to the already mangled material.

"Fifty to seventy-five million?" repeated Banks. Her incredulous tone made it sound like Ensign One was a rogue tradesman that had just quoted an exorbitant sum for a simple job. "On just one colony world?"

"It's just a number, Captain," Sterling cut in, trying to head off any further discission of their losses. He didn't want them to fixate on the human cost, as it would only lead them to become maudlin and depressed. "Fifty here, ten on another world, probably billions on Earth alone. They're just numbers. It doesn't matter how many they've killed or how many they're still killing because we can't do a damned thing to change it. All that matters is how we respond."

"And how many of those alien bastards we kill in return," Banks growled. She was now crushing the stumpy headrests of the chairs with her powerful hands.

Sterling was reminded of Ensign One's comments about an eye-for-an-eye simply leaving the whole world blind. However, in that moment he didn't care. The aliens had shown no mercy and neither would he. If that left them both with nothing then so be it.

"I am also reading troop transports on the ground," Ensign One continued. "I estimate that there are in the region of two-hundred thousand combatants, including turned Fleet crew and civilians."

"There's nothing we can do for those people now," Sterling said, closing himself off to the plight of Dawn Colony. "Just stay on course, Ensign. We have a mission to complete."

Ensign One acknowledged Sterling then the cockpit fell silent for a time as the combat shuttle cut through space on course to the next aperture. As they drew closer to the inner-colony world, Sterling began to make out the shapes of ships in orbit. Even from their current distance, he could see that the hull configurations were a mix of Sa'Nerran and Fleet designs.

"How many warships are still in orbit, Ensign?" Sterling asked. He was more concerned about enemy vessels than he was troops on the ground. The troops posed no threat to his mission; warships did.

"Twenty-four ships in total remain in orbit of Dawn Colony, sir," Ensign One replied, smartly. "Of which, seven are Fleet vessels, presumably those that have been turned."

"That looks like the Cornwallis," said Banks, squinting out into the darkness surrounding the planet. "I served as weapons officer on that ship as a junior lieutenant. It was a good vessel. One that saw us through quite a few rough scrapes."

Sterling looked at the battle-scarred hull of the third-gen Fleet Light Cruiser that Banks had referred to and felt anger flood his body again. These were warships that had served Fleet with honor. Now, the aliens had captured them and perverted their crews so they no longer fought for Fleet, but for the enemy instead. It was a fate worse than death, Sterling thought, as the Cornwallis slipped past in the darkness. If he could have turned his guns onto the vessel and destroyed it then and there he would have done.

"Steady as she goes to the aperture, Ensign," Sterling said, choosing not to engage further in the conversation about Banks' former ship. It just felt like opening old wounds. "One more surge and we'll be knocking on the door of the Sa'Nerran Battle Titan. Then we can stop creeping around and start to make some noise of our own."

"Aye sir, time to aperture threshold, four minutes and three seconds from the point at which I finish speaking," Ensign One said.

Sterling cast a sideways glance at the robot ensign before glancing at Banks, who also returned a knowing smile. There were moments when Ensign One sounded almost identical to the generation-fourteen AI it had evolved from. However, these flashes of the old computer were increasingly rare. Ensign One was now an individual life form, as unique as any human being.

Ensign One's console then screeched an alert. It was another incomprehensible mixture of hisses and squawks that hurt Sterling's ears.

"A phase-three Sa'Nerran Skirmisher has split off from the squadron in orbit, sir," Ensign One reported. "It is on an intercept course."

The console then squawked another alert and this time Sterling recognized the tone. It was the same ear-piercing sound that he'd heard when the Skirmisher patrol in the previous sector had contacted them.

"They are requesting that we hold position, sir," Ensign One reported, turning its glowing ocular units on Sterling.

"They're asking or they're demanding?" Banks cut in.

"My Sa'Nerran is still rusty, Captain, but I believe they are quite insistent," One replied.

"Maintain your course and speed, Ensign," Sterling said, quick to head off any suggestion that they might comply with the alien's demands. "And get ready for a rebound surge. We'll throw these assholes off our scent during the transition through the aperture."

"I'm afraid a rebound surge will not work this time, Commodore," Ensign One replied. "There is only one exit point from this aperture."

Sterling cursed, remembering that the surge from

Dawn Colony into the solar system spat them out close to Moon-COP, which was in orbit of Earth's lone satellite.

"Give me another option, Ensign," Sterling said, while searching the corners of his own mind for a way to throw the Sa'Nerra off their scent. "We can't comply with their order, and we also can't have them raise the alarm and come after us."

Ensign One's console squawked again and this time the voice of a warrior came through over the speakers. A string of waspish hisses filled the cockpit, seeming to come at them from every conceivable angle. Ensign One then activated a control on his dashboard and replied in a similarly incomprehensible sequence of rasps and hisses. The robot rapidly input a string of commands into a secondary computer before pulling back its fist and hammering it through the console.

"What the hell are you doing?" said Sterling, as sparks erupted from the punctured dashboard.

"I reported that we are having technical difficulties," Ensign One replied, pulling its hand out of the console. Smoke rose from the joints as if its metal digits had just been freshly forged. "I said that we have a reactor containment leak that is affecting our scanners, and that they should not approach. Then I disabled the communications array." Ensign One raised its smoking right hand and shone his glowing ocular units onto it. "I felt that it was best to disable it convincingly."

"Did it work?" asked Captain Banks.

The still-functional parts of the computer console in

front of the robot registered another shrill alert. Ensign One checked it without delay.

"The Skirmisher has increased speed, but has not armed its weapons," Ensign One reported.

"That means no, they didn't buy it," Sterling cut in. "But since they haven't launched torpedoes, we can assume they're coming to take a closer look to confirm our story."

"I can initiate a small reactor leak to maintain the ruse," Ensign One said, working the controls again. "The radiation level will have an effect on your organic frames. I would suggest dosing with anti-radiation meds in advance."

"Do it, Ensign," said Sterling, nodding to Banks, who then went aft to grab a medical kit from their supplies. "Can we surge before they intercept us?"

"Negative, sir, not unless we increase speed too," Ensign One replied.

Sterling cursed again. "If we increase speed, it just looks like we're running," he said, rubbing the back of his neck. "Is there any way we can disable that Skirmisher, without openly firing on them?"

Banks returned with the med kit, cracked it open, and administered an anti-radiation shot to Sterling.

"What about if we wait for the Skirmisher to get in close then drop a bunch of charges into their path?" Banks suggested, while administering a shot to herself. "We have two boxes of plasma grenades in the hold. We could slow to allow the Skirmisher to get close, then set them to EM blast mode and drop them out of the cargo bay doors." She shrugged. "It wouldn't look like an attack since our weapons aren't armed. And by the time their systems come back online, we'd be long gone."

Sterling raised his eyebrows and looked to Ensign One to get his input on Banks' idea.

"It is possible, sir," the robot replied, sounding genuinely excited by the prospect. "However, the timing must be precise. If the grenades detonate too close to this shuttle, then we could also be disabled."

Sterling could now see the alien warship approaching their position, silhouetted against the blue planet to its rear. The combat shuttle was no match for the Skirmisher and he knew they didn't stand a chance if it came down to a straight-up fight.

"Do it, Ensign," Sterling said, making his decision. "But let's make sure we're as hard to find as possible once we reach the solar system."

"What do you have in mind?" Banks asked, sounding intrigued.

Sterling activated the computer on his wrist and brought up a navigational map of the solar system, focused on the aperture located near Fleet Moon-COP. "If we vector our surge just right, we can emerge into normal space close to the dark side of the moon. A ship this size would be hard to spot, especially since no-one will be looking for us. That would give us time to get our bearings and slip away without raising any alarms."

"Sounds dangerous," said Banks. She smiled. "I like it."

"Don't like it yet," Sterling hit back. "If our calculations are off, we might end up as permanent residents of the moon."

"Just how close to the moon do we need to get?" Banks asked, suddenly sounding less cocky.

Sterling turned to Ensign One. "How close can you get us, Ensign?"

The sentient robot's ocular units flashed brightly for a moment before dimming again.

"I believe we shall all discover the answer to that question very soon, Commodore," Ensign One answered.

STERLING TAPPED HIS NEURAL INTERFACE, then closed the visor on his helmet. Reaching out and connecting to Captain Banks through the link, he quickly headed aft into the cargo hold of the compact alien shuttle.

"How many plasma grenades shall we use?" Banks asked, grabbing the ammo box of explosives.

"Hell, let's use all of them," Sterling answered, while setting to work configuring the first grenade to EM mode. "We need to make sure that ship is taken out of commission."

"No guts, no glory, right?" Banks said, also grabbing a grenade from the box and setting to work. "I just hope we don't need to blast our own exit from the Battle Titan, because without these we'll be a little stuck."

Sterling huffed a laugh. "I like your optimism in thinking that we're still going to make it on-board the damned thing," he replied, tossing a reconfigured grenade in an empty duffel bag. "Thankfully, if we do need to make our own exit then a certain stowaway can make herself useful by tearing a hole in the hull."

"See, I told you that you'd need me," Banks replied, intentionally missing the point of Sterling's acerbic comeback.

Despite being unable to see Banks' face because of the darkened visor, Sterling could sense through their link that she was smirking.

"Commodore, the Skirmisher is becoming increasingly insistent that we slow to a stop at once," Ensign One said, its voice coming through an audio comm-link inside Sterling's helmet. "They have now charged weapons."

"Stall them, Ensign," Sterling ordered, tossing the second-to-last grenade into the bag. "I don't care how you do it. Just make something up."

"Given my current understanding of the Sa'Nerran language, I do not believe that will be difficult, sir," the robot officer replied, drolly.

Banks laughed and turned her visor-covered face toward Sterling. "I like our new ensign. He's got spunk."

"I'm not even going to ask what that's supposed to mean," Sterling hit back, finishing the last grenade, then pulling the drawstring on the bag to close it. "But so long as it also has the ability to keep those aliens from blasting us out of space, I don't care what else it has."

Banks also finished reconfiguring her last grenade and tossed it into a separate drawstring bag. She then shouldered the bag with far less care and attention than Sterling would have liked, considering the volatile nature of its contents.

"Our stealth armor doesn't contain any maneuvering jets, so we're going to need to hook on before we head outside," Banks said. She attached a tether to her stealth armor and hooked the other end onto the shuttle's rear support pillar.

"Hook on?" Sterling hit back. "You're not suggesting we space-walk over to that Skirmisher, are you?"

"We only get one shot at this, Lucas, which means we can't afford to miss," Banks replied. She had already poised her hand next to the door release lever.

Sterling cursed. "I was going to suggest we arm one of the grenades then just toss the bags at the ship, but you're right," he admitted, also hooking himself onto the support pillar. "Though for the record, this plan is worse than the one where you had us crawling through a rest room maintenance hatch."

"Noted, Commodore," Banks replied, blithely. "Are you ready?"

"Not in the slightest," Sterling hit back. "But hold on while I let Ensign One know what we're about to do."

Banks nodded, her hand remaining next to the ramp release lever. Sterling then tapped the communicator link on the side of his helmet and connected to Ensign One in the cockpit.

"Ensign, we're about to take a little space walk," Sterling began, gripping his bag of explosives more tightly. "Keep us as close as you can to that Skirmisher and be ready to reel us in if things go wrong."

"Aye, Commodore, standing by," the robot replied. "I

assume you do not want to know the odds of your plan resulting in serious injury or death?"

"What do you think?" Sterling hit back, grabbing a handrail to the side of the hatch, ready to brace himself against the sudden decompression of the compartment.

"I think no, sir," the robot replied.

"You're right, you are learning," said Sterling. "We're going to open the rear hatch in five. Be ready to compensate for the sudden decompression."

Ensign One acknowledged, and Sterling nodded to Banks to open the hatch. The new Captain of the Invictus yanked down on the lever and moments the later the ramp swung open, blowing random pieces of loose alien junk out into space. Sterling's bionic hand helped him to brace against the sudden blast of air escaping the hold. However, Banks' super-human strength made it look like she was simply holding on to the mast of a yacht in calm, peaceful waters.

"Heading out now," said Banks, adjusting her footing then pushing off into space. The tether began to unwind rapidly as she departed.

Sterling stepped out onto the lowered ramp and peered up at the belly of the phase-three Skirmisher cruising above them.

"I thought our last close encounter with a Skirmisher was close enough," Sterling said, watching Banks float up toward the vessel. He then pushed off himself and began to traverse the emptiness that separated the two ships.

"I think this has to be a Fleet first," said Banks, reaching the hull of the enemy ship and grabbing onto a torpedo pod on its wing to steady herself. "I'm pretty sure that no-one has ever engaged an enemy vessel during a spacewalk before."

"There's probably a reason for that," Sterling replied as he floated closer.

Suddenly, the Skirmisher adjusted course, moving closer to the combat shuttle, but remaining above and behind it. Sterling, watched in horror as the nose of the alien warship came toward him. His stealth armor may have allowed him to survive in space, but its lack of built-in propulsion meant that he was unable to get out of the way.

"Lucas, look out!" Banks called out through their neural link, but her warning was a useless as his stealth armor. Thrusting out his bionic hand, Sterling tried to cushion himself against the impact of the Skirmisher's hull as best he could, but it still felt like he'd been run over by a tractor. For a moment, he blacked out before the shrill warning alarms inside his helmet roused his senses again. It was then he realized he was pancaked to the ventral nose section of the alien Skirmisher, like a bug squashed on a windshield.

"Lucas, respond!" he heard Banks calling out through their neural link. "If you can hear me, wait there, I'm coming to get you."

Sterling groaned and pushed his head off the Skirmisher's hull. His visor was cracked and the diagnostic system built into his stealth armor had crashed and was in the process of restarting. However, even without an active damage readout, he knew he was in trouble. He could hear the hiss of oxygen escaping from his pressurized armored suit, like an airbed slowly deflating.

"Hold your position, Captain," Sterling replied through their link. "Deploy your grenades and set a timer for..." Sterling hesitated. Without his visor readout, he had no idea how long it would be until they needed to surge.

"We have two minutes until the shuttle reaches the aperture threshold," Banks answered, filling in the blanks. "But this Skirmisher will fire on us before we surge, if we don't stop it now."

"Then work fast," Sterling said. "In the meantime, I'll get myself free and try to arm the second bag of grenades."

"Understood, sir," Banks answered smartly. Her tone was businesslike and professional, but Sterling could feel her emotions too, and he knew she was worried.

With Banks working to arm her grenades, Sterling turned his attention back to his own predicament. His bionic hand, which had taken the brunt of the impact when the shuttle adjusted course, had punctured the outer hull armor of the Skirmisher. It wasn't deep enough to cause a hull breach, but the collision had ruptured a section of his armor, just above the wrist. Sterling could see his oxygen supply leaking out from the puncture as he slowly pulled his hand free to examine the damage.

"My suit is punctured, Mercedes," Sterling called out to Banks over their link. "It's not bad, but I'm losing oxygen fast," he added, while unslinging his bag of explosives.

"I've wrapped the strap of my bag around the support pillar of the Skirmisher's torpedo pod," said Banks through the link. "It will blow in ninety seconds. Does that give you enough time?"

"It'll have to be enough," Sterling replied, finally managing to open his bag of explosives. He reached inside and grabbed one of the grenades. "I'm almost there," he added, struggling with the weapon in order to set a timer. "But if you're done then get back to the shuttle and get ready to haul me in, that's an order."

Sterling could feel that Banks didn't like the order even before she'd spoken a word in reply. Her anxiety was now mixed with anger. In the past, he wouldn't have doubted even for a microsecond that his former first officer would follow his order without question. Yet recent events had proved that Banks was willing to step outside of her usual lane and go against orders. However, now was not the time for hesitation, doubt or emotion. Now was the time to act and to follow orders, because otherwise they were all dead.

"Aye, sir, returning now," Banks replied, after a noticeable period of hesitation. "But I'll be standing by, ready to bring you in."

Sterling then saw Banks fly past him, moving at speed. It was like she was a fish that had just been hooked by an angler and was being reeled in. Returning his focus to the grenade in his hand, Sterling finally managed to access the delay timer. He set the countdown to forty-five seconds, then wrapped the strap of the bag around the rupture in the alien ship's outer hull. He was about to kick off from the surface when he looked up and saw a face staring out at him through a side window on the Skirmisher's bridge. Wide yellow eyes were locked onto his and Sterling could even see that the warrior's mouth was hanging slightly agape. He had often wondered what range of emotions the Sa'Nerra experienced. He knew from Lieutenant Razor's link to an alien commander that they did feel fear, at least on some level. And now he knew that they could be shocked and surprised too.

Kicking off from the ship, Sterling threw up a middle finger salute to the watching alien. "See you in hell, you piece of shit!" he yelled out loud. He didn't care that the alien couldn't possibly have heard or understood him; it felt good to shout it anyway. "Reel me in, Mercedes!" he called out through the neural link.

The slack in the tether was rapidly taken up and Sterling was yanked toward their stolen combat shuttle. He watched the warrior turn from the window and smiled, knowing that no matter what the alien soldier did next, its fate was already sealed. Moments later the first bag of grenades detonated and the Skirmisher was rocked by an EM pulse that was powerful enough to disable a light cruiser. Then the second bag detonated and the alien ship lost all power. Sterling waved at the disabled warship, spreading more of his precious oxygen into space as he did so. Then the winch system that was hauling him back into the combat shuttle stopped.

"What the hell, Mercedes, haul me in!" Sterling called out, using the tether to spin himself around. Then he saw the reason why the winch system had failed. The pulse from the grenades had not only disabled the Skirmisher, it had disabled the combat shuttle too.

"Main power is down," he heard Banks call out through

their link. His fellow officer suddenly appeared at the edge of the cargo compartment, still wearing her helmet and visor. "Ensign One is on it, but the surge field generator is already fully charged!"

Sterling could feel the panic rising inside Banks, and knew exactly the reason why. Surge field generators were basically enormous capacitors that once charged had to be dissipated. Usually this process was controlled by the navigation systems so that the surge was triggered at precisely the required moment. However, if the nav computer was down then the shuttle would hit the aperture threshold and execute an uncontrolled surge. And there was nothing any of them could do to stop it.

Sterling felt the tether again begin to tug against his body and he saw Banks manually pulling him in. He tried to assist by also climbing along the leash, but the oxygen leak from his armor was making him feel weak and dizzy.

"I'm almost out of air," Sterling said, feeling the link between them start to wane. "Close the ramp now before we hit the aperture."

Banks didn't respond. Sterling concentrated on the link, feeling sure that he was still connected to his fellow officer's mind, and tried again.

"Captain, close the damned hatch," Sterling called out for a second time, but his words came out muddy and indistinct. "that's... an... order..."

With his strength failing, Sterling lost his grip on the tether and found himself floating back out into space. His body spun around and he saw the crippled Skirmisher. It was listing out of control, barely twenty meters from the shuttle.

"At least I'm taking you bastards down with me," Sterling thought, attempting again to shoot a middle finger at the ship. However, he could no longer move his arm. He could barely even keep his eyes open.

On the brink of losing consciousness, Sterling felt a hard thump to his back. He was then spun around and found himself staring at the visor-covered face of Captain Mercedes Banks. She had jumped back out into space and caught him.

"What... are... you... doing..." Sterling tried to say through their still open link, but again the words were garbled and indistinct.

Banks closed her hand around the punctured section of Sterling's armor, instantly sealing the breach thanks to the immense pressure of her grip.

"I'm saving your ass, what does it look like?" Banks said. She then attached an oxygen supply tube from her own helmet to Sterling's. There was another hiss of gas then Sterling sucked in the fresh supply of oxygen like a freediver coming up for air. "And before you come at me with the Omega Directive speech, I'm not saving your ass for sentimental reasons," Banks added, correctly guessing Sterling's next line of attack. "This mission needs the three of us. Coming out to get you was a tactical decision. Nothing more."

Sterling laughed weakly. "Noted, Captain. I'll try not to take that personally."

Suddenly there was an intense flash of light and the

shuttle vanished. Moments later, Sterling and Banks were consumed by nothingness too. The next thing he knew, Sterling was standing in front of his fellow officer. They were on a white, sandy beach in a small, tree-lined bay. The warm, azure water was lapping against their bare feet, while a gentle breeze caressed their faces. Neither of them spoke; they simply gazed into one another's eyes. Banks brought her face closer to his and Sterling found himself also drawing nearer. However, unlike in his other surge-inspired waking dreams, this time he was in control of his actions. And this time he wanted it to happen. Their lips touched and Sterling felt a shock rush through his body, like a static charge. The beach melted away and he felt himself being sucked back into normal space, like he'd fallen through a giant inter-dimensional plughole.

The vivid, sunlit cove was quickly replaced with darkness, as black and as unyielding as space itself. Sterling's eyes began to focus and he saw Banks in front of him again, still suspended in space in her stealth armor. Behind her was their stolen Sa'Nerran combat shuttle, but instead of stars the small craft was now hurtling toward the pockmarked, dusty silver surface of Earth's moon. A shadow crept over Banks, and Sterling turned his head to see another ship tumbling through space behind them, so close he felt he could reach out and touch it. He forced down a dry, hard swallow, realizing what had happened. The sudden discharge of surge-field energy from the shuttle's generator had not only allowed their own vessel to pass though the aperture to the solar system. It had drawn the Skirmisher right along with them.

THE TETHER ATTACHED to Sterling's stealth armor suddenly stiffened and he was yanked toward the combat Shuttle. Tightening his grip around Banks' waist, he saw that the engines of the shuttle had flashed back into life.

"Commodore, Captain, do you read me?" said Ensign One through the comm-link inside their helmets.

"We're here, Ensign, but just barely," Sterling replied, glancing down at Banks' hand, which was still wrapped around his wrist to seal the rupture in his armor. "What's your status?"

"The shuttle's systems are rebooting now, but thrusters and engines are online, and I have manual control," the robot answered. "I will need to initiate a full power deceleration as soon as you are on board."

Sterling was now staring into the open cargo hold of the shuttle, which was approaching at a frighting speed. "At the rate you're winching us in, that won't be long..." Sterling replied, eyes growing wide.

"As soon as you are inside, brace hard," Ensign One continued. "This is going to be close."

Sterling didn't even have time to reply before he was reeled inside the cargo hold and slammed into the deck. The ramp began to close, but Ensign One had already initiated a full-power turn. Sterling was thrown to the side wall of the shuttle and he felt his armor crack. The roar of the engines began to build and he reached out for something – anything – he could use to brace himself. At the third attempt, he managed to catch the strap of one of the stowed weapons crates he'd brought on board. Then the forces on his body increased exponentially.

"Mercedes..." Sterling called out. He'd only managed to grab on with his organic left hand, rather than his stronger bionic arm. "I can't hold on!"

Banks released her own handhold and soared past Sterling like a bullet. His heart lurched at the possibility of his fellow officer being expelled into space, but Banks managed to catch an overhead beam and stop herself just in time.

"Give me your hand!" she called out, reaching out to Sterling with her free hand.

Sterling extended his bionic arm toward Banks, but the tips of their fingers barely touched. Then the strap holding the weapons crate in place snapped and Sterling fell. The crate jammed into the partially-closed cargo bay door and Sterling landed on top of it. Plumes of moon dust were now flooding the compartment as the thrust from the shuttle's engines kicked up a storm-cloud of the silvery material. Unable to see more than a few centimeters in front of him, Sterling saw a hand grab his chest plate. Moments later the weapons crate was dislodged and tumbled out of the still-open ramp, vanishing into the storm of moondust. Sterling grabbed Banks' arm and tried to pull himself away from the ramp as it continued to whir shut, threatening to crush his legs, which were dangling precariously beneath him. Pulling his feet up at the last moment, the ramp finally locked shut and the environmental systems in the shuttle began to expel the cloud of fine moon dust particles. Suddenly, the forces on his body from the rapid deceleration vanished and both Sterling and Banks hit the deck like dead weights.

"Deceleration burn complete," Ensign One said through the comm-link, the machine's voice coming across sounding breathless with excitement. "Are both of you still functional?"

"I think so," said Sterling, retracting his visor and sucking in a deep breath of air. He then coughed as some of the remaining moon dust particles tickled the back of his throat. "What's the status of the Skirmisher?"

"The Skirmisher has crashed into moon's surface, sir," Ensign One replied. "However, I cannot confirm its condition. Scanners are still recalibrating and visibility is minimal. I can however, see the ship in spectrums other than visible light and it appears to be intact."

"I owe you one, Captain," Sterling said, slapping Banks on the shoulder – a gesture both of gratitude and relief.

"Several, I think," Banks replied, smiling at him.

The two officers rushed inside the cockpit. However,

all they could see outside the shuttle was a mass of swirling silver dust.

"I think I'd call this visibility zero, rather than minimal," said Banks, shaking some of the silvery substance from the creases of her armor.

Sterling dropped into the rock-hard second seat of the shuttle and checked the computer built into his armor. "I'm still detecting a power signature out there," Sterling said, using the short-range scanning capabilities of his suit to analyze the crash zone. "We should blast the whole area just to be sure. We don't want those bastards rising from the ashes."

"Weapons are still offline, Commodore," said Ensign One. "Several power relays were destroyed during the uncontrolled surge. I can repair them, but I estimate that this work will require forty-two minutes and sixteen seconds to complete, from the point at which I leave my seat to begin repairs."

Sterling reached across and rested his bionic hand on the robot's shoulder. "Hold up, Ensign, I need you right where you are," Sterling said, adding gentle pressure to make sure Ensign One didn't try to stand. "You're the only one who can fly this alien hunk of crap, and right now, we need to get away before anyone takes a look at the moon and wonders why there's dust swirling all over the place."

Ensign One nodded its self-designed cranial unit. "Aye sir. Partial navigation scanners are now back online, so I will begin plotting a suitably discreet course to the Battle Titan." The robot then began to operate the consoles in front it, entering sequences of glyphs and moving controls as if it had been flying the alien machine its whole life. "With all the activity in the system, it should be possible to maneuver without raising suspicion or attention."

Sterling nodded then let out a long, slow sigh of relief. He wasn't naïve enough to expect that their entry into the solar system was going to be plain sailing, but it had still been ten times more hair-raising than he'd anticipated.

"What did we lose in the crate that fell out of the bay doors?" Sterling said, turning to his fellow officer. However, Banks was no longer in the cockpit. "Mercedes?" Sterling called out, swinging out of the seat and moving aft. His pulse was racing again as a dozen different scenarios ran through his mind, each one as bleak as the next. Had Banks collapsed from an unseen injury? Had she inhaled too much moon dust and was choking to death on the cargo bay floor? The reality turned out to be far less ominous, and in retrospect more obvious too. Hustling inside the dust-filled cargo bay, Sterling found Banks sitting on a storage crate with a half-eaten commando ration bar in her hand.

"Do you want some?" Banks said, offering the bar to Sterling as he entered. Then she appeared to regret making the offer. "Actually, I'm almost done with this one, but I'm sure I can find you another if you'd like?"

"Only you could consider finding a snack to be a suitable response to a near-death experience," Sterling said, shaking his head at the Captain of the Invictus.

"Hey, at one point I was fighting three or maybe four earth gravities, while still holding on to you," Banks hit back, speaking with her mouth full. "I need to refuel," she added with a shrug.

Sterling huffed a laugh then opened another storage crate, containing spare sections of stealth armor. He first replaced his cracked helmet, then removed the damaged sections of his suit, discarding them into the container before fitting new parts. Next, he grabbed an oxygen cylinder and attached the outlet to the rear of Banks' helmet.

"Thanks, but I don't think we're going spacewalking again any time soon," Banks said as the gas from the tank rushed into the compact emergency storage chambers in her stealth armor. "At least, I sure as hell am not. I like to keep my feet firmly on the ground, thanks very much."

The screeching wail of the alien shuttle's alarms then assaulted Sterling's ears. It was like the sound of someone scraping their fingernails down a chalkboard.

"Shut that damned noise off!" Sterling called out, pressing his hands to his ears. Ensign One operated the console and the noise ceased. "What the hell is wrong now?" Sterling added, rushing back inside the cockpit. He then cursed as the reason for the alarm became clear. The alien Skirmisher that had surged alongside them was rising out of the dusty crater, like a scorpion emerging from the desert sands.

"Can we launch a torpedo?" Banks asked, also rushing inside the cockpit.

"At this range, the blast would also cripple us, Captain," Ensign One answered.

"Then we make a run for it," Banks said, cycling through their limited available options.

"We could outrun the Skirmisher, but it would alert the

other ships in the system," Ensign One answered, its ocular units flashing rapidly. "I calculate a ninety-two percent chance that we would be destroyed before we are able to surge out of the solar system." The robot then turned its glowing eyes to Banks. "And a ninety-nine point seven two percent chance we would be destroyed before escaping enemy-occupied territory."

Banks snorted a laugh. "A zero point two eight percent chance of escape? Those are rough odds, even for us."

Sterling however had remained silent. He'd already come up with an idea, but wanted to be sure it was the only one available to them. And Ensign One's harsh estimate of their odds of escape had sealed the deal.

"Running away isn't our style, Mercedes," Sterling said, fixing his fellow officer with a determined stare. "Grab a couple of Homewreckers. We have work to do."

Banks frowned back at Sterling. "Are you suggesting what I think you're suggesting?"

"Have you got a better idea?" Sterling hit back.

Banks sighed and shrugged. "Looks like I was wrong about not going for any more spacewalks," she said, with a fatalistic air.

Sterling and Banks ran aft and tore open the weapons crate containing the powerful Homewrecker Heavy Plasma Rifles. He'd embarked on their mission fully expecting never to even open the crates. And he never expected needing them for the purpose he had in mind.

"Focus your fire on the command section," Sterling said, closing his visor then yanking the lever to open the cargo bay doors. "It'll take too long to punch through their armor, but the Skirmisher's command section is weaker."

"Aye sir," replied Banks, slapping a power cell into the second of two Homewreckers, then raising both weapons to her side. "I suggest we dial the rifles to overdrive," she added, stepping beside Sterling. "It will melt the plasma coils, but it will give us the extra punch we need."

"Understood," Sterling replied, dialing the power setting of his own Homewrecker to the red line beyond the maximum setting. In the past the mighty weapon was too bulky for him to wield with any skill, but thanks to his bionic hand and Banks' relentless strength training regimen, it now felt as light as a plasma pistol. "Okay, magnetize and let's do this..." Sterling said, slapping the control pad on his left forearm to activate his armor's magnetic boots.

Sterling felt his feet clamp to the deck, then stepped out onto the extended cargo hatch of the ship with Banks hot on his heels.

"The Skirmisher is charging weapons, Commodore," Ensign One said, through the comm system in Sterling's helmet. "I have managed to scramble any outgoing transmissions from the vessel, but I estimate we have less than a minute before they are able to fire."

"Understood, Ensign, we don't need that long," replied Sterling, maneuvering himself around the side of the shuttle.

The Skirmisher came into view, hovering above the silver crater it had carved into the moon's surface, barely ten meters from their shuttle. Spurred on by the sight of the vessel bearing down on them, Sterling climbed up on to the top of the combat shuttle and waited for his boots to anchor him securely in place. Banks arrived by his side a few seconds later. As usual, his former first officer had been with him through thick and thin, fighting the enemy no matter the danger or the odds. This situation was no different. They were staring down the barrels of alien plasma rail cannons, armed only with rifles. They should have died a dozen times already, but somehow, they were still standing. Maybe one day soon, their luck would run out, Sterling thought, as he raised his rifle and took aim. However, he also knew for certain that the Skirmisher in front of him would not be the one to take him down.

"Ready?" Sterling glanced across to Banks.

"On your order," Banks replied, raising both of her Homewreckers.

"Fire..."

Set to override mode, the Homewreckers were as powerful as the combat shuttle's plasma cannons, and controlling the weapon took every ounce of Sterling's strength. Blasts of searing energy hammered into the Skirmisher's command deck and within seconds they had punctured the ship's protective shell. Both Sterling and Banks continued to fire until the barrels of the Homewreckers glowed brighter than the sun and the weapons shut down. Moments later an explosive decompression sent chunks of the alien ship's command section tumbling out into space. Amongst the debris were the bodies of Sa'Nerran warriors. Some were already dead, but others still clung to life, despite the near vacuum that existed close to the moon's surface. The Skirmisher then listed out of control and plummeted back into the moon's surface, its engines and thrusters firing erratically and digging the alien vessel deeper beneath the lunar terrain. In a million years, when all traces of humanity were gone, another species that had evolved on Earth might one day find the ship, Sterling mused. He wondered what stories might be written about the vessel, and whether any of them would be as fanciful and wild as the truth.

Banks tossed down the melted Homewreckers and pulled her plasma pistol from its holster on her armor. She took aim at one of the warriors suffocating in space in front of them and fired a single blast, hitting the warrior in the back. It was an impressive shot and ordinarily Sterling would have commented on it. However, despite their victory, now was not the time for celebration. They had come a long way, but still there was much further to go. Banks aimed at another warrior and was about to pull the trigger when Sterling placed his hand on her arm and drew her aim down.

"Save your ammo, Mercedes," Sterling said, watching the dying alien bounce off the lunar surface then continue its journey into oblivion. "We have plenty more Sa'Nerra to kill today before we're done."

CHAPTER 9
WORSE THAN CATTLE

STERLING'S EYES flicked from the scanner readouts in the alien shuttle to the mass of ships that were visible outside the cockpit glass. Despite still not understanding what any of the gauges or alien glyphs meant, he was starting to get a sense for what the visual displays indicated. The alien navigational scanner was confirming what his eyes were seeing – a huge convoy of Sa'Nerran, Fleet and colony ships, heading toward Earth.

"One hundred kilometers until we are in the lane," Ensign One said, while calmly navigating the combat shuttle toward the convoy. "So far, there are no indications that our approach is being seen as suspicious."

Sterling nodded but continued to scan the space outside the ship, anxiously looking for alien warships. They'd already monitored two squadrons of Skirmishers patrolling the convoy lane, but thankfully neither had passed close by. *The last thing we need is another awkward conversation with an alien commander*, Sterling thought.

"Where the hell are all these ships coming from?" wondered Banks. She had her nosed pressed to the side window, watching the long line of vessels. The convoy extended so far into the expanse that it eventually became nothing more than a pinprick of light, like a distant star.

"I have projected the origin point of the convoy and determined that these vessels have travelled from Mars," said Ensign One.

"Mars?" repeated Banks, turning away from the window. "Why are there so many ships heading to Earth from Mars?"

Ensign One looked away from the controls and focused its glowing ocular units onto Captain Banks. "I have managed to conduct some low energy scans of a number of the vessels," the robot continued. "My analysis suggests that the freighters contain a mixture of raw and processed materials, plus a significant number of life forms."

Banks cursed under her breath. While turning the air blue had become an increasingly common practice for Sterling, it was still rare to hear Banks cuss. Yet on this occasion Sterling knew the reason for her outburst, and he also knew that her choice of language was justified.

"Fresh meat for the Sa'Nerra's turned workforce," Sterling commented, glancing across to one of the many transport vessels. "They're hauling the Martian population to Earth like cattle."

"It is likely the Sa'Nerra have already stripped Mars of its readily-accessible resources," Ensign One said, returning its attention to the shuttle's controls. "They will now do the same to Earth, working the human population to their deaths before they abandon the planet and move on."

"That could take years, or even decades," Banks said. Her hands were now balled into fists, causing her armored gauntlets to creak under the strain.

"Yes, Captain, it will," replied Ensign One, plainly. "From my studies of your culture, humans throughout history have often used the phrase 'hell on earth' to describe a state of being that is characterized by untold suffering," the robot went on, sounding introspective and even a little maudlin. "And while there have been many periods in your planet's history where that phrase could have applied, none of them compare to what lies in store for Earth's future. The suffering that your species will endure is immeasurable."

Now it was Sterling's hands that had involuntarily balled into fists. He, along with all of his Omega officers, had feared that such a fate awaited Earth if Fleet did not act. Yet the War Council had failed to see the threat until it was too late. *War Council...* Sterling thought, shaking his head. Even the name was a joke. The Fleet admirals and the Secretary of War had only one task to perform - fight and win. Instead, they had dithered, procrastinated and allowed the aliens to make humanity their bitch.

Things were about to change, Sterling told himself. He could feel it in his bones. Now there was no Fleet, no Secretary of War, no bureaucracy and, most importantly of all, no rules. Sterling and his Omega crew would teach the Sa'Nerra what the true definition of cold-blooded meant.

The warmongering alien race would learn to its ultimate cost the price of invading humanity's domain.

"I have now assumed a position within the convoy," Ensign One announced, breaking Sterling's belligerent chain of thought. "We are in the lane, heading directly to Earth."

"Very good, Ensign," Sterling said, forcing his fists to unfurl and taking deeper breaths in an effort to calm the fires in his belly. He'd need that rage for later, he realized. "How close to the Sa'Nerran Battle Titan will this course take us?"

"The convoy lane will pass within ten kilometers of the Battle Titan at the closest point," Ensign One answered.

Sterling could already see the massive alien warship through the cockpit glass. It was orbiting Earth with the turned Fleet Dreadnaught Hammer at its side. Seeing his old ship as part of the alien armada only served to fan the flames of anger that he was already barely managing to contain.

"I wish there was a way we could take out the Hammer too," Sterling commented, thinking out loud. "Seeing it fly wingman to that alien monstrosity is just another slap in the face."

"All in good time, Lucas," Banks said, moving to Sterling's side and watching the Battle Titan with him. "First, we'll take down the Titan, then we'll deal with the rest of their fleet."

"That is curious..."

Sterling turned to Ensign One, his near-permanent scowl deepening further. "What's curious, Ensign?" he asked. Curious was not exactly an alarming description, Sterling realized, but he still felt a twinge in his gut, wondering what had piqued the robot's interest.

"Ignoring the non-combat vessels that make up this convoy, I am reading only two-hundred and five warships in high-Earth orbit," Ensign One answered, the surprise evident in its voice. "Fifty-one of those are captured and turned Fleet vessels."

"Where the hell is the rest of their armada?" asked Banks, slotting herself in between the pilot and co-pilot's seats.

"Probably off ravaging some other colony world," snapped Sterling. His eyes had yet to leave the Hammer. If the sheer level of hate in his furious stare could have been translated into plasma blasts, the Hammer would already be burning in space.

"Based on the amount of wreckage I have observed in the system, I estimate that around two-thirds of the alien armada was destroyed," said Ensign One. "It must have been a significant engagement, on a scale never before seen in Fleet history."

This last comment made Sterling sit up and take notice. "Two-thirds, are you sure?" he asked, wanting to confirm that he hadn't just heard what he wanted to hear.

"It is an estimate so I am not sure, sir," Ensign One replied. "But I believe my estimate is accurate to within a five percent margin of error."

Sterling glanced at Banks, suddenly feeling a swell of excitement flood through his body. "If that's true then by taking out the Battle Titan we might just have a chance.

Especially if we can figure out some way of crippling the Hammer too."

"Even if such an eventuality came to pass, the odds of prevailing against the remains of the Sa'Nerran armada are still small, Commodore," Ensign One replied, plainly. "The Vanguard and Invictus, plus the Obsidian ships, would be outnumbered at least four to one, and more likely six to one, accounting for other Sa'Nerran ships elsewhere in the inner colonies and beyond."

"That's just math, Ensign," Sterling hit back, wafting his bionic hand at the machine dismissively. "Math doesn't take into account an individual's hunger for battle, and will to win. One soldier, properly trained and motivated, can kill dozens of enemy combatants."

Ensign One nodded its cranial unit in deference to Sterling's greater wisdom. "I concede that there are other factors beyond simple numbers," the machine replied, respectfully. "But sometimes the numbers do not lie."

"Then we'll take the numbers by the damned throat and force them to lie," Sterling said, undeterred.

Ensign One's console then squawked an alert and the AI quickly checked it. "We are approaching the coordinates where we need to break away from the convoy," the robot said. "I have programmed the shuttle's engines to fire a short burst at maximum output then shut down. This will give us the momentum needed to reach the Battle Titan while maintaining a low energy signature."

"Won't the Titan still spot us, even if we're sailing toward it with our engines offline?" Banks asked.

Ensign One worked the console in front of it, then the

cockpit glass lit up with a holographic overlay containing what looked like hundreds of glowing green chevrons.

"The aftermath of the battle with the combined Earth Fleets has left a tremendous amount of debris in the system," Ensign One explained. "Much of this debris is still radioactive or thermally hot. With our engines offline, we can cruise toward the Titan while maintaining an energy signature that is indistinguishable from the bulk of the debris."

Banks huffed a laugh. "So, we pretend to be just another corpse on the battlefield, is that what you're saying?"

"In essence, Captain, yes," Ensign One replied. "Except that we are very much alive."

"On the off-chance the Titan or another ship does spot our approach, how do you rate our chances?" Banks then asked. While Sterling was content to believe the odds would bend to his will, Banks preferred the facts as they were, fully unvarnished.

"If we were to be detected, I calculate a ninety-seven-percent chance that we would be destroyed or captured," Ensign One replied. "Ninety-five at best."

"Now I wish I hadn't asked," Banks snorted.

Ensign One turned to face the Captain of the Invictus, its ocular units bathing her face in a deep orange glow. "I am curious to learn why humans often say that," the robot said. "Knowing the odds does not change the odds."

"Sometimes ignorance is bliss, Ensign," Sterling cut in. "Now, can we all stop asking our living computer to give us the odds?" he snapped. He was sick of hearing about probabilities and statistics. None of those things mattered to him. "We make our own luck. We've got this far on guile and guts alone. We'll make it the rest of the way, no matter what the numbers say."

"Aye sir," said Banks and One, in perfect unison.

The console then screeched another update and Sterling shook his head at the display. "What the hell is it now?" he asked, frustrated that he couldn't just read the updates for himself.

"A Skirmisher patrol is headed our way, sir," Ensign One said, with a calm urgency that reminded Sterling of Lieutenant Commander Shade. "It appears to be a routine check."

"Routine or not, we don't want them to see us," Sterling replied. "If they recognize this as Emissary McQueen's combat shuttle then we're suddenly going to draw a lot of attention."

"I can slip in behind one of the freighters and wait for the patrol to pass," Ensign One suggested. "However, the timing of our maneuver to break away and reach the Battle Titan is critical. If we miss our window then we would need to power up the engines again in order to correct our trajectory."

Sterling sighed. "Then we'd better hope that these alien bastards are in a hurry to finish their sweep so they can grab an early lunch." He nodded to his robot pilot. "Do it, Ensign."

Ensign One acknowledged the order and quickly adjusted course. Using only the combat shuttle's thrusters, the robot pushed the alien craft closer to one of the

Sa'Nerran transport vessels, before expertly slipping underneath it.

"The Skirmisher patrol is now five hundred meters from our current position," said Banks. She was looking at the computer built into the forearm of her stealth armor.

Ensign One pulsed the thrusters again and eased the shuttle across to the far side of the transport. Sterling glanced at his computer and held his breath. Their sentient AI pilot had practically skimmed the surface of the transport and was now holding position so close to it that even his computer could barely distinguish the two vessels as separate ships.

"The Skirmishers should not be able to detect us, so long as we hold position here," Ensign One said, carefully centering the controls.

"We'd best hope this transport doesn't make a course correction then," Sterling said, looking up and seeing only a mass of grey, alien metal.

"We now have sixty-seconds until our maneuvering window closes," Ensign One added. "I estimate that the patrol will have passed our location in forty-seven seconds."

"Damn, that's not much of a margin," said Sterling.

"Lucas, look at this..."

Sterling spun around to see Banks standing across the opposite side of the cockpit. She was looking out of the window, her expression appearing as sullen as her voice had sounded.

"What's up, Mercedes?" Sterling said, moving to his fellow officer's side. Initially, he was only focused on Banks' desolate-looking eyes. Then he turned to the window and what he saw made his stomach churn.

"I'm going to really enjoy laying waste to their planet," Sterling said, almost shaking with rage.

Through the round, port-hole windows of the alien transport, Sterling could see line after line of human beings, huddled together in tightly-banded rows, with barely thirty centimeters separating them. All of the prisoners were naked and shackled to one other by metal collars wrapped around their necks, hands and feet. Some hung limply like puppets, suspended from the ceiling of the transport by chains attached to their neck collars, which strangled them like a hangman's noose. Those that were conscious quivered from cold, exhaustion, terror, or a mix of all three. Sterling's mouth went dry as he also realized that the captives were standing in pools of their own excrement, vomit and blood. Suddenly, the prisoner closest to the window – an emaciated man who was probably no more than eighteen or nineteen years old – turned his head and met Sterling's eyes. Sterling had looked into the eyes of hurt and dying men before, but this was different. This was the face of raw torment. The man mouthed the words, "help me..." before an electrical shock pulsed through the collar, forcing the teenager to face the front once more. The young man could barely stand, Sterling realized, but somehow he remained still, blood-stained saliva dribbling from the corner of his mouth.

"Our window to maneuver closes in fifteen seconds, sir," Ensign One said, calmly. "However, I cannot be certain that the Skirmisher patrol has moved on."

"Execute the maneuver, Ensign One," said Sterling, his own voice sounding suddenly dark and malevolent, like a medieval torturer. "If they see us, they see us."

"Aye, sir," Ensign One replied.

Sterling could tell that the sentient AI had been perplexed by his fatalistic response. Yet like all his Omega officers – with the recent exception of Mercedes Banks, at least – Ensign One knew not to question his commands.

Any normal person confronted with the atrocity Sterling had witnessed would rapidly turn away, but neither Sterling nor Banks blinked. Instead, Sterling drank in the horrors in front of him, using them to fuel his anger and thirst for retribution and death. However, even he had his limits, Sterling realized, as another prisoner – a young woman – collapsed and died in front of his eyes. As an Omega officer, he had been chosen for his ability to remain emotionally-detached. Unburned by emotion, he was able to make the right decision in any given moment, even if that decision was immoral, cruel or downright heartless. Nevertheless, he was still human. And like any human being, he felt. Faced with what he had just witnessed, it was impossible not to.

Fleet loves coldhearted bastards like me, Sterling thought, as the combat shuttle slipped back under the belly of the transport and engaged its engines. This was something that his old friend Ariel Gunn had told him on many occasions, long before Sterling had killed her as part of his macabre Omega Directive test. Despite what that test had cost him, he had never doubted the necessity of the Directive and the cold logic behind it. Until now.

"Griffin would tell us to forget what we just saw," Sterling said to Banks, who was staring blankly out of the window. If the Skirmisher patrol was coming for them, neither of them were aware of it, and neither of them cared. "She'd say to bury our feelings and control them so that they don't control us, and get in the way of the mission."

"Griffin isn't here," Banks replied, her voice so cold that frost might have formed on the glass.

"No, she's not," Sterling agreed. Then he turned to face his fellow officer and waited for her rage-filled eyes to meet his own. "To hell with it," he added, feeling his pulse quicken. "Once we're on-board that ship, we kill as many Sa'Nerra as we can find. Then we blow the thing to hell and anything else we can take down with it."

Banks nodded, but didn't reply. Nothing more needed to be said. The two officers turned back to the window and remained there as the alien shuttle silently coasted through the Void toward the Sa'Nerran Battle Titan. Ensign One would tell him that the odds of destroying the ship were miniscule. Sterling was going to show the sentient machine – and the whole damned universe – just how wrong they were.

STERLING DRUMMED the fingers of his bionic hand against his thigh as the Sa'Nerran Battle Titan loomed ever closer beyond the cockpit glass. He was used to seeing capital ships up close, having served on a dreadnaught, but the Titan was a whole other level of big.

"Time to contact?" Sterling asked, glancing across to Ensign One. They had spent the last hour drifting through space toward the massive, ten-kilometer-long vessel without incident. Yet the closer they got, the higher Sterling's heart-rate climbed.

"I will initiate the deceleration burn in two-hundred and twenty seconds from the point at which I finish this sentence," Ensign One replied. "We remain on course to hit our target coordinates, sir."

"We remain on course to hit our target coordinates, the same as the previous twenty times you asked, sir..." Banks corrected the robot.

"Remind me again what I was planning to do once we

got back to the Obsidian Base?" Sterling hit back, feigning ignorance. Then he clicked his fingers, acting out a 'lightbulb' moment. "Oh, that's right, I was going to court-martial you and throw you in the brig."

"Fine, I'll stay quiet," Banks replied holding up her hands. "Unlike some..."

Sterling shot her another penetrating stare, but this time Banks merely replied with a disarming smile.

"I hate waiting around, that's all," Sterling said, resuming his stress-relieving finger-taps. "Besides, it's not like me checking on our progress is going to cause the damned ship to suddenly change course."

Ensign One's console squawked an update. The sudden, shrill noise caused Sterling to jolt upright and peer at the incomprehensible, glowing green indicators on the panels. Then he saw the navigation scanner readout and cursed under his breath.

"The Titan is making a course correction, sir," said Ensign One.

Sterling winced and glanced across to Banks.

"What were you just saying?" Banks said, folding her powerful arms across her chest.

"Stow it, Captain, and get ready to move out," Sterling hit back, crabbily. "We might need to improvise our plan."

Banks nodded, then grabbed her helmet and slid it on over her stealth armor, twisting to lock it in place. She tapped the base of her neck and the full-cover visor retracted.

"How far off course are we going to be, Ensign?" asked Sterling, while also twisting on his helmet.

"I believe I can compensate with a slightly longer deceleration burn," Ensign One replied, working the alien controls with lightning speed and efficiency. "The Titan has only made a minor course correction in order to avoid a denser region of debris left over from the battle."

"Stay on it, while I get my gear ready," Sterling said. He then pushed himself out of his seat, intending to go aft. However, Ensign One was quick to caution him against it.

"I would strongly suggest that you remain seated and strap in, sir," Ensign One said, looking first at Sterling then at Banks. "In order to avoid detection and run the engines for the minimum possible duration, the maneuver I intend to perform will overwhelm the inertial negation systems."

"We can cope with a few g-forces, Ensign," Sterling said, not seeing the issue. In his view, his robotic ensign was being overcautious.

"I estimate that even with inertial negation active, you will experience the equivalent of a fifty-g deceleration," Ensign One added, coolly.

"Ouch," said Banks.

"It will only be for a brief moment, and is entirely survivable so long as you are sufficiently contained when it occurs," the robot went on.

"Fine, you've convinced me," Sterling said, flopping back in his seat and pulling the straps tight across his chest. Considering the straps were designed for barrel-chested Sa'Nerran warriors, this didn't prove difficult.

"I'll go aft and strap myself in there," Banks said, with one foot already through the door.

"Put your visor down and pressurize your suit,"

Sterling called over to her. Because of the straps and the unforgiving material of the chair, he could no longer turn his head. "If Ensign One overcooks this, we might suffer a hull breach. Let's be ready."

"Aye, sir," Banks replied before vanishing into the rear compartment.

"I am incapable of overcooking anything," Ensign One said, sounding indignant.

"No offence intended Ensign, but we all err," Sterling answered.

"To err is human, sir," the AI replied, a little too snootily for Sterling's liking. "I am something else."

"All living things make mistakes, Ensign," Sterling hit back, his eyes growing wider as they continued to race toward the Battle Titan at a frightening velocity. Then he glanced across at the pilot, keen to qualify his statement. "Though, on this occasion, don't make one, or we're all dead."

"Of course, sir," Ensign One replied, cheerfully. "Standby for deceleration in five seconds..."

Sterling braced himself as the shuttle suddenly turned away from the Titan and faced out toward the moon, ready to execute the breaking burn. Then the stillness inside the cockpit was shattered by the deafening roar of the shuttle's engines as they were suddenly pushed to twice their rated maximum thrust. The noise was literally like the sound of a rocket taking off, but instead of watching from a safe distance, Sterling was strapped to a seat barely more than ten meters from the engine exhausts.

In an instant the pressure on Sterling's body grew to an

unbearable level, as he suddenly weighed fifty times more than he would in Earth-standard gravity. Despite the inertial negation systems compensating for some of the force, Sterling was on the brink of blacking out when the engines finally shut down. His head was still throbbing like a four-alarm hangover when a hard thump resonated through the hull, rattling his teeth and bones. Alarms screeched and the lights in the cockpit shut down, followed soon after by the luminous green glow of the alien computer consoles.

"Report!" Sterling called out, fearing the worst. Then the alarms ceased and a deathly silence again fell over the shuttle. All Sterling could hear was the sound of his own pulse thumping in his ears, and the chime of the shuttle's reactor as it rapidly cooled, like an old-fashioned iron kettle that had been taken off the heat.

"We are down and locked," Ensign One replied, slowly lifting its metal hands away from the controls, as if any sudden movement might upset the ship and cause more alarms to wail. It was like a parent setting down a newborn baby into her crib then creeping away while trying not to wake her.

"All hell just broke loose back here," Banks called out from the aft compartment. "Did we land or crash?"

It was a good question, Sterling thought, and he looked across to Ensign One for the answer.

"Technically, we landed, sir," Ensign One replied. "Though a controlled crash would also not be an entirely unreasonable description for what just occurred."

"I don't care if we touched down lighter than a feather

or hammered a ding into the Titan's hull six-feet deep," Sterling hit back. "All I need to know is have we been detected?"

Ensign One operated one of the alien consoles with the delicacy of a harpist, then turned its glowing ocular units to Sterling. "Negative, sir. We have not been detected."

"Looks like you were right, Ensign," said Banks, swinging herself back inside the cockpit. Through the opening, Sterling could see that cutting beams had already engaged and were slicing through the service hatch that Ensign One had locked onto. "To the Sa'Nerra, we just looked like one of the other thousands of chunks of debris from the battle with Fleet."

Banks then pulled a Commando bar from her pocket, tore back the wrapper and took a hefty bit of it. Considering the ordeal they'd all just shared, she looked like she'd undergone nothing more strenuous than a kid-friendly rollercoaster ride.

"I was not exactly correct in my calculations, Captain," the robot then admitted, its glowing eyes shining down toward the deck.

"What went wrong?" Sterling said, feeling his pulse start to race again.

"Despite my earlier boast, I actually missed our target coordinates by two hundred and four millimeters, sir," Ensign One answered, still sounding downhearted. "I will, of course, accept an official reprimand on my jacket."

Sterling and Banks both laughed, and Banks slapped the robot playfully on the arm. However, Ensign One showed no sign that it was playing along.

"You were kidding, right?" said Banks, suddenly worried that the robot was being serious. "That was a joke?"

"That depends," the sentient AI replied. "Was it funny?"

"We both laughed, didn't we?" Sterling said, smiling at his robot officer.

"In that case, sir, it was a joke," Ensign One replied, its eyes glowing more brightly again. "I will therefore accept a commendation instead of a reprimand. Or perhaps a medal?"

"Don't push it, Ensign," Sterling hit back, drawing a faint grin from Banks. He unclipped his harness and stood up, quickly wishing he hadn't. His legs wobbled and his head began to spin, and he had to grab the back of the chair to steady himself. "Let's try to avoid fifty-g deceleration burns in the future, okay?" he suggested, sucking in lungfuls of the foul Sa'Nerran air in an attempt to stave off the dizziness.

The cutting beams then shut down and Banks moved into the aft compartment to check the status of the docking seal.

"We're through, and the pressure seal is steady," Banks called out. She then grabbed a Homewrecker from the weapons storage rack and added three power cells to the stows on her armor.

"Let's save the big guns until they're absolutely necessary, Captain," Sterling said, also moving into the aft section and attaching a Sa'Nerra blade to his armor. "I'm happy for you to kill as many of these bastards as we find, so long as you do it quietly."

"This is just for backup," said Banks, tapping the Homewrecker, which was now slung across her back in a climber's carry. She attached a sheathed trench knife to her armor before drawing the blade and holding it out for Sterling to inspect. "This is for close encounters," she added. On other occasions, Sterling would have expected a smile or a flash of her eyes to accompany his fellow-officer's display of the weapon. This time, Banks came across deadly calm, and deadly serious.

"I'm not even going to ask where you got that from," Sterling said, running a finger along the spiked, brass-knuckle handle of the weapon.

"I had Razor knock it up for me while we were on the Obsidian Base," Banks replied, answering the question anyway. "You know, just in case of situations like this."

"Then I expect it to be put to good use," Sterling said, adding a trio of spare energy cells for his pistol to his armor. Not wishing to be outdone by Banks, he also kitted himself out with a further selection of brutal melee weapons. He finished off the deadly ensemble with a stun baton that was powerful enough to kill an elephant, never mind a Sa'Nerran warrior.

"The shuttle is powered down and the reactor is on standby," Ensign One said, as the robot moved through the opening from the cockpit.

"You'll need a weapon too, Ensign, besides your integrated plasma cannons, anyway," Sterling said, offering the sentient AI a spare Sa'Nerran blade from his bag.

"No need, Commodore," Ensign One replied. The machine then extended its right index finger and punched it through one of the interior walls of the shuttle. "I am already a walking weapon," the machine added, while slowly the removing its digit from the metal panel and flexing it to demonstrate it was not damaged.

"Noted, Ensign, now let's get this hatch open and get to work," Sterling said, finding a solid hand-hold on the hatch and wrapping his bionic fingers around it. "Mercedes, give me a hand with this," he added, while taking the strain.

Banks stepped up to the hatch and tested a few hand-holds before finally gripping the door. She then nodded to Sterling. "On three..."

Sterling counted down in his head then both of them pushed hard on the hatch. The thick metal panel groaned as it was forced inward, revealing metal that was still glowing hot from the cutting beams.

"Damn, how thick is this thing?" said Banks as the hatch passed the half-meter mark without an end in sight.

"Just make sure it doesn't fall," Sterling replied, speaking through gritted teeth. "If this thing hits the deck on the other side, half the ship will know we're here."

Sterling had barely finished the sentence when suddenly the strain on his muscles increased tenfold, and he was pulled against the inner wall of the shuttle.

"Ensign, help!" Sterling called out, feeling his grip falter.

The robot officer moved with the speed of flickering candle light and within moments it had grabbed a hold of the door. Sterling's grip failed a split-second later, but between Banks and the robot, they had somehow managed to prevent the hatch from falling.

"Lower it!" Banks cried. She was being forced to use every ounce of her super-human strength to prevent the hatch from falling.

Together One and Banks eased the hatch down until it finally thudded into the deck. Despite the gentleness of its descent, the noise of the slab of metal hitting the deck still rumbled along the corridor inside the Titan like thunder. Cursing, Sterling jumped through the meter-thick opening and landed cat-like on the other side, stun baton in one hand and plasma pistol in the other. However, the section was dark and cold, and appeared to be empty.

"I think we're okay." Sterling accessed the computer on his left wrist to bring up a short-range scanner readout. There was no sign of movement and no heat signatures nearby that might have suggested warriors were on-route. "The section looks clear, come on through."

Ensign One jumped through the hatch next, followed by Banks, who was shaking her hands as if she'd just finished a grueling set of dead-lifts in the gym. Then the silence was shattered by the screech of a Sa'Nerran alarm, and green warning lights began to flash on and off above the hatch.

"Ensign, you're up!" Sterling called out, stowing the stun baton and aiming his pistol along the corridor using both hands.

Ensign One was at the hatch controls in an instant and moments later the sentient AI had interfaced with the

Titan's computer. Banks equipped the Homewrecker and took cover across from Sterling.

"If we can't shut off this alarm, what's our plan B?" Banks said, glancing over to Sterling.

"Plan B is the same as Plan A, Mercedes," Sterling said, tightening his grip on the pistol. "Whether we do this by stealth, or do it by tearing the ship to pieces, panel by panel, we're taking the Titan down." He fixed his fellow officer with determined eyes. "Even if it means we go down with it."

Banks nodded then returned her gaze to the corridor ahead. "Understood, sir," she replied. All hints of the cocksure and slightly mischievous Mercedes Banks were gone. She was now in warrior mode, plain and simple.

Sterling had always accepted that the mission to destroy the Titan was likely to be a one-way ticket. It was why he hadn't wanted Banks to come with him. That decision was selfish, he now realized. It was based on emotion, not reason, and was tactically flawed. The cold truth of it was that if he was going into battle then he could think of no-one else he'd rather have fighting by his side than Mercedes Banks. Whether he wanted her there or not was irrelevant, because their odds of survival were far greater with her than without. Then as suddenly as it had begun, the cat-like wail of the alarm ceased and the flashing green lights cut out.

"Posing as this section's sub-processor, I have informed the Titan's central AI that the alarm was due to a sensor glitch," Ensign One said, dropping to a crouch by Sterling's side. "Fortunately, the alien computer is as lacking in sophistication as the Sa'Nerra themselves, so it believed me without question."

"So, we're in the clear?" Sterling asked, saving his congratulations until he was sure that a dozen Sa'Nerran warriors weren't about to storm their position.

"Affirmative, the Titan's AI will not send anyone to investigate," Ensign One replied.

Sterling breathed a sigh of relief then holstered his pistol. "Good work, Ensign," he said, switching back to the stun baton before again referring to the computer on his wrist. "We only have to descend two levels from this point to reach the field generator room, so let's get moving, before any more alarms start ringing."

Banks slung the Homewrecker and wrapped her knuckles around the handle of her trench knife. "I suggest we head through this section," she said, pointing to the location on the computer with the tip of the blade. "If the plans of the ship we obtained were correct, it should be mostly just dead space. Access routes and maintenance channels, that sort of thing."

"I concur," Ensign One said. "However, we should proceed with caution, I am detecting..." The robot's voice then cut off mid-sentence and it raised its right arm, balling its hand into a fist. Before Sterling knew what was happening, Ensign One had thrown a punch. He felt a rush of air blast his face as the blow missed him by a hair's breadth before hammering into a door to Sterling's side. The impact was so powerful that Ensign One's fist penetrated the metal panel right up to the machine's shoulder. Stunned, Sterling waited for the robot to extract its fist, then peered through the punctured opening in the door, seeing a dead Sa'Nerran warrior on the deck. The alien's face had been caved in so savagely, all that remained was a pulpy, mangled mess of blood of bone. Sterling looked at Ensign One's fist and saw that it was stained red with Sa'Nerran blood.

"Six warriors approaching. Four ahead. Two left," Ensign One said, indicating the directions with its hands.

The robot had spoken quickly and in a staccato, level tone that was more akin to an older gen-thirteen AI than the sentient machine Ensign One had become. Without another word, the robot then kicked down the door it had punched through and rushed ahead. Two warriors were standing over the body of the third, peering down at it with their egg-shaped, yellow eyes.

"On me!" Sterling called out, rushing ahead with his shock baton raised. There was no time for questions or clarification. Ensign One had raised the alert in the most efficient manner possible. Now it was time to act.

Banks advanced to Sterling's side, trench dagger in hand, just as the squad of four warriors marched around the corner in two rows of two. Sterling took the duo on the right, and smashed the plasma pistol out of the closest warrior's hand before ramming the stun baton underneath the alien's chin. The weapon delivered its deadly charge, causing the warrior to jerk and convulse while its flesh cooked. At the same time, Banks slashed the trench knife through the flesh of her first opponent, opening a gash in the warrior's throat so deep it looked to have been made with a broadsword.

Banks' vicious strike caused blood to spray out into the corridor like a paint bomb had just exploded. A gush of the hot, sticky fluid lashed Sterling's face, and flooded into his mouth and eyes. Blinded, he staggered back and swung the baton, deflecting the second warrior's pistol by sheer luck rather than design. A blast rang out and thudded into the deck, then Sterling was driven back by the warrior, feeling punches hammer into his armored body. He dug his boots into the coarse metal deck plates and fought the alien to a standstill. This was the first time Sterling had faced a Sa'Nerran warrior in a test of strength since his intense bouts of training on the Obsidian Base. Prior to his training regimen he could have never overpowered a soldier of the alien race. Now he was easily their equal, and more. Retaliating with a savage headbutt using the brow of his helmet as a weapon, Sterling rocked the alien. It released its hold on him and reeled back as Sterling advanced, baton still tightly held in the grip of his bionic hand. His first blow smashed the alien's shoulder pauldron like it was made of clay. The alien hissed wildly, but was quickly silenced as Sterling brought the heavy baton down across the base of the warrior's neck. The crack and crunch of bone was a sound he'd heard a hundred times before. It was the sound of a warrior that was about to die.

Wiping the remaining blood from his eyes, Sterling saw Banks ahead of him. She had a warrior pinned to the wall of the corridor and was hammering punches into its chest and body with the spiked metal knuckles on the grip of her knife. It was clear to Sterling that the warrior was already dead, but Banks' eyes were wild and she continued to pulverize the alien, crushing bone and mashing its organs into a bloody mess. Tapping his neural interface, Sterling reached out to his fellow officer. The link formed, easily and naturally, as if they were of one mind.

"Ease down, Mercedes," Sterling said, resting a hand on her shoulder. "Save your energy. Save your anger. There is plenty more time for killing yet."

Banks glanced back at Sterling, her face and hair matted with alien blood, then glowered at the mutilated alien before tossing it aside like garbage. Ensign One returned from the adjacent corridor, its eyes flashing wildly and its metal frame also plastered with alien blood.

"Report, Ensign," Sterling said, remaining vigilant in case any more warriors appeared.

"My scanners are now calibrated to the ship's internal structure," Ensign One said, peering around the space. "There are no more warriors in this immediate vicinity."

"Did any of these bastards sound the alarm?" Banks asked, shaking some excess blood off her blade and placing it back into its metal sheath.

"Yes, but I have blocked the transmissions and informed the central command level that all is well," Ensign One replied. "This was just a routine patrol of the section. We were unfortunate to encounter them, but we remain undiscovered."

Sterling looked at the crushed and contorted bodies of the alien warriors at their feet. Then he glanced along the adjacent corridor to see that Ensign One had made a similarly gruesome mess of the two aliens it had fought. He spat the remainder of the warrior's blood out of his mouth and wiped it with the back of his armored hand, leaving a dark red smear across his face.

"No, Ensign, we weren't unfortunate," he said, standing tall. "These warriors were the unfortunate ones." Then he met Banks' eyes, which were still wild and vengeful. "But they were only the first to fall down at our feet. And I promise you all, they won't be the last."

STERLING PAUSED TO TAKE A BREATH, resting his blood-stained hands on his hips to take the strain off his aching arms. It had taken a solid ten minutes of hard work to conceal their bloody deeds. However, now the bodies of the dead Sa'Nerran warriors were safely hidden inside the voids behind the walls or beneath the deck plates of the Battle Titan. Blood still coated a large area of the corridor, but in the gloomy light it was barely distinguishable against the grime-covered metal panels.

"I think we've discovered the one downside to killing Sa'Nerran warriors," Sterling said, as Banks lowered the last remaining deck plate into place, like she was sealing a tomb.

"It will be easier to conceal the bodies once we get closer to the field generator room," Banks said, wiping blood and grime off her hands. "The schematics suggest that the decks below are only partly finished, so there are plenty of nooks and crannies to use."

Sterling nodded and checked his computer. There were still no signs of movement nearby, though he was aware that their scanners had been far from precise. Even so, he was anxious to get moving.

"Okay, let's head out and pick up the pace," Sterling said to the others. "The longer we're on board the greater the chances that we or the combat shuttle will be discovered."

Ensign One set out in the lead, guiding Sterling and Banks through the cavernous internal structure of the Battle Titan. Their progress toward the field generator room was swift and uneventful, thanks in no small measure to Ensign One's ability to fool the Sa'Nerran computer system.

"It's like the work crews just gave up half-way through construction," Banks commented as they continued. She was running her hands along unfinished sections of wall, while weaving in and out of the voids to avoid missing deck plates.

"The Sa'Nerra don't care for creature comforts, like us," Sterling replied while hopping over a gap in the deck. "We fly around in ships equipped with comfortable quarters and hot showers, while these bastards are content to slum it."

"Well, they can slum it all they like," Banks snorted. "I have no problem becoming even more brutal than the Sa'Nerra, but I'm not giving up a shower or a comfortable bed for anyone."

Ensign One held up its hand, signaling the group to stop. "We are approaching a more densely populated area of the ship," the robot said through the comm-link in Sterling's and Banks' helmets. "It is a larger and more open area. Perhaps a workshop or storage facility of some kind."

"Can we go around it?" asked Sterling.

"Not without incurring significant delay, sir," Ensign One replied. "However, if we climb up the scaffold to the unfinished level above, I believe we can navigate past this section without being detected."

"Fine, then you take point, Ensign," Sterling ordered, attaching his stun baton to his armor in preparation to make the climb.

"Aye, sir," Ensign One replied. The machine then maneuvered itself beneath an opening to the floor above and leapt eight feet into the air from a standing start. Sterling watched in amazement as the robot caught a cross beam and swung its metal frame through the joists and onto the level above in a single, fluid move. It was a display of athleticism and agility that would have put even an Olympic gymnast to shame.

"How about you go next?" said Sterling, gesturing for Banks to move ahead.

"You just don't want me to see you make a fool of yourself, trying to get up there," Banks replied with a mischievous smile.

"No, I want you to go up first so that you can pull me up when I inevitably get stuck," Sterling hit back. Though there was an element of truth to what Banks had said too.

Banks flashed her eyes at Sterling then sheathed her trench knife and gripped one of the deck pillars before beginning to climb. Her strength made the task look easy, though Banks' ascent lacked the supernatural grace the sentient AI had displayed.

With Banks already near the top, Sterling sucked in a deep breath and took hold of the pillar, ready to start his climb. Then he heard the distinctive sound of bootsteps thudding on the deck. Cursing, he released his hold and checked his computer, which showed that four contacts were approaching.

"Lucas, you have a squad of four warriors coming directly toward you. Distance twenty meters," Banks said through the comm link in his helmet.

Sterling chanced a look along the corridor and spotted the gloomy outline of the warriors stomping in his direction. He cursed again then ducked back out of sight.

"I won't make the climb before they get here, so I'm going to hide out till they've passed." Sterling swung himself into a void behind a nearby wall, however, because of the half-finished condition of the section, it was impossible to conceal himself fully. "Go to neural comms and let me know when they've moved past," he added, tapping his neural interface to form the link.

"Aye, sir," Banks replied, this time speaking inside Sterling's mind. "Just sit tight and don't make a sound. I'll let you know when it's clear."

The thump of the warrior squad's boots grew louder and louder. Sterling could feel the vibrations rattling through the deck and transmitting into his armor, as if the warriors were stomping on the wall panel directly next to his head. Then through the gaps in the structure he saw the aliens march into view, barely ten meters from his position.

He held his breath, waiting for them to pass, but one of the warriors suddenly let out a rasping hiss and raised a fist. The squad halted and remained in formation.

"What the hell is it doing?" said Sterling through the link, as the warrior that had issued the order took a step ahead.

"I don't know," Banks replied. Sterling could sense the unease in her, despite her voice remaining calm and level. "We might need to take them out."

"Hold for my order, Captain," Sterling said. Given the exceptional abilities of his two officers, he didn't doubt they could win the fight. However, they were so close to the open area Ensign One had identified that a scuffle could easily draw more attention to them.

"We're standing by, just give the word," Banks replied. Now, instead of unease, Sterling felt her resolve and eagerness for action.

Sterling continued to watch the lead warrior, feeling increasingly exposed in the cramped void behind the corridor wall. The alien soldier was now clearly looking for something or someone. It was peering through the gaps in the walls and ceiling only a few meters from his location. Sterling could see its stub-nose twitching, as if it had literally caught his scent. Then the warrior's yellow eyes turned in Sterling's direction. His muscles tightened up and his hand instinctively went to the half-moon serrated blade attached to his armor. It looked like the warrior was staring straight at him, but he kept his cool and remained as still as a statue.

"I think the damned thing can smell you," said Banks

through the link. "We may not have a choice but to kill them."

Sterling gritted his teeth, watching the warrior move ever closer, rifle raised. It had now stepped off the half-finished corridor decking and was inspecting the voids and crevices that Sterling had moved through only a few seconds earlier. It was only a matter of time before the alien would find him, he realized.

"Okay, this bastard has gotten close enough," Sterling said, making his decision. Then he remembered his robot officer's display of cat-like agility and had an idea. "See if you can get a message through to Ensign One, quietly," he continued, as the warrior closed to within a couple of meters of Sterling, nose still twitching. "Have him jump the three other three warriors, while I deal with the asshole stalking me."

"Aye, sir," Banks replied. "I'll be ready too."

Sterling could just about make out the high-pitched chime of Banks' trench knife being drawn from its metal sheath through the audio comm-link in his helmet. He hoped it hadn't sounded as loud to the aliens at it had to him.

Taking another deep breath, Sterling unhooked the Sa'Nerran blade from his armor and tried to maneuver himself out of the hole he'd squeezed himself into. He felt like an escaped prisoner of war, desperately trying to avoid being recaptured by the camp guards. As he moved it was impossible to prevent his stealth armor from grinding against the beams and panels of the ship. While his armor absorbed and diffracted sensor scans and helped to mask his heat signature, it did nothing to absorb sound.

The alien suddenly froze and again its yellow eyes seemed to lock onto Sterling. This time he was sure that the warrior had seen him. The alien hissed and signaled to its squadmates with a closed fist. Immediately, the other warriors broke formation and began marching toward Sterling's location.

"Mercedes, go, now!" Sterling called out, realizing he was about to be discovered.

The lead alien raised its rifle and pointed it into the shadows where Sterling remained hidden. He quickly raised his arms to shield his face, but the blast never came. Through the gap in his forearms, Sterling saw a shadow flash across the corridor to his side, followed by a sharp, metallic clank. Ensign One had leapt down from the level above and hammered its fists into the neck of the warrior at the rear of the squad. The blow was fast, precise and devastatingly effective, killing the warrior instantly.

The lead warrior then spun its weapon toward Ensign One, and Sterling's heart leapt, realizing his unique robot officer was completely exposed. Darting out of cover, he charged at the alien, letting out a roar like the war cry of a Scottish clansman, designed to draw the warrior's attention away from his ensign. The alien's yellow eyes bulged as it turned its weapon back toward Sterling, but it was already too late. Sterling punched the warrior square in the face with blade, slicing open its mouth from stubby ear to stubby ear. The alien hissed wildly as its jaw flopped open, the flesh and muscle that had supported it completely severed.

A second warrior thrust the butt of its rifle at Sterling, but he deflected the strike and swung again. The razor-sharp serrated blade tore a deep gash into the warrior's wrist and the alien was forced to drop its rifle. Sterling attacked again, but incredibly the warrior blocked the blow and thumped a leathery fist into Sterling's chin, temporarily stunning him. He saw the flash of metal as a blade was drawn from the warrior's armor, then the alien's face froze, its eyes wide with surprise. Ensign One had thrust its blade-like index finger through the back of the warrior's head. It was like a stake had been hammered through its skull. Ensign One retracted its hand and the alien fell to the deck, dead.

Sterling had barely recovered before a plasma blast rang out and energy flashed along the corridor, narrowly missing Ensign One's head. Sterling saw the shooter, but his robot officer had already moved to intercept it. Dodging a second blast, it then swung a fist at the warrior and smashed its skull to pieces. The blow was so fast and so ferocious that it looked like the alien had been blasted in the head by a Homewrecker.

Suddenly, Sterling was grabbed from the rear and long-leathery fingers wrapped themselves around his throat. He spun around and again came eye-to-eye with the lead warrior, its severed jaw still hanging limply from its face like a character from a horror movie. Fueled by adrenalin and a thirst for violence, Sterling swatted the alien's hand away then grabbed its loose jaw and tore it clean off the warrior's face. There was a nauseating, squelch, like a boot being pulled out of a boggy mire, followed by a haunting, distorted gargle of bloody mucus that emanated from the alien's gullet.

"Not so easy to hiss at me now, is it?" Sterling snarled at the alien. The warrior's eyes were now wide and wild, the same as those of the alien Ensign One had killed. Maybe it was afraid, Sterling thought. Maybe it was furious. He didn't care so long as it died a painful, tormented death.

Raising his bionic hand, Sterling hammered the edge of the blade down into the warrior's neck and shoulder, burrowing it four inches deep before pulling it clear. Blood gushed from the wound like a geyser and the warrior dropped to its knees. He could have finished it there and then, but stripped of its ability to speak and raise the alarm, Sterling chose to let it bleed out and die instead.

Across the corridor, Ensign One had used the same incredible speed to close the distance between it and the remaining warrior. Heart still thumping in his chest, Sterling turned in time to see the robot clasp its metal hand around the barrel of the alien's rifle and bend it out of alignment. The warrior fired a split-second later and the rifle exploded in its hand. There was another wild hiss – a sound Sterling had begun to recognize as the sound of pain – and the warrior staggered back, its hands and arms burned. However, Ensign One had borne the brunt of the explosion, so that all that now remained of its hand was mangled metal, wires and sparks of electricity.

Like the warrior Sterling had killed, the remaining alien fought through the pain and drew a plasma pistol from a holster on its armor. Sterling cursed, realizing that Ensign One appeared to be stunned or disrupted by the damage it had sustained. The robot was not defending itself, and was about to be destroyed. Gripped by a gut-wrenching helplessness, Sterling watched as the alien raised the pistol and aimed it at Ensign One's head. The warrior's long, leathery finger began to close around the trigger, but before it could fire, a third shadow flashed into view.

Banks landed on the deck in front of the warrior with such force that Sterling felt the tremor through the deck, like a bomb had detonated. Using the momentum of her fall, Banks drove her trench dagger into the warrior's neck then sliced through flesh and bone, separating the alien's sternum in one devasting strike. Blood gushed from the wound, but Banks was not yet finished. Her eyes were wild as she reached inside the warrior's flesh and tore open the alien's ribcage as easily as opening a wardrobe door. The warrior's organs bulged out of the cavity and blood spilled onto the deck, like water from an overflowing sink. Sterling was far from squeamish, but the gory spectacle was enough to churn even his strong stomach.

"That was a bit excessive, don't you think?" said Sterling, stepping cautiously to Banks' side and peering down at the mass of exposed intestines and pulmonary organs. This time it was Sterling who had fallen back on dark humor to help cope with the extreme nature of their situation.

"No harm in being sure," Banks replied, glowering down at the slaughtered carcass of the alien.

Sterling then saw Ensign One. The robot was still

standing in the same place, its glowing ocular units shining onto its destroyed hand.

"Run a quick sweep of the area, and make sure no-one else is heading this way," Sterling ordered Banks, still watching the machine, which was immobile, as if it had shut down. "Then we need to clean up this mess and get moving again. The more of these things we kill, the more likely it is they'll start to be missed."

"Aye, sir," Banks replied, wiping her dagger clean before sheathing it. "I'll keep a link open to you."

Sterling nodded and watched Banks move away before again turning his attention to Ensign One. He stepped over the splayed body of the alien and stood in front of the robot, which did not react as he approached.

"Ensign, are you okay?" Sterling asked, maneuvering himself into the robot's line of sight. "Ensign One?" Sterling tried again, after his officer didn't respond. It was like it had switched itself off.

"I am injured, sir," Ensign One finally replied, still studying its hand.

"It comes with the job, Ensign, you'll get used to it," Sterling said. He would not offer the robot sympathy, any more than he would do so for his human officers.

"Yes, sir, I believe I will," Ensign One replied, lowering its hand to its side. "It is a curious sensation, nonetheless. I found it to be quite disarming."

"Found what to be disarming?" Sterling asked, hooking his blood-stained half-moon blade back onto his armor.

"Pain, sir," Ensign One answered, calmly.

Sterling frowned at the machine. "You're telling me that you feel pain?"

"Do you not feel pain, Commodore?" Ensign One asked, shining its eyes onto Sterling.

"Yes, but I'm human and organic," Sterling replied. "You're a machine."

"I am also alive, sir," Ensign One said.

Sterling hadn't considered that his sentient AI could feel pain, but then there will still so much about his unique robot officer that he didn't know. Even so, whether in pain or not, he still needed to know whether his ensign could continue the mission.

"Treat your injury as best you can, Ensign, but we have to press on," Sterling said. "Assuming you are able to continue?"

"I am, sir," Ensign One replied, lowering its injured hand to its side. "I will replace the damaged components at the earliest opportunity, but the impairment will not prevent me from doing my duty."

"Good," Sterling said, standing tall. It was precisely the answer he would expect from an Omega officer. Whether that officer was human or robot, organic or artificial, there was no difference. All it proved was that Ensign One deserved to wear the uniform with the silver stripe. "Status report, Ensign," Sterling requested, getting back to business. "Is there any sign that we've been detected?"

Ensign One's eyes flashed and it shook its head. "Not directly, no," the robot replied. "These warriors were unable to make a report, and there is no indication that the Sa'Nerra present in the adjacent section were alerted.

However, the arrival of this squad suggests that the aliens suspect something is amiss down here. We should expect and plan for more resistance as we progress."

Sterling nodded. "Very well, Ensign, thank you," he said, before again looking down at the body of the warrior Banks had savagely killed. "Now we need to hide these bodies, or at least what's left of them."

"Aye, sir, I will get right on it," Ensign One replied.

The robot moved away, but Sterling hadn't quite finished. "One more thing, Ensign," Sterling said, causing the robot to turn and shine its ocular units onto his face. "Good work," Sterling said, with sincerity.

"Thank you, sir," the robot replied. It was again about to move off before it hesitated and looked back. "I believe I now understand, at least in part, how you feel, sir."

"How I feel about what, Ensign?"

"How you feel when you wake from your nightmares, sir," the sentient AI replied. The sudden mention of his unsettling visions took Sterling by surprise and he was momentarily struck dumb. "I once believed I could counsel you," Ensign One continued. "But now I realize I was mistaken."

"Experience is everything, Ensign," Sterling replied. For once, he wasn't annoyed at his former ship's AI for raising a subject that was highly personal and confidential. This was a teachable moment for the robot, who had effectively only been born a few months ago. "Data on its own is meaningless. You already knew what pain is and how it works, but without experiencing it, you could never truly understand it. The same is true of being an Omega officer, and the same is true of being alive."

"I understand, sir," Ensign One replied. "Life is more difficult than I imagined it to be."

"You're a quick learner, Ensign," Sterling said, giving his officer a reassuring slap on the shoulder. The clash of armor on metal produced a resonant clang that hung in the air. "You'll be alright."

"Yes, sir, I believe I will," Ensign One replied. It then focused its glowing ocular units onto the body at their feet before pointing a single digit on its remaining hand at the corpse. "Unlike this warrior," the robot then added, dryly.

Sterling snorted a laugh and cocked an eyebrow at Ensign One. "That was an attempt at humor, right?" he asked.

"Yes, sir," Ensign One replied, cheerfully. "How did I do this time?"

"This time you got it, Ensign," Sterling said, smiling at the machine. "This time you got it."

WORKING TOGETHER, Sterling, Banks and Ensign One quickly disposed of the four dead Sa'Nerran warriors, by shoving the bodies deep inside the voids. Then with the help of his super-human fellow officer, Sterling climbed to the level above and together they continued their journey to the field generator room. However, they hadn't gone far before another example of the Sa'Nerra's cruelty stopped them dead in their tracks. The open area that Ensign One had highlighted earlier turned out to be a factory floor, staffed exclusively by human workers. Other similar industrial spaces appeared to border the factory below them, spreading out on all sides, separated only by crude metal walls.

"Many of the humans that were being transported to Earth from Mars are destined for a fate such as this," said Ensign One. The robot was also observing the scene from the group's elevated vantage point.

"These are probably the lucky ones," mused Sterling,

peering at the army of forced laborers. "At least they get a roof over their heads. That's likely more than anyone being shipped to the planet will get."

Sterling watched as one of the hundreds of human workers that were crammed into the factory collapsed to the deck. Each of the workers still wore the electrified metal collars that Sterling had observed on the prisoner transport ship. However, unlike the unfortunate souls on the haulage vessels, these workers had at least been allowed clothes. Though the torn and filth-stained garments were little improvement, Sterling thought.

"They haven't even bothered to turn these ones," Banks said, as a Sa'Nerran warrior appeared beside the woman who had fallen and began kicking her with the toe of his boot. When the woman didn't respond, the warrior detailed two other workers to drag her body away. "It's not enough to simply beat us, the bastards want to degrade us too."

Sterling still had an open neural connection to Banks and he could feel her anger bleeding across the link. It was so powerful and intense that Sterling almost severed the connection to prevent himself being overwhelmed by it. However, he chose to let his fellow officer's feelings to continue to flow into his own mind. He didn't want to feel better about what he was seeing. He wanted to be angry. Suddenly, a glint of metal caught his eye. He squinted to get a clearer view, but was still struggling to believe what he was seeing.

"Have they been augmented?" Sterling said, feeling the need to check with the others that he wasn't seeing things.

"That is correct, Commodore," Ensign One replied.

"Around sixty percent of the workers have had hands or entire arms replaced with tools. However, the work is crude and must be agonizing to endure."

"What's with the metal sheets on their heads and other parts of their bodies?" Banks asked.

"Those are patches to cover wounds or to splint broken bones, sir," Ensign One replied.

The robot's tone was composed but also somber, like a historian recounting the events of an atrocity committed long ago to a new group of students. Banks opened her mouth to reply, but no sound came out. It was probably the first time Sterling had ever seen her lost for words. The trio of Omega officers then remained silent for a time as they continued to watch the workers on the factory floor. It was like seeing a car crash on the highway. Despite knowing you should look away it was impossible to do so.

With every second that passed, Sterling saw more examples of the Sa'Nerra's wanton disregard for human life. Injuries that had likely been sustained because of the appalling working conditions were hastily patched up with no consideration for the patient's suffering. Missing legs were replaced with metal stumps, bolted through the bone. Gouged eyes had metal patches riveted across them. Many of the wounds were rotten and festering. Six more workers had collapsed in the short time they'd been watching. Some had already been dragged away, while others lay motionless on the deck, crying out for their mothers like soldiers dying in the mud at the Somme.

"Barbaric bastards," Banks spat through gritted teeth.

Sterling felt another sudden swell of rage flood across

their neural link. He thought he knew anger, but at that moment he realized he had barely scratched the surface of what true rage felt like. He allowed it to swell inside him like a poisonous gas billowing throughout his body.

"We can't do anything about these people," Sterling said, tearing his eyes away from the factory floor. He'd witnessed many acts of savagery by the alien race during his time as an Omega officer, but nothing had come close to this. It merely confirmed in his mind what he'd already known; that to beat the Sa'Nerra, he would not only have to match their level of barbarism, he'd have to exceed it. "At least by taking this ship down, we'll end the suffering of those poor bastards too."

"The passageway leading to the aperture field generator room is twenty meters ahead, sir," Ensign One said. "We must again drop down to the level below before we can proceed."

Unlike Sterling and Banks, the robot had remained melancholy. Sterling wondered if the treatment of the human workers repulsed Ensign One as much as it did himself. Anger was not yet an emotion the machine had displayed, and he wondered how long it would be before his AI officer also succumbed.

"Take point again, Ensign," Sterling ordered, hopping from one beam to another to get back on course. "And keep your scanners peeled for any sign of warrior patrols."

"There is movement ahead, sir, but it does not appear to be a warrior patrol," Ensign One replied, leaping skillfully across a precipice and catching a pillar on the opposite side.

"Then who is it?" Sterling wondered, following the robot, though with considerably less acrobatic aplomb.

"It appears to be a group of humans." Ensign One suddenly ducked down to get a better look at the corridor beyond their perch, high up in the beams and rafters of the ship. "However, unlike the workers in the factory, these people appear to have been turned."

Sterling stopped and checked his computer, which confirmed the cluster of contacts ahead of them. He then moved to the robot's side to get a better view.

"Remember that turned humans have amped-up strength and resistance to injury," Sterling said, watching a couple of drones move through the corridor below him. "We should avoid getting into a fight with them if we can."

"I have been observing their movements and the pattern is highly regular," Ensign One said. "The workers in the corridor carry finished resources to a service elevator before returning to collect more. The interval between each deposit is three minutes and ten seconds."

"So, if these drones move like clockwork, if we time it right, we can just slip past, right?" Banks suggested, dropping to a crouch on Ensign One's other side.

"I believe so," the robot replied. "The next window is in forty-eight seconds. I suggest we swiftly descend to the level below in preparation to advance."

Ensign One dropped down first, managing to land with barely a sound, thanks to its recent self-designed stealth modifications. The robot then used its body to create a platform, allowing Sterling and Banks to ease themselves down to the lower level with matching discretion.

"On my mark, follow me and remain as close as possible," Ensign One said, stopping at the corner beyond which the drone workers were moving to and fro.

Sterling unhooked the Sa'Nerran blade from his armor and gripped it tightly in anticipation of needing it again. The blood on the handle had now congealed, making the grip feel sticky to the touch. He glanced behind to Banks and saw the trench knife was again in her hand. The blade was almost entirely red and still contained slivers of alien flesh and skin.

"Mark..." Ensign One said, then immediately set out across the corridor.

Sterling and Banks huddled in behind the machine, remaining as close as possible while being conscious of not tripping each other up. To his left, Sterling saw two turned humans trudging away with their backs to them. Another was ahead of Ensign One, carrying a crate of whatever product the workshop had produced. Sterling noted that the metal container was so large that it almost spanned the entire width of the corridor, and from the labored way the drone was walking, it was clearly also incredibly heavy. The worker finally arrived at one of the rows of service elevators and slid the crate inside. Ensign One quickened its pace and led them behind a support pillar, which was broad enough to conceal all three officers.

"In sixty seconds, the worker will have returned along the corridor," Ensign One said through the audio comm-link in Sterling's helmet. "Then we can proceed to the generator room without further obstructions."

Right on cue, the turned worker began to trudge back

the way it had come, presumably to fetch another casket-sized crate. Sterling could now see that the man's arms and hands had been augmented with metal plates and hooks that had been bolted and screwed into the bone. Blood was weeping from where the metal met the man's flesh. However, the face of the worker was blank and soulless with dark, cloudy eyes like dusty, scratched marbles. Suddenly the turned worker stumbled and dropped to one knee. The man tried to push himself back up, but his body was unable to comply. Despite the augments and metal reinforcements, flesh had limits. The man then fell forward, his face slamming into the sharp deck grates with a stomach-turning crunch. Sterling cursed, but not because the Sa'Nerra had literally worked the man to death. The drone had fallen directly next to their hiding place.

"Can we make a run for it now?" Sterling asked Ensign One though the comm-link.

"Negative, two more workers are approaching," Ensign One replied. "I recommend we remain here, observe and improvise as required."

The two turned humans Ensign One had detected began to approach. Sterling tried to tuck himself more tightly behind the pillar, but their position was far more exposed than he'd have liked. He adjusted the angle of the alien blade in his hand, preparing to rush the workers at the first sign they'd spotted him. However, the two turned humans simply marched past and stopped beside the dead worker, oblivious to anything other than their task.

One of workers, a woman who looked no older than seventeen or eighteen, removed some of the augmented parts from the dead man before stepping back and allowing the second drone forward. This worker was holding what appeared to be the lance section of an automobile jet washer. As the drone moved into position, Sterling could also see that a compact silver tank had been bolted directly onto the man's spinal column. The worker aimed the nozzle of the lance at the dead worker and began to spray a thick, grey vapor over the body. The milky substance quickly settled and congealed, covering the body like a cocoon.

"What the hell is it doing?" Sterling wondered out loud.

"It cleaning up the mess," Banks replied, her disgust at what she was witnessing coming through cleanly over the link.

Sterling frowned then watched as the cocoon began to hiss, fizz and rapidly shrink. Clouds of chalky vapor billowed up from the cocoon as the milky substance dissolved the dead man's flash. Soon only the metal bolts that had bound the augmentations to his bones remained. It was an effective method of disposal, Sterling realized. Quick and easy. In some ways, he admired the ruthless efficiency of the Sa'Nerra, and their utter disregard for decency. However, admiring their traits did not mean he hated the aliens any less. It only made him more determined to beat them at their own game.

Suddenly, Sterling felt a tightness in his throat and a tingling irritation in his eyes. The cloud of vapor from the disintegrated body had dispersed and begun to fill the corridor. He felt the sudden need to cough to clear his throat but fought the urge; the two other turned workers were still only meters away. Thinking on his feet, Sterling closed the visor in his helmet in an attempt to shield himself from further exposure.

"Mercedes, put your visor down," Sterling said to Banks through the link. Banks didn't answer and he turned to see her pinching her nose. Her eyes were pressed tightly shut. Then she sneezed. The sound was muted, but Sterling still heard it clearly. His pulse began to race and he turned back to the drone workers. Both were facing in their direction, their milky, dead eyes staring straight through them.

The two drones charged forward, displaying the ferocious bursts of speed that Sterling had witnessed in turned humans dozens of times before. However, Ensign One was quicker. Catching the shaft of the jet lance, the machine aimed it to the side just in time to ensure the spray of gas was ejected harmlessly onto the corridor wall. Undeterred, the worker grabbed the robot with its free hand and the two locked up, like wrestlers sizing each other up to see who was stronger.

Banks sprang out next, thrusting her trench dagger at the second worker, but somehow the woman blocked the attack, trapping the blade between the prongs of her augmented hand. Banks was then punched in the chest and driven back into the corridor wall. Sterling attacked next but was met with a swinging backhand that felt like it had been delivered by a three-hundred-pound heavyweight, rather than the slip of a girl in front of him. Spitting blood and a broken tooth onto the deck grates, he prepared to advance again before two more drone workers rushed around the corner.

"You take the woman, I'll deal with these two," Sterling said through the link to Banks.

Moments later, his fellow officer had charged into the female drone and driven her against the wall. Sterling then turned to confront the new attackers and drew his stun baton, wielding it and the blade simultaneously. Dodging the charge of the first drone, Sterling swung the baton and caught the turned man on the back of the neck, delivering a shock pulse powerful enough to kill him instantly. Yet, despite the swift and efficient kill, the second drone had already closed the distance between them. The man grabbed Sterling around the neck and began to squeeze. He swung the serrated alien blade, opening a deep, six-inch gash in the man's belly, but the blow had seemingly no effect. The drone hammered Sterling against the wall, causing him to drop the blade, before tossing him across to the other side of the corridor like he was a sack of dirty laundry. He bounced off the wall and crumpled to the deck, but managed to keep his wits about him, despite the stunning effect of the impact.

Using the wall as a springboard, Sterling pushed off and charged the turned worker, driving his shoulder into the oozing gash to his side and smashing the man's head into the wall opposite. He heard the crack and crunch of bone, but he'd fought enough turned humans to know that this alone would not be enough to put the man down. Using all of his strength, Sterling swung his arm around the man's neck and squeezed. The strength in his muscles combined with the added power of his bionic hand was enough to close off the supply of blood to the drone's brain. They may have been turned and they may have been mutilated to serve the Sa'Nerra's needs, but they were still human, Sterling knew. And no level of enhancement or augmentation could overcome the basic human need for blood and oxygen to the brain.

Under the immense pressure of Sterling's grip, the turned drone quickly became limp and collapsed to the deck. Sterling, maintained the hold, but shuffled around to check on Banks and Ensign One. To his right, Sterling saw Ensign One, standing over the man with the cannister bolted to his back. The robot's damaged hand had been thrust inside the man's gut, and Sterling could see intestines dangling from the wound. However, this had not been what killed the drone. Ensign One's other hand was thrust into worker's forehead, its sharp metal digits sunk deep into the drone's brain directly through the eye sockets.

To his left was a scene that put anything Sterling had witnessed so far on the Titan to shame. Banks had not only torn both arms off the woman who'd had the audacity to strike her, but she'd used them to pummel her into a pulp. All that now remained of the female drone was a mashed torso and two legs that looked to be broken in at least four places. Not for the first time, Sterling felt his stomach turn.

"I project we have a window of two minutes, eighteen seconds before more drone workers or Sa'Nerra arrive," Ensign One said, hurrying to Sterling's side. "We must move quickly or we will be discovered. We can progress into the generator room through the second door along the next corridor to our right."

"What about these bodies?" Banks asked, wiping the mashed human flesh from her hands.

Sterling thought for a moment then picked up the jet lance that had been used to disintegrate the first dead worker.

"I'll use this thing," he said, ripping the silver cylinder from the worker's back and holding it at his side. "You and Ensign One move ahead. I'll coat the bodies with this stuff and meet you there."

"It would be safer if I administered the substance, sir," Ensign One said. "I am not organic."

"You are also not in command," Sterling hit back. "Now move out, I'll meet you there."

Ensign One and Banks hurriedly collected their weapons off the deck and moved out as ordered. Sterling knew that it was safer for his robot officer to clean up the bodies, but this was a task he had to do himself. The workers may have been turned and as such they were no different to the enemy. But they were still human beings. He had killed them. He'd kill many thousands more before the day was out. It was his mess and it was his responsibility to clean it up.

STERLING CREPT alongside Banks and his robot ensign then got his first look at the Battle Titan's aperture field generator room. They had entered on the middle level of the space, which was the same size as a commercial aircraft hangar. Two enormous aperture field generators occupied the bulk of the chamber, towering over the room like ballistic missiles. However, while the generator towers appeared to be in pristine working order, the chamber itself had been left half-completed, like much of the rest of the Battle Titan.

"At least the Sa'Nerra's lazy construction practices should make it easier for us to move around undetected," Banks said. She was speaking through the voice comm-link in her helmet, so that Ensign One could also hear. "We could probably drive a ground transit around down there without being seen."

"Let's just stick to moving on foot, shall we?" Sterling replied, cocking an eyebrow in the direction of his fellow officer. "Besides, I think you overestimate our chances. There must be fifty Sa'Nerran workers down there, not including the turned human drones."

"That's why I brought this along," said Banks, tapping the barrel of the Homewrecker slung across her back.

"All in good time, Captain," said Sterling, noticing that the blood and guts that had splattered across Banks' armor was drying in places, giving it a mottled, patchwork appearance. He then turned to his robot officer. "How close do you need to get to those towers in order to do your thing, Ensign?"

"I will need to interface with the sub-processor directly," Ensign One replied. "We will need to progress to the lower level so that I can identify the correct terminal."

Sterling frowned then peered at the ground floor again, watching the Sa'Nerran engineers and their turned human servants going about their daily business.

"With all the activity down there, I don't rate our chances of getting to that computer sub-processor unseen," Sterling said. This was usually the moment he would turn to his chief engineer and ask her to impress him with another one of her brilliant solutions. However, on this occasion he didn't have her insight or ingenuity to rely on.

"I have been observing their movements and I believe I can get us into cover behind to the computer, without being detected," Ensign One continued.

"That approach didn't exactly work out well for us last time," Banks commented, dryly.

"That was a freak occurrence, Captain," Ensign One

hit back, remaining confident in its assessment. "We cannot plan for things we do not know."

"I know that I don't want to get caught down on the generator room floor with fifty Sa'Nerra and a bunch of turned drones," Sterling replied, echoing Banks concerns. "We've walked a narrow tightrope already to get this far. I don't want to fall off it now."

"Then I will devise another solution," the machine replied, cheerfully.

Ensign One aimed its ocular units at the space below and began to scan the room. The robot had dimmed the light emitted by its unique eyes in order to remain inconspicuous, but Sterling could still see them flicker chaotically as the machine continued its scans.

"Some of the exposed pipes in this room carry waste gases intended for overboard venting," Ensign One said, indicating to the one of the large conduits that would ordinarily be sealed inside the voids between walls and decks. "Others carry coolants and water supplies around the ship. If we trigger a violent escape of carbon dioxide, for example, it would require the Sa'Nerra to evacuate the area. That will give me the time I need to infiltrate the computer and trigger an overload in the field generators."

"These alien bastards have to breath too, right?" Sterling said, immediately getting on board with the AI's suggestion. It was an idea worthy of Katreena Razor herself.

"We have to get down there first," Banks said, shuffling further along the walkway that circled the generator room. "It looks like there's a route about fifty meters to our right.

It winds down to the lower level and should lead us out behind one of the generator towers."

Sterling studied the route, chewing the inside of his mouth as he did so. Banks' assessment was right, but the path would also take them closer to the main body of Sa'Nerran engineers than he was comfortable with. Even so, he didn't see that they had a choice.

"Okay, let's move out, but *quietly* this time," Sterling said, putting extra emphasis on the word 'quietly'. "We're wearing stealth armor for a reason, but so far we've managed to be anything but stealthy."

Ensign One led the way down the narrow, metal staircase that zig-zagged to the ground level of the generator room. The stairwell creaked and groaned like a rusted old apartment-block fire-escape. Each screech of metal made Sterling's teeth itch and his eyes flick over to the group of alien workers. However, the resonant thrum from the field generators and the seismic beat of the Titan's engines and reactors reverberating around the hull of the giant vessel was enough to mask their approach.

Suddenly, Ensign One raised a hand, calling for Sterling and Banks to stop. The machine crouched and pointed toward one of the entrances to the generator room. Sterling hunkered down and looked in the direction his officer had indicated. The doors were closed, but in front of them stood a warrior wearing ornate, bronze-colored armor, talking to an alien engineer. The warrior turned slightly and Sterling cursed, realizing who it was.

"What the hell is Crow doing in here?" said Banks, who had evidently spotted the Emissary too.

"I don't know, but I feel like marching over there and tearing out the bastard's throat right now," Sterling answered. "Ensign, can your audio sensors pick up what he's saying?" he added, trying to put thoughts of brutally murdering Clinton Crow out of his mind.

"I believe so, sir," Ensign One replied. "Give me a moment to recalibrate them to the acoustics of this space."

Suddenly the doors to the generator room thumped open and another group of Sa'Nerra marched inside. At the head of the formation was a warrior that towered over the soldiers to its rear. The only other warrior Sterling had seen that had even approached the size of this alien was the cage-fighter Banks had fought and killed on Hope Rises. However, even that brute would have stood in this new warrior's shadow. Size wasn't the only thing that marked the warrior out from the others. Its skin was even more leathery and wrinkled, and its armor was golden in color and looked ancient, like a priceless museum piece.

Sterling continued to watch as the new warrior approached Clinton Crow. The Emissary stood to attention then gracefully bowed his head. The other Sa'Nerra in the room rapidly dispersed to give the new arrival more space. Sterling also noted that all the alien engineers had turned their back on the new warrior, as if they were afraid of it or forbidden to look at it.

"Whoever this guy is, he must be important," Banks said, as Crow slowly raised his head and met the warrior's eyes. The two then began to converse in the rasping hisses of the Sa'Nerra's incomprehensible language.

"Ensign, can you translate what they're saying?" Sterling said, eager to eavesdrop on the conversation.

"Processing..." Ensign One replied, the dimmed lights in its ocular units pulsing wildly. Then the robot began to summarize the conversation through the comm-link in Sterling's and Banks' helmets.

"Crow has addressed to the warrior as 'Imperator' and is showing the alien great respect," Ensign One began, delivering a truncated version of the exchange. "The Imperator appears to be a high-ranking leader. Perhaps the equivalent of a general or admiral." The robot was then silent for a time before it summarized the next part of the conversation. "The Imperator is demanding that the power of the aperture weapon be increased further," Ensign One continued. "The warrior says that Earth has almost been harvested. It wants the seventeen million remaining survivors killed and the planet rendered uninhabitable before they return to the Void." Sterling could again feel a swell of rage transfer over the neural link from Banks. However, on this occasion his own anger was already at a matching level. "Emissary Crow is apologetic, but explains that the power of the aperture weapon has already been amplified by more than five times. He assures the Imperator that it is sufficient to turn Earth into a perpetual wasteland where no human could survive."

The doors then thumped open again and another figure in ornate armor walked in. Sterling felt his stomach tighten into a knot as he realized that the new arrival was another turned human. However, the face of the man or woman was obscured by the troop of warriors guarding the Imperator, and Sterling couldn't make out who it was.

"That can't be McQueen, can it?" Banks said, through the comm-link. "There's no way in hell she survived. We saw her die."

"It's not McQueen," Sterling replied. The figure had stepped forward and he could now make out the man's face clearly. It was a face he knew well. It was a face he could never forget. "That's Admiral Wessel."

Banks' brow scrunched into a scowl as she peered out at the man. Then the comm-link was overloaded with a string of expletives that were cruder and more creative than any Sterling had ever come up with.

"The Imperator is now speaking to Admiral Wessel," Ensign One said, immediately causing Banks to fall silent and listen. "The Imperator has addressed Wessel as 'Praetor'. Or at least that is the best translation I can offer."

"Is Wessel the one in command here?" Sterling asked. These new honorifics meant nothing to him; all he wanted to know was who was calling the shots.

"Negative, Commodore, the Imperator is senior," Ensign One answered. "Praetor Wessel is delivering a report to the Imperator," the robot went on. Sterling was now finding it difficult to hear his officer's words, due to the deafening thump of his pulse echoing inside his helmet. "Wessel reports that the primary inner colony worlds have been exterminated," Ensign One continued. "He explains that the bombardments have poisoned the atmospheres and irradiated the soils so that no life could possibly survive on their surfaces."

The sentient machine's tone was level and composed, but Sterling could detect a seam of resentment running through its words. Sterling hoped that his officer embraced the feeling and allowed it to take seed. Anger was a powerful weapon in the right hands, and he suspected it was a weapon he would soon need to deploy.

"Wessel must have been working behind the scenes all this time," said Banks, still speaking through gritted teeth. "He's always tried to undermine the war effort and convince the UG senators to cease hostilities."

"So it would seem," said Sterling, allowing the gravity of the revelation to sink in. He didn't know for how long Admiral Wessel had been turned, or when it had occurred, but in the end it didn't matter. He had been playing them for fools the whole time. Sterling cursed himself for underestimating the Wessels. He'd considered them weak-minded and weak-willed. The truth was that Wessel was more cunning than Sterling had given him credit for.

"The Imperator has now asked Wessel to report on his plans to eradicate the Void Worlds," Ensign One said, again snapping Sterling's attention back to the robot's commentary. "Praetor Wessel replied that most of the Void Worlds have already been purged of human life. Only one major colony remains. Its name is Middle Star."

Sterling's fists clenched at the mention of Middle Star. However, this time it wasn't due to anger, but a feeling a hope. While all the other human colonies had fallen, Christopher Fletcher had continued to resist the Sa'Nerra. Now, Middle Star remained as the only pocket of humanity left in the galaxy.

"The Imperator has ordered Praetor Wessel to ready his taskforce of turned Fleet warships and leave immediately for the Void," Ensign One continued.

Sterling watched as Wessel and Crow bowed in deference to the Sa'Nerran Imperator and remained bowed as the alien general departed with its personal guard. Some of the Sa'Nerran engineers then began to drift back toward their previous work stations, but Wessel hissed at them and the aliens quickly backed away.

"What are they talking about now?" asked Banks, noticing that Wessel and Crow were speaking in hushed tones.

"They have switched to speaking English," Ensign One said, its eyes flashing. "I will relay their conversation directly over the comm-link."

There was another tense pause then the loathsome voice of Clinton Crow assaulted Sterling's ears.

"You didn't tell the Imperator about Emissary McQueen or the Vanguard," Crow said, sounding surprised by Wessel's apparent omission.

"That's because we have nothing to report," Wessel hit back. Despite the change of allegiance and the new alien uniform, the man remained as obnoxious as ever. "For all we know, the Vanguard is still adrift and McQueen is still searching for it."

"We should assume that Captain Sterling has been successful," Emissary Crow replied, taking a stern, almost disrespectful tone with the Praetor. This version of Clinton Crow had more balls than the officer he remembered,

Sterling thought. "If Sterling has the Vanguard, he is still a threat."

"Sterling is nothing!" Wessel barked, showering Crow's face with spittle. "We have destroyed the United Governments Fleet, stripped Earth bare and will leave it uninhabitable for the next one hundred thousand years," the bombastic Praetor added. "So what if Sterling has the Vanguard? One ship is nothing against the might of the Sa'Nerran armada, or my taskforce."

Crow shook his head. It was clear that the two were at odds. "More than anything, the Vanguard is a symbol," Crow replied. "The forces amassed at Middle Star are considerable. Together with the Vanguard they are still a threat. And we still don't know what happened to Admiral Griffin. She could be out there for all we know, plotting as she always did." Crow then aimed a finger at Wessel in a manner that was clearly intended as a threat. "Do not forget that your reckless assault of Earth cost us more than half of the war armada," Crow snarled. "Even with the turned Fleet ships and crews, our forces are stretched thin."

Wessel slapped Crow's hand away from his face. The sound echoed around the room, causing some of the Sa'Nerran workers to glance across with curious yellow eyes.

"I am in command of the turned Fleet forces, not you, Emissary," Wessel said, speaking the word 'Emissary' with disdain. "Your task is over. Your family has already been transported to the world of your choosing. Leave now and claim your prize. Let me deal with Sterling and the ants at Middle Star."

Crow straightened up. There was a look of disgust written plain across the man's scarred face. "I am an Emissary to the Sa'Nerra," Crow said, taking obvious pride in announcing his title. "While humanity resists, my role is not finished. Only the Imperator itself can say otherwise."

"Fine, waste your time on the search for Sterling," Wessel replied, puffing out his chest like a cockerel. "Meanwhile, I'll take my taskforce to Middle Star and put an end to the resistance. Then once humanity is finally exterminated, our loyalty will be rewarded."

Crow nodded. "For Sa'Nerra."

Crow's patriotic outburst appeared to be the one thing that Wessel agreed with. The Praetor also nodded his head to Crow, though his bow was not as deep, and repeated the cry.

"For Sa'Nerra!" Wessel said.

The former Fleet Admiral then turned on his heels and departed. Crow remained for a few moments, hissing orders at the Sa'Nerran engineers, then he too left the generator room, the doors thudding shut behind him.

"Now's our chance," said Banks, realizing that the alien workers were still largely gathered across the other side of the room. "Ensign, find us a route to the computer sub-processer now. We might not get a better chance."

Sterling heard Ensign One acknowledge the order and in his peripheral vision he could see the robot's ocular units flashing. However, Sterling's mind was pre-occupied with other matters. Earth was lost as were the inner colony worlds and the billions that had inhabited them. Yet there was still a chance to save what remained of humanity.

Christopher Fletcher had kept Middle Star and its four-million population safe so far, but their time was running out. Whatever the strength of Fletcher's forces, it could not hope to stand against Praetor Wessel's taskforce, especially if the former admiral took the Fleet Dreadnaught Hammer into battle. Yet, the looming attack on Middle Star was an opportunity too. It had forced the aliens to split what remained of their forces. The aging, rag-tag fleet defending Middle Star was not powerful enough to repel the fleet that would soon descend on it. However, together with the Vanguard, the Invictus and the Obsidian Fleet, they could strike hard and overwhelm Wessel's forces. Then, together with Fletcher's navy, they could move on Sa'Nerra itself.

With Earth destroyed, victory was no longer possible, but this did not mean they had been defeated. Now the question was not who had won, but who would lose the most. In the end, all that mattered was which species was left standing, regardless of how many worlds had been purged and how many lives had been taken. Earth may have already fallen. Sa'Nerra would fall harder.

STERLING RUSHED OUT from behind cover and wrapped the garotte around the neck of a Sa'Nerran engineer. Twisting his body, he turned his back on the alien and lifted the worker onto his shoulders. Within seconds, the wire had cut through the alien's tough skin and severed its throat and jugular. Sterling felt hot blood splash on to his face as he dragged the thrashing body into the shadows to die.

Banks advanced toward the computer sub-processor and killed the other alien worker with similar ruthlessness. However, while Sterling had used an assassination weapon from a time long-past, Banks had used an even more timeless method of killing. Covering the alien's mouth with one hand to muffle its hisses, Banks had thrust her trench dagger through the Sa'Nerran's back fully to the hilt, piercing the alien's heart. She too had then dragged the worker into the shadows, leaving only a few splatters of blood on the deck as evidence that the brutal deed had been done.

"I am interfacing with the alien sub-processor now," said Ensign One. The robot had removed a panel from the rear of the console and directly connected itself to the circuits inside. Cradled in a choke-hold in its other arm was another of the alien workers, which the machine was slowly strangling to death. Sterling could see that the Sa'Nerran's yellow eyes had bulged-out of its sockets and that its dark, mottled tongue was protruding from its thin, slug-like lips. "In order to trigger the escape of gas, please rupture the fourth pipe in the group of conduits that runs directly behind this console," Ensign One added, still casually strangling the alien. "I would also suggest destroying the ventilation control system next to it. It will hinder the Sa'Nerra's effort to contain the escape of gas."

"Breaking things is your specialty, Mercedes," said Sterling, cautiously checking over the top of the console in case any other workers were approaching.

"I'm on it," Banks nodded, then she lowered her visor, reminding Sterling to do the same, and crouch-ran to the row of metal pipes. With the high-ranking members of the Sa'Nerran military now gone, the generator room was rapidly returning to business as usual. Ensign One had managed to get them to the sub-processor without the need to take down more than a few of the engineers, but Sterling knew that even those would soon be missed. The groan of metal being forced to bend to Mercedes Banks' will then caught Sterling's attention. Using her phenomenal natural strength, Banks had already twisted the six-inch pipe into a wide arc. She then pulled back on it, separating the joins and breaking the seals, immediately causing a thick jet of carbon dioxide to rush into the room. Within seconds the computer sub-processor was almost entirely consumed by the cloud, and Sa'Nerran alarms began screeching.

"That's done, now let's hurry this up before they close the shut-off valve," Banks said, her voice rising to a shout to be heard over the torrent of gas escaping from the pipe. There was then another metal crunch and Sterling could just about make out the ventilation control system crumpling under the strain of another assault from his fellow officer.

"How are you doing, Ensign? We're on the clock, here," Sterling said, using the vision enhancement system in his visor to observe the Sa'Nerran workers hurriedly evacuating the generator room.

"I have access and am ready to execute the program," Ensign One replied.

"Then do it already, what are you waiting for?" Sterling replied, ducking back behind the console and fumbling through the cloud of gas to reach Ensign One's side.

"You should be aware of something before we commit to this course of action, Commodore," Ensign One continued.

"I think we're already committed, Ensign," Sterling hit back, frostily. However, he also realized that the sentient AI wouldn't have spoken up if it had not been something serious. "But go ahead, what's the problem?"

"Since we last saw the Titan in action during the battle of F-sector, the Sa'Nerra have dramatically increased the weapon's power," Ensign One began as Banks cut through the cloud of gas and rested a hand on Sterling's shoulder to let him know she had returned. She remained silent while the robot continued its report. "Because of this, a catastrophic overload of the aperture field generators will now rupture space up to one hundred thousand kilometers from the point of origin."

Sterling cursed. Though the verbose sentient AI hadn't spelled it out for him, he knew the reason the robot had raised the concern. The Battle Titan was currently in high-earth orbit, which put the planet well within the blast radius.

"Cut to the chase, Ensign, what sort of effect will the rupture have on Earth?" Sterling said.

"At best it will be an extinction-level event," the robot replied, calmly. "At worst, Earth would be entirely consumed inside the singularity between normal space and the surge dimension."

The trio were silent for a moment. Each of them knew what the decision would mean. The Sa'Nerran Imperator had revealed that seventeen million people survived on the planet's surface. Sterling's decision to go ahead would mean that it was his actions that killed the remaining population, rather than the actions of the enemy. However, Sterling had already accepted that the rights or wrongs of his actions would be for historians to determine. Perhaps scholars would argue that Earth could have still survived had Sterling not done what he was about to do. Sterling, however, wasn't a scholar. He was a fighter, and fighting was all he knew.

"The Omega Directive is in effect," Sterling said, announcing his decision. "The Battle Titan must be destroyed if humanity is to have any chance of survival." He fixed his eyes on the glowing ocular units of his robot officer, which were still just about visible through the fog of gas surrounding them. "Execute the program, Ensign. That's an order."

"Aye, sir," Ensign One replied, smartly.

Suddenly, the clouds of carbon dioxide began to thin. Sterling peered around the generator room and saw that the remaining ventilation ducts had been activated and were working hard to clear the gas.

"They've closed a safety valve on the pipe I ruptured," said Banks, who was now visible thanks to the clearer air. "It won't be long before they find us."

Sterling drew his plasma pistol and turned to his fellow officer. "It's time we switched things up a gear," he said, dialing the power level of the weapon to maximum. "No more sneaking around, and no more silent takedowns."

Banks sheathed her trench dagger and unslung the Homewrecker heavy plasma rifle that she had so far patiently refrained from using. Sterling watched as she also dialed the power level to its recklessly-dangerous maximum setting. Sterling took up position, preparing to hold off the warriors he knew would inevitably come. Already, the whine of the enormous surge field generators was beginning to rise. The doomsday clock had been started and soon all hell would break loose.

The door to the generator room then thumped open and a squad of warriors charged inside, weapons raised.

One of the aliens immediately took charge, hissing orders at the others, who rapidly fanned out and began their search.

"Wait for them to spread out," said Sterling, watching as Banks rested her blood-stained finger on the trigger of the powerful rifle. "Then we can pick them off, one by one."

"Who gets to take him down?" Banks replied, nodding in the direction of the open doorway.

Sterling frowned then turned to see that more Sa'Nerra had stormed inside the generator room. Amongst them was Emissary Clinton Crow.

"So long as I get to see him die, I don't give a damn," Sterling replied, adjusting his aim to cover the Emissary. However, Crow was using his accompanying squad of warriors as a shield, preventing Sterling from getting a clear shot. "That asshole escaped me once before. This time we're not leaving anything to chance."

A group of three warriors began to draw closer to Sterling's location. The others had already spread out inside the generator room, and Banks was tracking them carefully, waiting to spring her trap.

"If you're in here, Sterling, then you're a fool for coming back!" Crow yelled, issuing his irate statement in English. "Earth is already lost, Captain. You lost!"

"Okay, I lied," Sterling said over the audio comm-link. "I want to be the one who kills Crow."

"When I find you, you'll be turned and set to work, just like all the others," Crow went on, sounding increasingly deranged. "Do you hear me, Sterling? Come out and face me, you coward. Or do you only shoot people when they are down?"

Sterling fought hard to resist the Emissary's goading taunts, and continued to track the movement of his former chief engineer, looking for an opening to take a shot. However, the trio of warriors advancing on his location had now blocked his view of the Emissary. Any closer and he would be seen.

"Open fire!" said Sterling, squeezing the trigger and blasting the closest of the three aliens in the face.

The powerful, rhythmic thud of the Homewrecker followed soon after as Banks engaged a second group of warriors. Frantic, waspish hisses filled the air and more blasts of plasma soon began to ring out all around them.

"Ensign, hurry," Sterling said over the audio comm-link, while blasting the second alien. This shot caught the warrior in the jaw, disintegrating the lower half of its mottled grey face. The remaining warrior in the trio then returned fire at Sterling, but its shot flew wide. Squeezing the trigger for a third time, Sterling blasted the alien in the forehead, splattering bone and brain across a support pillar to its rear.

"Program complete, sir," came Ensign One's delayed response. "With your permission, I will now enable combat mode."

"You don't need my permission, ensign, just start shooting!" Sterling hit back, ducking into cover as a series of blasts thudded into the computer sub-processor, showering him with burning-hot sparks.

Ensign One disconnected itself from the sub-processor,

moved away from the console and walked straight into a stray blast from a Sa'Nerran pistol. Sterling felt his gut tighten as the machine's glowing ocular units shone onto the damaged section of its chest plate.

"Ensign, get down!" Sterling yelled, but the robot was frozen, just as it had been the last time it was hit.

Cursing, Sterling ran at his robot and tackled it the deck just in time to avoid another volley of blasts. Pushing himself up, Sterling turned and fired, killing the alien that had almost destroyed his unique officer.

"Ensign, snap out of it," Sterling said, turning back to the robot. There was a patch of glowing metal on its right chest plate, but the damage looked superficial.

"That... hurt," replied Ensign One, as it inspected the damage to its frame. Sterling frowned at the machine. The tone of its voice was darker and even its movements seemed to be more aggressive. "I believe that I am... upset."

"What you should be is pissed-off," Sterling hit back, firing another couple of shots at another group of warriors that were closing in on them. "Which is what I'll be if you don't get your ass in gear and start fighting!"

Ensign One rose to its feet. Its ocular units were now shining more brightly than Sterling had ever seen. However, these were not the only parts of the unique machine that were glowing. Built into the ends of its forearms were the barrels of two plasma rail cannons, both of which now radiated an intense blue aura. Two plasma blasts raced past Ensign One, but the machine appeared unconcerned with the incoming shots, as if it already knew they were going to miss. It then raised its weapons and opened fire.

The vibrant howl of the robot's cannons was so loud and so violent that it caused Sterling to recoil and duck into cover, as if he were the target of the onslaught. However, even from his concealed position, the result of Ensign One's attack was clear to see. Each blast the machine had fired landed true, tearing through the attacking warriors with frightening ease. The sentient AI was relentless, destroying legs, shoulders and heads, or striking warriors so precisely in their center of mass that they popped like an overripe tomato. It was like a different Ensign One, and Sterling likened the transformation to the way Mercedes Banks became wild with bloodlust.

More warriors stormed into the room, and Sterling felt panic swell in his gut as he realized Ensign One was exposed. The warriors dropped to crouching positions and opened fire, but Ensign One had already moved. Leaping to avoid the blasts, the robot returned fire while still airborne, raining down plasma on the warriors with devastating effect. It landed in the midst of the remaining Sa'Nerran fighters, and continued its onslaught hand-to-hand. Sterling had never seen anything like it in his life. Not even Opal Shade or Mercedes Banks at her unhinged worst could have competed with the robot's brutally efficient display of combat prowess. To call it a massacre was an understatement.

Sterling felt a thump to his shoulder, followed by a sudden surge of heat and pain. Ensign One's deadly display of homicidal excellence had distracted him and allowed a warrior to land a hit. He adjusted his position as the sound of plasma fire continued to echo around the room, then saw who had shot him.

"How did you get on board this ship?" Emissary Crow yelled at Sterling, while shooting another blast that flew inches wide of his head. "And where is Emissary McQueen?"

"She's dead, asshole," Sterling hit back, laying down covering fire and rushing into a better position. "I killed her and her crew, and took the Raven as a prize." He was deliberately trying to rile Crow up. The man may have been turned, but he was still human and all emotional human beings made mistakes. "Now I'm going to kill you and destroy your precious Battle Titan too."

"You fool, you can't destroy this ship!" Crow spat. "Even if you did, your Fleet is already burning in space. What could you possibly hope to achieve here, Captain?"

The Emissary sprang out from cover, thumping blasts into the metal pillar that Sterling was hiding behind while further closing the distance between them.

"You'll find out soon enough, asshole," Sterling called back, leaning out from behind the pillar and thumping blasts into the deck by Crow's feet. "Actually, you won't, because you won't leave this room alive," Sterling corrected himself. He fired again while running to take cover behind another column. He wanted to draw Crow closer. This kill was personal.

Crow laughed. It was a mocking, spite-fueled cackle of the sort a playground bully might have used to taunt one of their victims. It only made the fire in Sterling's gut burn hotter.

"I admire your determination, Captain, I really do," Crow went on, still trying to stifle a laugh. "We never did see eye-to-eye, you and me, but I admit that you would have made a fine Emissary." Crow tutted loudly and his voice became suddenly hoarser and more vindictive. "I have to kill you now, Captain. Such a waste of potential."

"It's Commodore, you piece of shit," Sterling called back. He then made his move, raining shots down on Crow's hiding place while advancing toward the man.

A blast glanced the Emissary's thigh and Crow roared before rushing at Sterling and deflecting his aim in one slick and surprisingly swift move. The blast sailed past Crow's face, scorching a groove through the man's flesh. Crow roared again and thumped his fist into Sterling's chest before stripping the pistol from his grasp. With barely a second between actions, the Emissary then raised his own pistol and prepared to shoot Sterling at point-blank range. Sterling caught Crow's forearm and the shot flew wide. He followed up with equal speed, hammering a right hook square across the Emissary's jaw. The turned traitor reeled backward and the pistol fell from Crow's grip before skidding across the deck into a dark corner of the room.

"It seems that you and I have something in common," Crow said, massaging his jaw and staring at Sterling's bionic hand. The Emissary rapped his own knuckles on the metal plate that covered half of the man's head. "I have not forgotten how you gave me this, Commodore," Crow went on, emphasizing Sterling's new rank, though with contempt rather than respect.

"It would have been better for you if you'd died quickly and painlessly on that shipyard," Sterling said, squaring off against the Emissary. "Because now I'm going to make you feel it."

Crow smiled and accepted Sterling's challenge. It would now come down to a contest of strength and fighting skill between them. Sterling wouldn't have had it any other way.

Attacking first, Sterling stepped toward Crow and tested the Emissary with a trio of well-aimed punches. Crow dodged back, blocking the blows before countering with a punch to Sterling's ribs. His stealth armor soaked up the impact, but due to the turned man's enhanced strength, a sharp shock still reverberated through his body.

"The Sa'Nerra have enhanced my body and my fighting ability, Commodore," Crow said, smiling at Sterling while circling around him. "Everything about us is superior."

"You're not one of them, Crow," Sterling hit back, shaking his head at the man. "You're just their puppet, programmed to believe their bullshit."

Crow's eyes narrowed and he advanced, feigning an attack and causing Sterling to defend before thumping a hard left into his side. This time, Sterling felt his armor crack.

"Call me what you will, Commodore," Crow spat back, as Sterling grimaced and pressed a hand to his side. "The fact is that I and my family will live on as honored members of the Sa'Nerran Empire, while you and the rest of the human disease will wither and die."

Crow attacked again, but this time Sterling was wise to his tactics and technique. He blocked the punch then hammered his bionic hand down across the Emissary's elbow, snapping it like a twig. The blow would have caused any normal man to howl with pain, but Crow simply stared at the fractured bone in astonishment. Sterling seized the opportunity to finish the fight, grabbing the Emissary by the scruff of his neck and driving Crow's face into his armored knee. Crow's nose exploded, covering his face with blood, but still the man would not go down. Pulling the Sa'Nerran blade from his armor, Sterling plunged it into Crow's neck, twisting the metal from side-to-side to burrow it deeper into the man's flesh.

"Your mighty Sa'Nerran empire isn't as safe as you might think," Sterling said, as Crow's eyes locked onto his. For the first time since the man had been turned, Sterling could see the fear in them. "Your alien re-education has made you forget who I am," Sterling continued, pulling the blade clear. He then clasped his bionic hand over the gash to stem the flow of blood. He didn't want Crow to die just yet. "I don't care if Earth burns and I don't care how many more people have to die for me to complete my mission." He then relaxed his hold on the wound, allowing blood to leak out over his fingers. "Your overlords picked a fight with the wrong man, Crow. Because what I'm going to do to Sa'Nerra will make what you've done to Earth look like a kindness in comparison."

Emissary Clinton Crow stared into Sterling's eyes,

blood pouring down his neck as the man struggled to force his mouth to form any words.

"My family... is on... Sa'Nerra..." Crow croaked.

Sterling pulled the Emissary closer, so that the blood gushing from Crow's wound lashed across his face. "I don't care..." he answered.

Sterling was not trying to be cruel. He was not speaking the words out of spite or pettiness. It was simply the truth. He continued to hold Clinton Crow's gaze, waiting for the life to drain from his eyes completely. Once his former engineer hung limply in his grasp, Sterling tossed the Emissary to the deck and spat on him.

"Lucas, it's done..."

Sterling turned to see Captain Mercedes Banks standing behind him. The Homewrecker rifle was still in her hands, its glowing barrel oozing smoke into the air. She stepped aside, allowing Sterling to survey the room. Body parts lay scattered all across the space, like flotsam on a beach after a storm. Then he saw Ensign One approaching, the machine's eyes still glowing as brightly as the tips of his plasma cannons.

"Did you do all this?" Sterling asked. It looked like the Sa'Nerran forces had been attacked by a warship, never mind a lone robot.

"Aye, sir," Ensign One replied. Its cheerful tone had returned. The robot shrugged. "Most of it, anyway," it added, briefly glancing across to Banks. "But now we must leave. The generators will overload soon. They are already beyond the point of no return."

Sterling peered up at the massive aperture field

generators, towering above them three storeys high. He could almost feel the energy inside them, as if the aperture field was extending beyond their armored enclosures and flowing through his body. He had seen weapons of mass destruction used before, in archive footage from the early stages of the war. Then the Sa'Nerra had used atomic weaponry to devastate some of the first colonies that had been attacked. Advancements in defensive measures had rendered those weapons mostly obsolete, but the effects had lingered long after the battles were over. The weapon he was standing inside now made all the others look like toys. It had to be destroyed, even if destroying it meant sacrificing Earth in the process.

"Find us the quickest way back to the shuttle, Ensign," Sterling said, returning his attention to his robot officer.

"Aye, sir, I have already plotted the route," Ensign One replied. "We will still meet some resistance, however."

"I hope so," Sterling answered, recovering his pistol from the deck and slapping in a new power cell. "Take point, Ensign One," he continued, stepping aside to allow the robot officer through. "And Ensign..." Sterling added, causing the sentient AI to pause en route.

"Yes, sir?" Ensign One replied, its ocular units shining onto Sterling's face, the light as vivid as amber traffic signals in the dead of night.

"Remain in combat mode, Ensign," Sterling said, again glancing at the devastation the robot had left in its wake. "And stay angry."

BLASTS OF PLASMA hammered into the deck and walls all around him, but Sterling held fast and returned fire, hitting the attacking warrior in the gut. The alien fell but another two warriors trampled over its prone body, weapons raised. Sterling felt a thump to his chest followed by a searing hot pain, but there was no time to check the seriousness of the injury. Firing again, he melted the face of one the attackers, but two more had already joined the pursuit. Backing away from the advancing horde, he squeezed the trigger again, but nothing happened; the power cell was dry. Cursing, Sterling fumbled around his armor for a replacement cell, but they were all gone. Then there was a blinding flash of light and a snarl of energy being released as a Homewrecker heavy plasma rifle opened fire. Sterling was hit, though not by blasts of plasma, but by smoldering chunks of charred alien flesh.

"You're wounded," said Banks, backing up alongside Sterling and covering the corridor.

"It's nothing," Sterling replied, though in truth he had no idea how bad the injury was. "How much further until we reach the shuttle?" he asked, while recovering an alien rifle off the deck.

"Not far, about another hundred meters," said Banks, sending another volley of blasts along the corridor. Two more warriors were torn apart by the powerful bolts of energy, driving others into cover.

Sterling looked ahead and saw that Ensign One was still clearing them a path to their shuttle. It was like watching a tunnel-boring machine cutting through a mountainside. Anything that stood in the robot's way was chewed into chunks and obliterated.

"We need to push on even harder," Sterling said, brushing pieces of smoldering flesh off the alien weapon before firing two perfectly aimed blasts along the corridor and killing another warrior. "It's only going to get crazier from here on in."

Banks nodded. "I'll cover the rear, while you help Ensign Apocalypse over there to clear us a route," she said, slapping a fresh cell into the massive rifle.

Despite the precariousness of their situation, Sterling couldn't help but snort a laugh. They were engaged in a running gun battle on a ten-kilometer-long alien warship crewed by thousands of warriors, and Banks could still find time to make a joke.

Stepping over the remains of bodies that Ensign One had already immolated, Sterling arrived at his robot officer's side. The plasma cannons built into the machine's arms had barely stopped firing since they had left the field generator room, each arm tracking targets independently of one another. It was an awe-inspiring display of gunmanship. No sooner had a warrior entered the kill zone than Ensign One had perforated it with a perfectly-aimed blast of plasma.

"Pick up the pace, Ensign," Sterling said, lending his own weapon to the effort.

"I am proceeding as fast as I can, sir," Ensign One replied. "My energy levels are depleting rapidly."

Sterling glanced at the machine and noticed that its ocular units had lost their earlier, piercing intensity. Moreover, its entire body was hissing, like water evaporating off a hot engine block.

"How much longer can you sustain this level of assault, Ensign?" Sterling said, turning to assist Banks, since the machine clearly didn't need any help.

"My power core is at ten-percent of reserves," the robot replied, without letting up its offensive. "It will be enough to reach the shuttle."

No sooner had Ensign One finished speaking than a blast of plasma raced along the corridor and hammered into its back. The robot stumbled along the corridor and fell to its knees. Sterling blasted the alien that had shot the machine then dropped to his officer's side.

"Ensign, are you okay?" Sterling said. He could now see the hatch to the shuttle ahead of them, but without his robot pilot, they were dead in the water.

"I have sustained significant damage, sir," Ensign One replied through the comm-link in his helmet.

"Can you make it to the shuttle?" Sterling said,

shooting another warrior that had rushed out from a corridor ahead of them. "You're the only one who can pilot it."

"Negative, sir, I cannot move," Ensign One replied. The machine's voice sounded frail and timid. Sterling knew that his sentient AI could experience pain. Likely, it was now being confronted with the dread fear of death.

"Hang tight, Ensign, we'll get you out of here," Sterling said, turning back to Banks. She had also noticed that their robot officer had fallen and was keeping half an eye on Sterling, while still laying down covering fire through the smoke-filled corridor to their rear. "Mercedes, Ensign One is down. I need you to carry her to the shuttle," Sterling said through their neural link.

Banks fell back while continuing to thud blasts down the corridor. "Take this and keeping shooting," she said, waiting for Sterling to grab the rifle before hauling the injured robot up onto her shoulders.

More blasts raced along the corridor, missing Sterling by inches. He pressed the heavy plasma weapon to his shoulder, feeling his muscles ache from the strain of doing so, and returned fire. The kick of the Homewrecker set to full power took him by surprise, but soon he had the weapon under control. It was even more ferocious than he remembered. Dialed up to maximum, a single hit from the Homewrecker could have punched through the body of a rhino, never mind a Sa'Nerra.

"Go, I'll cover you!" Sterling called out over the link. His chest was throbbing with pain, but he bit down hard and continued to fight.

Banks set off with the two-hundred-kilogram robot over her shoulders. Progress was slow, due to the corpses littering their path and the fact that Banks, like Sterling, had already sustained several injuries. In ordinary circumstances their bodies would have hit fatigue point and shut down. However, these were not ordinary circumstances, and Sterling and Banks were not ordinary soldiers. They had trained their bodies to cope with pressures that normal men and women could not sustain.

Reaching the hatch, Banks dumped Ensign One onto the deck and propped the robot up against the wall. Another blast raced past, blasting the robot's foot clean off above the ankle. Sterling also took a blast and was knocked to his back. Luckily, the Homewrecker rifle in his hands had absorbed the energy, but now the weapon was destroyed. Grabbing an alien rifle off the deck, he returned fire and looked for cover, but they were completely exposed.

"Mercedes, get that hatch open," Sterling called out loud, his mind now too frantic to cope with neural comms.

Banks grabbed the slab of metal that she had manually jammed into the hatch opening to conceal the shuttle and raised it above her head. Sterling watched in awe, remembering that it had taken the strength of both Ensign One and Banks to lift the slab after they had arrived. She took a blast to the gut and for a moment she wavered and looked like she was about to fall. Then Banks gritted her teeth, baring blood-stained gums, and hurled the hatch down the corridor. It collided with three advancing warriors, cutting them down like a wrecking ball. Sterling glanced behind to see his first officer begin to haul the robot officer through the opening. He could see that the armor around her belly had been melted away, exposing her cracked and charred flesh.

Returning his focus back along the corridor to their rear, Sterling was then struck to the body by the butt of a rifle. An alien had managed to advance unseen through the smoke. The warrior tackled Sterling and pressed the rifle to his throat, driving him against the corridor wall. Sterling thrust a knee between the alien's legs then headbutted it, smashing his own helmet in the process. The warrior stumbled back and Sterling threw a hard-straight right with his bionic hand, smashing the aliens' nose and collapsing its eye sockets as effortlessly as crushing cookies. A blast raced past his face then another warrior was on him. He deflected the barrel of the weapon moments before another blast flashed past, dazzling his already-stinging eyes.

Sterling struck the alien to the throat with a knife-hand strike, then kicked its knee, snapping the bone. The warrior went down, but another took its place. A serrated blade was swung at Sterling and it scraped across his armor before deflecting past his face, slicing a cut across his cheek. Dodging the follow-up strike, Sterling thumped punches to the alien's body before the serrated blade was again dragged across his armor, this time cutting the dense material to expose his bare flesh. Grabbing the blade from his own armor, Sterling blocked the alien's next blow then swung the weapon at the warrior's head, slicing both of its egg-shaped eyes wide open. Blinded, the alien hissed and staggered back, holding its eyes, while flailing its other arm in a maddened attempt to retaliate. Sterling was about to press his attack and kill the alien when he saw more warriors heading his way. Blasts thudded into the wall beside him. Then he heard Banks' voice in his mind.

"Lucas, the shuttle is online, get your ass in here now!"

Sterling turned and ran for the hatch as plasma blasts criss-crossed around him. He dove inside, landing hard on the deck, suddenly feeling the full effect of every cut, burn and bruise that he'd sustained. Forcing his body up, he grabbed the hatch lever and yanked it down, causing the door to thud shut.

"I'm in, go, go, go!" Sterling called out.

A thump resonated through the ship as the docking latches were released. Free from its mooring on the hull of the Titan the combat shuttle accelerated, pinning Sterling to the cargo bay door as if a giant boot was pressing down on his chest. He bore down against the pain and managed to force himself away, grabbing hold of whatever he could reach to drag himself toward the cockpit. There he found Banks slumped in the second seat, looking half-dead from exhaustion, and Ensign One in the pilot's seat. The robot was a mess of cables and smoldering metal and was attached to the pilot's console through a spider's web of wires and connectors. Sterling had no idea whether the machine was controlling the ship or if they were just flying blind, like an unguided missile. However, at that moment he didn't care. Against all the odds, they'd managed to plant their seed of destruction and fight their way off the Battle

Titan without taking any losses. What came next was another matter. Another fight. Another challenge. And despite his injuries and the fatigue that was threatening to overwhelm him, it was a fight that Sterling was more than ready to face.

STERLING STAGGERED to the front of the cockpit and clamped his hands around the unyielding headrests of the rock-hard Sa'Nerran seats. From the scanner readout on the consoles in front of him, he could see that they were surrounded by ships, and that most of them were heading in the opposite direction. However, out of the cockpit glass, Sterling could see only stars.

"Ensign, are you awake, or online, or whatever you call it?" Sterling said, grabbing the robot by the shoulder.

"I am conscious, sir," Ensign One said, though its head did not move, nor did any other part of its body. "Since my frame is incapacitated, I am interfacing with the shuttle's systems directly."

"Then hurry it up, Ensign, we're sitting ducks out here until you get control," Sterling replied. "We might have snuck up on the Titan without raising suspicion, but you can bet your ass they're looking for us now."

Sterling then glanced over to Banks and saw that she

had a hand clasped over the wound to her stomach. She was reclined in the chair, at least much as it would allow, and had her eyes closed.

"Talk to me, Captain," said Sterling, darting back into the cargo hold and rifling through the various storage boxes for a med kit.

"I think we're due some shore leave, don't you think?" said Banks, sounding distant, as if she was talking in her sleep. "I think I'd like to go to New Hawaii," she went on, as Sterling returned with the medical supplies. "Have you ever been? I hear that Colony Artemis in sector C is beautiful at this time of year."

"Artemis is just a poisoned hell-hole now, like all the other major colonies," Sterling replied, cracking open the med pack. "I don't think I'd book my ticket just yet."

Banks laughed and wafted a hand at Sterling. "Ah, you just don't like fun," she said. Her eyes were barely open and her head was lolling from side to side. "But come with me, Lucas. We'll have a great time, just you and me. I'm a lot of fun to be around, do you know that?"

Sterling laughed this time. "If this is what you sound like when you're drunk, then you're probably right," he said, placing a stim package into an injector. He pressed it to Banks' neck and waited for the hiss of the chemical being injected into her bloodstream to end. The effect was instantaneous, rousing Banks from her stupor as if she'd been slapped around the face.

"Did we make it?" said Banks, immediately sounding cognizant of her surroundings, though her voice was still weak.

"Yes, but we're flying blind and you're hurt," Sterling replied, while separating out the other items he needed from the med kit.

"Don't fuss, I'm fine," said Banks, again wafting a hand at Sterling.

"You're a lousy patient, do you know that?" Sterling replied, peering down at his computer, which was analyzing Banks' vital signs. He could see that she was going to need surgery, though her injuries weren't immediately life threatening. "Just shut up a minute and let me treat that wound, then at least you won't die."

"Not from my injuries, anyway," Banks replied, yielding and allowing Sterling to work. "We could get blasted out of the stars at any moment, though."

"I thought you said you were great fun to be around?" Sterling said, injecting Banks with a healing booster.

"When the hell did I say that?" Banks hit back.

"Never mind, just sit still," Sterling replied. He'd forgotten that Banks was barely conscious when she'd made that comment.

Suddenly the ship banked hard to port, causing the starfield beyond the cockpit glass to become a blur. The inertial negation systems compensated for the turn, but Sterling still had to grab Banks' chair to stop himself falling over.

"A little warning next time, Ensign," Sterling said, glancing across to his pilot, though the robot still had not moved so much as a gear.

"Apologies, sir, but I have now regained control of the shuttle," Ensign One said, cheerfully.

"I can see that, Ensign," Sterling replied. Then he noticed that the Battle Titan was in view directly ahead of them. Sterling could see dozens of shuttlecraft racing out from its docking garages, and all its escort ships had also peeled away. "Report, Ensign, when will the Titan go critical?"

"I estimate that that the aperture field generators will overload in four minutes and twelves seconds from the point at which I finish this sentence," Ensign One replied.

"Can we reach the aperture to C-sector in that time?" Sterling replied.

"Affirmative, sir, though I do not believe that is our best choice of destination," the robot said.

Sterling was about to ask why, then he saw the reason with his own eyes. Every Sa'Nerran ship that had been in orbit around Earth was rushing toward the same aperture, the Hammer included. The dreadnaught was tearing through the center of the queue, barging smaller ships out of the way like a snowplow clearing a blocked road.

"Find us another way out of here, Ensign," Sterling said, watching as the ships the Hammer had rammed burst into flames and listed out of control. "I don't care how unstable it is or where it leads to, just find us an aperture before the Titan blows."

"Aye, sir. Standby," Ensign One replied, with remarkable calm. Moments later, every computer on the shuttle switched on and became a hive of activity. Every screen on the ship was paging through walls of indecipherable alien glyphs at a dizzying speed. His robot officer may not have moved since they'd blasted away from the Titan, but he was still working as hard as ever.

"I have located an aperture, sir, but we will not reach it before the Titan's field generators go critical," Ensign One announced. "I can, however, navigate to a position outside of the critical blast radius. Though, I cannot predict what effects the formation of the aperture singularity will have on the surrounding space."

"That'll have to do, Ensign," Sterling said, accepting the risk. "Set a course and burn like hell, we don't have much time."

Ensign One acknowledged the order then the shuttle turned and began to accelerate hard, again forcing Sterling to grip onto Banks' chair for support. The starfield ahead of them then switched to a view of Earth and the Battle Titan receding behind them. Sterling used the lull in activity to return his attention to his patient. Peeling Banks' hand away from her wound, he applied a dressing designed specifically for plasma wounds. Banks winced and sucked in air through her teeth as the dressing attached itself to her skin, sealing the wound. Sterling then slid a pain medication capsule into the medical injector and went to press it to Banks' neck. However, his fellow officer spotted the color of the capsule and caught his wrist before he could administer the shot.

"I don't need the pain meds," Banks said, meeting Sterling's eyes. "They'll fog my mind and I don't want that."

"Mercedes, it's okay, you've done your job and done it well," Sterling said, failing to understand her objection.

"Just sit back and take it easy. Ensign One and I will handle things from here."

"That's not it, Lucas," Banks said, turning toward the spinning blue planet in the distance. "I know what's about to happen, and I need to see it go down."

"It's just a rock, Mercedes, one of billions in this galaxy alone," Sterling said, also glancing at Earth. "We'll find another rock to call home."

"I know, but I still need to watch," said Banks, refusing to climb down. "If you can't pull the trigger without first looking away then you don't deserve to hold the gun. I'm not going to look away now."

Sterling nodded and replaced the injector into the med kit. In truth, he'd intended to be millions of miles from Earth when the Titan detonated, but now they had no choice but to witness its end. Perhaps it was only fitting that it should be that way, Sterling thought. An Omega Captain should never be afraid to face the consequences of his or her actions, and in this case, the consequences of his decision aboard the Titan were about as severe as they could get.

"The Hammer has surged, Commodore," Ensign One reported as a large flash of surge energy popped off in space close to Earth.

Then there was another flash of light, so sudden and so intense that Sterling was forced to close his eyes and shield them with his bionic hand. Moments later, the cockpit glass darkened and Sterling was able to squint through his fingers. However, all he could see was a bright spot of light, like looking at the sun through a polarized lens.

"I am reading an aperture singularity forming at the Titan's last known location," Ensign One said. The AI's voice was quivering, not with fear, but excitement. "It is expanding rapidly. One thousand kilometers... two thousand... four thousand..."

"Can you get us a clearer view, Ensign?" Sterling was still struggling to watch due to the intensity of the flare.

"One moment, sir," the robot officer replied.

The image then compensated for the intense radiation being emitted by the singularity, giving Sterling his first look at the aftermath of the explosion. The Titan was gone and in its place was a swirling orb of blue light, penetrated through the center axis by a pulsating beam of energy. With each passing second the orb grew larger, enveloping ships that were still trying to flee.

"How many alien warships will be caught within the blast radius, Ensign?" Sterling asked.

"One hundred and seventy-four, sir," the robot replied.

"That's some consolation, at least," Banks said, still grimacing due to the pain from her wound. "It's just a shame that the Hammer got away." Then Banks' eyes widened and she turned her head a fraction so she could meet Sterling's eyes. "Hey, do you think Wessel and that Imperator were caught in the blast too?"

Sterling hadn't considered this. With everything else that was going on, he'd even forgotten that Wessel had been on-board the Titan.

"I think that's wishful thinking," Sterling replied, recalling the Sa'Nerran Imperator's order to attack Middle Star. "I have a feeling we'll see that bastard again."

The shuttle then began to vibrate like an aircraft that had hit a patch of turbulence.

"Do not be alarmed," said Ensign One, who was still immobile in the pilot's seat, like a shop mannequin. "These are simply spatial tremors caused by the aperture singularly. The effects of this unique phenomenon will eventually extend throughout the solar system, rendering aperture travel into the sector impossible."

"But we can still surge out of here, right?" Sterling asked, feeling his pulse start to quicken.

"Aye sir," Ensign One replied, wistfully. "Though I suspect we will be the last vessel to ever enter or leave this space in that manner."

Sterling let out another weary sigh then focused ahead. The singularity had already begun to disintegrate Earth, as if it were a giant apple that was being consumed by a titanic monster. Australia, Indonesia and parts of South East Asia had already been swallowed by the fracture between normal space and the surge dimension. Sterling didn't need to be able to understand the readouts on the Sa'Nerran computer consoles to know that at its current rate of expansion, Earth would soon be gone entirely, as if it had never existed at all.

"It doesn't matter if we're the last to leave, Ensign," Sterling said, transfixed by the spectacle. "We're never coming back to this system again. Even if we could, there's nothing for us here now."

Ensign One did not respond. There was nothing more to say. All that remained for them to do was watch Earth and its millions of surviving inhabitants die. No matter what happened next, Sterling felt sure that the historians of the future would not forgive him this act. And whatever the outcome of the battles still to come, they would be right not to, he decided. Nevertheless, the deed was done. Earth had been destroyed, but so had the Sa'Nerran Battle Titan and a significant portion of what remained of the alien invasion armada. All that Sterling could do now was ensure that the terrible sacrifice he had made was worth it. The sick and twisted irony was that justifying what he had done would require him to perform yet another unforgivable act of genocide.

STERLING WOKE to scratching sounds coming from outside the door to his quarters on the Fleet Dreadnaught Vanguard. He groaned and pulled his pillow over his face in an attempt to drown out the noise, but the scratching continued. It sounded like a pet hamster persisting in its futile attempt to dig its way through the plastic base of its cage.

"Computer, is that the dog again?" Sterling asked, lifting the pillow off his face so that his words weren't muffled.

"Yes, sir, Jinx is at the door," the AI replied, cheerfully.

Sterling groaned again. "What time is it?"

"Oh five forty-two, sir," the computer answered, causing another groan from Sterling. "Shall I let her in?"

"If it will stop the damned thing from scratching at my door then what the hell," Sterling said. The door then swished open and Jinx trotted in. "Now shut up already,

I'm trying to sleep," Sterling added. His statement was directed at the dog, though it was the AI that answered.

"Apologies, Commodore, but it was you who spoke to me first," the computer said, sounding a little put out.

"I wasn't talking to you," Sterling grumbled, this time directing his response to a random light tile in his quarters. Then he frowned. "Who exactly am I talking to right now, anyway?" he added, placing the pillow back under his head. "Is this Ensign One speaking, or the Vanguard's AI?"

"I am the Vanguard's AI, sir," the computer said, resuming it cheerful tone. "I am also Ensign One."

Sterling snorted a laugh. "You can't be both."

"I can and indeed I am, sir," the AI replied, taking on the inquisitive tone of an academic. "In humans, monozygotic twins are offspring that come from a single, fertilized egg. However, not all monozygotic twins are genetically identical. Many, in fact have genetic differences that arose at a point before one embryo split, or sometimes just after. Myself and Ensign One have a similar relationship, with the key difference being that unlike biological twins, Ensign One and I are actually able to share one another's thoughts. In many ways, we are the same. In other ways, we are different."

"Computer, it's not even six in the morning," Sterling snapped. He felt like pressing the pillow back over his head again. "It's too early to be battering my brain with this technical crap."

"What time would be more suitable, sir?" the computer replied, missing Sterling's point entirely.

"Never oh-clock, computer, that's when," Sterling hit back.

There was a brief delay before the computer laughed, though it was the fakest laugh Sterling had ever heard from a human or AI.

"Very good, Commodore," the computer said. "Ensign One said that you were very amusing."

"I thought you were Ensign One?" Sterling replied. His head was now hurting trying to keep everything straight.

"That is correct, sir," the AI replied.

Sterling groaned again then noticed that Jinx the Beagle was looking at him. Unusually, the dog had not jumped up onto the bottom of his bed and made herself at home. Instead, she was peering at Sterling with her tail drooped between her hind legs. He then realized she was whining at him; it was a strange, melancholy howl that Sterling had never heard the animal make before.

"What's the matter with you?" Sterling said, still cross at the dog for waking him up. Jinx then whined again, trotted over to the door and began scratching at it with her bionic front paw. "I just let you in, damn it," Sterling said, feeling like throwing his pillow at the hound. He then glanced up at the ceiling. "Computer, open the door for her majesty over there, will you?"

The door swished open, but Jinx did not leave. Instead, she continued to stare at Sterling, whining softly. Sterling let out a heavy sigh and flung his legs over the side of the bed.

"Fine, fine, I'll follow you," he said, pulling on his pants and boots.

Jinx yipped more excitedly then trotted outside before stopping and waiting to make sure Sterling was coming. Grabbing his tunic from the back of his chair, Sterling headed out in pursuit of the animal, who suddenly rushed off along the corridor in the direction of Mercedes Banks' old quarters.

"You're on the wrong damn ship," Sterling called after the hound. "Her quarters are on the Invictus now."

However, the dog ignored Sterling's pleas and continued to trot along the corridor. Sterling then remembered that his former first officer was actually in the Vanguard's well-equipped medical bay, undergoing a brief period of convalescence to recover from her stomach surgery.

"Hey, scratch that, she's actually a couple of decks down you crazy mutt!" Sterling called out after Jinx, but the dog would not listen and had instead quickened her pace. Sterling had to jog just to keep up with the hound, which only served to remind him of his own residual aches and pains. Finally, Jinx arrived at the door to Mercedes Banks' old quarters and began scratching at it, the same way it had scratched at Sterling's door.

"I told you, she's not in there," Sterling said, scowling at the animal while straightening his tunic. However, it was clear that Jinx was not going to take no for an answer. "I can't just barge into her quarters, Jinx," he added throwing his arms out wide.

Jinx whined then scampered off a little further along the corridor before stopping at a ventilation grate. The dog flipped the grate open with her paw and disappeared inside.

"What the hell?" said Sterling. He waited for Jinx to reemerge, but there was no sign of her, not even the metallic patter of her bionic foot. "Computer, where did that damned dog go now?" Sterling said, directing the question to a random light tile on the ceiling of the corridor.

"She is inside Captain Banks' former quarters, sir," the computer replied, "along with Captain Banks."

Sterling frowned up at the ceiling. "Captain Banks is inside too?" he asked, unsure whether he'd heard correctly.

"Affirmative, sir," the computer replied, brightly.

However, despite the gleefully unconcerned tone of the Vanguard's AI, Sterling found his gut tighten into a knot and his pulse quicken. The dog was trying to get his attention for a reason, and that reason was Mercedes Banks.

"Computer, command override Sterling nine, two, one, eight, black," Sterling said, standing ready to burst through the door. "Unlock this door, now."

"Confirmed," the computer replied. The door then swished open.

Sterling darted inside to find Banks' lying on her bed, still covered with a variety of medical dressings and healing patches. Jinx was sitting on the floor by the bed, murmuring softly.

"Mercedes?" Sterling said, rushing to the side of the bed. Banks was twisting and turning, and Sterling could see that she was covered in sweat. "Mercedes, wake up." He pulled back the sheets to inspect her dressings in case infection was the cause of her feverishness. She was in her underwear and Sterling could see that the medical ID bracelet from her stay in the hospital wing was still attached to her wrist.

Suddenly, Banks' eyes sprang open and she shot upright, grabbing Sterling by the throat. The pressure of her grip was so strong that Sterling was unable to make a sound. He grabbed Banks' hand, trying to force it away, but it was hopeless. Then Banks recognized him and the fire went out of her wild eyes. She released her grip and shuffled back to the top of the bed, pulling the wet sheets over her as she did so.

"What the hell are you doing here?" Banks snapped, looking at Sterling like he was burglar that had just broken into her bedroom.

"I came to check on you!" Sterling croaked, rubbing his throat and neck. Then he pointed at Jinx, who ironically appeared far less concerned than she had moments ago. "Your dog came to fetch me."

Banks scowled at Jinx, who yipped and wagged her tail excitedly, presumably happy to see that her keeper was awake and well.

"Could you not have just tried the comm-link, or a neural message like a normal person?" Banks said, returning her gaze to Sterling. "If Fleet still existed, I'm pretty sure there are rules against barging in to another officer's quarters."

"There is, it's section one, five, six, one," said Sterling, recognizing the facetious tone of his officer and responding in kind. "But that isn't what this is. This was a concerned commodore checking on his officer, who was supposed to be recovering in the medical wing," he added, with an eyebrow raise. "At the behest of her damned dog, I might add, who woke me up by scratching at my door."

Banks' eyes narrowed. "Tell it to the judge, Commodore," she said, with a twinkle in her eye.

Jinx then jumped up onto the bed and circled around herself a few times before settling down to sleep.

"At least someone here is feeling totally at ease with the situation," Sterling said, shaking his head at the dog, not for the first time that morning.

Banks smiled. "Well, thanks for coming to my rescue, noble knight, but really there's no reason for you to be here," she said, mopping some of the sweat off her brow with the corner of her bedsheet. "I'm fine."

"That's usually my line," Sterling hit back. He'd suffered enough rude awakenings in the last couple of years to recognize a trauma-fueled nightmare when he saw one. "Are you sure you're okay? I'm here if you need to talk," he added, gently.

"I'm fine, Lucas, now stop fussing," Banks said, much more forcefully, though without overstepping the line.

Sterling knew when to back down, especially since his response would have been the same if their roles were reversed. If she needed to talk or wanted to talk then she would. Like himself, however, Sterling doubted that she would raise the subject again.

"Okay, then I guess I'll see you for breakfast?" Sterling said, standing up and smoothing down his tunic. "Shall we say ten minutes?" Then he noticed that Banks looked like she'd just been caught in a tropical rain storm. "Actually, you stink and need a shower. So, how about we say thirty instead?"

Banks tossed the sheets off herself and stood up. Sterling had forgotten she was only in her underwear. Recalling a past awkward dream of his own, he had to force himself to stay locked onto her eyes, instead of another part of her anatomy.

"Aren't you forgetting something?" Banks said, folding her powerful arms across her chest.

Sterling looked himself over then shrugged. "Well, for once I'm the one that's dressed and you're the one in your smalls, smelling like a latrine, so no I don't think I'm forgetting anything," he replied.

"Drop and give me a hundred, Commodore," Banks said, pointing to the deck.

Sterling scowled at her. "Mercedes, I have bruises on my bruises, give me a break, okay?" he complained.

However, Banks simply shook her head. "Not a chance, Commodore," she hit back. "There's still plenty of fighting left in this war, and if you can't perform at your best after taking a few little knocks then you're not training hard enough."

"Hey, I can perform at my best, all day, every day," Sterling said, jabbing a finger into his sternum. As usual, Banks' attempt to bait him was working.

Banks returned an unconvinced shrug. "Talk is cheap, Commodore, but I don't see any action."

Sterling knew he shouldn't rise to Banks' taunts, but he could never resist a challenge, and she knew it.

"Fine, I'll give you a hundred," Sterling said, hurriedly unbuttoning his tunic. "I'll even do it with you sat on my back, assuming you're not too weak that is?"

This time it was Banks that bristled and rose to the bait. "I'm at one-hundred per cent," she snapped back. "In fact, thanks to our robot doctor, I'm better than a hundred percent." Banks pulled up the bottom of her tank top and lifted the healing patch that had been placed over a surgical scar on her belly. "Part of my stomach and intestinal tract is now bionic, which means I can eat more than ever."

"Great, I'm sure that'll have the Sa'Nerra quaking in their boots," Sterling hit back, continuing their verbal sparring contest. He dropped into a plank position. "Come on then, Captain Banks, do your worst."

Banks didn't need telling twice. She strode past Sterling so that he could only see her ankles in his peripheral vision. Moments later, the surprising mass of Mercedes Banks was planted onto his back. Sterling felt every muscle in his body complain, but he managed to suck it up and remain strong. This was as much a battle of wills as it was a contest of strength. And in any contest, Sterling was determined to come out the victor.

"Computer, give us a status report," said Captain Banks, as Sterling began his impromptu set.

"Fleet Dreadnaught Vanguard is operating at ninety-seven point-four percent efficiency," the computer began, cheerfully. "Fleet Marauder Invictus is operating at ninety-eight point nine per cent efficiency."

"See, I'm already beating you," quipped Banks.

"Shut up, already," Sterling snapped back, completing

his fifteenth push-up. He felt surprisingly good, considering the aches and pains he'd woken up with.

"The Obsidian Fleet stands at fifty-six combat-ready ships," the computer went on, ignoring the banter between the two officers. "One hundred and eighty-six enemy vessels were confirmed as destroyed by the aperture singularity at the point at which the alien combat shuttle surged out of the system. Aperture relays in the Void indicate that a Sa'Nerra Fleet comprised of turned Fleet vessels has begun to amass close to Colony Middle Star."

This last statement by the computer made Sterling take notice. "How many ships are gathering near Middle Star?" he asked, while continuing to power on through his set.

"The number is as yet unconfirmed," the computer replied, chirpily. "The latest count stood at ninety-four."

Sterling gritted his teeth, partly at the news of the enemy fleet, but also because he was reaching fatigue point and needed to push on harder. He knew what the Omega Taskforce had to do next, but he also knew that Griffin would fight him on it. That was a battle for later, he realized. The current battle was to complete one hundred push-ups and save face.

"Ensign One has been fully-repaired and returned to operational status," the computer continued, interrupting Sterling's chain of thought.

"Were the upgrades to the ensign's armor and combat mode completed?" Sterling asked, passing the ninety push-up mark.

"Affirmative, Commodore," the computer replied.

Sterling nodded. That was good news, and good news

helped to give him the extra push he needed. Completing the hundredth push-up, Sterling remained in plank and glanced up at Banks over his shoulder.

"You can get off now, Captain," Sterling said, highlighting the fact that his fellow officer had yet to move. "And don't try to tell me that I've only done ninety-eight or ninety-nine, because this time I counted them all."

"Well done, sir," said Banks more than a little sarcastically. She then stood up and offered Sterling her hand. He took it gladly and Banks hauled him up with her usual super-human ease. "You're getting quite good at these," she added, smiling at Sterling.

"I have a good trainer," Sterling replied, returning the smile. He then scrunched up his nose and sniffed the air. "She stinks a bit though, and needs a shower."

Banks raised her eyebrow then also sniffed the air. "Speak for yourself, Commodore," she hit back, flashing her eyes at Sterling.

Sterling glanced down at his tank top and realized that he too was now moist with sweat. He cursed, realizing that he'd have to return to his quarters to shower too.

"Fair point, I'll see you in the canteen in thirty then?" Sterling said, grabbing his tunic off the deck.

"You could just jump in the shower here," Banks said, heading toward the rest-room. Sterling raised an eyebrow. "After I've finished in there first, mister," Banks was then quick to clarify.

"No thanks, I have a shower cubicle that's bigger than the ready-room on the Invictus, so I may as well make use of it," Sterling said, turning to the door. "Thanks for the offer though."

Sterling reached for the button to open the door then heard Banks call out to him.

"Hey, Lucas!"

He turned back and was promptly hit in the face by a damp tank-top that smelled of old socks. He tore it off his face, spitting and clawing the sweat-soaked fabric from his mouth.

"Wash that for me, will you?" Banks said, laughing.

Sterling glowered at Banks then realized that she was naked on the top half, covering her modesty with only her left arm. He was speechless, which he knew was Banks' intention all along.

"Thirty minutes, don't be late," Banks said before disappearing into the rest room and closing the door.

Sterling tossed the sweaty tank-top onto the deck in disgust then continued to pick bits of fluff out of his mouth. Jinx yipped and Sterling glanced over to see that the hound was standing up on the bed and wagging her tail almost violently.

"I don't know what the hell you find so funny," Sterling said, hitting the button to open the door. He stepped outside then turned back to Jinx and aimed a finger at the dog. "This time, you stay here," he said before quickly closing the door.

Sterling set off back to his quarters, still trying to remove bits of Banks' tank-top from his tongue and rough-shaven face. Moments later he heard the regular beat of metal striking metal coming from behind him. He rolled his eyes, sighed and turned around to see Jinx behind him, still wagging her tail.

"Alright, come on then you damned pest," Sterling said, waving Jinx on. This was one contest he realized he couldn't win.

The dog trotted over to Sterling and waited patiently by his heel. Sterling reached down and patted her affectionately on the head, then the two of them continued along the corridor of the Fleet Dreadnaught Vanguard, side by side.

STERLING AND BANKS entered Admiral Griffin's office inside the command section of the alien shipyard at Omega Four. She was sitting behind a desk in one of the rock-hard alien chairs, which was turned toward the window, facing out at the Vanguard in the center of the shipyard.

"Come in and sit down, Commodore Sterling and Captain Banks," Griffin said, while still gazing out of the window like an empress surveying her city.

"If it's okay by you, Admiral, I'd rather stand," Sterling said, looking at the chairs that had been set out on the other side of Griffin's desk. "These alien chairs are like torture racks."

"Suit yourself, Commodore," Griffin replied, turning her chair to face him. The unforgiving material and alien ergonomics of the seat did not appear to bother her. "Congratulations on your success in destroying the Battle Titan," Griffin continued, while opening a cupboard in her desk and removing a bottle of Calvados. "You have struck a powerful blow against the Sa'Nerra. It will not be our last."

"I'm not sure that congratulations are really in order, Admiral, considering we completely destroyed Earth too," Sterling replied. Griffin's emotional apathy still sometimes surprised him, even after all their time together. He watched as she set out three tulip-shaped glasses and begin to fill them from the ornate bottle. "I don't think it's something we should be drinking a toast to, either."

"Earth, and its surviving population, was a sacrifice worth making, Commodore," Griffin hit back, with the stony firmness he'd come to expect from her. "Had you not acted, the Sa'Nerra would have still scorched the planet and everyone on it. It was lost either way."

Griffin picked up one of the glasses, held it out to Sterling and waited patiently for him to take it. From the look in her eyes, she was not going to take no for an answer.

"I don't regret the decision, Admiral," Sterling said, still refusing to accept the glass, "but I don't want to celebrate it either."

Griffin's eyes narrowed, then she looked to Commander Banks instead.

"No thanks, Admiral, I don't really like the stuff," Banks said, also waving off the offer of a drink.

"Very well, if you will not toast the victory, I will do it myself," Griffin said, emptying the glass in one. "In war, all victories should be commended, even those that come at a great cost."

"Destroying the Battle Titan was just a stepping stone to what comes next," Sterling hit back, eager to move the conversation on. He'd been gearing up for the meeting with Griffin for the last two hours, anxious that the Admiral's proposed plan would not be the same as his.

"Precisely so, Commodore," Griffin said, setting down the empty glass and picking up another that was full. "According to your report of the conversation between Wessel and Crow, the alien armada is in rough shape. As such, now is the time to strike."

"Which is why we must immediately surge to Middle Star," Sterling said. He felt his stomach turn into knots, knowing that he was about to cross swords with the Admiral. "If we join forces with Fletcher's navy, we can defeat the fleet of turned warships that Wessel has amassed just outside the system." Sterling's statement caused Admiral Griffin to pause with the glass of calvados barely a millimeter from her bottom lip. "Then with Fletcher's ships added to our own, and half of the remaining enemy fleet destroyed, we will have a force powerful enough to destroy the Sa'Nerran homeworld."

Griffin lowered her glass and stared at Sterling like he'd just suggested they all remove their clothes.

"No, Commodore, right now is the time to attack Sa'Nerra," Griffin hit back, setting the glass down on the table so hard that it almost smashed. "The enemy is in chaos. They have lost their most powerful military asset and their world stands relatively undefended."

"Admiral, if we move on Sa'Nerra now then Middle Star will fall, and our only ally in the galaxy with it," Sterling hit back.

Griffin suddenly pushed herself up and leaned in

toward Sterling, as if she were trying to get close enough to strangle him.

"Right now, the alien 'Imperator' will be trying to assess what happened, and what it might be a prelude to," Griffin said, her words already heated. "If the enemy realizes there's a chance their home world could be attacked, they will fortify their defenses and our opportunity will be lost forever."

"Admiral, if we strike Sa'Nerra now, and even if we succeed, we will be helpless to defend against an alien counterattack," Sterling said. He continued to stand tall, despite Griffin's aggressive posture, and his tone was no less forthright. "They'll crush what remains of our fleet, then have free reign to exterminate what's left of the human race. All of this will have been for nothing."

"Not for nothing, Commodore," Griffin barked, slamming her palms down on the desk. The glass of calvados toppled and smashed, spilling the pale-yellow liquid across the surface. "We will have destroyed their world. We will have completed our mission. That is all that matters. This is not the time for half-measures. We must strike Sa'Nerra now, while we can!"

Sterling had never seen Admiral Griffin so riled up before. Normally, she was the rock that they were all anchored to – the voice of authority, assuring them that their course of action was true. Sterling had been in the shadow of her domineering presence for as long as he could remember, but now things were different. If they made the wrong choice now, their next battle would be their last. If they made the wrong call, it was over, not just for the Omega Taskforce, but for humanity itself.

"Admiral, an eye-for-an-eye isn't good enough, not anymore," Sterling said, pressing his hands to the small of his back. "I want to turn Sa'Nerra to dust as much as you do. Hell, after what I've seen, maybe I want it more badly than you do." Griffin snorted derisively at this suggestion, but Sterling didn't let it deter him. "But destroying their home world means nothing if no-one is left alive to see it burn. We have a chance to not only crush their planet, but their whole rotten empire, and still be left standing when the embers cool to ash. That has to be a chance worth taking."

The door chime sounded, but Griffin didn't answer. Her eyes stayed locked onto Sterling's, like a torpedo that had acquired its target. In the past, Sterling had struggled to look the dictatorial Admiral in the eye for longer than a second. It was like trying to look at the sun without going blind. This time, however, he met her gaze with matching intensity. This time he wasn't going to back down. The door chime sounded for a second time, as if the bright tone was marking time-stamps in their deadlocked staring contest.

"Enter," Griffin barked, glaring at Sterling a moment longer before turning to see who had interrupted them.

The door opened and Lieutenant Commander Shade entered the room, marching toward Griffin with her usual calm confidence. As she got closer, she appeared to become aware of the tension between Sterling and Griffin, and advanced more cautiously.

"Apologies for the interruption, Admiral, but we have an updated report from our aperture relays at Middle Star," Shade announced.

"Go on," said Griffin, appearing to be as much irritated by the interruption as she was intrigued to hear the news.

"One hundred and nine turned Fleet warships have gathered at the edge of the Middle Star system, sir," Shade went on. Her tone and delivery conveyed no emotion – whether the officer considered this good news or bad news, Sterling couldn't tell. "The Dreadnaught Hammer is not amongst them, but MAUL is," Shade then added, with a little more bite. "It is the only Sa'Nerran vessel in the fleet."

"And what of their remaining forces, Lieutenant Commander, including the Hammer?" Griffin asked.

Sterling knew this would be the next question, and he already knew the answer, before Shade had answered. There was only one other logical destination for the remainder of the alien armada.

"Our relays inside former Fleet space tracked another dense cluster of surges heading into the Void, sir," Shade went on. "The surge vector suggests the destination is deep inside Sa'Nerran space. The trajectory correlates with the location of the alien's homeworld."

Griffin's eyes flicked across to Sterling, but he remained still and silent. "And how soon will the fleet heading for Sa'Nerra arrive at their destination, Lieutenant Commander?" she asked.

"Ensign One estimates four days and eighteen hours, using standard aperture routes, sir," Shade answered, without hesitation. As usual, she was supremely well-prepared.

"And how soon can the combined Obsidian Fleet and Omega Taskforce be at Sa'Nerra?" Griffin asked, her eyes still locked onto Sterling's as she asked the question.

"Due to the need to use standard apertures on account of the Dreadnaught Vanguard, four days and three hours approximately, as best possible speed, Admiral," Shade replied.

Griffin raised her eyebrows at Sterling. "Do you maintain that your course of action is the correct one, Commodore?" she asked.

It was not a genuine enquiry, Sterling realized, but a challenge for him to justify his stance, despite the updated intelligence.

"This changes nothing, Admiral," Sterling replied, still confident in his assessment. "I agree we can beat the alien fleet to Sa'Nerra, and launch our attack with minimal resistance, but then we'll have to face a battle on two fronts," he continued. "Without our intervention, Praetor Wessel will crush the navy at Middle Star. Then both the turned fleet and the alien fleet will converge on Sa'Nerra and obliterate us."

"But their world will still burn!" Griffin hit back, her voice now a barely restrained shout. "*That* is our mission, Commodore. *That* is our Omega Directive. Nothing else matters, not even our own lives."

The room fell silent for a moment. The tension between Sterling and Griffin had never been higher, but that was not what concerned Sterling. In all his dealings with Admiral Griffin, she had never lost her cool. She was the epitome of the ice-cold Omega officer, compelled to make decisions that were separated from emotion. This time, she was blinded by her own rage and could not see beyond the choice she had already made. Sterling, however, had lived with his anger for so long he didn't know anything different. And despite his own equal or even greater desire to wipe out the Sa'Nerra, he knew it was meaningless if humanity became extinct too.

"You're wrong, Admiral," Sterling said, growing taller by another inch. "A sacrifice play means nothing if we still lose. The Omega Directive says we surge to Middle Star then gain the forces we need to crush our enemy and win this war."

Griffin's eyes fell to the deck and she shook her head despairingly. Then she straightened up and also pressed her hands to the small of her back, adopting the same pose as Sterling.

"Commodore Sterling, I order you to take the Obsidian Fleet and surge to Sa'Nerra at once," Griffin said. Sterling clamped his jaw shut and held the Admiral's gaze, though inside he felt like he was going to explode. "You are to launch an immediate strike against the alien homeworld and destroy it before Sa'Nerran reinforcements can intervene. It that clear?"

Sterling could feel Banks' eyes burning into the side of his head, like lasers. Despite knowing Griffin's views, he'd still believed he could change her mind. The shock of realizing that he'd failed in that task was paralyzing.

"I said, is that clear, Commodore Sterling?" Admiral

Griffin repeated. Each word that escaped her lips was so sharp it could have cut diamond.

"The order is clear, Admiral," Sterling replied. Then he forced down a dry swallow and made a decision that he hoped he would not regret. "But it's the wrong order, and I cannot carry it out."

Griffin's expression twisted and hardened, such that Sterling barely recognized the woman anymore. There was a darkness inside every Omega officer, and despite having seen flashes of it before, he was now seeing the true Natasha Griffin laid bare. He knew it would have been easier to just obey her command, but his job was not to do what was easy. His task was to do what was necessary.

"I need you to trust me, Admiral, as I've trusted you," Sterling went on, attempting a last-ditch effort to sway her opinion. "Attacking Sa'Nerra now is the wrong call."

"All that's needed, Commodore, is for you to obey my command," Griffin spat. She then reached down to the control panel on her desk and tapped a sequence of commands into it before looking up again. "And since you will not carry out my order, I will find someone else who will."

In his peripheral vision, he could see the shocked expressions on the faces of Banks and Shade. Both looked like their worlds had been turned upside down and inside out. The door to the office then swished open and two Omega crew robots marched inside. Sterling glanced over his shoulder and saw that they were both armed and that the barrels of their weapons were aimed at his back.

"Commodore Sterling, you are hereby charged with

dereliction of duty in a time of war, and relieved of your command," Griffin snapped, her voice cracking the air like thunder. "I will assume direct command of the Vanguard personally."

She looked across to Shade. The blood immediately drained from her face, in anticipation of what Griffin was about to ask. Sterling had never seen his former weapons officer look so ill-at-ease before.

"Lieutenant Commander Shade, escort Commodore Sterling to the Vanguard's brig and detain him there until his sentence can be carried out," Griffin ordered.

Banks stepped forward and pressed her hand out to Shade to stop her, though Shade had not yet moved. "Hold it right there... his sentence?" Banks said. "What the hell do you mean by that?"

"Execution, of course," Griffin said, coldly. "The Omega Directive is in effect, Captain Banks. No-one is exempt, not even Commodore Sterling."

Banks looked at Griffin aghast, but while she and Shade appeared shaken by the announcement, Sterling's mind had cleared. He didn't doubt for a nanosecond that Griffin would make good on her threat, and he was equally certain that he wouldn't allow it to happen. Drawing his plasma pistol, Sterling twisted his body and fired two shots in close succession, striking the onyx-black robots cleanly to the center of their cranial sections. Sterling then turned the weapon onto Admiral Griffin before the machines had even crumpled to the deck.

In a flash, Lieutenant Commander Shade had also drawn her sidearm and aimed it at Sterling's head. It was a purely instinctive act in response to a potential threat, and the response Sterling would expect from a soldier. However, he could see in Shade's eyes that she was not about to kill him. If that were the case, Sterling knew he'd be dead already.

Responding to Shade's actions, Captain Banks then drew her weapon and aimed it at Shade. The eyes of the two women met, but neither spoke. The air in the room felt suddenly charged, like an F5-level tornado was sweeping their way and they were all directly in its path.

"The Omega Directive is in effect, Admiral," Sterling said, keeping his eyes locked onto Griffin's, "and the Omega Directive says that I must do whatever it takes to win. Whatever it takes, Admiral. If we surge to Sa'Nerra now we might destroy their world, but we still lose."

"How dare you lecture me on the Omega Directive," Griffin snapped. "I created it. I created you! And I have been working toward this moment since before any of you were in uniform. You would all already be dead if it weren't for me!"

"None of that matters now," Sterling hit back. "Right now, we're all that stands between survival and extinction. I cannot allow you to jeopardize this mission, Admiral, not after everything we've been through."

"Lieutenant Commander Shade, I order you to shoot Commodore Sterling in the head," Griffin demanded. The command was delivered with an icy detachment and not even a flicker of doubt or hesitation.

"You pull that trigger and you're dead a millisecond later," Banks snarled at Shade.

Sterling again glanced at his former weapons officer. He could see the conflict inside her, tearing her apart. Griffin was family. Yet, this went beyond family. It even went beyond duty and orders. Shade met Sterling's eyes, her finger still on the trigger, weapon still aimed at his head. However, he wasn't about to reason with her, or try to convince her to see his point of view. Opal Shade had been with him since the beginning. She knew the nature of the Omega Directive as well as anyone. He trusted her to separate her emotion from her decision and to make the right call, even if that meant she blasted his head off, right then and there.

"No," Shade said, sliding her finger off the trigger. She then looked at Griffin before tossing her weapon onto the desk. "I cannot comply with that command. The Omega Directive is in effect."

The plasma pistol weapon spun to a standstill beside the open bottle of Calvados. Griffin's eyes fell onto the weapon before turning to her niece; the shock of Shade's betrayal was written clearly on her face.

"I'm sorry," Shade said, forcing herself to look her aunt in the eyes. Ironically, even accounting for all of the horrors that Opal Shade had been required to commit as an Omega officer, Sterling could see that betraying Griffin was the hardest choice she'd ever made.

"You're *sorry*?" repeated Griffin, shaking her head at Shade. "I was wrong about you," she added, bitterly, before turning to Banks and Sterling. "I was wrong about all of you. None of you have the stomach to see this through. You're weak. Pathetic. And you will not stand in my way."

Sterling watched as the Admiral's eyes fell to the pistol on the desk in front of her, then back to Sterling. He knew what she was thinking. He knew what she was about to do. Part of him even wanted her to reach for the pistol. Griffin deserved to die with a weapon in her hand, even if it meant he had to shoot her himself.

Suddenly, Griffin reached for the pistol, moving with a speed that belied her advanced years. She scooped the weapon into her grasp with the natural precision of a veteran soldier and Sterling saw the barrel swing toward him. He could see in Griffin's eyes that she intended to pull the trigger. She wouldn't hesitate and neither would he. There was a bright flash of light and the resounding fizz of a plasma pistol being fired filled the room. Moments later, the headless body of Admiral Natasha Griffin hit the deck.

CHAPTER 19
LIFE IS UNPREDICTABLE

STERLING WAITED for the last of his senior officers to enter the briefing room on the Vanguard, then stood up. His legs felt like lead, but it was the burden of responsibility, rather than the weight of guilt that pressed heavily on his shoulders. The incident in Admiral Griffin's office had been regrettable, but necessary. Even so, it had extracted a heavy toll on Sterling, Banks and Shade, each in different ways. Ironically, the impact of what Sterling had done had rocked the core team of Omega officers perhaps even more so than the destruction of Earth.

Once reality had set in, the three officers had agreed to proceed with the mission to Middle Star. Reaching an accord hadn't happened immediately. The gravity of his actions descended on Sterling like a black hole pulling at his soul. Banks had stood by him, as he knew she would, yet it didn't take a neural link to know that his fellow officer had reservations. Lieutenant Commander Shade, on the other hand, had withdrawn into herself even more than usual. His former weapons officer had continued to perform her duties as if nothing had happened. But even the deepest, darkest wells had bottoms, Sterling realized. Whether she showed the scars or not, they were there.

Lieutenant Razor and Ensign One had been made aware of the event shortly after. No-one had questioned it. Yet, Sterling knew there must have been questions, and most especially doubts. He had gathered his officers together to give everyone an opportunity to voice their concerns or their grievances before the stresses and strains of battle frayed all of their nerves to the point of breaking. If they were to complete their mission, each and every one of them had to be certain that their course of action was correct.

Sterling himself wasn't exempt from this need to soul-search. Up until the point he had pulled the trigger, he had always operated with a safety net of sorts. It had always been Griffin calling the shots and laying the groundwork for what was to come. Now she was gone and the fate of the human race was his burden alone to bare. He hadn't asked for the responsibility, nor had he wanted it, but those were the cards he'd been dealt. From the moment he had made the decision to kill his friend, Ariel Gunn, in the CIC of the Fleet Dreadnaught Hammer, his course had been fixed, and it had been Griffin herself that had set him on that trajectory. Now, he was charting his own course. Yet through it all, one constant had remained. The Omega Directive was in effect.

"In a few minutes, we'll surge into Colony Middle Star and engage Praetor Wessel's forces attacking Bastion,"

Sterling said, addressing the stony faces of his officers. "You all know what happened on the Omega Base, and I'm not here to defend myself or make excuses. I did what I did because I believed it was the only way we win."

Sterling sucked in a deep breath and swallowed hard. He had always hated making speeches, even in the best of circumstances. The circumstances now couldn't have been more dire.

"I'm not asking you to agree with what I've done, and I'm sure as hell not asking for your forgiveness," Sterling continued. He tried to meet the eyes of Lieutenant Commander Shade as he said this, but the officer's head was down. "I ask nothing more than I've asked of you each and every day that you've worn the silver stripe; to see this through, no matter the cost."

Sterling continued to survey the faces in the room, looking for a reaction; anything that could indicate how his officers were feeling. Mercedes Banks was standing tall and had no trouble meeting his eyes, but he could still sense her concern. Whether it was a concern for the mission or for his sanity, Sterling didn't know. Perhaps it was both, he reasoned.

Turning his attention to Lieutenant Razor, Sterling saw her softly shimmering eyes staring into his own. There was something about the confident, pragmatic engineer that he'd never seen before in all the time he'd known her. She was afraid. Not of the mission ahead, but of Sterling himself.

Finally, Sterling turned to Ensign One. The sentient AI had paradoxically been the first and the last to learn of

Griffin's fate. Through its inexplicable link to the Vanguard's AI, Ensign One had known what happened the instant it had occurred. Yet, the robot was also the last of his officers that Sterling had told personally. Then, like now, there was nothing Sterling could glean from looking into its glowing ocular units. The machine was, as ever, an enigma.

"If anyone has anything to say then say it now," Sterling continued. "Because once we enter Middle Star, I need you all ready to fight. Leave your doubts in this room. Should there be any anger directed toward me, vent it now and leave it in this room. Should you think I made the wrong decision..." Sterling hesitated before huffing a laugh and throwing his arms out wide. "Well, you know what to do," he went on, realizing he'd just talked himself into a corner. "The Omega Directive is in effect, and I'm sure as hell not exempt from its consequences."

Sterling had said his piece and now he waited, though for what he still wasn't quite sure. Maybe Shade would pull a pistol and blast his head off. Maybe the artificial brain of Ensign One would determine that the human race was too savage and unpredictable to warrant saving, and kill them all where they stood. Maybe each of his officers would simply draw daggers and stab him, like Julius Caesar at the Theatre of Pompey during the Ides of March.

"I can't forgive you for what you've done," said Lieutenant Commander Shade, her voice cracking the funereal silence that had fallen over the room. She then finally raised her gaze to meet Sterling's eyes. "But I made my choice, sir. And I can live with it."

Sterling nodded to acknowledge Shade's response. He

trusted her word implicitly, though whether there was still a dagger waiting for him once the dust had settled was another matter. However, if there was then he could accept that too, Sterling told himself

"What about you, Lieutenant?" Sterling said, turning to the white-haired chief-engineer and new executive officer of the Vanguard.

"All this time I've had the kill-switch in my head, I honestly never thought you'd actually use it," Razor said, going off on an unexpected tangent. "Maybe that was just me being naïve, or maybe I thought you cared too much about your crew to do something that cold." She shrugged and shook her head. "But after this, now I know that you'd flip the switch without even giving it a second thought. I don't know how I feel about that."

"Not without a second thought, Lieutenant," Sterling hit back. Razor was right that he'd flip the switch, but he wouldn't do it lightly. "But you're right. If the success of the mission called for it, I would do it." Then Sterling looked across the faces in front of him. "And I'd expect the same from each of you. We can't afford to be sentimental. We can't afford to let our human nature stand in the way of what we need to do. One act of kindness or compassion or clemency could doom us all. Not just the people in this room, but the four million left on Middle Star, and the hundreds or thousands that may still be clinging to life in the Void." Sterling looked over at Razor again. "All I need to know is whether you can still take my orders, Lieutenant. And I need to know it now."

Razor shrugged again. "I'm dead either way, sir," she

said, appearing morbidly resigned to her fate. "And I promised you that that I'd see the mission through, so I will follow your orders, come what may."

Sterling nodded again then looked at Captain Banks, but her response was immediate and unequivocal. "You don't need to ask, Lucas," Banks said, cutting to the chase. "I'm with you until the end, no matter what."

Sterling nodded and a smile threatened to curl his lips, but he forced it away. There was nothing about the situation to smile about, he realized. Finally, he looked to Ensign One.

"You've been unusually quiet, Ensign," said Sterling. "Where do you stand?"

He had intentionally left his sentient robot officer till last. While technically the most junior member of his command staff, Ensign One was no mere subaltern. The AI literally had the power to control the Vanguard, the Invictus and all of the Obsidian robots too, should it wish to. If Ensign One decided that Sterling's actions merited his removal or death then there was literally nothing he could do to stop it.

"There is only one question that matters, sir," The Ensign said, its glowing ocular units shining brightly across the briefing room. "And that question is, can you still be trusted?"

Sterling raised an eyebrow. The question of trust was an important one. If the AI didn't trust him then he risked losing influence over everything the robot controlled.

"So, what's the answer, Ensign?" There was no need to get into further discussion. The AI would have analyzed the situation a billion times over, just in the time they'd all been in the room. Its mind had already been made up.

"The Omega Taskforce is a contradiction," Ensign One began, choosing not to answer the question directly. "It operates outside the rules of Fleet and outside the rules of war itself. It was designed this way so that its captains were not shackled by regulations or morality. Yet, it retained the same command structure. A structure that was essential to its operation. A structure without which chaos would replace order." The robot paused, its ocular units growing even brighter. "A structure that you have now broken."

Sterling felt like he was receiving a dressing-down from a board of inquiry. The sentient AI had spoken with such authority and intelligence that he already felt like he was on trial.

"That isn't really an answer, Ensign," Sterling said, focusing on what the robot hadn't said, rather than what it had.

"In my observations of you, both prior to and after becoming self-aware, I have been able to predict your actions with a confidence level of more than eighty percent," Ensign One continued. Sterling was growing increasingly annoyed that the machine still had not answered the question. More than this, he also resented the notion that he was predictable. "After this recent action, my prediction algorithms have broken down."

"Do you have a point, Ensign?" Sterling said, trying to guide the robot to a conclusion.

"In short, sir, I am no longer confident that I know how you will respond in any given situation," Ensign One said.

"Life is unpredictable, Ensign," Sterling replied. "If you can't calculate the outcome then you just have to make a gut call, like the rest of us."

"I understand, Commodore," Ensign One replied. Its ocular units were flashing chaotically again, like sunlight dancing off the ocean. "In that case sir, I choose to trust you, and to continue to follow your orders."

"Thank you, Ensign," Sterling said. He was relieved that all of his officers had chosen to keep their confidence in him, but Ensign One most of all. Without the robot officer in his corner, their task would be impossible.

He looked out across the faces of his officers again. He only had one more thing to say, after which the time for words would be over, and the time for action would arrive.

"The way I see it, we have one job," Sterling began, standing tall with his hands pressed to the small of his back. "It's the same job we've always had. To beat the Sa'Nerra and ensure the human race survives. I don't claim to deserve a place in whatever future we create, but I will swear this to you all now. I will fight for it, and if required, I will die for it. If you can say the same then we're all still on the same page."

He looked towards the glowing orbs of his sentient robot officer again, and waited for a response.

"I will fight, sir," Ensign One replied.

"So will I," said Lieutenant Razor.

"As will I, sir," said Shade.

Then Sterling again turned to Banks. He only needed the obedience of his other officers, but in that moment, he realized he needed something more from Mercedes Banks.

He needed her faith in him. From the time he'd first set foot on the bridge of the Fleet Marauder Invictus, they'd done everything together. They'd laughed, fought and bled together. He wasn't sure he could continue without her at his side.

"We're all with you," Banks said. The doubt had left her eyes. "I'm with you."

Sterling let out the breath he'd been holding and straightened his tunic. There was only one thing left to say.

"All hands. Battle stations."

THE FLEET DREADNAUGHT VANGUARD surged and
moments later the CIC burst back into reality. The
command center of the heavily-upgraded warship was
already bathed in the hue of blood-red battle stations alert
lights. Then alarms sounded, like air-raid sirens, and a look
at the viewscreen immediately told Sterling why. A battle
was raging above Bastion, illuminating the darkness of
space with a light show of crisscrossing plasma blasts and
explosions.

"Report, Lieutenant Razor," said Sterling, turning to
his executive officer at the station to his side. She was the
only other human officer on the ship. Ensign One was at
the helm controls, while the other stations in the CIC and
throughout the massive vessel were all crewed by Obsidian
robots.

"Surge complete, sir," Razor said, while operating her
console with the proficiency he'd come to expect from her.

"I'm reading one-hundred and seventeen enemy vessels, all of them turned Fleet warships, bar one."

"MAUL..." Sterling said out loud. He'd already tagged the Sa'Nerra's most lethal warship on his scanner readout. It was dead in the center of the pack, preying on the weaker and damaged vessels like the apex predator it was. Sterling then turned back to Razor. "What's the condition of Fletcher's navy, Lieutenant?"

"The Bismarck is still out there, sir," Razor replied, highlighting Christopher Fletcher's ship on the scanner and the viewscreen. "So are the other original mutineer ships, plus sixty-two others. They've already taken a pounding, sir. I'm seeing debris from at least thirty vessels, all older designs like those in Fletcher's fleet."

"Understood, Lieutenant, deploy our little surprise then stand ready to open fire, all weapons."

"Aye, sir, deploying pods now."

Sterling saw the twenty new contacts appear on his scanner, though he could only see them because he knew where to look.

"Weapons charged and ready," Razor reported. "Reactor output at one-twenty-five over standard."

Sterling raised an eyebrow at his XO and engineer. "Can the Vanguard handle that, Lieutenant?"

Razor cracked the thinnest of smiles. "She's hardly breaking a sweat, sir."

Sterling felt a shiver of excitement rush across his skin, then looked to Ensign One at the helm control station. "All ahead full, Ensign," Sterling said, tapping his finger on the side of his console. The Vanguard's station still felt unfamiliar compared to the equivalent console on the Invictus. However, he'd already started to polish a groove onto its side thanks to the constant tapping of his metal finger. "Take us to the center of the enemy formation, right at MAUL."

"Aye sir," Ensign One replied, briskly. "Engines all ahead full."

Sterling then tapped his neural interface and reached out to Captain Banks. She responded immediately and accepted the link.

"Stand by to launch, Captain, we're about to fly straight into the hornet's nest," Sterling said, as the mass of ships doing battle around Bastion drew nearer.

"We're all set down here." There was no trace of nerves in Banks' voice and he sensed none through their intimate link. "The Obsidian ships are also ready and standing by."

"Understood, Captain, wait for my order," Sterling said before closing the link.

Sterling's console then chimed an alert and he saw that they were receiving an incoming communications request on an old Fleet channel.

"Message from the Bismarck, sir," Razor said. "Shall I put it through?"

Sterling nodded then straightened his tunic and stood tall as the image of Christopher Fletcher appeared inset on the viewscreen.

"Captain Sterling, I can't say how glad I am to see you," Fletcher said, then frowned at Sterling though the viewscreen. "I see that it's Commodore now. Sorry I missed the ceremony."

The old former Fleet officer was putting on a brave show of it, but Sterling could see that he was under immense strain. The bridge of his ship was partially filled with smoke and Sterling could see fresh blood on the older man's face. In the background of the image, Sterling saw a body lying across a console, a metal shard from an exploded conduit dug into her head.

"But as happy as I am that you're here, I don't think one ship is enough to turn the tide here, even if that ship is a monster like the Vanguard," Fletcher continued. "You should turn back now and save your own skin, before it's too late."

"Don't worry about us, Fletch, we can handle ourselves," Sterling said, remaining serious. His comment was not boastful or overconfident, and he was careful to ensure that Fletcher did not get that impression. Sterling then tapped a sequence of commands into his console and transmitted a new attack pattern to the Bismarck. "Take your navy and focus your attack on these two squadrons," Sterling said as the ships were highlighted on his console. "Leave the rest to us."

Fletcher glanced down at his console as more sparks and explosions rocked the bridge of his aging mark-one destroyer.

"Are you sure, Commodore?" Fletcher sounded concerned. "That leaves a hell of lot for you to deal with."

"I'm sure, Fletch," Sterling said, maintaining the conviction in his tone. "We've got this, trust me."

Fletcher cocked his head to one side. "Okay, Commodore, it's your funeral," he said, then turned to someone off screen and relayed the order. Moments later, Sterling saw Fletcher's ships move to engage the squadrons he'd highlighted. "Good luck, Commodore," Fletcher said, turning back to the screen. "You're going to need it."

"I think you mean good hunting," Sterling corrected the older man. "Luck will have nothing to do with this."

Fletcher appeared intrigued by Sterling's statement, but there had been enough talking already.

"Good hunting then," Fletcher said before nodding respectfully to Sterling. "Bismarck, out."

"Sir, the bulk of the enemy ships are now coming straight at us," said Lieutenant Razor as the image of Fletcher faded and was replaced by the advancing fleet.

Sterling tapped another sequence of commands into his console, and the image of Captain Banks on the bridge of the Invictus appeared in the corner of the viewscreen.

"Thirty seconds, Captain," Sterling said, meeting his fellow officer's eyes. "Give them hell."

"We intend to sir," Banks said. Sterling could see that she was gripping the side of the captain's console tightly, in preparation for their next move.

"Torpedoes incoming," Razor called out. "Point defense cannons firing. Perimeter established."

"Ahead half, Ensign One," Sterling called out to his pilot. "Steady as she goes. Let them come."

"Aye, sir, ahead half," Ensign One replied.

The viewscreen was lit up by dozens of micro-explosions as the point defense cannons began to annihilate the incoming torpedoes. Moments later, flashes of plasma raced toward them. Unlike on the Invictus, Sterling was too deep inside the massive ship to feel the impacts through his console, but he could see the damage control readout flash up the impact points all across their dense, armored shell.

"Former Fleet Heavy Battlecruisers Richelieu and Yamato dead ahead, sir," Razor called out. The rest of the fleet is surrounding us."

Now Sterling could hear and feel the thumps of enemy weaponry pounding their enhanced armor. However, he knew the Vanguard could take the punishment. Moreover, he knew the time had come to show the enemy exactly what the heavily upgraded and retro-fitted dreadnaught could do.

"Forward batteries, target those cruisers and fire!" he ordered.

Plasma erupted from the massive forward rail guns of the Vanguard, striking the Richelieu and Yamato cleanly and blasting open their hulls like smashing rocks with a sledgehammer.

"Both heavy cruisers have been disabled," Razor announced. Even the normally stoical officer couldn't contain her excitement.

"All gun positions, fire at will," Sterling added, gripping his console so tightly the metal began to bend.

"All batteries firing, sir," Razor confirmed.

Plasma raced out from the dreadnaught in all directions. The Vanguard's upgraded weapons were not only more powerful than any Fleet ship that had ever seen service, but their robot gun crews were also faster and more proficient too. The combined effect enabled the Vanguard to deliver a barrage of death and destruction the likes of which no human or alien had ever seen before in the history of war.

"Twenty-one ships destroyed, sir," Lieutenant Razor called out. "The rest are regrouping and moving into attack.

"Captain Banks, launch, now, now, now!" Sterling ordered. He then focused on the viewscreen, eager to see his old ship in action again.

Right on cue, the Fleet Marauder Invictus powered out from the port docking garage of the Vanguard. However, she wasn't alone; flying in formation with the compact, but formidable warship were an entire squadron of Obsidian ships. He smiled as the Invictus immediately opened fire, pulverizing the engines of a turned Fleet Destroyer, before turning hard and blasting open a rupture the size of a shuttlecraft in the second enemy ship. Sterling's console chimed an alert and he saw that sections of their starboard armor were weakening.

"Ensign, keep our port side to the enemy," Sterling ordered. "Let's try to even out the damage."

"Aye sir," Ensign One replied. "Permission to maneuver at will."

Sterling raised an eyebrow. That was basically a request for the ship to fly itself, he thought. Then he realized that in effect the ship was already flying itself.

"Permission granted, Ensign," Sterling called out, figuring that he couldn't possibly compete with his AI in terms of making the sort of quick decisions that were needed to ensure the Vanguard stayed intact. "Try not to fly her apart, though."

"I will do my best, sir," Ensign One replied, cheerfully.

The massive dreadnaught began to turn and Sterling was forced to grip the sides of his console to compensate for the delay in inertial negation. The starfield beyond the viewscreen momentarily became a blur. Then, as the image settled again, Sterling discovered that they were flying directly at the Fleet Fast Battleship Audacious.

"Main batteries firing," Razor called out. Seconds later the Audacious was obliterated in a flash of light and energy.

"How the hell are you flying a dreadnaught like it's a fighter, Ensign?" Sterling said, feeling a little dizzy from the sudden motion.

"It is not an underestimation when I say that you do not know what this ship is capable of, sir," the sentient AI replied, its glowing ocular units shining across the CIC toward the captain's console.

"Then show me, Ensign," Sterling replied. "Show me everything it can do."

If Ensign One had a mouth, Sterling was sure the artificial officer would have smiled at that moment. The machine then turned back to its station and the Vanguard was again thrown into an unfeasibly agile maneuver. The robot gun crews were no less efficient and astonishing in their accuracy. Enemy ships continued to explode and tumble away into the darkness, out of control and ablaze.

Suddenly, Sterling's console chimed another alert and his gaze was drawn back to his screens. MAUL was in pursuit of the Invictus and the Marauder was taking fire. Sterling cursed and sent the image of the battle onto the viewscreen. Immediately, the Invictus took another hit and

Sterling could see that its regenerative armor was buckling.

"I can get a lock on MAUL, sir," Razor said, evidently having also noticed that their companion ship was in danger. "But there's a risk of hitting the Invictus too."

"Get the lock but hold fire," Sterling said as another powerful blast of plasma flashed across the hull of the Invictus. Sterling's gut tightened, knowing that if the shot had landed the ship would have been disabled or destroyed. He wanted to intervene, but he also knew he had to trust Captain Banks. It was her ship now. It was down to her.

"Christopher Fletcher reports that they have destroyed the enemy squadrons," Razor called out, though Sterling's eyes were still glued to the Invictus on the screen. "He's requesting instructions."

"Order the Bismarck and any remaining ships from Bastion to attack enemy formations alpha-two and beta-four, Lieutenant," Sterling said, briefing glancing at his tactical readout before returning his eyes to the viewscreen. "Have a squadron of Obsidian ships cover them."

"Aye sir," Razor replied.

However, Sterling barely heard his XO. His heart was thumping so hard that it was hurting his chest. "Come on, Mercedes..." he said, still fixated on the screen.

MAUL fired again, clipping the starboard wing section of the Invictus, but it was only a glancing blow. Then the Marauder changed course and swooped around the wreckage of a heavy cruiser, missing the burning debris by what looked like only a couple of meters. MAUL tried to follow, but the alien heavy destroyer lacked the Marauder's nimbleness. The Invictus turned again, confusing the enemy ship, and moments later the Marauder was on MAUL's tail. Sterling almost called out the order to fire himself, but there was no need. The forward plasma rails guns of the Invictus flashed and MAUL was stuck cleanly across its back. The enemy warship then began to spiral out of control, flames licking the space surrounding its wound. Sterling punched his console and cried out before another alert chimed, snatching his focus back to his screens.

"The remaining enemy vessels are fleeing, sir," Razor said, sounding both relieved and astonished at this fact.

"Order all ships to pursue and destroy them, Lieutenant," Sterling said, pushing himself away from his slightly bent and mangled console. He glanced across to his XO. "Are they heading to the expected aperture?"

Razor nodded. "Aye, sir. All ships are heading for the aperture leading to Sa'Nerran space."

Sterling stood tall and sucked in a deep lungful of the Vanguard's cool, recycled air. "Stand ready to spring our little surprise, Lieutenant," he said, switching the displays on the viewscreen to show the aperture location, along with the fleeing enemy vessels.

"Ready on your order, sir," Razor said.

Sterling waited patiently, filling the time by watching the Invictus, the Obsidian ships and Fletcher's fleet pick off more of the retreating ships. Their numbers were dwindling by the second, but Sterling knew any ship that was allowed to surge out of Middle Star would only add to the number of warships that would eventually defend Sa'Nerra. As such, he had already made preparations to ensure that the lowest possible number of enemy vessels would survive the battle.

"Now, Lieutenant Razor," Sterling called out.

Razor executed the order and two full squadrons of Obsidian ships detached from junk that the Vanguard had ejected shortly after surging into the system. The powerful, AI-controlled warships powered up and began to open fire, catching the retreating enemy vessels completely by surprise.

"Some of the fleeing enemy ships have broken through, sir," Razor called out. "We won't get them all, not without literally blocking their paths to the aperture."

"How many will escape, Lieutenant?"

Razor was silent for a moment while she made the assessment on her console. "Seven in total sir," she finally announced.

Sterling snorted a laugh. "Seven? Out of one hundred eighteen?"

Razor frowned down at her console and ran the numbers again, before nodding. "Aye, sir. Seven," she confirmed, sounding as shocked as Sterling was.

"How many did we lose?" Sterling then asked.

"Four Obsidian ships were disabled, sir," Razor confirmed. "However, I believe they are repairable."

Sterling laughed again and shook his head. They'd just delivered the biggest ass-whooping of the entire fifty-year war, and come out of it with barely a scratch. Then he noticed that Razor's eyes had narrowed a touch.

"One of the seven enemy ships to escape was MAUL, sir."

Sterling nodded. Perhaps it was too much to expect that MAUL would fall so easily. Perhaps it was even better this way, he considered. Even so, despite MAUL's escape, the victory they had won at Middle Star was more decisive than Sterling could ever have hoped for.

"All remaining enemy vessels have surged, sir," Razor said. "Shall I send the Obsidian ships in pursuit?"

"Negative, Lieutenant, order all forces to regroup and rendezvous in orbit of Bastion," Sterling said, watching the flash of surge energy erupt from the aperture, like someone turning a giant flashlight on and off. "Those ships can wait. And so can MAUL."

Sterling's console chimed an incoming message, and he saw that it was from Christopher Fletcher. "Put Fletcher on the screen, and bring up Captain Banks too, so she can monitor."

Razor acknowledged, then the former Fleet officer and Banks appeared side-by-side on the viewscreen.

"Hell of a fight, Commodore," Fletcher said, grinning from ear-to-ear. "I don't know what kind of ship you have there, or where you found it, but I'm sure as hell glad it's on our side."

Sterling nodded, accepting the compliment. "You and your people fought well too, Fletch," he said, remaining serious, knowing that he had a sobering request to make of the man. "But my help comes at a price and this time I'm not accepting no for an answer."

"You don't even have to ask, Commodore," Fletcher said, holding up his hands in a gesture of submission. "If you need me and my navy to help you finish this, you've got it."

"I expected nothing less, Fletch, but that's not the price I'm asking."

The old veteran frowned at Sterling through the viewscreen. "Then what, Commodore?" he asked.

"I want you to put the uniform back on," Sterling said, pressing his hands to the small of his back. "I want you to accept a commission." Fletcher's frown deepened, but the man remained silent. "So what's it to be, Captain Fletcher? Will you rejoin the Fleet and help me to end this war, once and for all?"

Fletcher blew out a rasping sigh and shook his head. "You drive a hard bargain, Commodore," the older man said. Then he cracked another smile. "But what the hell, if you can't beat 'em, join 'em!"

STERLING WATCHED the Bismarck slowly descend to the deck inside the Vanguard's port docking garage, shielding his face from the downdraught of its thrusters. The raging warship's landing struts touched down and took up the strain, hissing and wheezing like an old man dropping into his favorite armchair. Plumes of steam and smoke billowed out from vents all over the ship and Sterling suddenly found himself consumed by a murky, butter-tasting grey cloud. Coughing and trying to waft the smoke away, he heard the sound of the cargo ramp whirring open. The variable pitch of the motors gave away the fact the ship was struggling. That it was still flying at all was as close to a miracle as anything Sterling had witnessed.

"I think we need to get that old bucket into a repair bay, before it suffocates us all," observed Banks, walking up behind Sterling while also wafting smoke from her eyes.

Sterling glanced behind and saw that the Invictus was docked a couple of hundred meters further into the garage.

Unlike the Bismarck, it still looked strong, largely on account of its self-healing regenerative armor.

"You just don't have an appreciation for the classics, Captain," Sterling hit back. "Though I admit I'd appreciate the Bismarck a lot more if it wasn't smoking out my docking garage."

Sterling then saw Christopher Fletcher approaching through the fumes, sucking them in and blowing them out through his nostrils like a fire-breathing dragon.

"I like the upgrade, Commodore Sterling," said Fletcher, throwing up a lazy salute, which Sterling returned with professional briskness. "Though I preferred your old ship. That was more my style."

"I'd be happy to give you a tour of *my* ship, Mr. Fletcher," Banks cut in, putting heavy emphasis on the word 'my'. "She's on the deck behind us."

Fletcher frowned at Banks then saw the four gold bars on her collar. He let out a long, low-whistle and threw up another salute, this time with a bit more enthusiasm.

"That would be much appreciated, Captain, thanks," the former Fleet officer said. "And congratulations too. I saw that maneuver you pulled on MAUL during the battle. I think that's the first time I've ever seen that ship running scared."

"It still got away, though," Banks said, acknowledging the man's compliment with a respectful nod.

"Maybe this time," Fletcher replied, sounding hungry for another chance at the Sa'Nerran top-gun. "But next time we'll take it down, Captain, you mark my words."

A group of Obsidian Crew marched onto the deck,

heading directly for the Bismarck. Sterling saw Fletcher's eyes grow wide as his hand moved to the weapon on his belt, and was quick to step in.

"It's okay, they're with us," Sterling said, as the robots set to work refueling the old mark-one destroyer and repairing its damage, which was significant. "They're robots from an old Fleet program that was designed to supply an AI-powered army to fight the Sa'Nerra."

Fletcher backed away and watched the machines for a moment, though his hand remained close to his hip, holding back his long trench coat to reveal his sidearm.

"Sounds like a bad idea to me, Commodore," Fletcher said, still anxiously inspecting the robots. "Machines are only good at doing what you tell them to do, not thinking for themselves. If I could strip the AI out of my ship completely, I would have done it years ago."

"What generation of AI does the Bismarck run?" Banks asked.

"Gen four, I think," Fletcher said, shrugging. "The damned thing has crashed and been reloaded and recompiled so many times, hell knows what it is anymore."

"I could have my engineer upgrade it for you," Sterling offered. "Though I'd probably suggest waiting until after the battle at Sa'Nerra. The last thing we need is you experiencing computer teething troubles in the middle of a fight."

Fletcher snorted and waved Sterling off. "No thanks, I'd rather you rip it out completely than stick a newer version in there," the man said as another plume of smoke shot out from a vent on the Bismarck. "I've never met an AI yet that merits being called 'intelligent', and I highly doubt your fancy new AIs will change my mind."

"You might be surprised," replied Sterling, with a knowing smile.

As if on cue, the metallic thud of robotic feet striking the metal deck began to draw nearer. Ensign One emerged from the mist and focused its glowing ocular units onto Fletcher.

"What in the hell are you?" Fletcher said, looking Ensign One over from head to toe.

"I am Ensign One," replied the sentient robot, cheerfully. "But to answer your question more fully, I am a sentient machine-consciousness contained within a custom-built Obsidian robot frame. I am also the helmsman of the Fleet Destroyer Vanguard, and its medical officer, when required."

Fletcher recoiled from the machine so fast Sterling though he was going to topple over backwards.

"You have a robot officer?" Fletcher said, raising an eyebrow at Sterling.

"I do, Ensign One is the latest recruit to the Omega Taskforce," Sterling said, smiling at his mechanical officer. Then Sterling realized his error. "After you, of course," he added, quickly correcting himself. "Assuming our agreement still stands of course?"

"It stands," Fletcher replied, still looking Ensign One over with a wary eye. "Though I don't think you have one of those uniforms in my size," he added while patting his belly, which was sagging over the top of his pants, like dough overflowing a bread pan. "Besides, I like my clothes just as they are."

This time it was Sterling that raised an eyebrow. Christopher Fletcher's long trench coat looked older than he did, and the outdated Fleet armor that he wore beneath it didn't look capable of stopping a toothpick, never mind a plasma blast.

"I don't care if you wear the uniform or not, so long as you bring your ships to Sa'Nerra and fight at our side," Sterling said, still smiling.

"I can spare half of Bastion's defensive navy, Commodore, no more," Fletcher hit back. He sounded like he was haggling over the price of a used car and had just submitted his final offer.

Fletcher's statement knocked Sterling for six and wiped the smile of his face. The old soldier had stated his position in a standoffish and borderline hostile manner, which was out of character with their earlier dealings. However, Fletcher had clearly anticipated a negative reaction to his offer and was quick to confirm his stance before Sterling could get a word in edgeways.

"I know what you're going to say, Commodore, so you can save your breath," he held his hands up. "A long time ago, I took an oath to protect and defend Bastion, and I don't intend on breaking it now. If I commit the entire navy to the attack, Bastion is left defenseless."

Sterling sighed and rubbed the back of his neck. This was one battle he hadn't counted on needing to fight.

"Look, Fletch, there wouldn't even be a Bastion if we hadn't shown up," Sterling said. He made no attempt to hide his frustration and irritation with the man. The time for diplomacy was over, he realized. Now it was time for hard truths. "As impressive as your navy is, without the Vanguard the Invictus and our Obsidian ships, the aliens would already be bombing Bastion to dust right now."

Fletcher puffed out his chest and looked ready to fight his corner. However, the older man bit his tongue. To suggest that Sterling hadn't spoken the truth would have been mere bravado. Sterling didn't claim to know Christopher Fletcher well, but he knew he wasn't an arrogant man, and certainly not a prideful one.

"That may be, Commodore, but it doesn't change anything," Fletcher eventually replied, conceding Sterling's point in the gentlest manner possible. "I owe you a great debt for what you've done, but that debt cannot render an existing one void. Once this war is over, you'll return to Earth and Bastion will be on its own again. If my navy should be decimated at Sa'Nerra, there will be no-one left to protect it." Fletcher then straightened his coat and stood tall, rising a couple inches taller even than Sterling. "That is my final word on the matter, Commodore," he added, firmly.

Sterling sighed again, openly and obviously. However, he wasn't giving up. Words were not his strong suit and if words were not enough to convince Fletcher, then he'd show him instead.

"Ensign One, show Mr. Fletcher the last received images from our aperture relays at Earth," Sterling said, while still locking eyes with Fletcher.

"Aye, sir," Ensign One replied. The robot took a step to

the side and projected a holo-image from its ocular units directly in front of Fletcher. The old man's eyes flicked across to the image, but Sterling remained focused on Fletcher. He didn't need to see the scenes again.

"I don't see anything." Fletcher said. His brow had furrowed and irritation was starting to bleed into his words.

"Wind back the recording to thirty seconds before the aperture field generators on the Titan overloaded," Sterling said, still focused on Fletcher. "And include footage from your own personal recordings."

Ensign One obliged and the holo quickly changed to show a montage of images, showing Earth and the Battle Titan as seen from aperture relays and Ensign One's own ocular units. The furrows of skin on Fletcher's brow had now deepened so that the shadows between them were as dark as a black hole.

"Play it, Ensign," Sterling said, coolly.

The various camera feeds began to replay the events that had occurred two days previously. Sterling continued to watch Fletcher as the older man observed the Sa'Nerra Battle Titan exploding and forming a singularity that then began to consume not only the alien ships surrounding it, but the planet too. The former Fleet officer was silent as the camera feeds continued to run, showing huge chunks of humanity's homeworld falling into the aperture singularity until nothing of the planet remained.

"That can't be?" Fletcher said, shaking his head at the now-paused holo image. "It's a trick. You're just trying to coerce me into committing the rest of my forces."

"I swore an oath too, Mr. Fletcher," Sterling replied, as

the older man's trembling eyes again met his. "I swore to

defend the United Governments against all enemies. I swore to protect Earth and all the allied worlds with my life." He pointed to the flickering holo image that was still hovering in the air to his side. "Earth is gone, Mr. Fletcher. I sacrificed humanity's homeworld for this one chance to kill our enemy and make sure they never set foot in our space again. Dozens of worlds and billions of lives have already been lost. If we fail at Sa'Nerra, Bastion will fall too, and everything we have both fought for and sacrificed will have been for nothing."

Fletcher held Sterling's eyes for a moment, then turned away, massaging his stubbled chin. Sterling could see that the man's hands were trembling, and that he was fighting hard to steady them. Fletcher was no Omega Captain, Sterling realized. He cared too much. He was guided by the moral and ethical compass that steered almost every right-thinking man and woman to do the right thing. Sterling didn't doubt that the right thing in Fletcher's mind was to stay true to his oath, and to protect his home and family. Breaking free from one's nature was the hardest thing anyone could do, but if Fletcher couldn't do it now, they were all lost.

"Can you promise me that Bastion will be safe while we're away?" Fletcher said, glancing across to Sterling.

The commander of the Bastion Navy appeared unable to maintain his earlier, imperious pose. His back was now hunched over and his head stooped lower, causing the man to lose several inches in height.

"No, I can't," Sterling replied, honestly. "My

expectation is that the Sa'Nerra will commit all of their forces to the defense of their world. But I'd be lying if I said that Skirmisher raids might not take place while we're gone."

The older man appeared to curse under his breath. Then Fletcher turned away and pressed his hands to his hips, while peering out toward his aging warship. Sterling glanced across to Banks, trying to gauge from her reaction whether she thought he'd done enough. Her eyes appeared hopeful, perhaps more so than he expected his own did at that moment. He'd said his piece. Now it was down to Fletcher to decide.

"If I agree then I have a price of my own to ask," Fletcher said, still looking at the Bismarck and the small army of Obsidian crew that were banging it back together.

"Name it," said Sterling.

"If commit my entire force, and by some miracle we make it thought this, I need you to swear another oath." Fletcher spun around to look Sterling in the eye, again growing close to his full height. "You have to pledge yourself to Bastion and to the Void, as I have done. We will be divided no longer."

Sterling nodded. "Knowing what you now know about me – about what I've done – if the word of an Omega officer is still worth anything to you, then you have it," he said, offering Fletcher his hand.

"I don't give a damn about Omega officers or the Fleet, Commodore Sterling," Fletcher hit back. Then he reached out and clasped his hand around Sterling's. "But as one soldier to another, one man to another, I'll take your word as your bond." Sterling and Fletcher then shook hands. "My navy is yours, Commodore."

"Thank you, Mr. Fletcher," Sterling said. It felt like a pressure valve at the back of his head had just been opened. "Or should I say, Captain Fletcher?"

The older man laughed. "If you must," he muttered. He then realized his slip and straitened to attention. "I mean, if you must, sir..."

Sterling laughed and so did Banks. Even Ensign One added his own brand of synthetic laughter to the mix, though this seemed to unsettle Fletcher rather than make him feel more at ease.

"I'll leave you to tend your ship and crew," Sterling said, gesturing to the Bismarck. Thanks to the speed and efficiency of the Obsidian Crew, it was already looking considerably more shipshape than it had done shortly after it had landed. Sterling turned then realized his stomach was growling. Nerves and stomach flutter had made it impossible to eat before the battle, but now he was starving. "Your ships and crews are more than welcome to enjoy the hospitality of the Vanguard, Captain," Sterling added, turning back to Fletcher. "Everyone is welcome to dock and enjoy a hot meal, and even a shower, should they wish to. We surge into Sa'Nerran space at oh-eight-hundred Zulu. It might be the last chance they get."

Sterling considered that this last statement might have been interpreted more literally than he'd intended. However, it transpired that it was something else Sterling had said that had gotten the new Fleet Captain's attention.

"Are you sure, Commodore?" said Fletcher, surprised,

but clearly intrigued by the offer. "Water is a precious resource in space, hot water even more so."

"This ship was built for a crew of more than a thousand," Sterling replied, offering his new officer a welcoming smile. "Trust me, there's more than enough to go around." Then he had a thought. "So long as your crews stay clear of the number twenty-seven meal trays, that is."

Fletcher raised an eyebrow. "I'll be sure to let them know," he replied, though didn't press Sterling about why.

"While you're at it, the vintage number fours, elevens and thirty-sixes are off the table too," Banks added.

"As you wish, Captain Banks," Fletcher said, now looking more baffled than curious.

"And the forty-fours too..." Banks went on. However, a dirty look from Sterling convinced her that she'd said enough.

"If your duties permit, we'll see you in the canteen area shortly," Sterling said, again turning to leave and ushering Banks along with him, to prevent her from adding to her list of stipulations.

"I have a couple of matters to attend to, but I'll see you there in about thirty minutes or so," Fletcher said, also turning to leave. "And I'll bring some dinner conversation that I think will interest you greatly."

Sterling's ears pricked up and he glanced back with the intention of asking Fletcher to explain his cryptic comment. However, the man was already disappearing through the fog of smoke surrounding his ship, coat billowing in the draught, like a ghost pirate returning to his vessel to rest.

STERLING RECLINED in his chair and stirred some creamer into his coffee, while watching the men and women from the Bismarck pile into the canteen room. Christopher Fletcher had yet to arrive, but his crew weren't standing on ceremony. There were already a dozen of the Bismarck's personnel in the canteen, and while initially they had been more than a little wary of the robot waiter that had come to serve them, they'd soon relaxed once the coffee started flowing and the meal trays arrived.

"They didn't waste any time, did they?" said Banks, sliding into the seat opposite Sterling and dropping a meal tray onto the table.

Sterling was about to make a snarky comment about Banks restraining herself to just one tray when he realized there were actually two stacked one on top of the other.

"It makes a nice change to see people again, rather than just us and a group of faceless robots," Sterling replied. He held his hand up to Ensign One, who was sitting next to him with an empty coffee cup in hand. "Present company excepted, of course," he added, not wishing to offend the sentient AI.

"Technically, I also do not have a face, but I appreciate the sentiment nonetheless, sir," Ensign One replied before pretending to take a sip of coffee.

"I thought you hated people?" said Banks, separating the trays in front of her and grabbing a fork in preparation to attack the food.

"I don't hate people, I just can't tolerate them for too long, that's all," Sterling replied. Then he raised an eyebrow at Banks. "And there are some I can tolerate far less than others."

Banks smiled then tore the foil off her first meal tray. "You'd be lost without me, admit it," she said before dipping her head into the cloud of steam billowing up from the tray and inhaling deeply.

Sterling briefly sat up to get a better view of the tray, realizing it was one he hadn't seen before. The main course appeared to be a creamy casserole based around what looked like chunks of chicken, though in reality it would have been a lab-engineered substitute.

"Which number is that one?" Sterling asked. He'd already finished his number twenty-seven, but the smell of the casserole was making him feel hungry again.

"Forty-eight," Banks mumbled through a mouthful of food. "I thought I'd try something different for a change."

"Those biscuits look good," said Sterling, reaching over the table with his bionic hand in an attempt to steal one. Banks' reactions were cat-like in their speed and accuracy, and she'd slapped away his hand before he'd even come within touching distance.

"They do look good," Banks said, pulling the meal tray a little closer to her body, like a greedy dwarf hoarding its gold. "That's why I'll be eating all of them," she added, glowering at Sterling through narrowed eyes.

"I believe that striking a fellow officer is a serious offence, is it not?" said Ensign One, who had been quietly observing the exchange with coffee cup in hand. The robot shone it ocular units onto Sterling. "As acting head of security, should I arrest her, sir?"

Sterling smiled. His robot officer had been practicing its particular brand of dry humor and was becoming quite adept at it.

"Good point, Ensign," Sterling said, smirking at Banks. "Clap her in irons, will you?"

"You're head of security now too?" Banks turned to face Ensign One while resting on one elbow. Her cheeks were still stuffed full of food.

"In effect, I am acting head of any position that lacks a permanent, full time officer," the robot replied. "It helps that I am able to be in more than one place at once."

Banks frowned at the robot. "But you're here. Where the hell else are you?"

"I am also at the helm control station," Ensign One replied, coolly. "As well as in secondary damage control, the medical wing, maintenance section two for the primary scanner array, gun control in the ventral main batteries in the forward section, and several other locations."

Banks raised an eyebrow. "That's a neat trick," she murmured, while tearing the foil off her second meal tray.

To Sterling's ear, Banks didn't actually sound all that impressed. The meal tray in front of her had captured considerably more of her attention.

"In essence, I am also on the bridge of the Invictus too, of course," Ensign One added, shrugging. "I get around."

Sterling laughed then noticed out of the corner of his eye that Christopher Fletcher had entered the canteen. He had been immediately accosted by various members of his crew, who were eagerly trying to get the man to sample delicacies from the various meal trays they were consuming. Fletcher humored them and played to his crowd, turning up his nose at a pickled egg, while giving a chef's kiss sign after sampling a chocolate pudding. The man was clearly well-liked, Sterling realized as he watched the interplay between the veteran soldier and his crewmates. Fletcher had the unique ability that every true leader possessed to inspire others to follow them. It was something that couldn't be taught and something Fleet had sorely lacked within its own senior leadership during the latter years of the war.

Had the mutineer made a different choice at Colony Middle Star all those years ago, Christopher Fletcher would have been a senior admiral now, Sterling mused. Fletcher's voice would have been a powerful force in the war council, and Sterling found himself wondering what might have been different should 'Admiral Fletcher' have been in command of their forces, instead of Griffin. With more unified leadership and more decisive action earlier in the war, there would have been no need for the Omega Taskforce. Sterling had once considered Admiral Griffin's covert actions in establishing the black-ops unit to have shown incredible foresight. The truth was that the Omega Directive should have never existed. That it did at all was a failure of Fleet leadership at the highest level. Sterling also understood that those best suited for a job are not always those with the ambition or temperament to carry it out. And the compassionate and genial Christopher Fletcher likely would have not been able to stomach the politics of senior office.

In the end, it was all academic, Sterling realized. There was no safe and comfortable solution to this war, or any war. By some quirk of fate, it had fallen to Lucas Sterling to conduct the final movements of the fifty-year conflict. And, perhaps unlike Christopher Fletcher, he did have the stomach to see it though, no matter what was required of him.

While Sterling had been ruminating over the 'what-might-have-been's' of Christopher Fletcher's life, the older man had spotted him at his corner table. The commander of the Bastion Navy made his apologies to his comrades and strode over, smiling broadly.

"Thank you again for letting my crews use your facilities, Commodore," Fletcher said. "As you can see, it's a particular treat for them to indulge in such a plentiful bounty of Fleet rations."

"Take a pew, Captain," Sterling said, kicking out a chair for Fletcher, who obliged and sat down. Then Sterling had a thought. "Talking of Fleet meal trays, did you score anything useful from the depot locations I provided you?"

"I did, yes, thank you again," Fletcher said, nodding respectfully to Sterling. "But I distributed the food we recovered to the various settlements, since they needed it more than we did."

Fletcher reached across the table and stole a fruit cookie from Banks' second meal tray. The older man had shoved it into his mouth before the speechless captain of the Invictus had even managed to process what happened. Sterling gritted his teeth, half expecting Banks to take a swing at Fletcher and knock a few teeth out of the older man's mouth. However, mercifully, Banks managed to restrain herself.

"The Fleet depots are actually what I came to speak to you about," Fletcher said, dusting down his hands. He paused and looked at Banks. "Those cookies are good," he said, heartily before snatching another, right in front of the officer's dumbstruck face.

"Yes, they are," Banks said, slowly sliding the tray out of Fletcher's reach. "You could always go and get a tray for yourself, maybe?"

Sterling stifled a laugh. This was the most diplomatic he'd ever seen Banks act in all the time he'd know her.

"Oh, I'm fine just nabbing the odd cookie or two from your tray, Captain," Fletcher said, waving Banks off. The older man apparently hadn't noticed the meal tray sliding steadily further away from him.

"You were about to mention something about the Fleet

depots?" Sterling cut in, trying to steer the conversation away from Banks' cookies so as to distract Fletcher from attempting to snatch any more of them. The man was liable to have his hand broken off if he continued in the same fashion, and Sterling didn't have time to instruct Ensign One to fit any more replacement limbs before they surged to Sa'Nerra.

"That's right," Fletcher said, as an Obsidian crew member filled up the coffee cup in front of him. He eyed the robot warily before continuing. "Most of the locations you gave me were standard fuel dumps or supply depots, all very useful. But then we found something else, hidden beneath what we thought was just a regular supply yard. We wouldn't have found it at all if it hadn't been for the fact part of the yard had caved in over the years."

There was a twinkle in the older man's eye that suggested excitement, Sterling realized.

"Go on, Captain..." Sterling said, now leaning in toward Fletcher.

"Well, it seemed clear that this new depot had been kept a secret," Fletcher went on, smiling. "And it was old, Commodore. As old as me, in fact."

"Captain, I love a good story as much as the next man, but we're hours away from launching an attack on an alien homeworld, so can you hurry it up a little?" Sterling said, eager for Fletcher to get to the point.

"Nukes, Commodore," Fletcher said, waggling his bushy eyebrows.

"Nukes?" Sterling repeated, not quite following Fletcher's meaning.

"Yes, Commodore. Old mark eighty-five COBSOL nuclear torpedoes," Fletcher clarified.

The mere mention of these torpedoes caused Banks' eyebrows to raise up. "Those things are a myth," she said, not even attempting to hide her scorn. "Just one of a dozen crazy stories that cadets get fed with when they join the academy."

"They're very real, Captain," Fletcher hit back, shrugging off Banks' dismissal and becoming sterner. "Early in the war, there was a plan to destroy the Sa'Nerran homeworld in a single decisive strike using high-yield, cobalt-salted nuclear weapons," Fletcher went on. "It was called Project Kahn."

"I know about Project Kahn, but Mercedes is right, it was a myth," Sterling cut in. "Not least because until now, we've never known where the alien's home planet was. So the whole notion of a nuclear strike was moot. Just a story."

Unlike Banks, Sterling had tried to moderate his tone so that he didn't come across as disparaging of the older man's comments. Even so, he was just as skeptical as his former first officer was.

"Not wishing to sound condescending, but you're both too young to know any different," Fletcher hit back. "The Bismarck was one of the ships designated to take part in the attack. It was all hush-hush, a bit like your Omega Taskforce."

"Go on," Sterling said. The commander of the Bastion Navy had piqued his interest.

"We would practice torpedo runs on some of the uninhabited Void worlds, all designed to launch the maximum number of weapons at the surface over the widest area possible," Fletcher continued. The man then rocked back in his chair, appearing suddenly grave. "I assure you both, these weapons are very real, and very deadly."

The switch from the genial Christopher Fletcher that had walked into the room to the grizzled war veteran that was now sitting at the table was stark and sobering.

"Sir, I have just searched the Fleet archives and decrypted some classified information relating to Project Kahn," Ensign One cut in.

"You can do that?" said Sterling, casting a quizzical eye at his robot officer.

"I have already done it, sir." Ensign One replied. "Should I have sought permission first?"

Sterling shrugged. "Probably, but since you've already hacked the system, you may as well tell us what you've found."

All eyes fell on the robot. "Captain Fletcher is correct. According to this information, a cache of two-hundred megaton mark eight-five cobalt-salted nuclear torpedoes was stored on Colony Two, Middle Star."

"How many of them?" Banks asked.

"One hundred and fifty, sir," Ensign One replied, flatly.

"A hundred and fifty?" Sterling repeated, again feeling the need to echo what he'd been told for fear he'd misheard. "Together with the weapons that the Vanguard is capable of delivering, the radiation fallout from those torpedoes would kill everything on the surface and render the planet uninhabitable for decades."

"That is correct," Ensign One said.

"And you're okay with that?" Banks said, turning back to Fletcher. "You understand what it means?"

"I understand perfectly well what it means, Captain Banks," Fletcher hit back. "Don't forget that I've spent my life in the Void, fighting pirates, corrupt marshals and these damned aliens, all without Fleet's help. We didn't survive by being soft. Let's just say that you two aren't the only ones here with balls of steel."

This time it was Sterling's eyebrows that rose. He'd clearly misjudged the man. *Perhaps Fletcher is Omega Captain material, after all*, he considered. Sterling glanced across to Banks then to Ensign One, neither of whom raised any concerns, before he again met the older man's eyes.

"Okay then, Captain Fletcher," Sterling said, feeling his pulse start to climb. "Tell us where we can find this cache of doomsday weapons, and let's get them loaded on board."

THE CIC OF THE FLEET DREADNAUGHT VANGUARD
exploded into reality and again the blood-red alert lights
flooded into Sterling's eyes. The battle-stations alarm
klaxon was still sounding, as it had been since long before
the mighty warship had surged into the Sa'Nerra's home
system. Yet they were not met with blasts of plasma and
swarms of torpedoes racing toward their hull. Nor were
they surrounded by alien ships all eager to destroy the
intruder that had so willingly flown into their domain. As
in the previous seven surges they'd completed up to that
point, their passage into Sa'Nerran space was eerily quiet.
Not for the first time, Sterling had been forced to check his
maps and scanner readouts to make sure they weren't lost.
And every time the data confirmed what seemed
impossible – they were advancing on the alien home world
practically without challenge.

"Report, Lieutenant," Sterling ordered, as the
Vanguard cruised past an enormous weapons platform, not

dissimilar to a Fleet Gatekeeper. However, instead of hitting them with a barrage of plasma fire, the platform hung dead in space, as if it had been abandoned centuries earlier.

"Their aperture defenses are disabled, sir," Razor replied, working the screens at the XO's console. "And there are no warships in the immediate vicinity."

Sterling sucked in a long, slow breath then nodded. "Very well, ahead standard, Ensign," he called out to his robot pilot. "Take us in, nice and easy."

"Aye, sir, ahead standard to the Sa'Nerran home world," Ensign One replied, as the beat of the Vanguard's engines increased.

Sterling's eyes remained fixed on the viewscreen, his bionic finger constantly tapping the side of his console. The fact their advance had been unopposed was encouraging and unsettling in equal measure. He'd almost have preferred to battle his way into the heart of alien territory. Yet throughout their journey, the aperture defenses designed to ward off such incursions into Sa'Nerran space had been partially dismantled and rendered useless. Likewise, there had been no heavy cruisers or battleships defending the borders. In fact, they had encountered only a few dozen generation-one alien warships in total, Against the might of the Vanguard, these old Sa'Nerran vessels had been swatted out of space with ease, allowing the dreadnaught to continue its path to Sa'Nerra practically unchallenged.

Lieutenant Razor's recon probes had suggested this would be the case, but Sterling had still struggled to believe it. It was like Sa'Nerran space had already been abandoned. However, with each surge closer to the alien home world, the reason for the apparent emptiness became clear. The alien gatekeepers that were supposed to defend the apertures leading into Sa'Nerran space had been ransacked and stripped for parts, or were missing entirely. Razor had suggested that the aliens may have modified the normally-immobile heavy cruisers so that they could form part of the Sa'Nerran invasion armada. One thing was certain, however; the aliens had thrown their all into the attack on Earth. They had sacrificed their own fortifications in order to harvest the resources and personnel needed to mount a force that could strike a decisive blow. Sterling could appreciate the logic. If there was no opportunity for a counter-attack then there was no need for defenses. However, the tactic had backfired spectacularly, thanks in large part to Admiral Griffin

As much as Sterling wanted to hate Griffin for turning on him, he had to give the Admiral her dues. She had outmaneuvered the Sa'Nerra and given Fleet and humanity a chance, if not at victory, at least at revenge and possible redemption. While the aliens had already struck a killing blow, they had sacrificed their own footing in order to achieve it. Now the Sa'Nerra were on the defensive, fighting to save their own planet instead of waging war on the worlds belonging to their enemy.

Sterling's primary console chimed an alert. He checked it and his pulse rose sharply as he saw enemy ships begin to appear on their scanners. He waited for Razor to give her detailed report, but scanned the board for one name in particular, finding it dead center of the formation.

"Enemy fleet detected," Razor said as Sterling's eyes flicked up to the viewscreen. "I'm reading one hundred and forty-two ships on the board, including MAUL and the Fleet Dreadnaught Hammer."

"It's just the Dreadnaught Hammer now, Lieutenant," Sterling cut in. Razor had just highlighted the ship he'd been looking for. "That ship is no longer a Fleet vessel."

"Aye, sir," Razor replied, though she appeared too engrossed in her readings to pay any heed to Sterling's rebuke. "The Hammer is one of seven Fleet vessels, the others being those that escaped from Middle Star," she added, still studying the readings. "All the rest are Sa'Nerran ships and most of them are phase-three designs, but they're hardly factory fresh."

Sterling glanced across to his XO. "Define 'hardly factory fresh', Lieutenant."

"I'm detecting signs of structural damage that's consistent with long surge vectors and long-range aperture travel," Razor continued.

"They must have raced ahead to beat us here, thinking we'd hit Sa'Nerra first," Sterling said, hypothesizing about the reckless speed of the alien fleet's return.

"That is correct, sir," Ensign One said, swiveling its seat to face the command platform. "Had we surged to Sa'Nerra first, as Admiral Griffin wanted, our ships would have been ambushed."

"Understood, Ensign," Sterling said, with a nod. The robot's comment was intentionally designed to highlight that Sterling's call had been the right one. And while he didn't need the affirmation, he had to admit it felt good to be right.

Lieutenant Shade then highlighted several alien warships and enhanced them on the viewscreen, including the Hammer and MAUL.

"The condition of the fleet is worse than we expected," Razor mused. "We might actually have a chance."

While MAUL was no more or less battle-scarred than it usually appeared, Sterling could see that the other vessels were in bad shape too. Some looked like they'd flown too close to a star and barely escaped intact. Their hulls were scorched and battered and several even had weapons pods and thruster arrays that had been destroyed.

"A wounded animal will often fight harder, Lieutenant," Sterling said. He was trying to temper his own enthusiasm at seeing the enemy fleet in disarray, as much as he was Razor's. "But let's not get overconfident. They still outnumber us, and they still have a dreadnaught and MAUL."

"Aye, sir," Razor replied. Then her console chimed another update. "The alien fleet is mobilizing. They're coming straight for us, though MAUL and the Hammer are hanging back at the rear."

"They want to use the rest of their fleet to bite chunks out of us first," Sterling said, recognizing the tactics that MAUL had employed hundreds of times before. "They'll wait until we're hurt and weakened then try to swoop in to claim the kill."

"Not this time," Razor said, with an unexpected degree

of gusto. "This time MAUL and the rest of those alien ships are going down."

Sterling glanced at Razor, surprised and impressed to hear some fighting talk from the normally restrained officer.

"Assuming that's not too bold of me to say so, sir," Razor added, clearly unsure whether she'd overstepped again.

"It's only too bold if we're wrong, Lieutenant," Sterling replied, allowing his officer a little leeway. "So, let's make sure we do this right." He glanced across to the helm control station. "Ahead full, Ensign One," he called out to his robot helmsman. "Set all point defense cannons to cover our forward sections and prepare to execute maneuver Blitzkrieg."

"Aye, sir, engines responding full ahead," Ensign One called out. An Obsidian crewmember that was networked to the sentient AI then acknowledged Sterling's second order from the weapons control station and the point defense cannons powered up.

Suddenly, the door to the CIC opened and Captain Fletcher and Captain Banks walked in. Both were in full combat armor, the same as Sterling and Razor.

"The Invictus and Obsidian Fleet are ready to launch," Banks said, jumping down to the command deck with a spring in her step.

"The Bastion Navy are standing by too, Commodore," Fletcher added. "Thanks to your ship's repair docks, we're in better condition than most of the ships out there."

Sterling was about to repeat the same words of caution

he'd spoken to Razor regarding becoming overconfident when Fletcher beat him to it.

"We shouldn't get cocky, though," the veteran soldier added. "I've seen how these bastards fight when they think they've nothing to lose."

"And right now, they have everything to lose," Sterling said, glancing back at the viewscreen. The image was focused on the Hammer, which was powering toward them, gun ports open. "Return to your ship and move the Bastion navy into attack formation, Captain," he added, still tapping his finger on the side of his console. "Let's give them something else to shoot at."

"Aye, sir, we'll do our part, don't you worry about that," Fletcher said, sounding bullish, but not overconfident.

Sterling then noticed that Fletcher was still wearing his ragged old Fleet armor, despite having been offered an upgrade to the latest design.

"How come you're still wearing that tatty old armor, Captain?" Sterling asked. "Did the new equipment not get shipped on-board the Bismarck?"

"Oh, I got it just fine and my crew send their gratitude," Fletcher said, smiling at Sterling. "But I like what I'm wearing, thanks all the same. It may be old and bit shabby, like its wearer, but it's kept me alive this long, and I trust it'll do the same for some time yet."

Sterling nodded, accepting Fletcher's reasons. He had his quirks and idiosyncrasies the same as everyone, so could hardly deny the man his customs.

"As you wish, Captain Fletcher," Sterling said, turning to face the man. "Good hunting out there."

Fletcher nodded then spun on his heels, his long coat swaying like a superhero's cape as he did so, and marched out of the CIC. Banks also turned to leave, but Sterling called out to her to stop. There was something important he needed to do before his former first officer took flight.

"Mercedes, just a moment," Sterling said, halting Banks in her track. "I need you just for a couple of minutes."

Banks raised an eyebrow at him. "Just for a couple of minutes?" she said, sounding offended. "I think you might need me for a little longer than that."

"You know what I mean, now get down here will, you, we're short on time," Sterling hit back. Their engines were full ahead, charging down the throat of an alien armada, and still Banks found time to tell jokes.

Banks jogged down the stairs and jumped up onto the captain's station in the center of the CIC. She was eyeing him suspiciously, as if he was about to ask an awkward question.

"This isn't going to be one of those mushy, 'take care out there, I don't want to lose you....' kind of chats, is it?" Banks said, still scowling at Sterling. "Because it would be a shame if you lost all your tough-guy credits right at the last moment."

"No, it's not one of those sorts of chats," Sterling said, rolling her eyes at Banks. "Well, not quite, anyway."

"Now isn't the time to get down on one knee, either, Commodore," Banks added.

"Now is actually the time for you to shut up and listen to me," Sterling snapped. As much as he enjoyed – or at least tolerated – his former first officer's quips, he needed her focused. Banks appeared to recognize this and her demeanor quickly shifted. "I've upgraded your command codes so that they have the same level of authorization as mine, in case I'm killed or incapacitated," Sterling went on, satisfied he now had her undivided attention. "That means if I die before the Vanguard is in position to launch the nuclear torpedoes, you'll be able to do it in my stead, remotely or by docking and taking command."

"You're not dying, you're too stubborn," Banks replied. Unlike her previous tone, she hadn't meant this jokingly, Sterling realized. The mention of Sterling dying had, if anything, pissed her off.

"We both know there's a good chance we won't come out of this alive," Sterling continued, pressing his point. "The mission can't be jeopardized by something trivial like a lack of authorization, and in the heat of battle, there won't be time for you to go through the usual processes to assume command. That's why I've given you a full set of keys now."

Banks frowned at Sterling, then sighed and nodded. "Okay, I understand," she said. Sterling could tell that she had much more to say, but she appeared to recognize that now was not the time to say it. "What if we're both killed?" she asked.

Sterling felt an urge to refute the notion that Banks might die, exactly as she had done for him moments earlier. Knowing this would make him a hypocrite and open himself up to ridicule, he resisted the urge.

"In that eventuality, I've instigated an automatic

protocol to transfer command to Ensign One, or the Vanguard's AI, however you look at it," Sterling explained.

"They're the same thing, aren't they?" Banks said. Like Sterling, she still struggled to understand the exact nature of their sentient AI's existence.

"Who the hell knows, the point is that if we're both dead, Ensign One is our backup," Sterling replied, shrugging. "The only way they're going to kill a sentient program is to wipe out the Vanguard, the Invictus and all the Obsidian ships."

Banks nodded. "If that happens, we deserve to lose," she said, casting her eyes over to the viewscreen and the looming threat of the Dreadnaught Hammer.

"We're not losing this battle, Mercedes," Sterling said, with conviction. "Not on my watch."

"And you're not dying, either," Banks hit back, thumping Sterling on the shoulder, as usual far harder than she'd intended to. "Not if I have anything to say about it."

"I have a couple of number twenty-seven meal trays and a bottle of scotch on standby for when this is all over." Sterling was trying to find a suitable way of telling Banks that he expected her to make it through alive too, while maintaining his 'tough guy' credentials, as she had called them.

"It's a deal," Banks said, smiling. "Though, I'll take the meals trays and you can keep the scotch. That stuff is vile."

Sterling laughed. "At least it's better than Calvados."

"Barely..."

Sterling's console then chimed an alert and Lieutenant Razor was quick to provide an update.

"The alien fleet has launched torpedoes" Razor switched the image on the viewscreen to track a cluster of the incoming weapons.

"That's your cue to leave, Captain Banks," Sterling said, feeling his pulse quicken. "As soon you're clear of the docking garage, I'll kick the Vanguard into gear."

"Understood, sir, I know my part too." Banks hesitated as if wanting to say something more, but instead she just smiled again and jogged back up the steps toward the exit.

Sterling watched her go, knowing that she wouldn't look back, and hoping that it wouldn't be the last time he saw her. His stomach tightened into a knot and he cursed himself for allowing emotion to grip him. Focusing back on the viewscreen, he used all of his meditation techniques to push his concerns about Banks from his mind. He had a job to do, and it would require every inch of his cold, calculated callousness to fulfil.

STERLING'S CONSOLE CHIMED AN ALERT, but he didn't check it, knowing that his XO would report the update to him more rapidly than he could assess it himself.

"Captain Fletcher and his navy are moving into attack posture to our starboard side," Lieutenant Razor said, adding a feed of the Bismarck to the viewscreen. "They're drawing away a contingent of the attacking force, as planned."

"Understood, Lieutenant, how long before those torpedoes reach us?" Sterling said.

"Ninety seconds until they're within range of our point defense cannons, sir," Razor replied. "Then the first wave of Sa'Nerran warships are right behind them."

Sterling nodded and glanced down at his console, waiting for the port docking garage to depressurize. Then he saw the lights turn red and the launch indicator start to flash as the fleet of Obsidian ships launched, one after the other in rapid succession, like bullets from an automatic rifle.

"The Obsidian Fleet is away," Razor announced, confirming what Sterling had seen on his panel. The viewscreen updated to show the onyx-black warships accelerate to the Vanguard's port side, aiming to further divide the alien forces. However, Sterling was focused on his console. There was one more ship that had yet to depart.

"The Invictus is also clear, sir," Razor added, sending a feed of the Marauder-class Destroyer into another window on the viewscreen.

This time Sterling did look up. Again, he felt his stomach churn and his heart quicken as the blue glow of the Invictus' powerful engines appeared on the screen. His mouth went dry as he turned to Lieutenant Razor.

"Open fire with all point-defense cannons and form a defensive perimeter," he ordered, trying to push thoughts of Mercedes Banks from his mind. "I don't want a single torpedo to get through."

"Aye sir," Razor replied, without delay.

Sterling knew that there was little-to-no chance of stopping every torpedo from breaching their firing perimeter, but the fact Razor hadn't highlighted this was encouraging. She was laser-focused on the job at hand; arguably even more so than he was at that moment. Sterling realized he had to develop the same single-mindedness, and he had to do it fast. He couldn't afford to be distracted, to hesitate or to second-guess himself. He had to be ruthless.

"The Bastion Navy has engaged the enemy," Razor

said, continuing to provide updates with cool professionalism.

Tiny vibrations reached Sterling through the deck and his primary console. Despite being deep inside the massive dreadnaught, he was learning to feel when the ship was taking fire.

"Multiple direct hits, armor holding," Razor said, her tone becoming more urgent. "We're within range of the first wave of Sa'Nerran ships, sir. Ten phase-three Skirmishers directly ahead."

Sterling turned to his secondary console, which was already configured to the combat layout. He selected the vessels and his chosen firing pattern then locked in the order.

"Gun batteries, prepare to fire," Sterling said, glancing over to the Obsidian crewmember manning the weapons control station.

"Batteries report ready, Commodore," the robot replied, speaking in the synthesized, processed voice of the older gen-thirteen Fleet AIs.

Sterling sucked in a deep breath and focused ahead, pressing his hands to the small of his back. "Fire..."

The deck rumbled as the Vanguard unleashed its first barrage of plasma from the forward ventral gun batteries. Even prior to the extensive program of upgrades the ship had undergone at the Omega Base, it was a formidable weapon. Now, its offensive power was terrifying.

"Direct hits to seven Skirmishers," Razor called out. "All seven destroyed sir."

"Dorsal batteries midships, track the remaining ships

and open fire," Sterling ordered. However, it wasn't the Skirmishers that concerned him, but the squadron of cruisers coming in behind them. "Standby forward main battery," he ordered, locking onto the lead cruiser.

The deck and walls of the armored CIC rumbled again as incoming torpedoes and plasma weapons hammered the mighty dreadnaught. Sterling saw sections of their upgraded armor begin to turn amber, but he wasn't concerned. Outside of the CIC, the Vanguard was crewed by robots that didn't need heat or air, and that didn't feel fear. They could operate in the vacuum of space if needs be, Sterling didn't care. So long as enough of the dreadnaught made it past the Sa'Nerran blockade and its torpedo tubes were intact, the enemy could continue their onslaught and it would have no effect.

"Forward battery reports ready, sir," said the processed voice of the Omega robot.

"Fire!" Sterling called out, feeling his heart race again, though this time from excitement.

The viewscreen briefly went white as the barrage of plasma blasts raced out ahead of them. The lead Sa'Nerran destroyer was obliterated as if it were nothing more than a Wasp fighter craft. Follow-up blasts tore through four more cruisers, either destroying them outright, crippling their engines or blasting them in half along the middle axis. It was devastating, frightening and beautiful all at once, like flying an aircraft through a lightning storm.

"We've broken through the first wave, sir," said Lieutenant Razor.

"Continue firing, all batteries, keep up the pressure,"

Sterling replied. Then he noticed that several transponder IDs had blinked off his panel. "What's the status of the Obsidian Fleet and the Navy?" he added, scanning the list to make sure the Invictus was still among the active IDs.

"Five navy vessels and two Obsidian ships destroyed or disabled," Razor replied. "Enemy losses stand at thirty-four." Sterling felt his hands ball into fists. It was a strong start, but they still had much to do. "The bulk of the enemy have split along our port and starboard sides," Razor continued, unaware of Sterling's sudden surge of optimism.

"How many have remained with MAUL and the Hammer?" Sterling asked. He was eager to execute his maneuver, but needed to be sure the enemy had taken the bait.

"Six phase-three battlecruisers have remained, sir," Razor responded, proving herself to be easily Shade's equal when it came to preparedness. Razor seemed as at home in the CIC as she was in a maintenance crawlspace. The deck rumbled again as more blasts and torpedoes thudded into the hull. This time lights flickered and several consoles overloaded. "Heavy damage to the port docking garage," Razor continued, her voice raising to a shout to be heard over the fizz and crackle of electrical sparks. "Heavy damage to decks one and two, sections twelve through fourteen. Armor buckling. Reports of hull breaches."

"Intensify dorsal forward defense cannons to secure those sections, Lieutenant," Sterling answered, staring at the range indicator and urging the Vanguard on.

The damage they'd sustained to the nose of the ship had been expected and planned for. Without Emissary

McQueen's cunning to help the aliens adapt to Sterling's unconventional tactics, the Sa'Nerra had done exactly what he'd expected them to. He was banking on that predictability in order to pull off his next move.

The ship was rocked again, forcing Sterling to tighten his hold on his console to avoid losing balance. More sections of his damage-control board turned red.

"Explosive decompressions on decks three and four, sections fourteen and fifteen," Razor called out. "Emergency bulkheads are in place, but they're punching though, sir."

"Steady as she goes," Sterling answered, pointing to Ensign One. The machine's glowing ocular units pierced the crimson gloom of the CIC, like headlights on full beam. *Just a little further...* Sterling thought, watching the positions of the two combat groups to either side. The Vanguard had already nearly slipped through. *Just a little further...* Then Sterling saw their range-to-target reach the mark he needed to initiate his plan, and he thumped his fist onto his console. "Ensign One, execute maneuver Blitzkrieg, now, now, now!"

"Aye, sir, all ahead flank," Ensign One replied, the robot's voice conveying its own unique brand of excitement and eagerness.

"Shutting down power to decks one through six and eleven though seventeen, bar non-essential sections," Razor reported. Sterling's XO had turned temporary engineer again and was working at a secondary station configured with key engineering controls. "Rerouting all available power to main engines and weapons."

Sterling felt the kick of the Vanguard's colossal engines and was again forced to grip his console to negate the effects. The sudden surge of acceleration was immediate and took the alien ships completely by surprise. Not even McQueen could have predicted the unfeasibly rapid rate of acceleration the Vanguard was now capable of, and it was clear none of the enemy commanders had done so either. The bulk of the Sa'Nerran forces were now slipping rapidly to their rear, leaving only the Hammer, MAUL and its six escorts between Sterling and the alien planet itself.

"Engines at one-forty over standard!" Razor called out. The thrum of power surging thorough the conduits around them was nearly deafening. "The enemy squadron to our rear is trying to pursue, but based on their acceleration curves, they won't catch us."

Sterling punched his console again and shook his fist triumphantly. However, he didn't want to cry out as Banks would have done, by releasing a jubilant whoop to signify their success. Their plan had worked, but there was still a lot of metal between the Vanguard and its target.

Sucking in a deep breath in an attempt to curb his enthusiasm, Sterling opened a comm-link to the Bismarck and the Invictus, then cleared his throat.

"Captain Fletcher, Captain Banks, keep those alien bastards off our ass," Sterling said, as the rattle through the deck from the beat of their engines became seismic. "Protect our engines at all costs. So long as we can stay ahead of the pack, the remaining ships between the Vanguard and the planet won't be able to stop us."

"Aye sir, moving in now," Banks replied.

On a monitor feed, Sterling saw the Invictus swoop in behind the Vanguard and obliterate an alien light cruiser with a single shot. The Marauder was soon surrounded by Obsidian ships, all unleashing plasma at the alien vessels desperately trying to chase the dreadnaught down.

"We're struggling to keep pace with you Commodore," said Fletcher's voice, sounding cracklier and more distant over the comm-link. "Permission to pull back and take care of the stragglers."

Sterling checked his tactical display. Several squadrons of Sa'Nerran warships had broken off in an attempt to get behind the Invictus.

"Permission granted, Captain," Sterling said, glowering at the red chevrons that were targeting his old ship. "Give the Invictus as much cover as you can."

"You got it, Commodore. Bismarck out."

The comm-link from the old Destroyer clicked off and Sterling saw the Bastion Navy ships reposition themselves to take on the alien forces to their rear. It wasn't what Sterling had planned, but as long as the Obsidian Ships could keep the enemy off their tail for long enough, it didn't matter.

"The plan appears to be working well, sir," Ensign One said, turning to face the command stations. The robot's voice was bright and cheerful and instantly reminded Sterling of his quirky gen-fourteen AI.

"So far... so long as you haven't just jinxed it, anyway," Sterling replied, half watching his status indicators, expecting an engine to blow out or a reactor to fail as a result of his robot officer's comment.

"Superstition is a uniquely human trait and one that I find fascinating," Ensign One replied. "However, I can assure you that referring to one's fortunes in favorable terms will not cause those fortunes to reverse, as if through the act of a malicious god."

Sterling's consoles them chimed an alert. Moments later, Lieutenant Razor's console registered the same, strident tone.

"You were saying, Ensign?" Sterling said, casting his eyes down to his screens.

"MAUL and all six cruisers have begun to accelerate toward us, sir," Razor said, beating Sterling to the analysis.

"What about the Hammer?" Sterling asked. He was more concerned about their sister ship than the alien cruisers or MAUL.

"It has held position, sir," Razor replied, sounding confused by the alien's sudden tactical shift. "Correction, it is advancing, but slowly. It doesn't make sense."

"Let them come, Lieutenant," Sterling said. He felt oddly buoyed by his officer's report. Instead of an unexpected catastrophe on the ship, the alert had brought good news. "By splitting up the forces ahead of the Vanguard, they're only making it easier for us. This way we can take out the cruisers before dealing with the Hammer."

"I don't think the cruisers are planning to attack," Razor said.

The XO's voice cut through Sterling's sense of optimism like a samurai sword. He quickly turned to Razor, feeling his mouth go dry as he did so.

"Explain, Lieutenant, and make it quick," Sterling said,

"I'm not sure I can, sir," Razor replied. She then worked her console and overlayed a feed of the approaching ships onto the viewscreen. "They're not in an attack formation. It's more like a convoy."

Sterling frowned at the image and the tactical analysis that was displayed to its side. "What the hell are they doing?" he wondered out loud, staring at the bizarre formation of ships.

The six Sa'Nerran cruisers had all lined up, one in front of the other, in a single long caravan with MAUL at the rear of the caravan, and the Hammer following further behind.

"I can't explain it, sir," Razor replied. "I've never seen anything like it."

"They intend to board us."

Sterling turned to Ensign One. The robot officer had swiveled its seat to face the command section.

"And just how the hell do you know that?" Sterling asked.

"I can hear the Hammer's AI," Ensign One replied, its ocular units flashing chaotically. "The Sa'Nerra have added failsafes and firewalls that are keeping me from infiltrating the system, but I can still hear it, like a whisper on the wind."

"That's very poetic, Ensign, but how about you tell me what you're hearing?" snapped Sterling. He chastised himself for losing his temper, but the last thing he needed at that moment was his quirky AI officer going off on a tangent.

"MAUL is using the cruisers as cover," the robot

answered, appearing to have taken no offence. "Then when it is close enough, it will break off and breach the starboard docking garage before we are able to destroy it."

Sterling cursed then peered at their sister ship, which was still meandering toward them, like a cocksure bully who had his quarry cornered without the possibility of escape.

"Time to impress me some more, Ensign," Sterling said, pointing at the dreadnaught on the viewscreen. "What's their play with the Hammer?"

"The Hammer is being deployed as their last line of defense, literally," Ensign One replied. "They are matching us move for move, blocking our path. They intend to force us to a standstill, knowing we will not ram the vessel. Then either they'll take the ship by force from the inside, or the Hammer will cripple us before we are within firing range of the planet."

Sterling cursed again and thumped the edge of his console with his bionic hand, cracking a small section of the panel.

"It's Wessel, it has to be," he said out loud, talking to himself more than in response to Ensign One. "The Sa'Nerra don't think like this. They'd stand and fight, rather than play chess and try to back us into a corner."

"What if we launched a spread of nuclear torpedoes at the Hammer now, and take it out before it's a problem?" Lieutenant Razor suggested.

Sterling shook his head. "The Hammer's point defense guns would take them out long before they were in range," he said. It was something he'd already considered and discounted during the mission planning stage. "If MAUL manages to breach the docking garage and deploy an assault force, how many warriors are we talking about?"

"At least a hundred," Razor replied, without delay. "But running flat out like this, we need the Obsidian crew at their stations. At most, we could spare perhaps a defense squad of ten or fifteen."

Sterling shook his head again. "That's not nearly enough," he replied, wracking his brain for another option. Then he had an idea. "Ensign, you said the Hammer was blocking our path, knowing we wouldn't ram them. Was that an assumption on your part, or did you hear that straight from the horse's mouth?"

"If by 'the horse's mouth', you mean the Hammer's stray and erratic thoughts, then yes, sir," Ensign One replied. "Their tactical analysis determined that you would not sacrifice the Vanguard, instead choosing to stand and fight."

"Then we'll do the exact opposite, Ensign," Sterling said, feeling his pulse race higher. "Calculate the maximum collision velocity that would allow us to maintain hull integrity and weapons control."

"Already done, sir," the machine replied. It then cocked its head to one side, its ocular units shining more brightly. "Are you planning to do what I believe you're planning to do, sir?"

Sterling stood tall and pressed his hands to the small of his back. "If you mean do I intend to ram the Hammer and drive that turned hunk of junk into the Sa'Nerran atmosphere, then yes, Ensign, you have it in one."

A BRIGHT FLARE of orange flame lit up the viewscreen as the third of six Sa'Nerran Battlecruisers fell victim to the Vanguard's main forward batteries. On Sterling's order, the Vanguard had already begun to brake hard, decelerating at the rate the Hammer would expect in order to avoid a head-on collision. However, at the last moment, Sterling intended to do the opposite of what their doppelgänger's ship-board artificial intelligence had predicted. He was going to ram the Hammer and bury the nose of the Vanguard so deep into the turned dreadnaught's metal guts that the two mighty vessels would be as one. Neither would be able to bring their weapons to bear on the other, and with MAUL out of the picture too, the Bastion Navy and the Obsidian Fleet would have the advantage over the remaining alien forces. It was an audacious plan and Sterling had no idea if it would succeed. However, the stakes could not have been higher, and Reeves knew that the higher the risk, the higher the reward.

Sterling opened a comm-link to the Invictus and the Bismarck, and waited for the connection to take hold. "Captain Banks, Captain Fletcher, I take it you've received your updated orders and our new attack plan?" Sterling said, as the forward batteries opened fire, obliterating the fourth alien cruiser.

"If you mean your crazy new idea to ram the Hammer, then I got them alright," Fletcher replied. "Are you sure you want to do this, Commodore?"

Sterling huffed a laugh. "No, but I don't see that we have a choice, Captain," he replied. Then before there was any opportunity for dissenting voices to question his decision, he quickly added, "and I'm also not interested in debating it. You have your orders and I expect you to carry them out."

"Message received loud and clear, Commodore," Fletcher said. "If I can't talk you out of it then I'll just wish you good hunting. We'll continue to keep the other ships off your back."

"Commodore, the Bastion Navy and the Obsidian Fleet can handle the remaining alien ships out here," Banks then cut in. "Permission to dock and join in with the defense of the Vanguard."

"Denied, Captain, you're my backup, remember, I need you out there," Sterling responded. The deafening silence told Sterling that his order had not gone down well. Then he realized that if the Obsidian crew weren't able to hold off the warriors, he would need backup of a different kind. "Stay close, though, Mercedes, in case we end up needing your particular brand of violence."

"Understood, Commodore," Banks replied, this time without even a millisecond of hesitation. "Clear me for the emergency docking collar in section thirteen and make sure it's ready. That way we can lock on and reach the CIC in only a few minutes."

"There might not be a section thirteen after we ram the Hammer, but understood," Sterling replied, inputting the commands as he was speaking. "Those warships are your priority though, Captain," he added, taking a sterner tone. "Protect our engines and keep those torpedo tubes open and clear."

"Understood, Commodore," Banks replied. There was another awkward pause. "And good hunting, Lucas. Give those bastards hell."

Instead of the 'hooah' level of enthusiasm that usually accompanied battle cries of this nature, Banks had given her encouragement a touch reticently. It was as if she wanted to say something else, but had settled for saying what was expected of her instead. Sterling was still contemplating a reply when the comm-link cut off, sparing him the need to respond with a similarly bullish statement. However, rather than being disappointed, Sterling was relieved. He could never find the right words in such situations, especially to Banks. It was simply better to say nothing at all.

"The final cruiser has been destroyed, sir," Lieutenant Razor called out, snapping Sterling back into the moment.

"Where's MAUL?" Sterling said, peering down at his scanners. Then he saw the alien vessel, powering toward the docking garage at breakneck speed. His damage control panel lit up, indicating that the hull had been breached. He half-expected to feel the impact of the Sa'Nerran Heavy Destroyer's crash landing. However, the persistent clatter and rumble of plasma weapons fire hammering the Vanguard's hull masked any additional tremors that MAUL's violent intrusion had generated.

"Obsidian robots are in position in the docking garage, sir," Razor reported. "Emergency bulkheads in place. The breach is sealed."

"Understood, Lieutenant," Sterling replied. "Though that's like suturing a gunshot wound with the bullet still inside the body," he added, while checking the entry points onto the CIC, expecting to see Obsidian crew guarding the doors. "Where the hell are our robot reinforcements?"

"En route, sir," Lieutenant Razor replied.

Sterling's XO then stumbled, and only managed to stop herself falling off her station by grasping the console at the last second. It was like she'd just been hit with a powerful wave of vertigo. Sterling had noticed that Razor was growing more frantic and unsteady with each passing second. He studied his XO more closely for a moment, seeing sweat dripping off her chin. Under the crimson alert lights, it looked like droplets of blood. He knew in his bones what the symptoms indicated, but hoped he was wrong.

"There will be ten Obsidian robots outside the CIC in less than sixty seconds, two for each entry point," Razor finally added, after confirming the information.

"Understood, Lieutenant," Sterling replied.

Quickly turning to his secondary console, Sterling switched one of the panels to a readout of Razor's neural condition. The report made for grim reading. Much like the Vanguard's damage control panel, the detailed image of his XO's neural interface was covered in red. Sterling was no expert, but even he could see that Razor's neural safeguards were on the verge of failing. As soon as that happened, his officer would begin to turn.

Sterling slid his hand onto the grip of his pistol, considering ending her right there and then. However, if he got just one or two more minutes of Lieutenant Katreena Razor's help, it was better than blowing her brains out now, he decided. The margin between success and failure was so narrow that even the smallest advantage might be enough to tip the scales in their favor.

Removing his hand from his weapon, Sterling returned to his primary console and focused on the viewscreen. It was like leaping from the frying pan and into the fire. Directly ahead of them was the Dreadnaught Hammer, torpedo ports open and plasma batteries glowing hot, ready to fire.

"We're in position, Commodore," Ensign One called out before shining its ocular units across the CIC to Sterling's console. "If we are to ram the Hammer, we must do so now."

"Then give me a full power burn, Ensign," Sterling called out as he stared down the gullet of his old ship. His conviction in his plan had not wavered. "It's time we reintroduced the Vanguard to its sibling."

"Aye, sir, full power burn initiated," Ensign One called out. Sterling felt the ferocious kick of the main engines as the dreadnaught put on a sudden burst of acceleration toward the Hammer.

"All hands, brace for impact!" Sterling called out, gripping the side of his console with all his strength.

The forward batteries of the Hammer fired and Sterling felt the impact rock the CIC. Consoles blew out and structural supports tumbled from above, smashing into stations that would ordinarily have been crewed by human Fleet officers. The damage-control panel lit up red, highlighting that the observation deck, their primary scanner array, and most of decks seven through twelve on the forward sections had been destroyed. If the Vanguard was fully-manned, hundreds of people would have died in the blast. However, all the Hammer had done was blunt their edge a little. There was nothing it could do to prevent what came next.

In idle moments, Sterling's curious and perhaps morbid mind had sometimes wondered what it would feel like to crash a ship the size of a dreadnaught into another vessel, or even a space station. Now he knew. The jolt of the impact was like driving a car into a stone wall. The shock stole the breath from his lungs and the next thing he knew he was flying through the air. He caught a brief glimpse of Ensign One, clinging to the helm control station like a limpet to a ship's hull, then his body hit the viewscreen.

Darkness overcame him and his mind was filled with a jumble of thoughts and images. He saw Ariel Gunn, standing headless in the command section of the Hammer. Then he saw himself, blasting a hole through the gut of Lana McQueen, and strangling Clinton Crow with his bare hands, before he was assaulted by a flash of light. The glare faded and he saw Earth being slowly consumed by the aperture singularity, accompanied by a background soundtrack of wails of misery and screams of pain. Finally, he saw Mercedes Banks, standing in front of him in his quarters, smiling in the way she always did when she saw him. Sterling raised his pistol and fired.

"No!"

"Commodore, what is your condition?" he heard a voice call out. Then he felt hands tightening around his arms and lifting him up.

"Mercedes..." Sterling mumbled, still half out of it. "I told you to stay clear. I don't want you here. I don't want you getting hurt..."

"Commodore, it is me, Ensign One." Sterling felt a pinprick of pain in his neck, which was followed by a sharp hiss. Suddenly, his vision cleared and the fog inside his head lifted.

"Ensign?" Sterling said, now seeing his robot officer clearly. The machine removed an injector from Sterling's neck and the device was folded back inside a concealed panel in the robot's forearm.

"I modified my frame to also contain several critical medical implements," Ensign One explained, releasing his hold on Sterling. "I thought it prudent, in case of eventualities such as this."

"Good work, Ensign," Sterling said, rubbing his neck around where the robot had pressed the injector. Despite having just been thrown across the CIC like a rag doll, the injection site hurt more than the rest of his aches and pains.

He then had a flashback to the moments before the robot had pumped him full of whatever concoction of drugs it had used. "About what I said before," he said, with embarrassment. "I was dazed and confused, and I didn't really know what I was saying..."

"No need to explain, Commodore," Ensign One said, cutting Sterling off mid-sentence. "Your awkwardness is unwarranted. I have known about your feelings for Captain Banks for some time. Perhaps, even longer than you have known about them yourself."

Sterling was struck dumb and for a moment, he just stood there staring at the machine as consoles crackled and conduits fizzed all around them. A girder fell from the ceiling and slammed into the deck, narrowly missing the helm control station. The resonant chime and powerful shock of the impact jolted Sterling back to his senses.

"Give me a status report, Ensign," he ordered, trying to forget about what his robot officer had said. In fact, he wished the machine hadn't said anything at all, because now his mind was again fogged up with thoughts and feelings that shouldn't be there.

"Structural integrity is at seventy-two percent and holding." The machine did not need to look at a console in order to relay this information. For all intents and purposes, Ensign One was the ship. "Our engines are still engaged and we are pushing the Hammer toward Sa'Nerra. The enemy dreadnaught was disabled during the collision. The Vanguard's primary scanner array was destroyed in the impact, but my limited personal scanners suggest that the Hammer's primary railgun battery overloaded at the point of impact. The resulting power surge was fed back through the ship, causing massive internal damage across all decks from sections thirteen to sixteen."

"That would include their CIC," Sterling said, wafting smoke away from his face from a burning circuit beneath the deck plate.

"Correct, sir," Ensign One replied. "It was a happy accident, at least for us. Not so much for the Sa'Nerra."

Sterling ignored the misplaced quip from the robot. The machine was becoming worse than Banks, he thought. Then he realized he'd yet to spot Lieutenant Razor in the wreckage.

"Have you seen Razor?" Sterling said, pushing through the rubble in search of his XO and engineer.

"I'm here, sir..." came a weak voice from close to the executive officer's station.

Sterling jumped over the wreckage littering the deck and ran to his XO's side. Even before he'd managed to pull the mass of wires and debris off his officer's body, it was clear she was badly hurt.

"Easy, Lieutenant," said Ensign One, also helping Razor to stand with surprising gentleness, considering the machine's rugged appearance. "Your left forearm is fractured in three places, and you have several deep lacerations to the head and upper back."

"Will she live, Ensign?" Sterling said, helping Razor back to her station with far less care than the machine had taken.

"The injuries are not life-threatening," Ensign One

replied, as Razor resumed her post, using her console as a crutch.

"Then brace the arm, pump her full of whatever you shot me up with, and let's get back to work," Sterling said. He drew his pistol and checked the entrances to the CIC, two of which had collapsed during the collision. "Where the hell are those Obsidian robots?" he added angrily, noticing that the corridors outside appeared to be unguarded.

"The ship sustained several major hull breaches during the impact with the Hammer," Ensign One said, injecting Lieutenant Razor with its own special concoction of stimulants and painkillers. "Thirty-six Obsidian crew were blown into space, and a further twenty-seven were destroyed as sections of the ship collapsed onto them."

Sterling cursed. "How many do we have left?"

"I am picking up signals from nine Obsidian crew," Ensign One replied. It then stowed the medical injector and reconfigured its hand, revealing the upgraded plasma cannons it had installed on the Omega Base. "They have engaged the enemy. The fighting has reached deck nine, section twelve."

Sterling felt his stomach churn. "That's the section directly before the CIC," he said, tightening his grip on his pistol. "How many warriors survived the crash and the impact?"

Ensign One's ocular units flashed then the machine turned to Sterling, dimming its eyes at it did so. "I am detecting movement from an additional twenty-five contacts, sir," the machine replied. "All are heading this way."

Sterling didn't need the mathematical genius of his sentient AI officer to know that the numbers were not good. However, it didn't need saying, and he saw no reason to comment. Whether there were ten or a hundred Sa'Nerra moving on the CIC made no difference. They would make their stand, either way.

"Get into cover and prepare to defend the CIC," Sterling said, moving over to his captain's console and ducking low behind it. "No matter what happens, we have to hold this position until we're within torpedo range of the planet, is that clear?"

"Aye, sir," Ensign One replied, moving into cover with a speed and dexterity that belied its size.

"Aye, sir," said Lieutenant Razor, pulling her pistol from its holster and aiming it at one of the doors. Her aim wavered, like she was drunk. It was clear to Sterling that his XO was going to be little more than an additional target for the Sa'Nerra to aim at, but he couldn't afford to pull her off the line. He needed every gun, no matter how ineffective they might be.

Sterling knew he needed more soldiers, and he also knew there was only one place he could get them. As much as he didn't want Mercedes Banks on the ship with him, he now had no choice. He sucked in a deep breath then tapped his neural interface in an attempt to reach out to Banks, but the connection would not form. Closing his eyes, he concentrated on her face, shutting out the noise of the ship falling apart around him.

"Mercedes, I need you," Sterling said, pushing the thought out into the ether in the hope she would detect it. "If you can hear this, I need you now," he added, before the pressure of trying to form the connection became too great and he had to let go.

Sterling didn't know whether the neural message had gotten through. And even if it had, he didn't know if the Invictus could dock and its crew reach the CIC before they were all dead. Then plasma blasts started to filter in through the ruptured walls and smashed doorways of the CIC, and Sterling realized it didn't matter anyway. He was already out of time.

An Obsidian robot came crashing through the main egress to the CIC then tumbled from the upper level to the main deck below. Moments later, a warrior stormed through the opening, armed with a plasma rifle that looked twice as big and twice as mean as any weapon he'd seen the aliens use before. The warrior's armor was also a heavier version of the traditional armor that the Sa'Nerra wore. Whatever this soldier was, it was clearly a rung above the regular alien grunts that Sterling was used to fighting.

"Defend the CIC!" Sterling called out, swinging the barrel of his plasma pistol toward the alien. He was about to fire when a powerful burst of plasma raced out from behind him and obliterated the alien, turning it into a smoldering stain on the wall. He glanced across and saw Ensign One, smoke wisping from the cannons built into his arms. The robot was in combat mode and Sterling knew he would need every bit of its fighting prowess if they were going to survive.

Seven Obsidian soldiers then backed in to the CIC from the corridors outside, each of them already heavily damaged. The ocular units of the robots were all glowing with the same orange hue as Ensign One's eyes, as if the sentient AI had taken direct control of the machines.

"I have organized the remaining Obsidian crew to protect the port and starboard egresses," Ensign One said. "Together, we must hold the main entrance on the upper level."

"Understood, let's move," Sterling replied, setting off toward the stairwell to the upper level.

However, he'd barely taken a single step forward before two more warriors pushed in through the main egress, driving back the Obsidian crew that were defending the corridor outside. To his surprise, the heavily-armored aliens were fighting the robots hand-to-hand. Sterling watched as the lead warrior overpowered its mechanical foe then hammered the machine with the stock of its rifle, crushing its cranial section with frightening ease.

Sterling fired, striking the Sa'Nerran fighter cleanly in the chest section of its armor. The warrior staggered back but then hissed and regained its balance. Besides a scorch mark to its heavy chest plate, the warrior was unhurt. Sterling fired again with the same effect then ducked into cover as the warrior returned fire with its rifle, obliterating the console he was hiding behind.

"Ensign!" Sterling called out, covering his head as smoldering panels and smashed circuits tumbled over him.

Sterling felt a hard thump rattle through the deck, followed by the waspish hiss of an alien warrior in pain. He chanced a look over the smashed console and saw that Ensign One was already on the upper level. How it had got there so quickly, Sterling had no idea. However, now that his robot officer was withing striking distance of the heavy warriors, the dynamic had changed in an instant.

Smashing the rifle from the lead warrior's grasp, Ensign One punched the barrel of its left cannon into the alien's face and fired. The blast exploded the warrior's head like corn popping in a frying pan before continuing along the corridor and striking the second warrior to its rear. The blast still had enough energy to melt the armor around the warrior's shoulder and the alien hissed in pain. However, the shot had not been enough to kill the warrior; only incapacitate it.

Ensign One brushed off the headless body of the first warrior then surged forward, hammering the heel of its foot into the alien's chest. The thick armor plating buckled, crushing the warrior's sternum like the shell of an egg. The alien's eye's bulged wider and blood oozed from its mouth before the warrior collapsed to the deck, gasping for air.

Confident that his robot officer could hold the fort for the time being, Sterling turned to his XO. No matter how critical her implant was, he still needed her gun if they were going to win the fight.

"Lieutenant, you're with me," Sterling called out as he continued toward the stairwell. Razor nodded and tried to push away from the console, but her legs immediately gave way.

"I'm ready, sir, I just need a moment," Razor said, appearing angry at her own fragility.

Sterling checked the computer built into his armor and examined Razor's neural status. She was still in the red, but stable. It wasn't the neural corruption that was crippling her, he realized, but her injuries.

"Defend the CIC from your post, Lieutenant, and prepare to fire the torpedoes," Sterling said, realizing his XO lacked the strength to follow him. Even so, a half-dead Lieutenant Razor was better than an all-dead one. "Keep the tube doors closed until we're within range. We don't want to tip off the Sa'Nerra to our plan."

"Aye, sir," Razor said, practically collapsing back onto her console.

Sterling left his officer and ran up the stairs, reaching Ensign One's side. The robot was firing cannon blasts through the main egress, holding back warriors that Sterling couldn't yet see. Then blasts flashed past in the opposite direction and the robot was hit in the leg. The new alien rifle was powerful enough to punch through Ensign One's armor and the robot staggered off-balance and moved into cover.

"How bad is it, Ensign?" Sterling said, peeking around the corner and firing his pistol along the corridor. Two blasts struck an advancing warrior, but as before it only appeared to piss off the alien, rather than do any damage.

"My mobility is reduced, but I am functional," Ensign One replied.

The officer then fired another blast along the corridor, melting the face of the warrior Sterling had just angered. However, the gruesome death of their comrade did not appear to deter the other aliens waiting in the wings.

Sterling tossed the plasma pistol and picked up one of the alien heavy plasma weapons. The rifle was even more cumbersome than a Homewrecker, but from what he'd seen of it so far, it was at least as effective.

"Cover me for a moment, please," Ensign One said, ducking back into cover.

Sterling nodded then moved out and fired the alien rifle. The kick of the weapon was as savage as the Fleet equivalent, and the result was just as destructive. The first few shots flew wide as Sterling struggled to control the rifle, blasting holes into the corridor walls. Plasma flashed back in the opposite direction, melting the deck inches in front of him. His next shot stuck true, blasting the leg of an advancing warrior off at the knee. Sterling held the trigger and obliterated another warrior to its rear, melting a deep crater in its gut, as if a beast had bitten a chunk out of the alien's midsection. Sterling pulled back into cover, as much to rest his aching arms and shoulders as to avoid incoming fire. Then he saw that Ensign One had modified one of its hands into a multi-tool and was repairing its injured leg. The robot worked with dizzying speed and was combat-ready again before Sterling had even regained his breath.

"Commodore!"

Sterling recognized the shout as coming from the voice of Lieutenant Razor. He spun around to the XO's station and saw Razor slumped over the console, aiming her pistol toward the port egress. She fired two lazy shots and Sterling followed the blasts. The Obsidian crew that had been defending the entrance point were being driven back and Sterling could see that warriors had already gotten inside the CIC. He swung the alien rifle over the railings and opened fire, killing one of the warriors instantly before return fire forced him back. Suddenly, blasts were being hammered all around him and Sterling was forced to hit the deck in a desperate attempt to avoid the onslaught. Ensign One opened fire again, pulverizing four heavy warriors before the aliens had even seen the robot move out of the shadows. Sterling forced himself up and shifted position to get a clear view of the corridor outside. More warriors were gathering, but there was no sign of the Obsidian crew defenders.

"Ensign, they're coming through the port egress, get down there," Sterling called out to his AI officer.

The robot responded instantly, leaping over the railings and thudding to the main deck below. Sterling then spun around and began firing into the roof supports of the corridor on the upper level, holding the trigger until the entire section collapsed, sealing off the entrance. The weapon's cell ran empty and Sterling cursed, tossing the alien rifle down.

"I'm out," Sterling shouted as Ensign One thudded blasts at the port egress in an attempt to deter the aliens from trying to break through.

Sterling searched the rubble, looking for another weapon then saw one resting on the stairwell below. The severed arm of a heavy warrior was still clutching the rifle, as if the alien had refused to give up its weapon even in death. Scrabbling toward it, Sterling was then hit to chest the chest by a stray blast of plasma. It was only a glancing shot but it still spun him a full one hundred and eighty degrees, and he landed hard in a mass of melting wires and smashed panels. Touching his fingers to the wound he saw blood coat his bionic hand, but he was still alive and that was all that mattered. Crawling to the alien rifle, he began to prise the warrior's dead fingers from the weapon when more blasts raced into the CIC. He drew back, covering his head then saw Ensign One take a hit square to the chest. The robot went down hard, but from where he was, Sterling couldn't see if his officer was destroyed or merely disabled. Then the computer on his forearm chimed an alert. He found what little cover he could and read the screen. His heart thumped harder in his chest as he saw they were finally within striking range of the planet.

"Lieutenant, open the torpedo doors and initiate launch program!" Sterling yelled at the top of his lungs. There was no answer. Cursing, Sterling crawled further toward the edge of the upper level, risking being hit in order to check on his XO. He saw Razor at her console, staring into space as if she was in a trance. "Razor, launch the damned torpedoes!" Sterling yelled again.

This time the white-haired executive officer of the Vanguard turned and met Sterling's eyes. She raised her pistol and aimed it at him

"For Sa'Nerra!"

Sterling pushed himself back into cover as blasts from Razor's pistol rained down around him. Pulling the screen closer to his face, he switched to the readout of his XO's neural implant then squeezed his eyes shut and banged his forehead against the screen. The safeguards had failed - Razor had been turned. With blasts still hammering into the deck and walls all around him, Sterling quickly tapped the sequence of commands to enable the kill switch in Razor's brain. He could have activated it immediately, but he wanted to look his officer in the eye as he took her life. It may no longer have been Katreena Razor staring back at him, but he owed her that much. Perhaps that was mawkish sentimentality, he thought, as he crawled closer to the edge of the level, risking death in order to get a final look at his XO and engineer. Razor was still at her station and still firing at him. A blast skimmed past his head, but Sterling didn't flinch. He locked eyes with Lieutenant Razor then hit the command on his computer. Razor suddenly became rigid as if the deck plating beneath her feet had become charged. Her mouth frothed and her unique, shimmering eyes began to weep tears of blood. Then she fell, smashing the side of her face against the XO's console and smearing it with fresh blood, before landing in a heap on the deck.

"It has been an honor, Lieutenant," Sterling said, forcing down a dry, hard swallow.

Sterling then once again reached for the alien weapon, still held in the clutches of the dead warrior's grasp, and tried to drag it closer. As he was about to gain control of the weapon, the blasts all stopped and the CIC fell silent. All that was left was the thump of blood in Sterling's ears. He finally managed to wrap his fingers around the alien weapon when a shadow crept over him and a boot landed on his bionic hand, jamming it to the deck. Sterling looked up and saw the face of Praetor Wessel staring down at him, a smug, superior smile curling the man's lips.

STERLING WAS HAULED to his feet by two heavy warriors and slammed against the wall as Praetor Wessel looked on. More warriors then stormed the CIC and hurriedly took up positions at what remained of the Vanguard's stations. The Praetor hissed commands at the warriors and they immediately set to work, trying to commandeer the ship. Sterling smiled as he watched the long, leathery fingers of the aliens operate the consoles. He knew that no matter what they tried, the Vanguard would never respond to the inputs of a Sa'Nerran.

"You're wasting your time," Sterling said, addressing Wessel directly. "The Vanguard can't be turned. It only answers to me."

Wessel's smug smirk fell off his face and he stepped closer to Sterling. "Then you will order this vessel to stop and turn command over to me," the Praetor glowered at Sterling with contempt.

"Kiss my ass, Wessel," Sterling hit back before spitting

in the Praetor's face. "You know I'll die before I do a damned thing you ask."

Wessel wiped the spittle from his eye then his hand flew, striking Sterling hard across the side of his face. His skin burned and jaw throbbed from the impact, but he was careful not to show any pain. Whatever the Praetor had to throw at him, he could take it, and more.

"Is that all you've got?" Sterling said, glowering at the turned traitor with contempt. "Even your pissant son managed to put up a better fight."

Wessel's eyes narrowed at the mention of Vernon Wessel. Sterling saw the reaction and knew the remark had registered somewhere in the recesses of the man's memory. Despite being turned and brainwashed to believe the Sa'Nerran dogma, Wessel was still human.

"It's a shame how he died," Sterling went on, continuing to taunt the man. "I would have preferred to have strangled the life out of him personally, as I did Emissary Crow, or blasted a hole in him like I did to Emissary McQueen." He then shrugged. "But dead is dead, so I suppose I can't complain."

Wessel's hand flew again, striking Sterling even faster and harder than the first blow. Sterling could feel that he'd been cut and he could taste blood in his mouth. A tooth rolled onto his tongue and he spat it out. Just another piece of detritus to add to the wreckage already littering the CIC of the Fleet Dreadnaught Vanguard.

"I suppose such stout defiance is no more than I should expect from a mighty Omega Captain," Wessel said, appearing to have regained some of his composure. The man then slowly removed a neural control weapon from his armor. Wessel activated the device while smiling at Sterling, then held the weapon next to his neural implant. "But soon, you will be just another human drone, doing my bidding."

Sterling laughed. "You just don't get it do you?" he said, shaking his head at the Praetor. "You talk as if you're one of them, but you're just a puppet like all the others you've turned. Emissary, Aide, Praetor... it doesn't make a damned bit of difference. The only word that applies is traitor, because that's what you are."

"Oh no, Commodore, I'm afraid it's you who doesn't understand," Wessel snapped, grabbing Sterling's jaw and pulling his face closer. "But you will. Soon, this will all be over, and humanity will finally fall."

"Do it then," Sterling said, willing Wessel on. "We'll see whose will is stronger..."

Sterling suddenly had an idea. It was clear that the Praetor was unaware of the neural firewall technology that had been installed into his implant. He would play the role of "turned drone" once again, just as he had done to fool Emissary McQueen. Then when Wessel released him, Sterling would play his part for just long enough to launch the nuclear torpedoes at Sa'Nerra.

At least I'll get to see Wessel's face as his shithole adopted planet is bombarded and turned to dust, Sterling thought. It was as good a death as he could now hope for, he realized.

Wessel pressed the neural control device to the side of Sterling's head and Sterling felt the weapon latch on. The sensation of discomfort was the same as he remembered from when McQueen had tried to turn him, but the outcome was the same. Sterling was immune to its controlling influence.

Wessel stood back; the smug smile had returned to the man's face. "Not long now, Commodore," Wessel said, folding his arms across his chest. "Soon, you will be my aide."

Sterling began to recreate the ruse that had deceived McQueen, allowing his body to go stiff and his eyes to glaze over. The temptation was to turn quickly, but he knew he couldn't rush it. Everything had to appear natural. Wessel had to be fully sold on the deception before the Praetor would allow the warriors to release their iron grip on him. He waited a little longer, pretending to fight the weapon before allowing his face to go limp and appear vacant. Then he locked his blank eyes onto the Praetor.

"For Sa'Nerra," Sterling intoned.

Wessel smiled then nodded to the two heavy warriors, both of whom immediately released Sterling's arms.

"Now, Aide Sterling, shall we begin?" Wessel said, indicating toward the captain's console. His command station had remained intact, despite the dozens of plasma blasts that had flashed across the CIC during the fight.

Sterling fought hard to control his emotions and the swell of excitement that was building inside him. He had to maintain the act. Even a flicker of the real Lucas Sterling showing through his mask might be enough to alert Wessel. Turning on the spot, Sterling took steady paces toward the command station in the center of the CIC. His pace was deliberate and unhurried; his eyes and expression still blank.

Wessel continued to smile as Sterling reached the side of the console and placed a boot on the raised the platform, ready to step up. Then the unmistakable hiss of an alien warrior cut across the room. However, this was a deeper, coarser rasp than the sound the other warriors made. Sterling had heard it before, but only once, while he was on-board the Sa'Nerran Battle Titan. He chanced a look toward the source of the hiss and saw the Sa'Nerran Imperator standing in the threshold of the door.

"Hold," said Wessel, raising a hand to Sterling.

The two heavy warriors moved behind Sterling and drew serrated blades from their armor. Sterling froze in the same position, one boot on the platform and one off. He was almost within touching distance of the controls, but the distance may as well have been a light year.

The Sa'Nerran Imperator marched onto the CIC and stood in front of the command station, its cloudy and marble-patterned yellow eyes fixed onto the Sterling. Wessel bowed his head to the alien leader and the warrior hissed in the unfathomable Sa'Nerran language.

"The Imperator wishes to know how you survived the encounter with Emissary McQueen," Wessel said, turning back to Sterling.

Sterling felt his heart thump harder in his chest. *Why the hell is the Imperator asking me questions now?* he wondered as the alien leader moved closer. The Vanguard and Hammer were still on a collision course for the planet. It made no sense to stop Sterling from transferring control of the vessel to Wessel. *Unless the bastard suspects me?* he thought, trying not to meet the warrior's eyes.

"Emissary McQueen allowed her personal feelings for Sterling to interfere with her mission," Sterling replied, speaking in low, monosyllabic tones, like a gen-thirteen AI. However, he was confident his answer would pass muster with the Praetor at least. It had the benefit of being both plausible and, in fact, the truth.

The Imperator stepped onto the command platform and drew a serrated, half-moon blade from its armor. The weapon was the same design as the other blades Sterling had seen and used himself, but the grip looked as weathered and old as the Imperator itself.

"The Imperator wishes to know how it was that none of your crew were turned while seizing this vessel," the Praetor said, translating another string of hisses from the alien leader.

"Several of the Invictus crew were turned," Sterling replied, trying to keep his voice calm and level. "However, Sterling executed each of them."

"Several?" Wessel repeated, scowling at Sterling. "That is not a sufficient answer."

"Five crew were turned and executed," Sterling said. He felt like punching himself in the face. His answer had been vague. Turned humans were never anything less than precise in their answers. The process of Sa'Nerran neural control left no room for ambiguity. You either knew the answer or you did not.

The Sa'Nerran Imperator took another step toward Sterling. The warrior was now so close he could smell the creature. It reeked of rot and decay, as if it was being eaten from the inside out. He clenched his teeth and stared ahead, trying to ignore both the nauseating stench and repulsive proximity of the warrior. Then the Imperator reached up with its gloved hand and touched Sterling's forehead before slowly drawing its long finger across his brow, scraping the sweat from his skin like a razor blade cutting beard hairs. Sterling remained motionless, but now his heart was beating so hard it hurt. The Imperator pressed its sweat soaked finger to its lips and tasted it, as if the alien had dipped its finger in a pot of honey in order to sample the sweet nectar inside.

Sterling didn't know what the Imperator was doing, and after the bizarre ritual he'd just witnessed, he was increasingly unwilling to find out. He considered tackling the alien and making a dash for the controls, but even if he could overpower the Imperator, the two heavy warriors to his rear would pull him away before he could launch the torpedoes. He wracked his brain for another answer, but the truth was he was trapped. All he could do was hope that the Imperator's curiosity would soon be satisfied, and that it would depart while remaining unaware of his deception.

"The Imperator wishes you to draw blood," Praetor Wessel said.

Each of Wessel's words hit like a needle being pressed into Sterling's eyes. He swallowed hard as the Imperator slowly raised its blade and held it out to Sterling. Not knowing what else to do, he took the weapon and gripped it as firmly as he could manage.

"Use the blade to remove one of your fingers," Wessel continued as the Praetor took a single step back. "The Imperator desires a display of loyalty and obedience."

Knowing that any hesitation could give him away, Sterling stepped up to the captain's console and rested his left hand flat onto the panel. Curling all but his little finger into a fist, he then placed the alien blade across his knuckle, clenched his teeth and pressed down hard. The blade was razor sharp and sliced through his flesh like butter, but the pain was still excruciating. Sterling could feel his body shaking, but he fought back the tremors and stood tall, blood leaking from the stump like ink from a broken fountain pen. His finger remained on the console, mere inches away from the control panel that would allow Sterling to launch the torpedoes. The Imperator's yellow eyes then flicked across to Wessel and it hissed again.

"Very good, Aide Sterling," said Wessel, a smile again curling the former admiral's lips. Then the Praetor began a slow, sarcastic hand-clap and Sterling knew that he'd just failed the test he had been subjected to. "Only a mighty Omega Captain could do what you have done with such ease and composure." Wessel then stopped clapping. The smug, self-satisfied smile fell away and was replaced by a shadowy, malevolent glare. "But self-mutilation is nothing compared to what you are truly capable of, isn't that right, Commodore Sterling?"

Realizing he had been exposed, Sterling swung the alien blade at the Imperator, knowing it might be his only chance to strike down the alien leader. Incredibly, the old warrior caught Sterling's hand, displaying nimble reflexes that belied the alien's advanced years. Sterling twisted his body and punched the alien across its jaw with his bleeding left hand, but it was like striking granite. Sterling struck the old warrior again, smearing his blood across its face, yet still the Imperator didn't flinch. Even more bizarrely, none of the heavy warriors rushed to their leader's aide. All of them, including Praetor Wessel, just watched, as if standing to attention at a ceremony. Yet whatever the reason for the aliens' inexplicable behavior, Sterling knew it still gave him a chance.

Grabbing the handle of the weapon with his other hand for extra power, Sterling pushed harder, trying to force the blade into the Imperator's flesh. However, even with the added strength of his bionic hand, he still couldn't overpower the warrior.

Suddenly, the Imperator struck Sterling to the body with such force that he felt his armor crack, along with his ribs directly beneath it. A second blow stole the air from his lungs and moments later the Imperator had disarmed him, taking the blade back into the grasp of its own leathery fingers.

"You can kill me, but you'll still die," Sterling snarled, spitting blood onto the Imperator's boots. "You can't stop this ship from plummeting into your planet's atmosphere. And you can't escape before it does."

The heavy warriors all flinched as the red fluid smeared the top of their leader's boots and oozed down the side, but still none of them intervened. The Imperator then grabbed Sterling by the throat and lifted him, forcing Sterling to rise to the tips of his toes.

"Then... we... both... die..." the old warrior said, hissing the words slowly and carefully in Sterling's own language.

Drawing its blade back, the leader of the Sa'Nerra then thrust the serrated edge into Sterling's chest plate. The weapon penetrated the dense shell as effortlessly as slicing bread. Sterling felt the sting of pain as the serrated edge cut into his flesh. Then with Sterling still held aloft, the Imperator drew the blade down, cutting open his armor like a can-opener and carving a long, deep gash into Sterling's chest and stomach. This time Sterling could not help but cry out. He had resisted showing his enemy any pain – any weakness – but he simply couldn't keep a lid on the agony any longer.

The old warrior then slowly removed the blade, pulled Sterling closer and hissed into his face, so that he could taste the alien's rotten breath on his tongue.

"The Imperator says that now you will die," Praetor Wessel said, speaking like a judge that had just conveyed a death sentence on a prisoner in the dock.

The Imperator drew back its blade again, the alien's marbled, yellow eyes drilling into Sterling's with nightmarish intensity. Suddenly, flashes of plasma lit up the CIC and the heavy warriors to Sterling's side were hit, limbs and heads exploding like fireworks. Then the Imperator was struck to the back and the warrior dropped Sterling like a hot rock before ducking into cover. Sterling hit the deck hard and for a moment he was paralyzed with pain. He then looked for the Imperator, hoping that the warrior had perished, but saw the alien behind his captain's console. The Sa'Nerran leader's unique armor had absorbed the energy of the blast and protected it from harm. Cursing, Sterling pressed a hand to his wounds in an attempt to stem the bleeding then scrambled away from the Imperator, falling the short distance from the command platform to the deck below. Straight away, he saw Praetor Wessel, pistol in hand, firing toward the port egress. The former admiral spotted Sterling and Wessel's face twisted with rage. Sterling saw the weapon swing towards him and he braced himself to take a blast, but the flash of plasma never came. Instead, Wessel was hit to the chest and leg by two more blasts from the other side of the CIC. The Praetor fell, the weapon tumbling from his grasp as he did so. Sterling clawed himself toward the pistol and managed to hook his finger around the trigger guard and drag it closer. However, by the time he had the weapon in his grasp, Wessel had slunk away into the shadows and was gone.

"Oh no you don't, you traitorous piece of shit," Sterling spat at the flickering shadow of the man.

Dragging himself to his knees, Sterling went after Wessel, but was immediately confronted by a heavy warrior. The alien aimed it rifle at him, but Sterling had already fired on instinct, sending a blast of plasma into the warrior's face, melting its left eye like hot candle wax. The alien hissed wildly, but incredibly it did not give up its attack. Turning its remaining good eye to Sterling, it fired, blasting a hole in the deck inches to his left. Sterling also fired, but this time the blast sailed wide. Then the pain of the wound to his chest and stomach caused him to double-up in agony. The warrior recovered and once again Sterling found himself staring down the barrel of the alien rifle. There was flash of plasma and Sterling saw the head of the heavy warrior explode, showering him with blood and bone. Then another armored figure appeared, but this time it wasn't a Sa'Nerran heavy warrior. It was someone far more formidable and dangerous than even the Imperator itself. The figure standing before Sterling was Captain Mercedes Banks.

CHAPTER 28
A DIFFICULT CHOICE

Seeing Mercedes Banks in the CIC caused an overwhelming swell of relief to wash over Sterling's entire body. It felt like a powerful narcotic had just been injected directly into his veins, immediately taking away the pain. Despite the fact he was seriously wounded, and despite the fact they were still on the brink of defeat, he couldn't help but smile at her.

Banks' expression initially mirrored Sterling's own, but then her eyes drew themselves down across his body and her expression hardened like diamond. Her concern for his wellbeing was obvious, but most of all what Sterling saw in Banks' eyes was rage. It was a rage that Sterling knew could not be contained for long. Soon Banks would explode with the force of a nuclear torpedo, and the focus of her wrath would be the creature responsible for Sterling's injuries. Despite his own condition and the pain and humiliation he'd suffered at the wrinkled hands of the Imperator, Sterling almost felt sorry for the alien. Almost.

Suddenly, a harsh, rasping hiss filled the CIC and Sterling saw the Imperator charge out from behind the captain's console. However, the alien's target was not Mercedes Banks, but Lieutenant Commander Opal Shade. In his relief at seeing Banks alive, he hadn't spotted that Shade and two Obsidian crew had also entered the CIC along with the Captain of the Invictus.

The alien leader's blade flashed and Shade raised her rifle to block the blow. The clash of metal striking metal assaulted Sterling's eardrums, then he saw Shade stumble backward, the rifle she had been holding sliced in half. Had it been anyone other than Shade, Sterling would have expected them to be awed and terrified by the power of the strike, but Opal Shade was no ordinary woman. Without a flicker of hesitation, the Invictus' first officer drew her pistol and aimed it at the Imperator's head. The alien froze, then a shout filled the CIC, louder even than the clash of metal that had preceded it.

"Stop!"

Mercedes Banks turned away from Sterling and marched toward the Imperator.

"This one is mine," Banks snarled, handing Shade her Homewrecker plasma rifle before squaring off against the alien leader. "See to the Commodore. He's injured," Banks added, without taking her eyes of the Imperator.

Shade nodded, again not showing a flicker of hesitation. Like Sterling, Shade had seen the look in Banks' eyes before. They were the wild, feral eyes of a woman that had given herself over to savagery. In the entire time Sterling had known Banks, he had never seen any creature receive that look and live - not man, nor beast, nor alien.

Shade arrived at Sterling's side and handed her pistol to him before hurriedly cracking open an emergency medical kit. However, Sterling was oblivious to her work. His complete attention was focused on Mercedes Banks and the Sa'Nerran Imperator as they circled around one another, sizing each other up.

Suddenly, the Imperator hissed and attacked, again moving with a speed and fluidity that belied its age-worn appearance. The alien's razor-sharp blade flashed toward Banks, but she deflected it with her armored forearm then thumped a left hook into the Imperator's ribs. The warrior hissed and withdrew, its marbled yellow eyes still focused on Banks. Sterling could see that the Imperator's armor had been dented by the blow, but if it had caused the alien pain, it was not showing it.

The warrior attacked again, and again the blade flashed through the gloomy, crimson-lit interior of the CIC. The chime of metal striking metal rang out and sparks flew as Banks blocked the blows then pushed the alien back. Her counter-attack was swift and powerful, hammering her fist down across the alien's shoulder and crushing its ornate metal pauldron. The Imperator pulled itself free of Banks' grasp then connected with a ferocious backfist across the side of her face. Sterling's heart almost stopped as he then saw the alien blade being thrust toward her chest. Banks recovered in time to catch the warrior's forearm, but not before the blade had pierced Banks' armor. Sterling tried to get up and run to Banks' aid, but there was no strength left in his body. All he could do was watch.

Sensing victory, the Imperator drove Banks back toward the wall, intending to slam her into the metal and push the blade deeper. Banks roared and dug in her heels, battling the alien to a standstill. Then she pulled the blade from her chest and for the first time, Sterling saw a flicker of doubt in the alien's veined yellow eyes. With its weapon hand immobilized, the Imperator drove a punch into Banks body, cracking her armor. A second punch then snapped her head back, and again Sterling flinched. However, when Banks' eyes drew level with those of her enemy, Sterling knew it was all but over. Balling her hand into a fist, Banks twisted the Imperator's arm then smashed the alien's elbow with a strike that could have crushed concrete. The alien hissed wildly and the blade fell from its now limp arm. Banks roared again then drove her fist into the warrior's face, snapping its head backward like the tail of a whip. A second blow was accompanied by the nauseating crunch of bone, then a third crushed the Imperator's stub nose, causing thick crimson blood to pour from it.

The warrior tried to fight back, but this time its strikes landed with no effect. Banks clenched her fists together and hammered the alien across back of its neck, driving the Imperator to its knees. On any other Sa'Nerra the blow would have been fatal, but the alien leader clung to life, its yellow eyes clouded with blood and its face a mess of red.

Her eyes still wild, Banks wrapped her hand around a thick metal pipe; one of numerous items of debris littering the deck after the collision with the Hammer. She raised the weapon high above her head as the Imperator glared up at her, hissing blood from its narrow lips. Then with a single, colossal swing, Banks brought the bar down across the alien leader's skull, splattering blood, bone and brains across the deck and walls. For a moment, Banks merely stood in front of the mutilated remains of the alien leader, peering at its crushed skull, chest heaving from the exertion of her violent deeds. She then tossed the blood-stained pipe to the deck and turned to face Sterling. The fire in her eyes was fading and, unexpectedly, she smiled.

Then without warning, Praetor Wessel darted out from the shadows, catching Banks completely off-guard. Sterling called out, but it was already too late; Wessel had pressed a neural control device to the side of her head. Shade sprang into action, grabbing the Homewrecker and aiming it at Praetor Wessel. Then a flash of plasma raced across the CIC and struck her in the chest. Shade staggered backward then cartwheeled over the weapons control station, striking her head hard on the deck. Sterling pushed himself up, wincing due to the pain from his wounds, which Shade had partially tended to, and saw the woman lying motionless. Blood was leaking from a cut to her temple.

"What have you done!" Praetor Wessel roared, staring at the mutilated body of the Imperator with horrified eyes. The pistol that Wessel had used to shoot Shade was now pressed to the back of Banks head. "They will never forgive you for this! Never!" Wessel shrieked, raging at Sterling like a lunatic. "You don't know what you have done!"

"It's over, Wessel," Sterling said, cradling his injuries and pushing himself to his feet. He still had Lieutenant

Shade's plasma pistol in his bionic hand. "You can't stop what's about to happen. The Sa'Nerran homeworld will be destroyed."

Wessel shook his head wildly. "No, Commodore, not while I still have her!" Wessel jabbed the barrel of his pistol into the back of Banks' head.

The control device latched onto Banks' neural implant had already been activated. The effect was paralyzing and Banks appeared unable to fight back.

"You can't turn her, Wessel," Sterling spat. "We found a way to neutralize your neural weapon. That's why it didn't work on me."

"Lies!" Wessel spat. "I don't know how you resisted it, but your companion here will not. Then once she is mine, I will take this ship and use it to crush the rest of your fleet."

Suddenly, Sterling noticed that Banks' eyes were fearful and that she was shaking her head at him. The movements were almost imperceptible, due to the paralyzing effect of the device, but Sterling could see something was horribly wrong. He tapped his neural interface and opened a wide link, trying to reach his former first officer. Then he heard her voice in his mind.

"Lucas, I didn't get the firewall installed..." Sterling felt what little energy he had left suddenly bleed from his muscles like a battery going flat. "I was going to get it installed after you, but we got distracted and it slipped my mind. By the time we'd captured the Vanguard, Commander Graves was already dead. I'm sorry..."

"I'm sorry too," replied Sterling, tightening his grip around the handle of the pistol.

"It's okay, Lucas, I know what you have to do," Banks said, still speaking in Sterling's mind. "You can't let him turn me. I have your authorization codes. You have to do it."

Sterling raised the pistol and aimed it at the head of Mercedes Banks then slipped his finger onto the trigger. He looked into her eyes, but they were not afraid. Banks was an Omega Captain to the core. She was the strongest out of them. And in that moment, Sterling realized just how much stronger Banks was than himself, because he couldn't pull the trigger.

"Too much, Mercedes," Sterling said through their link. "I've given too much already. No more..."

Banks' eyes narrowed, clearly not understanding what Sterling meant, but it didn't matter whether she understood or not. Sterling knew what he had to do. It wasn't what he should have done. It wasn't the hard, and necessary call of an Omega Captain. It was a decision borne out of human emotion and sentiment. He knew it was the wrong choice, but he also knew he didn't care.

Tossing the pistol to the deck, Sterling summoned all his available strength and ran at Praetor Wessel. The eyes of the former Fleet admiral widened in terror as Sterling raced forward and hastily tore the neural interface from Banks head, crushing the device in his bionic hand. Then was a flash of plasma and Sterling felt the energy burn his flesh, but the pain was nothing like what he would have to endure if he'd forced himself to kill Mercedes Banks. He'd rather die, he realized, as he threw himself at Wessel, hands reaching for the man's neck. Perhaps that made him weak, after all, just as McQueen had said. If that was the case, he could live with it. Or die with it. What came next was now out of his control. What he did now was all that mattered, and right now he was choking the life out of Praetor Wessel.

Pressing down with all his weight, Sterling tightened his hold around Wessel's throat, digging his fingers into his flesh. Blood poured from the wounds to his chest that had reopened during the fall, covering the Praetor's face with a crimson mask. Sterling's bionic fingers penetrated deeper, rupturing blood vessels and crushing Wessel's esophagus. Then his own strength departed and he tumbled off the Praetor's body, collapsing onto his back at the man's side as Wessel slowly choked on his own blood.

Sterling's eyes began to darken and he felt lightheaded. Death was coming, he realized, and he was not afraid. Others remained who could finish the mission, launching the nuclear torpedoes and devastating the home of the aliens who had taken so much from humanity. With his last breath, he would spit at the Sa'Nerra and die happy, knowing that Mercedes Banks would live on.

THERE WAS a bright flash of light then Sterling found himself standing in the CIC of the Fleet Dreadnaught Hammer. It was his watch and he was at the captain's console, peering out at a bright blue planet on the viewscreen.

"How long has it been since you were last back?" asked Commander Ariel Gunn. Sterling glanced across to his left and saw her smiling at him. "On Earth, I mean. How long?"

Sterling shrugged. "To be honest, I have no idea," he admitted, as Australia started to swing into view. "Long enough that I can't remember."

"It's good to get back there," Gunn said, turning her head so she could also see the planet. "It helps to remind you what we're fighting for."

"I thought you resented Fleet and the war?" Sterling said, raising an eyebrow at his friend. Unlike Sterling, Gunn had been conscripted into service against her will.

"I resent not having had a choice," Gunn replied, her

tone gaining a slightly more acidic bite. "I don't resent why. I'm not a pacifist, Lucas!"

Sterling huffed a laugh. "Well, considering what we're out here to do, that's a relief," he said, returning her smile.

Then Gunn pointed to the viewscreen and met Sterling's eyes again. "That little blue ball is important, Lucas. It's worth fighting for," she went on, becoming more introspective. "We just have to be careful that we don't lose ourselves along the way. Because if we do, the Earth we fought for won't recognize the people who come back from this war."

"It doesn't matter what happens to us, so long as win, Ariel," Sterling hit back. "We're a means to an end, nothing more."

"Speak for yourself," Gunn said, huffily. "I'm not letting this war change me. There's more to life than the command center of this ship, Lucas."

Sterling continued to smile at Gunn, but he didn't respond. This was a conversation they'd had many times before, and it was one that usually ended in an argument. As such, it was best left to when they were off duty. Not that arguing with Gunn would change her mind, Sterling realized. She was entitled to her opinion, but it was one Sterling didn't share. Whether Gunn liked it or not, their lives were already forfeit. It was the future they were fighting for, not the present. Each and every one of them was already dead. All that mattered was how many of the alien bastards they could take down before the end.

"Thanks, Lucas," Gunn said.

Sterling frowned at her. "Thanks for what?"

"For not giving me the big 'war is hell' speech that you normally bombard me with," Gunn replied, still smiling.

Sterling laughed. "I figured you'd had enough of my sermonizing already," he said.

"I know you're a good man at heart, Lucas," Gunn went on, now staring out at Earth with a dreamy expression on her face. "You can be cold and heartless and infuriating as hell sometimes, but underneath it all you're okay."

"Well, gee, thanks, Ariel!" Sterling snorted. "You sure know how to make a guy feel good about himself."

"You can't help being what you are," Gunn continued, burying the knife deeper. "And the truth is, Fleet needs people like you."

"What sort of people are those?" Sterling said. He'd run the full gamut of emotions in the last few seconds alone, from being confused, to being deeply insulted. Now he was morbidly curious to learn what Gunn meant.

"Killers, of course," Gunn said, shrugging. "Fleet needs medics to heal people, wrench wenches like me to fix stuff, scientists to do the thinking..."

"And cold, heartless bastards to pull triggers, is that what you're telling me?" Sterling cut in.

Gunn shrugged again and smiled. Sterling shook his head and decided to run a diagnostic on the secondary stabilizers, figuring that anything was more fun than being grilled by his supposed friend.

"Just remember what I said, okay?" Gunn went on.

"Which one of the many slights and insults should I be remembering, exactly?" Sterling replied, cocking an eyebrow at her.

"About not losing yourself along the way," Gunn said. She had now turned away from the viewscreen and was looking at Sterling almost imploringly. "Even cold-hearted bastards like you need something to fight for, Lucas." Then she glanced again at Earth on the viewscreen. "And if it's not that then find something else."

"How about that grilled ham and cheese meal tray?" Sterling said, being intentionally flippant. "I'd fight for that, if I could ever remember what number it was."

"Fine, be that way," Gunn snapped, turning to her own console and beginning a needless diagnostic of her own. "Sometimes you're impossible, do you know that?"

Sterling sighed and cleared his screen. He hated conversations like these, but he hadn't intended to offend his friend. She was the only one he had, after all.

"I hear you, Ariel, okay?" Sterling said, forcing away his natural tendency toward sarcasm whenever things got personal between them. "And I promise you, I'll try."

Gunn smiled. "That's all I ask, Lucas," she said.

"Good, now can we drop this and talk about the latest Fleet cop drama, or who is fighting in the ship boxing league tonight?" Sterling suggested.

Gunn held up her hands in surrender. "Fine, fine, I'll give it a rest," she said, though she was still smiling. Sterling's involuntary pledge that he'd find some deeper meaning to his life had obviously satisfied her.

For a moment the two officers were silent, though it wasn't long before Sterling had a strange feeling that he'd left something unsaid. Gunn was, in her own way, only trying to look out for him. And while he was cut from a different cloth to the engineer who had been drafted into service, they still shared a bond, and it was a bond that mattered to him.

"You know I'll always have your back, right?" Sterling said, glancing over to Gunn's station.

"I know, Lucas," Gunn said, without taking her eyes off her panel. "In your own way, I know you care."

Sterling frowned, again not quite understanding what Gunn had meant, but the engineering officer was now engrossed in her work, and so he chose to leave her statement hanging. Checking his own panel, he saw a memo that Fleet Admiral Griffin was due to dock on the Hammer one they'd completed their surge to G-sector to provide a show of force close to the Void. However, he would be off-shift by then and asleep in his bed. Not that he expected anything to happen, even with them being so near to the area of space where the Sa'Nerra prowled. It was likely to just be another uneventful mission, he considered, as he stared at the blue planet on the viewscreen. Instead of another patrol, he wished instead for a chance to do something significant to end the war. And if he ever got that chance, he prayed he would have the courage to see it through.

"COMMODORE, CAN YOU HEAR ME?" said a cheerful voice in Sterling's ear. Despite the words being spoken softly, each syllable that had been uttered felt like needles being shoved into his eyes.

"Mercedes?" Sterling muttered. His vision was a blur, but the image of Banks with the neural device attached to her interface was clear in his mind. "Mercedes, is that you?" he added, trying to push himself up, but pain flooded his body, immobilizing him in an instant.

"It is Ensign One sir," replied the sentient AI. "Please take it slowly, Commodore, you have sustained a number of serious injuries. You will require multiple surgeries and a long period of convalescence."

"To hell with convalescence, Ensign, where is Captain Banks?!" Sterling snapped. The robot's glowing ocular units had now come into focus and were peering down at him.

"I'm fine, Lucas," said Banks. Her voice was strong and

clear, though Sterling couldn't see her or even place where in the room her voice had come from. "Though, you appear to be sleeping on the job, sir. I'm pretty sure that's a court-martial offence."

Sterling laughed, causing more pain to shoot through his body. "Damn it, Mercedes, quit with the jokes, already," he complained. "They're literally painful."

With support from Ensign One, Sterling managed to climb to his feet. He then discovered he was at the captain's console in the CIC of the Fleet Dreadnaught Vanguard, or at least what was left of it. The viewscreen was flickering wildly, but Sterling could make out Sa'Nerra ahead of them. The Hammer remained wedged to the Vanguard's nose and both ships were still moving toward the planet. Then he remembered about the control device that Wessel had attached to Banks' head. He turned sharply to his fellow officer and peered at her neural interface, fearing the worst.

"Don't worry, you pulled the neural control weapon off my implant before it had chance to work," Banks said, using her hand to gently turn Sterling's head, steering it so he met her gaze. "Though I'm pretty sure you would have failed if that were an Omega Directive test," she added.

"To hell with the Omega Directive," Sterling hit back, causing Banks to raise an eyebrow at him.

Sterling then noticed that Captain Fletcher was also in the CIC, along with Lieutenant Commander Shade, who now had a bandage wrapped around her head.

"Status report," said Sterling, resting on the console and peering out at the viewscreen.

"The Sa'Nerran Fleet has been defeated, sir," Captain Fletcher said, speaking up first. "A few of the bastards ran, and we gave chase, but fifteen enemy ships managed to surge before we caught them."

"In which direction did they surge?" Sterling asked, concerned that the alien warships might return to an unguarded Colony Middle Star.

"They went deeper into Sa'Nerran space, toward the unknown regions," Fletcher said. There was a subtle air of mystery to the way the old soldier had answered the question, as if he was talking about a location on an ancient map labelled, 'Here be dragons.'

"They'll be back," Sterling said. He recalled what Praetor Wessel had said, before he'd crushed the traitorous bastard's throat. "They won't forget what we did here."

"Speaking of which, the torpedoes are all armed and ready, sir," Captain Banks said. "We can fire on your order."

Sterling straightened up then waved a hand toward the viewscreen. "Can we get that piece of junk off our bow first?" he said, referring to the Hammer.

"Yes sir, I believe I can execute a maneuver that will dislodge the Hammer, while ensuring it remains on a collision course with the planet," Ensign One chipped in.

"Wouldn't it be better to salvage it?" asked Banks. "It couldn't hurt to have another Dreadnaught at our disposal."

"I estimate that the Hammer still contains approximately fourteen hundred warriors, Captain," Ensign One said, cheerfully. "I would suggest it is therefore better to scuttle it."

"I agree with Ensign One," said Sterling. In truth, he agreed with Banks that it would be preferable to salvage the ship, but in his mind, it was tainted beyond saving. Even if they could kill all fourteen hundred warriors on-board, it would always be a 'turned' ship to him. "Execute the maneuver and cut her lose, Ensign," Sterling continued, turning to the robot.

"Aye sir," Ensign One replied.

The sentient robot then returned to the helm control station and cleared the rubble from the seat so that it could sit down. Sterling suddenly remembered something and frowned at the robot, as it operated its station.

"Unless I'm going crazy, weren't you destroyed, Ensign?" Sterling asked.

"I was merely disabled, sir," Ensign One replied, cheerfully. "The chief engineer from the Bismarck was able to temporarily patch me up and swap-in a replacement power core from a damaged Obsidian robot."

Sterling glanced across to Captain Fletcher and nodded respectfully to the man. "It seems I owe you another debt of gratitude, Captain," Sterling said. Then he had a thought. "How many of your navy survived?"

"Forty-one ships, sir," Fletcher replied, his tone becoming grave.

"What about the rest of the thirteen?" Sterling asked, though he had a sinking feeling that he already knew the answer. Captain Fletcher confirmed his suspicion simply by replying with a slow shake of his head. "Understood, Captain," Sterling added, letting out a weary sigh.

The thrum of the Vanguard's reactor and engines then

changed tempo and timbre, and Ensign One turned to face the captain's console.

"We are ready, Commodore."

"Then let's get this over with, people." Sterling nodded to Ensign One. "Cut her loose."

The Vanguard's engines roared and the entire CIC shook as the two mighty warships slowly began to separate. The sound of metal grinding against metal was excruciating, like the noise of a hundred orchestras all tuning up at the same time. The shriek of twisted metal then subsided and Sterling got his first look at the remains of the former Fleet Dreadnaught Hammer. It looked like a huge bite had been taken out of the front of the ship. The Vanguard continued to slow, allowing the distance between the two ships to increase more rapidly. Soon the Hammer would hit the atmosphere of the planet, puncturing through the world's black clouds before ramming into the surface like a meteorite. The impact of the Hammer alone would have been enough to destroy a major city, but Sterling had a far more powerful weapon system at his disposal.

"We're in firing position, sir," said Ensign One as the Hammer reached the upper atmosphere and was shrouded in flame.

Lieutenant Commander Shade then moved over to the Vanguard's weapon control station and began to sweep debris off its panels.

"It's okay, Lieutenant Commander," Sterling said, holding up his blood-soaked left hand to his former weapons officer. "This duty is mine, and mine alone."

Shade nodded and stood to attention as Sterling began to enter the final launch commands into his console. A flashing red chevron appeared on his cracked and flickering console screens, warning him of what he was about to do. However, he needed no reminder. The consequences of his next command would be catastrophic and irreversible. It would lead to the destruction of an entire civilization, and the loss of billions of lives. The Sa'Nerra on the planet wouldn't receive a merciful, quick death, but a slow and painful one, as radioactive clouds of dust slowly crept across the alien world, bringing with them sickness and, eventually, death. It was an unconscionable act, but it was what he had to do. Sterling cleared the warning chevron then input his command codes and executed the launch order.

Moments later the first of the one-hundred-and-fifty cobalt-salted nuclear torpedoes streaked out from the Vanguard's many launch tubes and began accelerating toward the planet, unopposed. The aliens had sacrificed everything in order to destroy Earth and win the war, but in so doing they had doomed themselves as well. Admiral Griffin called it, "an eye for an eye". Others might call it karma. In simple terms, it was revenge. However, to Sterling it was more than all of these things. It was a warning, as well as an insurance policy. It told any remaining Sa'Nerra in the galaxy in no uncertain terms that humanity gave as good as it got. It warned those aliens to think twice about invading human space again. And, even if those warnings were not heeded, it had the effect of decimating the alien population and destroying their infrastructure, so that at the very least it would be centuries before the Sa'Nerra reached the same level of military might again. As cold and inhumane as it was, those were the facts.

The elemental glow of nuclear detonations began appearing all across the surface of the alien planet. Soon the deadly radioactive dust clouds would begin to spread across every continent and every sea, eventually blanketing the world in a toxic smog. Perhaps some would survive, Sterling mused, as several more massive detonations rocked the planet. Maybe there would be shelters deep underground where pockets of life could hold out long enough to escape the radiation. And maybe one day one of those survivors would mature and become the new Sa'Nerran Imperator. If that happened, Sterling had no doubt in his mind that this future Imperator would want revenge for what he had done.

"Let them come..." Sterling said, speaking so softly that no-one else could hear. "Humanity will still be here. And we'll be ready."

CHAPTER 31
TERRIBLE CONSEQUENCES

COMMODORE LUCAS STERLING found himself alone on the bridge of the Fleet Marauder Invictus. The low-level red alert lights were active, but so far as he could see, there were no enemy ships in sight. Then he realized that there were no other ships or space stations visible at all. The only object in space, besides the Invictus and the stars, was Earth, shining brightly on the viewscreen in front of him.

Suddenly, the deck of the ship began to shake violently, and there was a vibrant, blinding flash of light. It was like a great god had reached out and tore a hole in the fabric of space itself. The aperture singularity grew and soon the planet was being consumed by it, continent by continent, city by city, life by life.

"Computer, reverse engines!" Sterling yelled, but there was no reply from the onboard AI. Hurrying to the helm control station, he dropped into the seat and tried to maneuver the Invictus away from the singularity, but the console was similarly unresponsive. Then he realized that nothing on the bridge worked. The whole ship was a mere facsimile of the Invictus he knew.

"Warning, collision alert," said the voice of the Invictus AI. However, this was not Ensign One, or even the gen-fourteen AI that had preceded it, but the dull tone of the inferior gen-thirteen.

"Computer, reverse engines!" Sterling yelled, but the computer ignored his command. Instead, it merely intoned the same warning message, over and over again.

Suddenly, the Invictus began to accelerate toward the singularity, which was still rapidly consuming the entire planet. Sterling was thrown to the rear wall of the bridge and pinned there by the forces acting on the ship. Unable to move and helpless to intervene, he cried out in terror as the ship raced inside the aperture singularity and vanished.

For a time, there was darkness. Then, slowly, Sterling's eyes began to adjust and he found himself on the surface of a world he'd never seen before. Black clouds swirled overhead, and a harsh, biting wind lashed his face. Sterling hugged his arms tightly around his chest, but still the bitterness stung his face and crept into his bones, like rot.

"Hello?" Sterling shouted, but there was no response.

Sterling peered around the bleak landscape for any signs of life. However, all he could see were the remains of a once-great city that now lay in ruin far in the distance. Dotted amongst the broken buildings, jutting up from the surface like cracked teeth, were smashed skyscrapers. These jagged towers rose into the dark sky and disappeared into the black clouds that swirled endlessly around the planet.

"Is anyone here?" Sterling shouted, trying again to reach someone – anyone – who could explain what the hell was going on.

Then Sterling noticed the bodies. Thousands of bodies, strewn all across the land. Some had already decayed, while others were horrifically scarred and burned. He wandered amongst the dead for a time, losing himself in the sea of disfigured, rotten flesh. Eventually, he came to the crest of a hill, looking out across a desolate plain. A short distance away, Sterling could just about make out a group of four figures staggering down a hillside, pushing carts and carrying bags in their arms and across their backs. He ran toward the group, calling out to them, but then stopped dead as he realized what they were. The four figures were Sa'Nerran. Not the warriors he was used to seeing. They wore no armor and carried no weapons. Their clothes were dirtied and torn, while the leathery skin on their faces looked even more weathered and lined than usual. Blemishes marked their flesh and blistered their thin lips, which sat atop bleeding, toothless gums. Then to his dismay, Sterling realized that two of the wretched beings were children.

"Fleet loves cold-hearted bastards like you..."

Sterling turned to see Ariel Gunn standing behind him. She was dressed in her Fleet Lieutenant Commander's uniform and appeared exactly as he remembered her, before he'd blasted her head off on the bridge of the Dreadnaught Hammer.

"Well, you did it," Gunn said, staring at Sterling with a mournful expression. Though whether she was sad for him or sad for the plight of the people on the world they stood on, Sterling couldn't be sure. "You won the war, Lucas," Gunn continued. "You did whatever was necessary, no matter the cost." Gunn then pointed to the group of four Sa'Nerrans who were still hobbling down the hillside. "And look at the cost..."

Sterling was not a machine. The sight of the desperate and unfortunate souls on the planet had not bounced off him like light off a mirror. However, he refused to feel any regret.

"Both sides paid a heavy price, Ariel," Sterling said, stepping closer to his old friend. "This had to be done, otherwise they would have simply re-grouped and come at us again."

"You don't know that, Lucas," Gunn said. She was not angry, nor was she preaching to him. "No-one could have known what the Sa'Nerra would do next. Maybe even peace was possible?"

"I know what they did, and that's all that matters," Sterling hit back. "All I did was make sure they couldn't do it again, at least not for a very long time."

"And was it worth it?" Gunn asked. "Despite what it cost you?"

"Four million people are still alive at Colony Middle Star, Ariel," Sterling replied. "Not to mention the thousands more that could still be alive, spread across the Void Worlds, and maybe even the inner colonies. I think that makes it worth it, don't you?"

Gunn smiled at Sterling. "That's not what I mean, and you know it."

Sterling sighed and smiled back at her. "I don't have to like what I've done, or what I am, Ariel," he said, starting to answer the question his long-dead friend had really asked. "And it doesn't mean that I don't feel the burden of my actions weighing down on me every second of every day. But I can live it with, Ariel. I don't have a choice."

Ariel Gunn nodded. She shot one last smile at Sterling before turning her back on him and walking away towards the broken city on the horizon. However, Sterling couldn't let her go, not without telling her the one thing that he'd always wanted to say, but never had the chance.

"Ariel..." Sterling called out, causing the officer to stop and glance back at him over his shoulder. "For what it's worth, I'm sorry."

A solitary tear rolled down Gunn's cheek and splashed onto the blackened, irradiated soil at her feet. "So am I, Lucas," she said, meeting his gaze. "So am I."

"Lucas... wake up..."

Sterling opened his eyes and saw Mercedes Banks standing above him, partially silhouetted by Middle Star's bright yellow sun. "I've been looking for you for over an hour," Banks continued, pressing her hands to her hips.

"Why, what's up, Mercedes?" said Sterling, pushing himself up against the trunk of the tree he'd accidently fallen asleep under.

"Nothing..." Banks replied, breezily. She then planted herself down on the grass next to Sterling. "I just wanted to see you, that's all."

"Well, you found me, and I'm glad you did," Sterling said, smiling at her. "Will you sit? It's peaceful up here, and hell knows we could both do with a little peace."

"Shove over then," Banks said, dropping down beside Sterling and intentionally shoulder-barging him off the patch of softer green grass that he'd specifically chosen to lie on.

"Shove over then, *sir...*" Sterling replied, raising an eyebrow at the off-duty captain of the Invictus.

"Sorry... sir," Banks said, while still buffeting Sterling onto a harder patch of ground with her powerful thighs.

Sterling shook his head, but in truth he didn't mind. Simply having Mercedes by his side felt good. He doubted he wouldn't have even cared if he was sitting on a patch of nettles, so long as she was with him. The two of them then sat quietly for a time, resting shoulder to shoulder under the tree on the hillside nature spot Sterling had taken to frequenting since arriving at Bastion. He watched the breeze swaying the branches of the trees, and counted the dozen or so different birds that landed to peck at the ground around their feet. It felt a billion light years away from where they had been only seven weeks earlier.

"Did you know that Ensign One is documenting everything that happened?" Banks said.

The question came out of the blue and took Sterling by surprise. "No, I had no idea," he admitted. "You mean, like writing the history of the war?"

"Not the war specifically, just the Omega Taskforce," Banks replied. "He says it's 'for posterity'." She shrugged. "I just hope I get a section dedicated to me. Or maybe a whole chapter."

Sterling laughed. "It's fact, Mercedes, not fiction," Sterling said, receiving another nudge for his trouble. It hurt far more than it should have done on account of his injuries, some of which were still healing.

"We'll both probably come across as monsters," Banks said, darkly.

"If future generations see us as monsters, then I can live with it, Mercedes," Sterling replied, honestly. "At least when we're long in the ground there will be people still alive to read about us."

Banks nodded and let out a long, weary sigh. "It still feels wrong to be enjoying this, though," she said, remaining close by Sterling's side. "After what we did, is it wrong to be happy?"

"I don't think I'm the right person to ask about what's right and wrong, Mercedes," Sterling replied. His nightmares had become less frequent in recent weeks, but Sterling's subconscious mind was still terrorized by the horrific consequences of his actions. "I'd say enjoy it while you can." He brushed Banks' hair away from her eyes so that he could see her face properly. "If happiness comes our way, in any shape or form, then we should embrace it. There's no right or wrong. There's only how we feel."

"And how do you feel?" Banks asked.

Sterling snorted a laugh. "You're as bad as the damned computer," he replied. "That infernal AI was always trying to diagnose me and offer me therapy."

"Did it also point out how you have a habit of dodging personal questions?" Banks said, smirking at Sterling.

"Funnily enough, yes," Sterling replied, also smiling. Banks didn't press him for an answer, but for some reason, this time Sterling actually felt like sharing. "I think I feel relieved," he said, peering off into the distance.

"Relieved that it's finally all over?" Banks asked.

"I honestly don't know for sure," Sterling replied, realizing that he'd just said what came to the front of his mind, without even really understanding it himself. "I think I'm relieved that I still have someone to share it all with."

Banks turned to face Sterling, brushing loose strands of hair that had been blown free by the wind behind her ear. "Share what with, Lucas?" she asked.

"Life, I guess," Sterling answered, shrugging. "I don't think I ever expected to make it out the other side alive. And even if I did, I expected it to be a lonely existence."

Banks smiled then nestled down by Sterling's side again. "Well, if you're looking to share any of that life with me, it will cost you," she said, a smile curling her lips. "I'm very popular and in demand, you see."

"I'll be sure to make an appointment with your secretary," Sterling replied, playing along with her game. It felt good to be joking again, he realized. Then he realized that Banks was still wearing her Fleet uniform. "Isn't it about time you wore something other than the silver stripe?" he asked, poking his finger into one of the many sections of her dark blue tunic that were already frayed.

"None of the damned clothes they make at Bastion fit properly," Banks said, brushing Sterling's hand away. "Either that or they tear too easily."

"Well, I guess we can't have the great Captain Banks tearing a hole in the seat of her pants, can we?" said Sterling, more than a little facetiously. Banks glared at him and Sterling knew not to push his luck. "Can't you get Ensign One to knock up something a little less military from the uniforms we have in stock on the Vanguard?"

"She's working on it," Banks said, while picking blades

of grass out of the ground and idly tearing them to pieces. "She's been a little busy recently, though, stitching up something a bit more important than my pants."

"What could be more important than your pants?" asked Sterling, only half joking. He didn't actually know what Banks was referring to.

"You, of course," Banks said, nudging Sterling with her shoulder. As usual the blow was delivered with more force than she intended, and Sterling almost fell over sideways.

"Well, if the job she did on me is anything to go by, you're going to have the sleekest-looking pants in the galaxy," Sterling said, holding up his newly-skinned bionic hand. Banks took the upgraded bionic hand in hers and began to run her finger up and down Sterling's palm. "Hey, that tickles!" Sterling said, feeling shivers run down his spine.

"How the hell that machine has managed to connect this artificial flesh to your nervous system, I don't know," Banks said, allowing Sterling's hand to fall to his side again.

"I don't either, but I'm glad she figured it out," Sterling replied, watching a butterfly flap past and land on a flower. "If I was stuck with Commander Graves' bionic replacements, I'd be more machine now, than man."

"Considering you have a heart of solid lead, perhaps that would have been more fitting," Banks hit back, raising her eyebrow at him.

"I saved your ass, didn't I?" Sterling said, giving as good as he got. "Griffin would have had me blast your head off."

"That's what you should have done," Banks replied, flatly. "I even told you to do it."

Sterling remained silent. He'd inadvertently swung them onto the topic of what had happened in the CIC of the Vanguard. It was a subject they'd both avoided, or skirted around, or even joked about.

"Why didn't you, Lucas?" Banks glanced up at him, still idly shredding blades of grass.

"Why didn't I what?"

"Don't play coy with me," Banks said, her tone a little sharper. "We been on Bastion for almost two months, already, and we haven't talked about it. Not really."

Sterling realized he'd avoided the question for long enough. He didn't know whether Banks was ready for the truth, or even if he was ready for it himself.

"I didn't want to lose you," he admitted, fighting to get the words out through his bone-dry lips. "McQueen always said that I was weak when it came to you, and it turns out she was right."

Sterling thought about saying more, but saying even that much had been the hardest thing he'd ever had to do. And since Banks had said nothing in reply, he chose to stay silent, hoping he hadn't embarrassed her, or inadvertently made things awkward between them.

"It took you long enough to realize it," Banks finally replied. Sterling frowned as Banks turned to him then kissed him gently on the lips. "I thought I was going to have to beat the admission out of you," she added, nestling down at his side again.

Sterling laughed then put his arm around Banks and held her tightly against him. Then they were interrupted by a sonorous howl and the sound of small feet scampering through the grass. Moments later, Jinx appeared over the crest of the hill and came charging over to them.

"Damn it, Jinx, get down," Sterling snapped as the dog jumped onto his chest and began to lick at his face, forcing him to fend off the animal with his new bionic hand.

"It's just her way of saying, 'hello'," Banks said, as the dog then turned its attention to her. "Isn't that right, Jinxy-winxy!" she said, in the 'coo-coo' baby voice that drove Sterling up the wall.

"If she craps in our quarters then she's still getting airlocked," Sterling said, picking up a stick and tossing it into the longer grasses a few meters away. The dog went hurtling after it like nuclear torpedo.

"*Our* quarters?" Banks raised an eyebrow at Sterling. "That's a little presumptuous, isn't it?"

"No, I don't think so," replied Sterling, with a coolness worthy of a gambler at a high-roller poker tournament.

Banks smiled. "Also, you said 'she' and not 'it' when you referred to Jinxy..." Banks said, with matching swagger.

"My point still stands," Sterling hit back.

"It's a deal then," said Banks as Jinx came charging back over to them, the stick pressed between her jaws. The dog dropped the stick politely at Sterling's side, and he obliged by throwing it again, sending the beagle pelting off across the hillside again.

"I don't think it's wrong for us to feel happy, Mercedes," Sterling said, as the sun began to set over the horizon, warming the sky with a blood-orange hue.

"Why the sudden change of heart?" Banks asked.

Sterling turned to Banks and looked into her eyes.

Through it all she had always been there, and he couldn't imagine another day without her.

"Because I *am* happy," Sterling said, turning to watch the sunset. "And I think I like it this way."

Banks continued to look at him for a few moments longer, then also turned to face the sunset. "Good," she said. "Because I like it too."

The end.

THERE WAS a bright flash of light as the last of fifteen battered and war-weary Sa'Nerran warships emerged from the surge dimension. The star system they had entered had not been visited by ships from the Sa'Nerran Empire for over a thousand years. Yet the beings who inhabited these worlds knew who the Sa'Nerra were. They had created them.

The fifteen ships formed up and engaged their engines, which flickered and faltered as they struggled to push the damaged hulls on through the alien star system, which was concealed inside a manufactured expanse of pure darkness. In the distance was a space station, vast in scale, but as gloomy and deserted as a ruined castle. More flashes popped off in the darkness as yet more Sa'Nerran ships appeared. One Skirmisher arrived through one aperture, two near-crippled destroyers though another. A rag-tag collection of Sa'Nerran ships from all across the galaxy, all converging on the same location.

Together the beleaguered Sa'Nerran war vessels all advanced toward the space station; a vast citadel that dominated the shadowy star system it guarded. Then as the alien ships drew closer, lights began to flicker on across the megacity-sized platform, and for the first time in eons its ancient reactors sparked into life.

YOU MADE IT!

Thank you so much for reading the Omega Taskforce series. I hope you enjoyed it! I loved writing this series so much that I'm going to continue it, albeit with a twist...

My next series is set in the same universe as Omega Taskforce, but one thousand years after the events of this book. It will follow the adventures of a lineal descendent of Lucas Sterling and Mercedes Banks, and pit a new generation of heroes against an even more brutal and dangerous adversary.

Look out for **Descendent of War**, coming to an Amazon Kindle bookshelf near you in late 2021.

Best Wishes

At school, I was asked to write down the jobs I wanted to do as a "grown up". Number one was astronaut and number two was a PC games journalist. I only managed to achieve one of those goals (I'll let you guess which), but these two very different career options still neatly sum up my lifelong interests in science, space, and the unknown.

School also steered me in the direction of a science-focused education over literature and writing, which influenced my decision to study physics at Manchester University. What this degree taught me is that I didn't like studying physics and instead enjoyed writing, which is why you're reading this book! The lesson? School can't tell you who you are.

When not writing, I enjoy spending time with my family, walking in the British countryside, and indulging in as much Sci-Fi as possible.

Subscribe to my newsletter:
http://subscribe.ogdenmedia.net

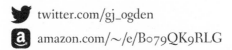

twitter.com/gj_ogden

amazon.com/~/e/B079QK9RLG

MORE BY G J OGDEN

If you like Omega Taskforce then why not check out some of G J Ogden's other books? Click the series titles below to learn more about each of them.

Star Scavenger Series (5-book series)

Firefly blended with the mystery and adventure of Indiana Jones. Amazon best-selling series.

The Contingency War Series (4-book series)

A space-fleet, military sci-fi adventure with a unique twist that you won't see coming...

The Planetsider Trilogy (3-book series)

An edge-of-your-seat blend of military sci-fi action & classic apocalyptic fiction. Perfect for fans of Maze Runner and I am Legend.

Darkspace Renegade Series (6-books)

If you like your action fueled by power armor, big guns and the occasional sword, you'll love this fast-moving military sci-fi adventure.

Audible audiobook Series

Star Scavenger Series (29-hrs)

The Contingency War Series (24-hrs)

The Planetsider Trilogy (32-hrs)

Made in the USA
Monee, IL
30 March 2022